MARIE GAMESON was born in Trinidad but spent her childhood in Barbados. As her knowledge of England was based entirely on the content of Enid Blyton books, when the family moved to the UK in 1974, Marie soon realised that you could never trust a writer to tell the truth. Marie and her mother co-wrote a book about the legacy of the Monmouth Rebels exiled to Barbados (The Turtle Run) which was published in 2016.

MARIE GAMESON

THE GIDDY CAREER OF MR GADD (DECEASED)

SALT

LONDON

PUBLISHED BY SALT PUBLISHING 2017

2 4 6 8 10 9 7 5 3 1

First published in Great Britain in 2017 by
Salt Publishing Ltd
International House, 24 Holborn Viaduct, London EC1A 2BN United Kingdom

www.saltpublishing.com

Salt Publishing Limited Reg. No. 5293401

A CIP catalogue record for this book is available from the British Library

ISBN 978 1 78463 118 5 (Paperback edition)
ISBN 978 1 78463 119 2 (Electronic edition)

Typeset in Neacademia by Salt Publishing

Printed and bound in Great Britain by Clays Ltd, St Ives plc

Salt Publishing Limited is committed to responsible forest management.
This book is made from Forest Stewardship Council™ certified paper.

For Kate

Chapter One

"I WISH YOU were dead."

I am sure that's what my mother just said, although she said it quietly, and her intended audience seemed to be the washing-up bowl in which her yellow-gloved hands are still immersed; certainly not me, for she jumps now when I walk further into the kitchen. Then she looks guilty, and I know for certain who she wants dead.

I'm amazed that there's anything left to wash up. I don't think we've had more than tea and cake, and I barely get a chance to wash up in my own house before Urs has whipped away anything that has been standing unattended for more than a nanosecond.

And now I can see my mother desperately hunting for something to fill the vacuum left by her last statement. "Dreadful news about Gary Glitter, isn't it? Your father would turn in his grave."

I will ignore the rubbish about my father – who is clearly not in a grave. As for Gary Glitter, I vaguely know the name; I think he did music. I haven't seen the news recently, but she's looking bothered, so I assume that he's either died or has said something unkind about God. "Awful," I say. "I didn't hear the details. Was it a car accident, or his heart?"

"She means that he's a paedophile," says Urs, who has silently conjured herself into the kitchen doorway. I will never understand how my sister moves so stealthily. She appears where before she was not, and disappears from where before she was.

"Oh right," I say, as if remembering. "Yes, dreadful."

"And it turns out that he was bald, all along," adds my mother.

"That's awful," I say again. I still don't really know who he is, but he's obviously alive, without hair, and damned.

My mother and Urs exchange a look, and I know that I have somehow failed again.

So that was my birthday, and fortunately it is over. My mother cried once – briefly – which I think was once less than last year. I am thirty years old, or thirty-one and a half depending on whether one is following the western or traditional Chinese calendar. I am back at work, which involves an efficient commute to my PC where I'm trying to translate a very long piece about investment opportunities in China into English. The article is actually more interesting in Mandarin.

"Thought you'd be up here. Winnie, I'm going now."

I turn around to see Urs who has appeared in my bedroom doorway, radiating waves of opprobrium; like my mother, when she sees Chinese characters on the screen, she reacts as if she has found me exploring a porn site. I didn't know she was here to be going, but she seems to slip into my place with the furtiveness of a thief.

"Oh, OK. Bye."

"Do you want to say anything to Mum?"

"Is she here as well?" I see Urs's face do that miniature slump, and add "I mean, is she still here?"

Urs sighs in that exasperated way. "I'm going to take her home. You could say goodbye."

"She said that she wished I was dead. Bit strong, I thought."

"I can't believe she said that."

"I'm sure she did."

"She just misses you." This is muttered as Urs turns around, but I think it is what she said. What is left of my family have an irritating habit of saying things so indistinctly that I'm never sure if they are trying to reveal something whilst showing that they know they should be trying to conceal it, or trying to conceal something and not making a very good job of it.

Urs is no longer in the doorway. I suppose if I'd been quicker I could have challenged Urs on what she meant by 'She just misses you' when I'm obviously still here, but I already know the answer. She means, of course, that Mum misses the old me, or to be more accurate, the young me. I have changed. I have changed substantially. I remember an ordained Buddhist monk telling me that everyone now called him by his new ordained name apart from his mother. ("It seemed a bit unfair to make her call me Padmasumra after she has been calling me Steve for forty-plus years"). I have not taken a new name, but I am no longer the person I was. And I am happy that it is this way.

I hear a muffled conversation downstairs, and then the front door close. I don't really understand what Urs's problem is: why would anyone wish the condition of hormonal teenage-hood on anyone? I really try to apply the Buddhist principle of detachment to whatever experience my senses tend to dump on my mind, and generally, I'm very accomplished at being dispassionate. But I'm afraid that when I see teenage girls, I feel a strong repulsion. It's the giggling, and the hyperbole, and the Oh My God, or even worse: Oh. My. God. Fortunately I have the insight to know that my negative reaction to teenage

3

girls is due to my own fear that I was once the same, and is therefore a vestige of ego and a useful sign that I must find a way of being more dispassionate about what irritates me.

Although I want to get back to a section on the investment potential of China's renewable energy, something compels me to look out the window. My mother's blonde ponytail seems to quiver with pique as she crosses the few feet from my front door to her white car, followed by Urs with her darker ponytail. They have a brief exchange by the driver's door but as they are side on to me, I can't see what they're saying. Whatever it is, some decision is reached and Urs takes the keys. My mother gets in the passenger seat. I clock that they had found a parking space right outside my house in this crowded south London terraced street, and then realise that my mother is wiping her eyes with her hands, stopping only to belt up. It is then that Urs looks up and sees me. I go back to my work but am drawn again to the window by a screech of brakes. Urs is giving one of those anal headshakes to an elderly man driving a brown car that is too big for him and too big for the street. She reverses out and he flounders into the space she just vacated, at such an acute angle that one wheel is on the pavement and the bonnet is nuzzling a young silver birch. Five seconds, it took, for the parking space to be filled. A new record for the street, I believe.

I go back to my PC but am distracted. I think my mother is silly for believing in God, but I wouldn't wish her dead for it, so I find her reaction to my godlessness a little extreme. I have been fairly successful at wiping out the memory banks of my childhood, but there's still the odd vestige of the past that makes its appearance with all the charm of a sodden sock stuck to the back of the washing machine.

Of course I could remember everything if I wanted to. But the only memory I want to bring back – and the earliest memory of the new me occurred a couple of years ago. I had hiked up a marble mountain in Taiwan's amazing Taroko Gorge and had what (ironically) I can only describe as a religious experience: I ceased to be me, I escaped the straightjacket of Ego and I flew with the wind. My head disappeared, and I had only the sensation of space above my neck. But most significantly, I realised – absolutely – that there is no God. My mother was sufficiently worried to fly out to Taiwan, where she took my 'Revelation' as a sign of some mental aberration brought on by eating too much rice and mixing with non-Catholics.

Someone is knocking on the door. It is insistent and irritating. Obviously not Urs or my mother, who let themselves in with no sense of impropriety, and – anyway – whose car is now heading towards Wimbledon. When I go downstairs and open the door, the elderly floundering parker stumbles into the doorway and looks at me with such a beaming smile that I involuntarily step back. He is about seventy-something, with wisps of hair forming an atoll around a bald dome, and wearing a shabby jacket with a tie. I have never seen him before.

"Winifred Rigby," he tells me, just in case I had forgotten my name.

"Win," I snap. God bless my mother for naming us after saints. Though I bet she regretted it later. St Winifred, patron saint of spinsters (she got that right), and pretty good at losing her head (she got that right too).

The elderly man looks confused. "Win," he says, unconvincingly. Then another beam. "You haven't changed at all.

Well, older of course. But I would have recognised the old you."

Oh God. Who is this weirdo?

"And you are?" I ask.

He wobbles and one hand clutches the door jamb. "Well, I'm here." Which I suppose is the answer my question deserved.

"Come into the kitchen," I say. I'm not sure I want a weirdo in my house, but he looks like he's about to keel over with septuagenarian excitement. Maybe he needs hydrating. I give him a glass of water. He shakily lifts the glass and drinks it all. I refill the glass and wait for him to tell me how he knows me and what he's doing here.

"It took me ages to track you down," he says, spilling more water than he's managed to get into his mouth.

"Should have just googled me," I say. "Though you'd have had more luck with 'Winnie Rigby'."

"Google?"

"Used the internet."

He frowns. "I hired a private detective. He found you straight away. He was very good."

"Yes, he probably just googled me."

"He did give me your phone number as well, but I thought a visit would be more in order, after all this time."

"How do you know me?" I ask.

"Well, you wrote about my father," he says. "Everything else you said came true. To be honest, I'd forgotten you for a while, but then I found your book while I was looking for some socks, and it all came back to me."

"Right."

He looks at me and must see my confusion. "Matching

6

socks," he adds. "And then I found your book - still safe."

"Couldn't have been me. I'm not a writer. I'm a translator." He's looking so blank that he couldn't have heard me. "I translate what other people write. I don't write."

"But you did," he says, shaking his tonsured head. "You wrote all about him." He leans forward. "Do you remember 'The Giddy Career of Mr Gadd (Deceased)'?"

"I think you have me muddled up with someone else." If he goes now, I still have two hours work time, before my evening headache kicks in. I make a show of looking at my watch, which - annoyingly - isn't on my wrist, and anyway, he is looking into thin air, so that my symbolic gesture is meaningless. "I'm afraid that I'm a bit short of time," I try, which is true, and add "time marches on", which isn't, but most people don't seem to know that.

He frowns. "No it doesn't. You were the only one who understood that. In fact I remember you saying that the past is always the present and the present is already history."

"Did I? When did I say that?" Where the hell is my watch? I can't remember if Urs was wearing it, and my mother has one of those nurse's pocket watches, so would be unlikely to pinch my timepiece. Though I could imagine her putting it in a 'safe place'; lots of my things seem to get squirrelled away into places so safe that I never see them again.

He sighs, and seemed to be trawling his brain for something. It is taking a long time. I stare ostentatiously at the kitchen clock, which stopped a few days ago at quarter past seven, so that (as I told Urs), I have to remember to only look at it twice a day. She didn't laugh. She just looked worried. I can't remember when she lost her sense of humour, but then again, I can't remember if she ever had one.

7

"It was a few years ago. Actually, it may have been quite a few years ago."

"What was?"

He looks at me, confused. "What was what?"

"What was a few years ago?"

"It was the answer to whatever you asked."

Now both of us are trawling our brains.

"You mentioned a book. You thought I wrote something."

He is nodding - quite vigorously for an old man - and there is something about his enthusiasm that tickles my brain. I have a fleeting vision of a man in the centre of a ring of children, but whether they are taunting him, or listening to him telling a story, I don't know. Maybe it's like one of those Chinese criticism sessions during the Cultural Revolution, where everyone had to take turns shouting accusations at the poor bugger in the middle.

"Who are you?" I said.

Now he's looking hurt. "How can you have forgotten me, Winifred?" He sighs. "Well, I suppose I was history, but I am the son of Gadd."

I can't say that's really cleared things up. "So - your father was Mr Gadd?"

"Yes, yes." More nodding.

"And this Mr Gadd is dead?"

He winces.

"Deceased?" I try. "Passed on?"

"Yes, yes. Only he hasn't. He keeps coming back. I don't know what to do with him. And then I remembered you. I can't believe I'd forgotten. But then I found your book again and it all came back."

"I'm afraid you've got the wrong person," I say. "I really have no idea what you're talking about."

8

"You remember that he wasn't a socialist at all – but he was quite an admirer of Keir Hardie, who – of course – you mentioned."

"Sorry – I still have no idea what you're talking about."

He rubs his hands over his face, and looks weary. "Then chaos is come again." He stops rubbing and freezes. Dead still. I wonder if he's having a stroke – or has died on his feet, but I can see that his eyes are moving. Not that I know if that is proof that someone isn't having a stroke.

"Did you hear that?" he says.

He lives. "Hear what?"

"He has a very deep voice. It was so loud just then. I thought that maybe you could . . ." He raises an index finger in the air. "Again. Just then. Like a deep rumble."

The truth is that I always hear a deep rumble. It is no longer an external sound but part of me – my connection with The Other Side. If I was lazy I would just call it my 'Om' as there are people I can say this to and they will immediately nod. Whereas if I say that ever since my happy event up a Taiwanese mountain I have carried a noise that's a cross between a Tibetan long horn and a waterfall at night – well, people just look confused.

"Just then. He calls my name. Can't you hear?"

I do hear something, actually, but it resolves itself into knocking on the door – frantic knocking. I go to answer it, but he clutches my arm. "Winifred, you must tell me what to do with him."

I gently disentangle myself and go to open the door, which I find is already open – my guest must have forgotten to close it. A woman – sixty-something, smartly dressed, is angrily banging the knocker of the open door; she looks me up and down, and then very directly to my face, says "Is my husband here?" I'm intrigued as to whether she also managed to find a parking space, but I see a minicab pulling away from outside the house.

"Depends who your husband is."

She spends a few seconds on my doormat making exasperated grunty sounds, then sidles past me.

"Well, do come in," I say, shutting the door, but the sarcasm falls on stony ground, for this termagant is storming the front room, and then the kitchen.

"Come out, Fred," she says sharply.

When I go in, I find that 'Fred' is hiding ineffectually in the broom cupboard, with more of him sticking out than sticking in. She turns on me.

"How long has he been coming here?"

"I don't know."

"You don't know?"

"How could I know? I have no idea where he set off from."

The withering look she gives me indicates that there are now two women on the planet who wish me dead, and my sympathy is with the elderly man who is being dragged out of the cupboard by a distaff hand clutching his jacket. I don't recall my mother ever being violent, but there is a similarity between the two women – something familiar about the contemptuous expression when people don't 'behave as they ought to'.

"You're not meant to drive," she shouts at him. Fred is mute and cowering, a strategy that seems to stoke her temper, for she grabs him again and virtually gives him a bum's rush out the kitchen into the hall. She is far too rough with him. I worry that she is going to propel Fred straight through my closed front door, but she pulls him to a standstill, and sidesteps around him to open it. He takes the opportunity to straighten a little and turn back to me.

"You have to help me, Winifred."

"Is this about your bloody father?" says Fred's wife. She takes his silence as affirmative, and grunts exasperation. "Superstitious nonsense." Then she manages to push him down the path at the same time as extricating his keys from a jacket pocket.

"Nice to meet you, Mrs Gadd," I say, with as much sarcasm as I can muster. She stops still on the path, the keys dangling in her hand.

"I am not Mrs Gadd. I have never been Mrs Gadd. And I will never be Mrs Gadd." Then she's off, shunting Fred forward as if he were a passive railway carriage.

Old Fred turns to give me a last beseeching look from the passenger seat of the long brown car, whilst she tries to reverse the car and simultaneously pull his seat belt across him.

As surreal birthdays go, I think this one lifts the cup.

I sense that my equilibrium has been nudged off-piste, so spend ten minutes on the cushion breathing slowly, until emptiness pours through my head and the comforting Om sound flows through my body. I don't talk to anyone about this. I once made the mistake of mentioning the phenomenon to Urs, but she sneered "There's no mystery, Win. It's just tinnitus." That sort of reaction doesn't really encourage one to share experiences again.

Urs rings later to check up on me. "I'm not coming back tonight," she announces, as though her presence was required or asked for (and it is neither). "I'm going to stay with Mum."

She leaves a silence, during which – presumably – I am either meant to express separation anxiety or guilt that my atheism has brought on one of Mum's downers. I'm afraid that I have zero sympathy, and I'm running rather low on anxiety. And anyway, at thirty-three, Urs still lives with our mother. Thirty-three! If that doesn't deserve an 'Oh. My. God' – I don't know what does.

"Righty-ho."

"Are you OK?"

"Well, I haven't changed since you last saw me. Except . . ."

"Yes?" she says.

"Do you know anyone called Fred Gadd?"

"Mmm – no. Rings no bells. Why?"

"Nothing."

"No, go on – why? Who is he?"

I already wish I hadn't mentioned him. "I just bumped into someone who thought he knew me. He wasn't very clear where from."

"What do you mean: bumped into? Where were you?"

"In the house."

I can hear her worry tumbling down the phone. "How did he get into the house?"

"He knocked on the door, and he seemed to know me."

"So you invited a man into the house? Just like that?"

"Don't worry – he was about a hundred and two." Another reason that our parents should not have named us after saints is that most female saints got canonised for refusing to get married. I don't know whether Urs has ever had an offer to refuse, but she will see sexual possibilities in all situations, and she thinks it's a Bad Thing.

"Exactly what happened, Winnie?"

"Look, it's really simple. An old man who I've never met before turned up on the doorstep, saying he knew me. And then his younger wife turned up, and dragged him away. That's it."

"Are you sure you're OK, Winnie? Do you want me to come back?"

"No. I mean yes I'm OK, but no - don't come round." Best not mention the mother of all headaches that is starting to suffocate my head. I must get to bed. Ironic, I know, that someone who has no sensation of her head should have such cracking headaches. I guess that's the downside of working with a screen all day. I say Goodbye and put the phone down. Hopefully I've put Urs's squirming mind at rest.

I can't sleep. Each time I think my mind is slipping into the much-needed shadows, I hear Fred Gadd (with a wife who isn't Mrs Gadd) beseech me: "You must tell me what to do with him". And when I have finally shut him up, an unwelcome phenomenon reappears: one that I haven't experienced for a while. Ever since I lost my head I can hear the constant deep throb of the Om humming through life, but right now it is being overlaid by a woman's voice, or at least I think it is the whisper of a woman - if whispers can have gender. Whoever she is, she whispers 'Thank God, thank God' over me, like a misguided mantra. And then the sound of someone tearing tissues in the room. There's no point switching on the light, because I know that no-one is there.

Chapter Two

I AM DRIFTING. I am floating. I am a shrivelled brown leaf, discarded by a tree to be borne by autumnal gusts through rural and industrial landscapes alike. I don't care where I'm carried, I don't mind where I land. I have no name. I am free.

And I have cramp, which unfortunately means the end of my flight. I stay on my cushion but stretch out my legs, and try to relive the sensation of detachment I just felt. Of course, it is important not to mistake these experiences for enlightenment; they are just the by-product of deep concentration, plus - I think - the letting go of all attachments. I have no delusions about my level of attainment, for someone more advanced would be able to meditate through both cramp and through the low cyclic rumble from downstairs, which is ousting my background Om as effectively as a single concertgoer's persistent cough can distract a music-loving audience.

Someone has put on the tumble drier in the kitchen, and there is something about the frequency of the sound that I find disrupting. I put away my cushion and come downstairs where I find Urs sitting at my kitchen table typing into a laptop. I don't understand what a bookkeeper does - other than to cover my kitchen table with stacks of paper - but I don't really mind her using my kitchen as an office. Anyway, she'll move as soon as I start making breakfast. My making breakfast seems to freak her out.

My mother, wearing her nurse's uniform, comes in from God Knows Where, and this I do mind.

"You're both here," I say, unnecessarily. "I didn't hear you come in, Mum."

"You had damp clothes sitting in the washing machine."

"I was trying to meditate."

"I'm not stopping you." (Does my mother know she's lying?) "But the clothes in the washing machine were still wet."

"Yes, I put them in last night, and I was going to take them out this morning to dry. After my meditation. Just because you've beaten me to it doesn't mean I wasn't going to do it."

They exchange one of their Mother-Elder Daughter meaningless glances, and Mum takes out her pocket watch and consults it, obviously deciding how much time she has to embark on whatever is the real reason for her visit this early; it surely can't be about sorting out my washing, nor would she have driven over here with the intention of disrupting my meditation. That is possible though: I knew a woman whose husband felt so threatened when she became a Buddhist that he ensured his trumpet practice coincided with her meditation time.

Now I notice that Mum's neck is bare.

"What happened to your crucifix?" I ask. "Or have they been banned in case you offend the sensibilities of Muslims and heathens?"

"I used to wear a cross, not a crucifix," she says, with more than a hint of impatience. "Crucifixes have Jesus on, crosses don't."

So that's sorted that out. I wait.

"This . . . man who turned up yesterday," she says. (I throw a reproachful glance at Urs, who is suddenly very interested in her laptop). "He was really here? In the house?"

"He was just a confused old chap. He wasn't after anything. He didn't try and do anything. He was just a bit muddled."

"Ursula said that he knew who you were."

"No, he knew my name, but he had obviously got me confused with someone else – a writer. It's no big deal. I'm not likely to see him again, am I?"

My mother looks at me. "I don't know. Are you?"

"Have either of you seen my watch?"

"Bathroom," says Urs.

"Maybe I'll skip breakfast. If there's nothing else, I'll get back to work." That strategy failed: my mother is still loitering in my kitchen. "I have quite a deadline," I say.

"So, how is your work going?" The question surprises me. My mother has zero interest in my work, doesn't understand my work, and therefore hates my work. I think it is the fact that neither she nor Urs can nose around my PC to see what I'm up to that makes her so detest my job – a position compounded by me writing notes for myself in Chinese, precisely to thwart their ceaseless mission to find out 'what I'm up to'; I once crept into the kitchen to find Urs desperately leafing through one of my Chinese dictionaries in an unsuccessful attempt to translate a reminder I had written myself to buy tofu.

"I've got loads on. I've got a large investment report to finish by close of today. Actually it's really interesting . . . is it better to invest in renewable energy or food products?"

Mother and Urs are looking concerned rather than interested.

"And then what?" Annoyingly, my mother is looking at Urs to answer this.

"And then nothing," said Urs quietly. "She hasn't got anything else."

Maybe I shouldn't have agreed to Urs doing my books. I knew at the time it was a ploy to see what I was up to rather than sororal charity, but what sane person would turn down the offer of having her tax returns filled in for nothing?

"Did this man offer you money?"

"What man?" And then I realise that my mother is talking about Fred. I roll my eyes and shake my head. I know how her mind is working.

I really don't know why there is this obsession with my supposed sex life. Taking up a religion that was alien to them was definitely a factor. The departure from what was considered 'the norm' was also a factor, but simply put, I changed, and moved outside their comfort zones, though it seems to me that any change moves some people out of their comfort zones. Our family never even went abroad for a holiday, such was my mother's fear of the unknown. I find this damp sock stuck somewhere at the back of my mind:

Dad (tentatively): We could probably afford to go to Thailand for ten days.

Mother (with a sharp intake of breath): The girls have never been on a plane before.

Me: Let's get on a plane!

Mother: It's a long journey. If you don't like flying, you can't just get off.

Urs: We can sleep. It will be like going to bed but waking up somewhere else.

Mother: No, I don't think so. Nothing wrong with Norfolk.

Dad: I didn't say there was anything wrong with Norfolk.

Mother: So why do you want to go to Thailand?

Dad: I didn't say I wanted to go there. I just said we could probably afford it.

The quashing of his idea must have affected him badly, because he took up his downtrodden stance in the back garden, smoking a wonky roll-up with tobacco sticking out of the ends, and holding an ashtray far out in front of him. Normally he played music when he was upset, but I picture him then smoking in twilight, so I guess it was too late for him to spin records. As for our summer holiday, we spent a week or so in Cromer or Crowborough; wherever it was, it was as windy as hell.

I'm not sure my poor father ever once got on a plane. There always seemed to be a reason why he couldn't. Only now does it occur to me that I should have invited him over to Taiwan. I spent many happy years there, improving my Chinese and supporting myself quite adequately by teaching English, so I could have invited him at least once. But that was before my mountain experience, and I was still selfish and ego-bound, and too busy sending missives home about how everything in the East was better. Whatever I said, my mother acted as if I had joined a brainwashing cult, and seems to have devoted her days since to a state of watchfulness for signs that I might 'return' to the dark side. She tricked me into coming back to visit my dying sister, but unfortunately had neglected to inform Urs that she must dress in a shroud and look viably-challenged. And so I returned voluntarily to find a healthy sister who hadn't changed, but who was united with my mother in an assertion that I had. As for my father, he must have finally worked up the nerve to flee from my mother, for he left soon after my return.

Maybe one day I could take him away. I will get back

to Taiwan just as soon as I've figured out a way of getting back the money that has been (inexplicably) removed from my account, on my instructions, according to the bank. This is why I only disclose half of my earnings to Urs. The rest is cash, paid by Chinese students who need help in translating essays, or by two-bit English translators who desperately accept agency work, and then find that they are incapable of translating the work they have been given. I will never be rich, but I am slowly building up enough money for the air fare back, and some basic living expenses until I get a decent teaching job.

"Are you OK, Winnie?" My mother's voice. We're in the kitchen.

"She'll come back in a second," says Urs, wearily.

It's time that mother and elder sister got out of my space. I take out the wok.

"What are you doing?" asks Mum, as though I had just extracted a land-mine from the cupboard.

"Breakfast." I wash some spinach. Usually, the comfortingly bland smell of rice fills the kitchen by the time I'm up, but I realise that today there is no such smell. I set the rice cooker each night to come on seven hours later, and I know I set it last night, because I leave myself a note to do so. Except that today, it has been switched off and the rice is sitting inertly in a bath of cold water.

"Who the fuck switched off my rice?"

"You can't have switched it on," says Urs.

"Actually . . . it was me," says Mother, at least having the grace to look guilty. "I saw the red light and thought you'd forgotten to switch something off. Sorry. Can't you just have cornflakes?"

19

Ten minutes later, I have my little house to myself. My mother has gone to work, wearing spinach, and there is a trail of drowned rice over the kitchen table, though none went in Urs's laptop – because I do have some morals. And because she snapped shut her laptop as soon as she saw me wrench the bowl from the rice cooker.

As I am eating my spinach with instant noodles, I brood over the level of interference in my life. And the inquisition about the old man. It occurs to me now that their concern wasn't that I had let a strange man into the house – but that the strange man didn't exist at all – a figment of my imagination. I'm almost starting to doubt myself.

Upstairs, I hit the keyboard to vanquish the screen saver. The screen resumes its display of a document outlining the investment potential of Chinese alternative energy companies. I'm about to tackle a piece on Biofuels.

Two hours later, it is all coming together; the final section is a summary of everything that has gone before, and needs little work to translate. I've learnt that it is good to take a break before the final polishing, so I will return to it later to double check that it reads smoothly. I am now aware that the Chinese are way ahead of us in terms of renewable energy – an amazing shift for a country that used to proudly show off its polluted rivers to western visitors as proof of industrial advance.

So, to quote my mother: And then what? It is Easter; the Chinese students have no essays they need help with, and there has been a dearth of would-be English translators needing to sub-contract work. I search for translation agencies asking for help (zilch), and review my profile on Translation websites: I had listed my specialisms as Finance, Legal (that was pushing it), and Technical; I can't think of anything else to add that will entice any organisation to send me work.

I won't starve – not for a few weeks, anyway – but at this rate I will have to plunder my secret Return-to-Taiwan fund. Right now I would even accept the shite assignments that I normally turn down, such as translation agencies offering some dreadful piece of work, like translating a badly scanned copy of a badly written exam paper by a bad student, who has no aptitude for Chinese, but has been told that it is the language of the future. But even these are not forthcoming.

When the phone rings, I briefly allow myself the luxury of imagining a desperate translation agency in need of a brilliant translator, but it is just Urs.

"Are you OK now?"

"I was OK before – until you two decided to wreck my breakfast."

"That was Mum, not me. She was really sorry, by the way. But it was an accident. You could control your temper a bit better."

"I could change the locks." (Though I wouldn't put it past either of them to put a ladder up to my bedroom sash window).

Urs sighs. "No, you can't. I'll tell Mum to back off."

"Thank you."

"Anything else I can do?"

"Yes, this is a silly question. Have I ever written anything? You know – had something published?"

Urs laughs – a laugh of derision rather than humour. "You? No. I don't remember you being at all creative." And then more suspiciously: "Why? What made you think you wrote something?"

"Oh, nothing. It doesn't matter."

"No, go on."

"OK. A different question. If I said 'chaos is come again' – would it mean anything to you?"

She repeats "Chaos is come again" several times. "It rings a bell, but I can't remember where from."

"It doesn't matter."

"Have you tried googling it?"

Of course I have. I google everything. "Yes," I say. "It's a Shakespeare quote. But then again, just about every quote seems to be from Shakespeare." Or from the Bible, but less of that.

A mini explosion of recognition comes down the phone. "I remember a teacher saying it years ago. But it really was years ago. And he wasn't a drama teacher."

"Do you remember his name?"

"God, now you're asking. I remember he was a bit eccentric. Why?"

"Oh, just trying to place a memory." Mother and Urs like it when I try and remember things, as though this offers me a road back to who (they say) I was. So I can hear Urs making approving sounds down the fibre optics.

"It's just come back to me: Mr Fallowfield. Do you remember him? He was History."

I was History. Son of Gadd.

I end the conversation as normally as I can, because I want to get downstairs and answer the door, (which is being urgently thumped) without alerting my sister to the fact that our old History teacher is probably on my doorstep, right now.

When I open the door, he is torn between greeting me and turning around to scan the street behind him. It is a warm day, but he is in his same shabby suit, with a faded tie, and probably the same shoes he wore to school almost fifteen years previously.

"I think I've shaken her off," he says, glancing behind him again, as if the street conceals snipers.

"Come in, Mr Fallowfield."

He beams. "You remember me." (Not exactly.) "But I think you're old enough to call me Fred."

Fred rejects my offer of tea (on account of his kidneys), and sherry (on account of his liver), but in the front room, he accepts a roll-up from me (on account that his wife wouldn't like it).

"She's become very interfering," he says, sadly. "She keeps hiding the car keys, and she's taken away my credit card. She found the bill from the private investigator, and his letter with your address." He has forgotten the roll-up, which goes out in the ashtray. But I don't mind; the thought of an old teacher accepting a fag from a former schoolgirl is satisfying enough. No need to inhale.

"Why Mr Fallowfield?" I ask. "I mean why aren't you Fred Gadd?"

"My wife's name is 'Maddy'. Maddy Fallowfield."

"You took her surname because she didn't want to be called 'Maddy Gadd'?"

"That's right. And because she hated my father." He goes silent for a moment, presumably reliving some fraught scene in their early relationship. "My father wasn't very nice to women, if I'm honest. But if I had realised what problems lay ahead when I gave up my name, I would have kept my surname."

"Problems?"

"There's no son of Gadd. I've left him in limbo. I don't

think he can move on." At this point, Fred Fallowfield, né Gadd, realises he's warm and takes off his jacket. I hold out a hand to take it, but he's suddenly distracted by my empty old armchair opposite; he hangs up the jacket on the carpet.

"But you are the son of Gadd. You said so."

"Yes, but I didn't keep his name. It's like he didn't have a son."

I have that same vision of him sitting in the centre of a circle of pupils. We are firing questions at him – history questions, and he is answering each one with joy, with triumph; he is happy. He is not the man who slumps before me now, who is definitely not happy. I wonder when chaos came and did not depart.

"You said that Mr Gadd kept coming back. What did you mean?"

Fred runs a weary hand over his hair-fringed dome. "Dreams. Sometimes I hear him call my name. But mainly I see him in dreams – always off to the side, just staring at me."

"OK, but these are your dreams. He is your creation. I mean, he's not really haunting you. Is he?"

Fred gives me a haunted look. "But he is. Particularly in the early hours. I wake up paralysed, and I can see the door open and he walks in – just the outline of him – but it is dark. Then he comes over and leans on my chest so that I can't breathe – and he whispers something, but I can never quite make it out."

"Sleep paralysis. Our minds wake up before our bodies. Every culture has folklore about the phenomenon. In the west, we tend to feminise it and call it the Old Hag. The Chinese call it Ghost pressing on the body."

"The Chinese have it right," he says, with a great weariness.

"He was just sitting there a moment ago." He nods at the empty armchair. "Gone now, of course. He disappears when I try and look directly at him."

The weird thing is that there is a depression in the arm-chair, which I hadn't noticed before. I know it is just auto-suggestion, and I'm annoyed to find that I am as susceptible as my peers-with-heads.

"Don't take offence," I say now - knowing that I would be offended if someone asked me this - "but have you been checked-out by a doctor?"

He grunts with exasperation. "Nurses, nurses - all the time. Do you know what day it is? Do you know where you are?"

"Do you know who the prime minister is?"

He meets my eyes. "Yes, yes - you're right. That question again and again. Sometimes I say 'Pitt the Younger', just to shut them up." He gives a withering look. "They don't even know who Pitt the Younger was."

He still hasn't told me who the prime minister is, and I have no idea what to say next, so I roll up a ciggie, which prompts him to fish his own from the ashtray and to lean forward to suck the flame from my lighter. He sucks too hard, and a flame creeps up the paper towards his nose, startling him into flinging it away. As a test of the flame retardant qualities of my sofa, it is a partially successful exercise.

"Sorry," says Fred, after I rescue the glowing butt from the little brown-rimmed crater on the central cushion.

"Let's go back to your father. Why do you think I can help you?"

"You wrote about him. The giddy career of Mr Gadd (deceased). You must remember."

"No, I don't."

He leans forward. "I always wanted to ask you, Winifred – why giddy? The giddy career always sounded a bit frivolous, and Mr Gadd was not a frivolous man – as you know. And neither were you. I wondered if you meant it literally, because of the heights he attained." I must look completely blank, because he immediately adds "the spiritual heights, of course", as if that would help.

"I'm afraid I don't remember any of this. Did I know him?"

"Not directly, but of course you knew me, and you had such a knack of picking things up. I mean I bet you didn't know Turner's wife, Sylvia – but you certainly picked that up, and wrote about it, didn't you?"

Did I? I doubt it. I only tend to remember what matters, which is all of my time in Taiwan, some of my time in university, and a few damp socks of teenagehood and childhood experiences. What Fred is describing sounds significant – significant to him, anyway – yet there are no bells ringing, not even a wisp of familiarity scratching my skull. As for writing anything – blank.

"So when exactly was this?" I ask. "Did we meet up when I was at university?"

"No, Winifred. When you were a pupil."

"Do you mean I was at school when I wrote this stuff? What? Like . . . do you mean history essays?"

"Not history, exactly," says Fred, looking a little ashamed. "But yes, they were nominally essays. To most people they would have appeared as assignments."

I start to wonder if Fred is a little odd rather than just a little old.

"Fred, whatever these essays were about, they're stories

from a schoolgirl, not Nostradamic scribblings. You're the one who's finding some meaning in them."

Fred closes his eyes:

"At the close of day, there is only the wisp of smoke to mark the death of dreams,

Survey your fallow fields, where weeds bind you to the present and free you from the crops of the past

With their roots in broken China, in imagined scenes of blue and white

The Willow bends to slake its thirst, while a pagoda tops a hill

Now just wish bone ash in which to grow your broken dreams

No easy road for the sun to rise again

And tomorrow brings chaos dressed up to pass for a day"

He opens his eyes and nods to me. "Do you see?"

"Not really. Did I write that?"

"I can't believe you don't remember," Fred says, and then he looks up and gives me an agonised look. "Did they give you ECT? I thought they might one day, you know. When those with dim eyes are bedazzled by brightness, they would rather darken the brilliance than welcome the light."

I think this is a compliment, and it's a tribute to him that he recognised my potential when I was presumably still an adolescent girl. "No, I never had ECT," I say. "No-one has done anything to me. To be honest, if I had any brilliance, you were the only one who recognised it."

He snorted. "Turner certainly didn't. That bloody mediocre idiot. I had to explain your biblical allusions to him."

"Who's Turner?"

Fred looks at me. "Well, he's dead now – isn't he? Just like you warned him."

"Oh. Well, who was Turner, then?"

He gives a heavy sigh. "What did they do to you? How can you have forgotten everything?"

"I haven't forgotten everything. I just choose not to remember it."

"Why on earth would you choose to forget?"

It is always tempting to talk about my experience up the mountain, but I have had such a negative reaction from people – Urs in particular – that I now keep that memory under lock and key; I literally visualise it as something in a big cave with a boulder rolled over the entrance. I don't know why people are so resistant – I assume once they have heard of my little awakening they feel that I am elevated and they are therefore (relatively) diminished; when, of course, the only person truly diminished by the experience is 'Me'.

But Fred will be different. He won't feel envy or threatened or belittled; in fact, my present condition will be confirmation that whatever potential he saw in me has been realised.

"Have you heard of *satori?*"

He shakes his head twice. And so I tell him about my experience in Taiwan, when I became headless; when I lost myself and all the fiddly, fumbly fetters of my petty existence. He listens with dull attention; a couple of times I notice that his eyes slide towards the empty armchair, and I wonder if I have an audience of two. When I have finished, he sits there mutely, staring ahead. I am strangely disappointed to see no joy in him after hearing about the only real thing that ever happened to me.

"So you're enlightened?"

"No, not enlightened. It's just an early sign. I really want to get back to Taiwan and practise more. I need to spend time in a monastery. I can't make any progress while I'm stuck over here."

"And this . . . experience . . . it wiped out your memory? Just like that?"

"Not at all. It's partly deliberate and partly that I no longer trust memories, so I can't be bothered to dig them out."

It was through meditation that I learnt about how flawed our memories are. We just register the emotion of an event and then store a narrative that supports that emotion. And occasionally an emotional response we've had to a situation now causes us to retrieve some semblance of the old memory and play with it and stain it further with whatever dye our present situation is coloured with, and then put that changed thing back into our brains. And then we remember that memory, which is even further removed from whatever it was originally connected with, and so the memory gets even more ego-fluff stuck to it.

"So you don't remember why you wrote what you wrote?"

"No. Sorry. Whatever I wrote when I was at school couldn't have meant that much to me."

"And you don't want to remember?"

"God, no. It's taken me years to get to this stage."

"But what about . . . ?" He chokes on the next word, so that I'm not sure whether he's said 'Gadd' or 'Dad'. And while I'm trying to figure out what he said, my seventy-something year old history teacher wraps his arms around his knees and starts rocking. I watch, baffled by this alien movement. His body is shaking.

I have the sinking feeling that Fred might be sobbing on my sofa.

I can't think of anything I said that should produce this

29

reaction. I find him a box of tissues, then go into the kitchen and make us jasmine tea, which I assume is kidney-friendly or liver-friendly or whatever friendly it needs to be. When I bring the mugs out to the front room, Fred has stopped sobbing, but is still hugging his knees, as hunched as a sick animal.

"OK," I say. "I'll try and help, but I don't know how."

He is pathetically grateful, and makes a lunge for my hands. Fortunately Urs had insisted that I get a tea-coloured carpet (though I doubt she foresaw this particular scene), and the jasmine tea will soon be pretty much indistinguishable from whatever else she or I have spilt over the last couple of years.

"Don't thank me," I say. "I haven't done anything yet."

"But you have, Winifred, you have. You have given me hope. You're a saint." He gives a shy chuckle. "Do you remember your story about the saints? Too dark for Turner, of course."

"No."

"About the people in a church singing that they would love to be in that number, when the saints come marching in? And how they would love it when the sun stopped shining and the moon turned blood red. And then the congregation heard the sound of marching and they fell silent with fear, and the windows of the church darkened, and the chancery turned caliginous, and the transepts turned tenebrous and the sun might as well have stopped shining, for its light was blocked by an army of saints peering through the stained glass windows . . ." - Fred's eyes are shut, his face enraptured by the words that I think he is reciting verbatim - ". . . Then the canonised corpses entered the church and they marched down the aisle. And the congregation were terrified and repulsed. For the saints were not just rotting bodies, but were missing body parts. Some had no fingers, no tongue, no ribs; a couple had no heads. And soon they were wrenching open the reliquaries, opening the ossuaries, manhandling the monstrances. Trying on relics for size. And then they start fighting amongst themselves. That finger is mine. Those were my ribs. Give me that leg bone, so that I may be whole for the Resurrection."

Oh God. A damp sock is twitching. Maybe I did write that.

He laughs. "You know, Turner had to read your essays with a dictionary in one hand. Drove him mad that a fourteen-year old girl used words that he didn't know."

That definitely sounds like me.

"Parvenu," says Fred, with a bit of a sneer.

Turner must have been my English teacher. The name is ringing a vague bell, though that might just be because Fred has mentioned him several times now.

Fred glances at the empty armchair, but Mr Gadd must be absent, for Fred's face turns back to me, and he is still smiling. "The other reason Turner hated your stories were that they were all 'morbid' – his words. I think you forced him to face his own mortality. Rather ironic, as it turned out."

I want to ask him how I warned Turner about his manner of dying, but Fred has got a zealous look in his eyes. "Morbidity! That's the answer. We need the intercession of the saints to help you remember."

"How, exactly?" I hope he isn't going to drag me into a church. Much as I try to forget, there are a few very smelly socks stuck to the back of my mind regarding the services and masses my mother made the young me sit through.

"We'll go to All Saints' Cemetery. Right now."

A cemetery sounds more palatable. "I haven't heard of that one. Where is it?"

"Nunhead cemetery," he says. "That's what they call it now."

Fred levers himself up and seems ready to go, but I take the mugs into the kitchen (Urs has a particular aversion to mugs that aren't left in the kitchen) and then I insist that we each have a drink of water and a banana before the journey, which I think is going to take at least a trip on the tube and then a train. He alternates the water and bites of banana as if they were medication he has to take, under sufferance, and then is by the front door, fidgeting impatiently.

"Toilet, maybe," I say. "While we're here."

He says he doesn't need to, but when I insist, he works his way up the stairs and is in the bathroom for a while. I rescue his glass from the bin, the banana skin from the washing bowl, and his jacket from the front room carpet. It jangles slightly, and I find a bunch of keys including a car key in a pocket; clearly, Mrs Fallowfield needs to work on her key-hiding skills.

Outside, Fred sets off down my short front path and stops on the pavement, looking discomfited.

"Someone's stolen my car," he says.

"Where did you park it?"

"Right there, by the tree." He points to a neighbour's car, which I suspect has been directly outside my house all day, and that is when I notice that Fred is now wearing my watch.

"There's a brown estate down there," I say, noticing that said car is straddling the pavement three houses down.

"Someone's moved it," says Fred. "I know I parked there."

And he had. Yesterday. Or whenever it was.

When we reach his car, he hands me the keys. "Probably

best if you drive. I get a little lost sometimes so have to use the TomTom and the woman's voice drives me mad." He pauses when he sees my hesitation. "You do know how to drive, don't you, Winifred?"

My father taught me, and he was a good teacher. Though I do remember driving into my parents' garage (which wasn't open), and my father saying: "Oh bollocks, your mother will be mad" and a green smear of paint on the very slightly crushed bonnet of our non-green car. Dad was right about a lot of things in those days. My mother was mad.

"Winifred?"

"Sorry?"

"You do know how to drive?"

I sit in the driver's seat and look at the dashboard. There's loads of things on there. I get out again. "I think best you drive, Fred. It's been a while."

I find the postcode of Nunhead cemetery on my phone, and Fred enters it on the sat-nav.

"Turn LEFT into Briscoe Road."

Her voice is a bit loud. Fred grimaces.

"She reminds me of my wife when she's trying to pretend that she's concealing her irritation when she really wants me to know that she's irritated. I don't suppose you know what I mean?"

"Yes, I do."

We set off, and are soon lost in a symphony of car horns.

Chapter Three

FRED SEEMS TO drive OK, though he groans every time the Irritating Lady tells him to go straight on. Actually she does not have much to say as we are mainly on one road: our journey is the above ground counterpart to the Northern line, as evidenced by the stations we're passing: Tooting Broadway, Tooting Bec, Balham, the three Claphams. It's a route I often take, but only as far as Borough.

There is a cage in the back of the car – but empty.

"You have a dog?" I ask.

"Dog? Yes. Well, no, well . . ."

"There's a dog cage in the back."

He rubs his eyes with one hand, and the car swerves slightly. "That's right. We used to have a dog. A black Labrador." He sighs. "Lovely creature. I often wonder what happened to Lucy."

I'm glad that I'm not driving. The traffic is heavy, and though the sheer volume of cars means we are moving at a sedate pace, I am finding it a bit busy. I notice that a red light is constantly illuminated on the dashboard: an outline of a car with a line sticking out the back. I have no idea what this means. We are driving a car with a fishing rod sticking out the back? Or the aerial is about to fall off? Anyway, whatever the red light is trying to tell Fred, he doesn't appear to have noticed, and the car seems to be going OK.

Bang.

"Oh no," Fred groans.

"It's not your fault. The traffic lights went green. They rolled backwards."

"No, I think I may have gone forwards," says Fred.

We have given the lightest of taps to an estate car in front. It's a silver estate – and it is stationary, which means that we can't get going again. I look behind to see if Fred can reverse, and I see that the boot door of our Volvo has elevated itself: presumably Mr or Mrs Fallowfield did not lock it securely. I might as well get out and see if the driver of the silver car is planning on going any time soon.

I get out and cast an eye back to see if cars are queuing up behind us. Yes, there's an instant queue, and a horn concerto serenades our little prang. I idly notice that car horns in unison – like church bells – strike a minor chord; it's a rather mournful tone, and I suspect one which will replay in my head tonight when I'm trying to sleep.

In the silver car ahead, the driver's door is pushed open, causing an impatient overtaking driver to swing abruptly out to the right. Then some legs appear, and eventually the rest of an elderly woman. It takes her a while to extricate herself, and she treats the door as a gigantic grab rail. I guess she's in her seventies.

"I'm so sorry," she says.

A girl with mousey pigtails climbs out of the passenger side and amazes me by getting taller and taller as she emerges. I had assumed she was about eight years old, but the way she is now towering over the side of the car and motioning with a 'hush' finger on her lips across the car roof at the elderly woman, well – she must be at least five foot twelve.

I'm wondering what sort of condition causes a child to grown so abnormally tall.

"Shhh Mum, you must never say you're sorry. Never."

It is only when I hear her talk that I realise that she is probably more my age. The pigtails have a sort of infantilising effect. It's a bit odd. And she's not really much taller than me.

"But I am," wails the old woman. "I thought I had it in first gear, but it didn't . . . what's the word? It didn't catch."

"You were just a bit slow with the handbrake. That's all. It wasn't your fault."

"I'm sure there's something wrong with the gears. I wish you'd let me buy a smaller car."

"Hello," I say. But they seem to be locked in a private family bubble, soundproofed against both my voice and the aggressive tooting of drivers who are having to pull out into the right-hand lane.

"There's nothing wrong with the gears, Mum. He shouldn't have gone into the back of you."

"But I didn't go when the lights went green."

"Shh Mum. Saying sorry affects your insurance."

"Hello," I try again.

"Diana," says Fred. I hadn't noticed him get out of the car, but he is leaning on the driver's door and staring intently at Pigtails.

It is funny how, whether distracted or dreaming, people with egos can hear their name. She instantly turns towards him. "How do you know who I am?"

"Do you know her?" I ask Fred.

Fred snorts. "Diana Candle." He looks at me and murmurs "She cried over Eva Braun's death." He closes his eyes as if landing a memory. "Yes, I'm sure it was Eva Braun. No-one else cried over Eva Braun. Not even her husband."

I'm struggling a little bit. I'm trying to remember which part of this day seemed normal. I try to ground myself but my usual Om sound is being overlaid by car horns.

"Winnie?" says pigtail girl/woman, staring at me.

"What? Winnie Rigby?" says her mother, and the twitches on her face indicate that she doesn't know whether to smile nervously, or frown nervously or just look nervous nervously.

Pigtails. Oh God. A damp sock is twitching. "Di?"

"ana," Pigtails and nervous mother chorus.

And back it comes. Diana, who I called Di (i.e. 'Die') - to wind her up - hung around me at school. And she hasn't changed that much, in that she's still a skinny girl with pigtails. I think she was a bit timid then. I'm not sure what she is now. Ill at ease, certainly. She seems to be vibrating with some uncomfortable energy. Surely not from having a little tap from Fallowfield's car. Really - we barely touched the silver tank.

I can see her staring at me, puzzled. And then a delighted grin, which must come from recognition.

"Winnie? This is so weird." And then she's looking at Fred, and her confusion is evident.

A car slows down, hoots three times, and the fat man in the passenger seat shouts out of the window "you should pull over instead of blocking the traffic." Diana screams back, "Why don't you just fuck off and die?", which is interesting, because she never ever used the D-word when I knew her. Mrs Candle makes indistinct clucking noises, like a distressed grouse, but whether these signal reproof at Diana's language, or fear that the man in the car will get out and thump her, I don't know.

As it is, the passenger looks a little taken back, but any

reciprocal action is thwarted when whoever is in the driving seat takes note of the honking cars behind him and pulls away.

"I'm sorry," says Diana to us. "I think I'm in shock. I had a bit of whip lash."

She massages the back of her neck and holds her hand out as if to confirm that it is indeed shaking. I check the cars for signs of damage.

"I'm sorry, I can't really place you," I hear Diana tell Fred. "You're not Winnie's . . . How do you know me?"

Fred sniffs a theatrical sniff. "I don't know you. I remember you." He looks at her nervous mother. "And I believe I remember you."

Diana's mother says, "Do you? Have we met?"

"I'll never forget the parents' evening when you asked me to teach cheerful history. Cheerful!"

"What's wrong with that?" asks Diana.

"There is no cheerful history." He looks at me. "Come on, Winifred, who said, 'Happy are the people whose annals are blank in history books'?"

"Um . . . Thomas Carlyle?" That came out of nowhere. I can't see any damage. I think that's what happens when one estate car hits another: not a lot.

"Of course," Fred beams. "Well done, Winifred. It was Thomas Carlyle."

I can't even see a scratch. Bending down is making me dizzy. I straighten up.

"Mr Fallowfield?" says Diana.

"Yes, Diana."

Then she looks at me and back at him and back at me, and I can see her confusion. "Where's your Dad?" she asks me.

I can guarantee that he will be standing outside Borough

station right now, but I'm not going to tell her that. "My parents split up a while ago." Was it two years? One year? I can't remember.

Mother and Daughter Candle both make sympathetic sounds.

"This is nice," says Mrs Candle, hanging onto the side of the car as if she would topple over without its support. "Isn't it lovely to bump into your old friend?"

"A lovely coincidence," says Di.

"Serendipitous," says Fred. He pats the top of his car door and looks at me. "But Winifred, I think it's time we . . ."

"I was saying that you should try and look up some old friends and see if they've moved on." I think Mrs Candle is talking to her daughter rather than to one of us.

Diana's smile disappears at her mother's words. "What do you mean, moved on?"

"I just meant . . ."

All this time, cars are still hooting and honking. I head-hop, and can see that through their eyes, we look like two parties who've stopped for some gossip by the traffic lights.

"I'd better shut the back before we set off," I say, hoping this will deliver unequivocal closing signals. And that is when Fred turns and sees the boot open.

"Lucy," cries Fred. "Oh, my God. My wife will kill me."

"You've lost a dog?" asks Mrs Candle, and I can see that her concern is genuine.

"A Labrador. A beautiful black Labrador." He seems on the verge of tears.

"Oh no," says Di. "How awful."

Great. We are bringing this to a close. I go to the back and pretend to shut the cage door (which in truth was already

39

shut). "The back shot up with the impact," I say. "Poor thing. She must have run off, terrified."

"Oh, my God," says Fred. "Poor, poor Lucy." He starts hyperventilating. I am now worried that he really thinks we have just lost his dog, which - for all I know - died three prime ministers ago.

And that was probably because Fred forgot to feed her.

He is now wheezing and clutching his left arm.

"Should we call an ambulance?" asks Mrs Candle, whilst Diana - I notice - has retreated to the passenger door.

"No, no," I say quickly. "He just needs to have his pills."

"I'm sure you'll find your dog," says Mrs Candle, now working her way up the car to the driver's door.

"Yes, I'm sure we will." I'm pretty sure we won't.

"I'll Facebook you, Win," calls Diana, now halfway in the car.

"Yes. Great." I do hate the way nouns become verbs.

"No," says Mrs Candle. "Come round and see us properly."

"OK." I have no idea where they live or what seeing someone 'properly' means, but at least they are going in the right direction.

A quick getaway is foiled by Mrs Candle having to work her way into her seat by using the door as a grab rail; once in and belted, she pulls out with such little warning that the cars behind brake with shrieks.

"Come on, Fred. Everything's OK now." Fred straightens up and watches me slam the back of the car. He seems to be in a state of suspension, so I gently take his non-heart-clutching arm and encourage him into the driver's side.

"Are you alright?" I ask, when I return to the passenger seat.

"Winifred. I'm having . . . I'm . . . Damn it. Have we just lost the dog?"

"No."

He sighs – I think with relief. "Oh good. My wife would kill me if I lost her again. I mean if Lucy had come back and then I'd lost her."

"Right. Don't worry, you haven't lost anything. Not today. We just pretended that we had."

"Ah." He gives a half-grin. "Yes, of course. To get rid of those blasted women. Good idea, Winifred."

But I am a little troubled as he pulls away to an elevated volume of horns. I try to disentangle this odd feeling of discomfort. I feel sorry that Mrs Candle seems so old now – I have a feeling that I liked her. But something else is troubling me: pretending to lose a dog was maybe not so good. Of all the five Buddhist precepts: no harmful action, no false speech, no stealing, no sexual misconduct, no intoxication – no false speech is the one I find easiest to follow. In fact, Urs sometimes whines at me "you could just lie once in a while", when I voice some unpalatable truth. But I have just told a few lies, and Winnie Rigby never, ever lies.

The path into Nunhead cemetery pulls you down into the nether world as if invisible hands were drawing you down to an oasis. It is something about the dampness that your body reacts to before your mind recognises what is happening. My spirits rise so noticeably that I wonder if I haven't been depressed these last few months.

I feel more at home here than I have felt anywhere else since my forced return to the UK.

I wish I had my camera, or at least I wish I had a camera, as I can't remember having owned one. I must have had one in Taiwan, but if I did, I can't remember what shots I took or what happened to it. The light is dim in here, but that just accentuates the solemnity of the sagging graves and sinking stones, whose uneven descent has left stone angels guarding their graves at crazy angles. In the neglected area of the cemetery we are now in, the statues are dressed in green, the graves being reclaimed by nature.

Despite his advanced years and a limping gait, Fred seems to keep up with me without too much effort. We are strangely in tune, choosing paths as if with one mind, stopping to read gravestones in synchronised arrest. There is no "shall we go this way?" or "I just want to look at this one more closely". No wonder we got on at school.

"Is Mr Gadd here?" I meant, of course, did Fred sense his father peeping out at him from behind a tree or a gravestone, but he takes me literally.

"No, no, of course not. He died overseas – as you know."

Maybe what I know will come back to me. All that I know is that I'm now feeling like I'm on a ghost ride in a funfair, being bombarded by little pastiches of human horror. Disembodied faces are briefly illuminated but without context. It is strange. One of those faces has pigtails.

"I knew Diana Candle at primary school," I find myself saying. "I remember now. She said her hamster was seven years old."

Fred frowns. "I thought hamsters only lived for a couple of years. Isn't that why parents purchase them? To introduce their children to impermanence and death?"

"Exactly. I remember telling Diana that it wasn't the same hamster, and that every time one died, her parents were rushing out to buy one that looked the same."

"You're really telling me that a girl of primary school age did not know about death?" asks Fred. "Were there no deaths in the family?"

"Now that you mention it, I do remember Mrs Candle saying that her mother had just gone on a long-term cruise to South America. I suspect she didn't come back."

Fred snorts.

And I now remember that Diana's mother was so annoyed about my 'hamster revelation' that she came around to see my mother to complain that I was exposing her daughter to unnecessary information. In fact, I remember crouching on the landing as my mother stood in the doorway and said "but surely Diana knows about death? She must know that people die?"

And Mrs Candle answering, "She's too young. You must promise me that Winifred will never mention death to her again."

My mother: "But Diana must know. The news is full of people dying."

Mrs Candle, in a brittle voice: "We don't let her watch the news. It's too realistic."

I can't remember exactly what my mother said next, but the gist of it was that she wasn't going to ask her daughter to censor the truth and that Mrs Candle should stop being so silly. (I can't actually remember what word my mother used: it is unlikely that she would have used 'silly' – maybe she said 'sensitive'). Anyway, it was from then on that I started calling Diana "Die", which she didn't like.

I suddenly feel a little flush of pride for my own mother. She stood up for me that day. Of course, her concept of death was cosseted by equally bizarre notions of the afterlife and eternal resurrection, but death was still a fact of life that she fully accepted we should understand. In fact, she exposed me to it in a refreshingly brutal manner. She must have felt sufficiently motivated to get us on a plane, as she took me and Urs for a long weekend in Venice so that we could visit the Basilica San Marco and ogle the ossuaries and feel reverence for the relics. Urs hated it, pronouncing the wizened bits of body "disgusting and creepy". I'm afraid that I was fascinated: my mother seemed so pleased with me, mistaking my morbid fascination for awe. And that's where I must have got my idea from: the day the Saints came marching in.

Turner. I can visualise him now: a florid face capped with long greasy hair punches its way out of the shadows. He had said to write something about 'Resurrection'. The boys wrote stories of footballers resuming their careers after repairs to cruciate ligaments and hamstrings, the girls wrote about Jesus – long tracts sounding suspiciously like they had been downloaded from a virtual bible. Except for two girls: I wrote about the saints marching back to reclaim their body parts, and Diana wrote a love story about a couple rekindling their relationship after a quarrel and going out for a nice meal. It has come back to me.

"How come you remember Diana?" I ask Fred. "It was fifteen years ago – probably more. You're not telling me that you remember every pupil in your classes?"

"I remember the best, Winifred," and he gives me his shy, sideways look. "And I remember the very worst. Though if I'm honest, I remember Diana because of her mother. You know, she said to me one parents' evening that I was only to teach cheerful history?"

"Yes, you said." Actually, I feel rather sorry that I called Diana 'Die'. The Candles were a bit precious about avoiding the 'bad' things in life, but it was a childish thing to do: verging on O.M.G. puerility.

We have reached a large mausoleum, presumably for a well-to-do family. One slab of stone has shifted slightly and I get down on my knees to peer into the darkness below. In the gloom I can see old coffins stacked – not our modern rectangle boxes with gleaming metal-effect handles, but the old-style Dracula-shaped coffins.

"That's amazing," I say. "You can actually see coffins down there. I can't believe that this place isn't visited by necrophiliac teenagers."

"Well, we do seem to have the place to ourselves," says Fred.

And that is when I notice that there is no-one else around. The odd little dribs and drabs of humanity that we have occasionally glimpsed on our stroll have disappeared. Blackbirds are in the trees whistling for the coming of twilight. We are completely alone apart from the worms, birds and corpses.

"What time is it?" I ask.

Mr Fallowfield casts a look at his wrist and reads my watch. "It's gone six o'clock." He makes a face. "I'll be late for tea. Blasted woman is very strict about meal times."

"This place probably shuts at five."

Sure enough, when we wander back to the main gate, it is securely fastened. We spend some time walking around the perimeter of the graveyard as the volume of the blackbirds' sad warnings increases, and is joined by the machine-gun chatter of magpies distressed by our presence. Now I can see why the cemetery is not frequented by necromancing teenagers or satanic worshippers: they can't get in at night. The huge metal fences are crowned with angled metal spikes. Which is sensible, but does mean that we can't get out.

"Oh dear, Winifred. What shall we do?" says Fred. "Chaos is come again." He sounds unsettled.

"Find the most sheltered spot we can." I have a brief fantasy about trying to shift the slab of stone and dropping down into the crypt, but abandon it, reluctantly. It would mean quite a drop into the darkness below. Moreover, it would be a very embarrassing scene in the morning, when early morning visitors to the cemetery would hear voices from the crypt below, calling for a ladder. Actually, it could be really funny.

Mr Fallowfield looks at me. "You mean – spend the night here?"

"Yes." Surely he can't be scared.

"But she'll kill me. I'm supposed to take pills in the evening. And eat. And I've got to tell her that I've lost Lucy. She's going to be furious."

"You haven't lost Lucy – or at least not today."

"Oh, of course, it wasn't today was it? But Maddy will still be furious."

"OK, OK." And actually, I have pills I'm meant to take in the evening. Though I suspect that my evening headache won't bother to visit tonight. In fact, I really feel good – better than I can remember. I don't know if it is the dampness or the peace or the proximity to death, but I feel alive.

"Can you get us out of here, Winifred?"

"I don't know. Part of the cemetery runs along a road. Let's check and see if they've bothered with the fence there."

Sure enough ("Brilliant, Winifred"), on the south side of the cemetery, the boundary is simply a six-foot wall. And here is a climbable tree that has generously grown a thick bough to the top of the wall. I can't remember the last time I shinned up a tree, or if in fact I ever did, but it's fairly easy. For me. I don't suppose tree-climbing is a U3A activity, for old Fred needs to be told exactly where to put a foot or hand, and to be pulled up in stages. Every step seems to hover on the edge of his joints giving way. He freezes in a crouched position, standing on the thick bough whilst clinging onto higher branches.

"It is the day when the keepers of the house tremble," he says mournfully.

"Sorry?"

He starts inching along the bough, reciting as he goes: "In the day when the keepers of the house shall tremble, and the strong men shall bow themselves, and the grinders cease because they are few, and those that look out of the windows be darkened . . ."

"Ecclesiastes?"

"Of course."

"Never understood what it meant, though."

"It means knees, back, teeth and eyes. Old age, Winifred, old age."

Whatever it means, the recitation seems to give him the courage to creep onwards a few feet. The final few steps along the branch involve me straddling the wall and supporting him across. The jump down is not too bad, and then I have to persuade him to hang down from the wall and accept my cupped hands as reliable footholds. Then he's down, safely.

It takes a little while to find the car, but we're soon in it and laughing with post-adventure euphoria; or at least

I'm laughing and Fred is trying to regain his breath under a smile of relief. There's a lull in the humour while we turn out pockets and the rucksack looking for the keys before I remember that the car was unlocked, and find the keys have got wedged in the crack in Fred's seat.

"Right," I say. "Better use the TomTom to get you home, then. Where do you live?"

Fred opens his mouth, but nothing comes out. He shuts his mouth, massages his temples and tries again. Nothing. He tries a run-up. "I live in . . . it's in . . ." He starts to panic.

"Forget it for a second," I say. "Tell me how Turner died, and how did I warn him?"

"Oh . . . er," and then Fred smiles when he's back on more familiar ground. "Well it was your brilliant – but if I'm honest, rather puzzling – piece about Lazarus. Like all your writing, it was quite brief. I think the theme was 'second chance' or some nonsense that Turner had come up with. You talked about the life of Lazarus after he'd been raised from the dead – which is, of course as far as most people would know. You had him doing all sorts to try and live a normal life: he took up hobbies, he tried internet dating, but no-one wanted to know him, because they thought he had crossed over. You said that he never smiled after he'd been raised from the dead – which I believe is supposed to be true. However . . ." he sighs. "To be honest, I mulled over that one quite a bit, but I couldn't see what you were driving at."

"I don't remember writing it, to be honest," I say. "But I get the theme. Pre-Reformation, people thought that if you'd had extreme unction, or last rites – in common speech – you had crossed over from life; you couldn't have sex again, for example. The Church could do nothing to dissuade the laymen that extreme unction was meant to be restorative rather than final." I could have added that all Catholics have pre-Reformation mindsets, so that this superstition about the last rites still holds.

"Turner wanted to get the education psychologists in, frankly. He would rather have had you labelled as 'disturbed' than admit that he couldn't make head nor tail of your writing. The funny thing was that when he tried to get others on side, he found himself outnumbered. One of the ladies - don't know if you remember Philly Muckett—"

Milly Fuck It. That's just come back. One of the boys thought of it, of course. Can't remember what she taught.

"—pointed out that the last line of your story was also the last line of a Sylvia Plath poem called 'Lady Lazarus'."

"Oh - right." I don't remember. Actually, I might do. I was probably interested in any writer who killed herself.

"Well, if that wasn't a warning to Turner, I don't know what was."

"Sorry - I don't follow."

Fred looks at me. "He called his glider 'Sylvia' - after his wife."

"He had a gliding accident?"

"Yes. It stalled apparently - though how something without an engine can stall, I don't know. I suspect he was trying something stupid to impress people, but whatever it was, down he came. A few years ago now. After I retired. I'm surprised you didn't hear about it."

"I was probably abroad." I am starting to wonder if Fred has overestimated me a little. The nearest I get to foretelling the future is knowing when Urs and my mother will be mad at me, and that doesn't take much prediction. And while I have no fond memories of Turner – actually, very few memories at all, apart from his unappealing face leering out at me during my earlier ghost ride, I don't think I would have wished him to end his mortal span in the crumpled wreck of a glider named after his wife.

"It's number eight, Skullbrook Road, Earlsfield."

"What is?"

"Where I live."

"Oh." I know Earlsfield is near the hospital where my mother works, but I wouldn't have a clue how to get there. I look at the sat-nav. "Do you know your postcode?"

"SW18 1AX." You couldn't believe he'd ever forgotten it.

It takes us quite a while to input the right postcode into the little box, but I assume we're successful because The Voice starts telling him where to go. I don't talk on the journey. I sense that Fred is finding it quite hard to drive now that the sun has cast its attentions elsewhere, and his gritted teeth are more due to having to concentrate than to a TomTom that sounds like his wife.

When the lady announces that we're in Skullbrook Road, Fred slows down. Presumably it is one of these old multi-storey terraced houses.

"Oh good," says Fred. "Her car's not there. She must have gone out. Evening classes most nights. So she says."

"What does she drive?"

"A brown Volvo."

"You have two brown Volvos?"

"No, no, just the one."

"Right. Um . . ."

"I thought you could come in and have a look at your essays. It would be the perfect time, as my wife's not in."

"I think you'll find that she is."

He parks and I call out Goodbye as I'm hurrying down the road. He calls after me, "What about my father?"

"I'll try and remember," I shout back, and if my words were caught by him, they may also have been caught by the angry woman who would never be Mrs Gadd, throwing open the front door, and no doubt very annoyed that she couldn't drive to her evening class tonight.

I run back to what seems to be the main street in Earlsfield. I have no idea how to get home, and I can't see a station.

A couple are walking arm-in-arm towards me. I wonder idly if they are brother and sister, as they both have brown hair and are wearing matching-coloured clothes, then I think it would be odd for a brother and sister to be walking together like that. They are a good-looking couple.

As they get nearer, I decide that they look sensible enough to know where the nearest tube station is, and am about to ask them, when the man releases his hold on the girl and lurches toward me with an excessive grin. He doesn't look drunk, and he is surely not going to proposition me in front of his girl-friend, so he might think he knows me. I look for clues; he's my age, very handsome, but he isn't tickling any damp socks.

"Winnie? It's you, isn't it?" He's still grinning, and the woman – who I now notice is equally stunning, and with similar blue eyes, is smiling, though more out of politeness than recognition, I think. He persists. "It is you, isn't it?"

"Yes, it's me," I say – confident of that much.

"How long has it been? Fifteen years? Fourteen years?"

That must make us school friends. "Too long for me to remember, I'm afraid. Were we at school together?"

He looks confused. "Yes, obviously. Though if I could forget that place too, I would."

The woman laughs. "I don't even know which school you went to."

"Fenner Brockway High," I say, keen to show this woman that I do remember something.

He draws her in with a proprietorial arm. "This is Karen."

Karen extends a hand, which I shake, whilst he tells her that I'm Winifred Rigby, but Win to her friends, and Winnie to her special friends.

She laughs. "Well that puts me in a difficult position. Shall I start off with Win?"

I tell her that's fine. I think her accent is Welsh.

He is staring at me, quite intensely, and announces that Karen is his partner, and that they've been together for years. Or maybe he meant four years.

"That's nice," I say. I'm getting hungry. I don't think I've had anything to eat since breakfast.

"So how've you been? You're not looking too bad. Good job?"

"Yes, not bad. I don't suppose you two know where the nearest tube station is?"

"Miles away," said Karen. "You'd have to get a bus."

"How did you manage to get lost round here?" he says. "Never mind – where are you trying to get to?"

"Colliers Wood."

"Ah, is that where you hang out now?" He strides the few steps to a bus stop and studies the bus routes.

"Can you help me out here?" I say quietly to Karen. "I am appalling at remembering names."

She looks amused. "I had a feeling you didn't recognise

him. Marty. Marty Wilcox." When I must still look non-plussed, she says, "Do you not remember him?"

"To be honest, my school days are a complete blank." Though of course, that's less true now than it was this morning.

"I went to a school like that," Karen says cheerfully.

"In Wales?"

"Yes. Near Newport."

"Got it," says Marty, wandering back to us. "If you get the 44 or 270, you could get off at Tooting Broadway. Or . . ." he looks at Karen, and I sense some attempt at telepathic communication is going on. ". . . you could come back to ours for a drink and a catch-up."

I could say that I don't drink and that the catch-up would be rather one-sided, but instead I just say "thank-you, but I would still have the problem of getting home afterwards."

"Are you working tomorrow?" asks Marty.

"What day is it tomorrow?"

"Saturday. You could stay over if you were stuck. We could put you on a bus in the morning."

If food had been on the menu too, I'd have said Yes, but I'm feeling rather light-headed, which means that I need to eat soon. I see a No 44 bus rolling towards the bus-stop.

"Next time," I say. "But I'd better catch that bus."

They look disappointed but resigned, and at the last second Marty leaps forward to wave his hand at the driver.

"It may be a request stop," he says.

"OK, thanks." The bus has stopped. As requested.

Marty grins proudly, as if he has just stopped a herd of wildebeests rather than a bus. "Perhaps you can come to ours next time."

"Yup." I can see there are loads of seats free. I won't have to share a seat with anyone's encroaching buttocks.

"Gadd be with you."

I am climbing the steps to the bus. I must have misheard. Was that Goodbye, or its longer version God Be With Ye, or has he just mentioned Gadd?

"Facebook me," I call over my shoulder.

They watch me get on the bus, and stay there looking at me and waving goodbye. Which is a bit embarrassing because – although I was the only person to embark – the driver does not pull away immediately, but sits there, humming his engine. And you can't keep waving goodbye without looking like a wally. I look at them to see how long they are going to keep up the valedictory hand flapping, and I see Marty say to Karen, "She could be the one". And Karen either answers "Baby" or "Maybe", and while I wonder what they mean, the bus pulls away.

Chapter Four

"I THOUGHT WE agreed that you don't smoke in the living room," says Urs. "You've ruined the sofa."

This is clearly rubbish, as the sofa still performs all the functions that one would expect of a sofa. I could understand her concern if a miniature person sat on the little cigarette pock-mark and fell through into a whirlpool of soft furnishings and sofa innards, but I don't think it's going to happen.

"Have you heard of Marty Wilcox?" I ask.

No answer. She's disappeared. I find her in a distorted heap on the staircase, trying to reach the 'test' button on the smoke alarm. Or maybe she's reached it and nothing is happening.

"The battery's gone," she says.

I repeat the question.

She makes a face. "Marty Wilcox. Yes, of course I remember him. Nasty bit of work."

"Is he?"

She sits on the staircase – evidently a preferable place of repose than the sofa with its dangerous sinkhole. "Well, he was. Why? Have you remembered him?"

"No," I say truthfully.

"Then why do you ask?"

"He Facebooked me this morning."

"Well, ignore him. Don't even think of replying."

Maybe now is not the time to mention that we are not only friends on Facebook, but have swapped a couple of messages and that I'm meeting him and Karen tonight in a pub in Earlsfield. He's even sent me a humorous shot of a map with the bus journey marked and three smiley faces stuck over the site of the pub.

"He's very good looking."

Urs puts her head in her hands.

"What?" I say.

She raises her head. "Yes, he was good-looking. You went out together. He was a total jerk and you chucked him when you realised he was two-timing you. Or maybe he was three-timing you – I can't remember. You were completely broken-hearted – a real bloody mess – and the strange thing was that once you chucked him, he couldn't accept it and he started stalking you – following you back from school. Dad had to warn him off."

"Really?" I can't imagine being broken-hearted over anyone. But then I would have been a teenager, and probably hormonally stupid.

"Yes, really."

"He's with someone now."

"Is he? Great." She looks relieved. "Just remember that Dad isn't around to sort out your problems anymore."

"I don't have any problems," I snap. "And why do you talk about Dad like he's dead? I see him all the time."

She looks very tired. "No, you don't."

I could argue, but there is no point. Certainly it is true that he won't be sorting out anyone's problems any more.

Urs suddenly does one of her weird mood swings and gives me a false smile. "Anyway – what did you get up to yesterday?"

I wrote it all down last night and I read it this morning and so much seemed to have happened that I wonder if yesterday was really one day or two. I sift through for something tame.

"Yesterday? I don't think I did much. But I bumped into Diana Candle. She was out shopping with her mother."

"Diana Candle? Oh God – I remember her. Well, that's great," says Urs.

"Was she? Great I mean?"

"Oh God, no," says Urs. "I thought she was a bit silly, to be honest. No, no – I take that back. I mean she was really nice."

"But silly?" First reactions are the true responses.

"No, no – not at all. Quite sweet really." (Now I know that Diana was very silly.). "It's great that you two remember each other. Will you get together and catch up?"

That phrase again: Catch up. Mrs Candle used it, Marty used it, and now Urs. What does it mean – I mean what does it really mean? Does it mean swapping CV content, or does it mean – as I suspect – that the unenlightened sense their path is running out ahead and that getting together with someone you knew in the past will somehow pull you back along the life path – the equivalent of a collegiate facelift?

"So will you see each other?" says Urs.

In truth, Diana has already sent me a Facebook invite, which I haven't accepted because I can see on her home page that she likes cats, including photos of them dressed as characters from Alice in Wonderland or the Three Musketeers. It reminds me of the Victorian's whimsical penchant for arranging stuffed squirrels in the pose of having a tea party.

"So will you see each other?" says Urs. She's sounding impatient.

"Not sure," I say. "I've got a lot on."

"Did you send off your investments piece?"

Fuck. Did I?

I trot up the stairs past Urs.

"You forgot, didn't you?"

"It's alright," I call back. "When they say the deadline is Friday, they mean they won't look at it before Monday. Anyway, I've done it. Pretty much."

I just need a couple of hours to check it over. My PC is on already, so I quickly kill the Facebook page and bring up both the original and English versions of the investment piece, side by side. I've reached the second page when I realise that Urs is standing silently at my shoulder. I know she would love to check the quality of my work, but is frustratingly (for her) hampered by having no idea what the original document says. To compound her frustration, I minimise my translated version and maximise the original.

"What does that say?"

"What does what say?" I ask.

She reaches over me to jab at the top paragraph. I sigh, and read it in Chinese.

"I mean what does it say in English?"

"If the non-perishable commodity is purchased and storage costs of the underlying assets are inevitable then a pure arbitrage can only be constructed if the futures contract is mispriced."

"It doesn't make sense to me."

"Yes, but you're not an investment banker," I point out.

"Would it make sense to an investment banker?"

"Yes," I say, firmly.

"But what does it mean?"

"I assume it means that a greedy investment banker gambling on making a quick profit is unlikely to get one."

"Oh." Urs pouts, and mutters that she'll put the kettle on.

Peace. She leaves me alone for long enough to satisfy myself that my translation is fit to send off. When she reappears with a mug of jasmine tea, I'm about to email the attachment.

"Do you think it will matter that you've sent it a day late?" she asks.

I change the date on my PC to yesterday's date. Then I send it.

"What now?" I say, as Urs is staring at me.

"Nothing. I'm just a bit surprised. Look - I don't have a problem with it at all. It's just that I would have thought that that counted as dishonest, and as we know, you never lie."

She's right. I've lied twice in two days. What is happening to me?

"I'm going out for a walk," I say.

"Good idea. I'll bring these." For a moment I think that Urs means that she will join me on the walk and will bring along the two mugs that she's holding, but I realise belatedly that she's making a point that she's having to clear up after me. Though not very well, as some tea slops over the rim of one mug.

"Thanks for the tea," I say. "Looks like you didn't drink yours." She just sighs.

Fortunately Urs doesn't accompany me on my walk, which is just as well, because I don't think she would cope with what lies at the end of my journey. I retrace yesterday's route above the northern line until I get to Balham, which is far enough - I think - to count for a walk in anyone's books, and then I get on a tube to Borough.

My father is standing outside the station, waiting for me, or at least, waiting for people to buy the Big Issue. He always looks a bit dismayed to see me - which I must admit, is a little bit wounding, but in truth he has no reason at all to feel ashamed. I rather admire him for choosing his tough life over the softer option of sharing a three bedroom house in Wimbledon with a cheerless wife. He always goes vague when I ask him where he lives, but I followed him (surreptitiously) late one Saturday afternoon and he ended up in a hostel a few streets away.

"Hi Dad."

He responds with his usual "Hi Ponytail," and a flicker of the lips rather than a smile. I don't know why he calls me Ponytail rather than Win, but I suspect he never liked the name and had two saintly daughters foisted upon him by our mother.

"How is it going?"

He says something that I can't catch – he has a tendency to put his head down and mumble when asked questions – but also holds up a fair wodge of magazines, and I can see yet more poking out of his rucksack. So it's not going that well by the look of it, but it's still earlyish, and he'll probably sell more as the commuters wend their way back to the station at the end of the day. No, it's Saturday today. It will be shoppers rather than commuters. I wonder if they will be more stingy because they have spent too much money on things they don't need, or will feel more guilty, because they are confronted by a poor man when their carrier bags scream that they have spent too much money on things they don't need. My poor old father.

His once-dark hair is now grey and his face is much more weathered than the face I remember from childhood, but his eyes are still a cloudy dark blue, unlike the light sky blue that Urs and I have got from our mother. I have a bit of a blank as

60

to his appearance during my teenage years, but presumably his hair was transitioning from dark to grey. He had his problems, but I don't recall him fading from our lives. It was more like I faded from his until his complete fall when I was in Taiwan.

"How are you?" he asks politely. At least his Brummie accent hasn't faded.

I tell him about Fred Fallowfield, whose father keeps haunting him, and that the old man seems to think that silly stories I wrote at school have some higher meaning for him. Dad looks blank, which is not surprising, as I realise that I've given him no context.

"You probably don't remember him. He was my old history teacher at school."

"Ah, history." He nods, and then smiles as a woman reaches out for a magazine and delivers the change into his other hand. She goes to walk in the station, but turns back towards me.

"You could at least buy one of his magazines," she says, and is gone before I can tell her to mind her own business. Let it go, let it go. I can only calm myself with the thought that whilst she deserves a kick up the backside, she has at least helped Dad out.

"Ursula said that you had to warn off an ex-boyfriend of mine. His name was Marty Wilcox. Do you remember him?"

Dad shakes his head. Not surprising; again, I have failed to give him any context.

"This was at school. A long while back."

"Are you a teacher?"

"No, I'm still a translator. Though teaching would certainly pay better." I smile as I say this, which usually makes other people smile, but after some seconds of no response, I join him in staring out at the stream of worry-line-faced humanity that bumps past us like a time-lapse sequence. Except of course, there are no lapses, and there is no time, and Dad and I are no more separate observers of this swirling mass than are two shrivelled brown leaves lying just outside an autumn eddy of discarded foliage.

There is no point pursuing this. Dad sometimes suffers from 'confused thought patterns' and today is obviously one of his bad days. I give him three pounds, accept a magazine, and refuse his bland offer to find me some change. And then I head into the station. As family visits go, this wasn't a success, and in terms of confirming Urs's account of Marty stalking me, it's been a complete failure.

Change, change, change. I am not like many. I accept change readily. I don't cling on. My father is no longer my father. Not if you define a father as someone who performs the conventional functions of a father rather than someone who has contributed chromosomes. I accept change. But I think part of the old him is still in there somewhere, just overlaid by confusion.

I feel a little down on the way home, and have to resort to extreme mindfulness to extinguish the dread I often feel after seeing him. I observe every movement of my body: I watch it as it rocks while the tube thunders on; I feel the muscles in the arm that holds the plastic rail above my head; I am aware of every position my body goes through as I bend and side-step to allow retail-saturated hoi polloi to move their bodies and shopping bags on and off the carriage.

"Are you OK?" asks a young man. He stays a respectful distance away, so must be a stranger rather than someone who recognises me. I assure him I'm fine, and when he looks confused, I wonder if I answered him in English or Chinese.

I think back to how I found my father. It was so weird that at the time I foolishly wondered if it was a supernaturally auspicious sign. I had to collect an urgent translation assignment from a company which was too stingy to courier it over. To save time looking for the building when I got there, I looked it up on Google maps and the photograph of nearby Borough station came up. All the faces of the passers-by were blanked out, apart from that of one man in the station entrance; he was standing in profile with his left arm thrust far out in ashtray-holding pose, except that whatever was really in his hand was obscured by a big blue bin. I knew then that I was looking at my father, but it was only when I went to see him that I realised it was Big Issue magazines he was holding.

I return to an Urs-free house and a mobile phone which seems to be flashing with annoyance that I forgot to take it with me. Three missed calls – all from the same number. My immediate hope that it is a desperate translation agency is quashed when it rings again; all the same, my spirits rise when I hear Fred's voice.

"Ah – finally. Thank heavens. The bloody woman has grounded me for a week."

"Your wife? Grounded you?"

"Yes, Maddy was furious about us taking the car. I had a bad time of it, Winifred, and worse, Mr Gadd is up to his tricks. Moving things, making noises, sitting on my chest in the middle of the night."

"I'm sorry to hear that, Fred."

"What does he want from me, Winifred?"

"What do you want from him?"

"What do you mean?"

I know there's no point telling him that Mr Gadd only exists in his head. "I mean just that. What do you want from him?"

Fred makes a growling noise, but goes silent for a few seconds. Then more seconds. I'm just starting to wonder if he's forgotten that I'm on the phone, when he says: "I want him to be settled. Just like you say in the penultimate paragraph: 'There was nowhere else to go for the unsettled'. I feel as if I have to do something for him, but I can't work out what it is that I need to do. It's like . . ." - (deep sigh) - "I've lost something Winifred. I feel as if I should know what he needs to be at peace, but I've lost the key."

"OK. I understand."

"You do?"

"Yes." And I think I do. I know that my mother and Urs are happier to treat Dad as if he took a long cruise to South America, but I think of him more as a man locked in sleep who could be woken with the right key. If I could just find it.

"Can you come round, Winifred? This evening?"

I'm sure I'm doing something this evening. I take my phone into the kitchen and scan my post-it notes on the noticeboard. "What about your wife?"

"She's gone to visit her sister. She's left me a ghastly microwave meal, so I assume she's not coming back until late."

Take clothes out of washing machine. (Can't remember if that was from yesterday. Must check).

Buy spinach and milk. (Damn - I could have done that on the way back from the station).

Ring Mum. (I don't remember writing that. I didn't. Urs's handwriting.)

Ask Dad if he remembers Marty (written in Chinese

64

because Urs gets irrational at any mention of him in the present tense. I can take that one down now).

Meet M and K at 7 pm (written in Chinese in case Urs gets incontinent with rage that I am meeting someone she has forbidden me from meeting).

"Oh, sorry Fred. I've got something on tonight."

"Oh. Oh dear, that's a shame. I just wanted to show you one piece of writing. I think it holds a clue."

"Whose writing?"

"Well – yours, of course. The one about the Chinese ghost marriage."

Needless to say, I don't remember. But it sounds interesting.

"I suppose I could pop in briefly. About six o'clock. But I can't stay long."

"Would you? Thank-you, Winifred. I would very much appreciate that."

He doesn't say goodbye, but I can hear vague off-stage sounds as though now he has occupied himself with whistling and banging cupboards, so I assume that is the end of the conversation, and kill the call on my phone. I attend to my post-it notes: I put my washed clothes into the tumbler drier, throw away the note about ringing my mother, and underline the reminder to buy spinach and milk, though in truth the milk is for guests – well, Urs.

Why does Fred want me to read a story on Chinese ghost marriages? More to the point, why did I write something on Chinese ghost marriages? If I did. I still don't have any proof that I wrote any of the stuff he's going on about.

I have a little time before I need to get ready, so I hit google. I am already familiar with the concept, but whether from my stay in Taiwan, or whether it was something I read when young, or at university, I don't know. There are different flavours in Singapore, Taiwan and across parts of China, but the gist is that those who die before they are married cannot be allowed to remain single in the Netherworld. A typical scenario would be a young male dying prematurely, and his parents searching out a suitable dead female and arranging a marriage. The wedding ceremony would pretty much follow the same ritual as one where the parties were still alive, except that some substitutes must be made for the bride and groom – which could be as prosaic as two ancestral tablets, or with representations of silver figurines or dolls of dough, or – more excitingly – dressed-up corpses.

In terms of what triggers the need for a ghost wedding, there seem to be two common events: one is that the single dead male starts making a nuisance of himself: appearing in his mother's dreams, disrupting the household with poltergeist-like activity, or causing illness in the family. The other is when the second surviving son is about to get married, for tradition states that he cannot be married before his elder brother. And here is where I have a problem: China has had a 'One Birth' policy since the late 1970s. Even with all the exemptions in place, I cannot imagine that many families have more than one son. So this sounds to me like the classic Western tendency to cling onto an outdated snapshot of Chinese culture. Even with apparent recent reports of 'Burke-and-Hare-type' murders of young girls so that their corpses could be sold as ghost brides, I am sceptical that this still goes on in modern China.

I catch the bus whose number Marty has thoughtfully written down for me, and recognise the bus-stop on the opposite side where they waved goodbye to me. Now I just need to retrace my steps to Skullbrook road. I've forgotten to bring an A to Z, but eventually find Fred's street, and then realise that I can't remember the number. I walk up and down several times, looking for something familiar, but the uniformity of the Victorian houses offers no help. On my fourth trip up the street, I hear a frantic banging on a window, and there is Fred. Number eight. A lucky number in Chinese. How could I have forgotten?

"You look a bit different," he says at the door.

I assume he means that I look a bit smarter, in that I've dispensed with my usual cargo trousers and sweatshirt.

"I'm going out later."

"I mean you look older than when I saw you last."

"Yesterday."

"What was?"

He gestures me into a very tidy living room and towards a sofa. He goes to sit on an armchair obliquely opposite, then seems to think better of it, and joins me on the sofa. Whether this is because his father is occupying the armchair or because he thinks that a side-to-side arrangement is better, I don't know. He certainly looks agitated, and very tired.

"Do you remember a Marty Wilcox in your class?" I ask. "He would have been the same year as me."

"Marty Wilcox." He shuts his eyes for a few seconds. "No – I don't believe so." Then he casts a look at the rejected armchair and rubs his eyes. "Winifred – I don't think I can stand much more of this."

"Mr Gadd?"

"He opened the freezer door. Must have been hours ago. Everything's half thawed out, and naturally Maddy will blame me."

"Hang on."

I find the kitchen and open the freezer. Sure enough, a quick grope of the contents reveals that the packets within are soft. Worse, the oven is on, though there is nothing inside. I don't think Mr Gadd is the culprit here. I turn it off and go back to the living room, where Fred has returned to his pathetic knee-hugging posture.

"What's worrying you, Fred?"

"I should have taken care of my mother better, Winifred. She was relatively young when she passed away. Well – probably the age I am now. But I think she could have lasted longer if I'd gone to visit more. I've re-read your piece and it's quite depressing about relationships in the afterlife."

"I'm sorry, but I really don't rem . . ."

Fred has reached out to the shelf under the coffee table and gently pulled out a rectangle of patterned cloth – or maybe it is a silk scarf. He uses both hands to pass it to me – a gesture of respect and reverence that I've only seen on formal occasions in Taiwan. I try to match his reverence by accepting it with both hands, and unwrap the cloth. Inside is a battered exercise book, open on a handwritten page. I don't recognise the writing.

"I wrote this?"

"Of course." He nods towards it, which I take as an instruction to read.

Mumu's Mama had her eye on Lulu as a potential daughter-in-law. Not only was she as demure as dough, and as softly spoken as a sough, but she was also blessed with a mother's hips. Mumu's Mama made sure to praise Lulu in front of Mumu, but her son just raised his eyes. And yet still she schemed. No matter what: it had to be.

68

It was a sad day when young Mumu died in a rice flailing
accident at the tender age of thirteen. The funeral was a silent
affair, as he was too young to have a wife and children to mourn
him loudly, or even quietly, and the attendees at the funeral
seemed embarrassed and inconvenienced at having to witness
his premature departure. Except for his Mama, who still held
out great hopes for his future.

Three years passed before Mumu's Mama declared that the
disruption of their household objects was not due to subsidence
but to Mumu's attempts to communicate his loneliness.

"We must find him a wife," she declared, to the chagrin of
her husband, who was busy filling out an insurance claim for
subsidence at the time. "He is lonely in Heaven," she opined.
"Whatever," said her husband, hoping that would be the end
of the matter.

The next day there was an earthquake. Whilst Mumu's
father sighed, and started filling out another insurance claim,
Mumu's Mama went to the market, where she heard that Lulu
had been squashed by a falling wall, and had expired – a sweet,
single, sixteen-year-old. Mumu's Mama rushed home to tell her
husband the good news.

"Now they can be wed," she declared.

Her husband was doubtful, so to prove him wrong, Mumu's
mother consulted an expert in mordant marital matters. The
man charged a heavy fee for drawing up the deceased parties'
horoscopes before shaking his head. "They are both cats," he
declared. "No good will come of this marriage."

(Did I really write this? There is no Year of the Cat in
Chinese astrology. Surely I would have known that. Or was I
deliberately signalling that this was pure fantasy?)

Mumu's father declared that the nuptials were a bad idea,

but Mumu's mother hollered that she would not consign her son to a loveless death.

"Being single is not so bad," declared her husband, ducking to avoid a wok made airborne through human forces rather than seismic ones.

And so the ghost marriage went ahead. Lulu and Mumu's mothers dressed up and discussed the beautiful babies that would be made in the afterlife, while the two fathers stood in a corner drinking and discussing fault lines.

Mumu was mad, and Lulu was livid. They had hated each other in high school, loathed each other in life, and detested each other in Death. But the marriage was binding, for whilst ghost marriages had been sanctified by the tradition of many centuries, no-one had yet invented ghost divorces.

The wrath of the dead teenagers was such that soon the harmonial honeymoon of Mumu and Lulu was traduced by trouble, and the familial homes of Mumu and Lulu were reduced to rubble.

"Now what do I tell the insurance company?" wailed Mumu's father, surveying the cairn that had once been his castle.

His wife pouted but held firm. "It's just a touch of subsidence."

Beneath the essay was written in red: 'Brevity and morbidity do not earn you high marks. Also, check your usage of Traduced.' Must have been Turner. Jerk.

All the same, I'm not sure what to make of it. The writing is neatly printed – more tidy than my adult writing style – but I don't really recognise it. I turn to the front of the battered book and see my name written in the same careful style. Was this really me? I feel that slight tingle you get when picking up things you last handled in a former life; I'm not sure it's that healthy.

All the same, I leaf through, finding the pieces named 'Lazarus' and 'When the Saints came marching in'. The same neat writing – each letter printed separately from its neighbour. I was obviously not into joined up writing; no wonder I love Chinese script: each character is written in isolation, rather than holding hands like emotionally retarded teenagers.

I turn back to the 'Subsidence' story – which I notice has the heading of 'Till Death do us part', and now I think that I did write it, for no-one else would have the temerity – or the originality – to subvert the theme so completely. I try very hard to remember. Even if I don't recall the story, I could see how the teenage me would have come up with it; I would already have had an interest in Chinese culture, and the story is really a bitter account of an interfering mother, whose bizarre superstitious beliefs and selfishly determined actions leave her husband homeless.

Oh God. Did I have foresight?

"So what were you trying to tell me?" asks Fred.

I must confess that I'd forgotten about him. "How did you interpret it?" I ask.

"I don't know, Winifred. I was wondering if you were warning me to take better care of my mother. It wasn't a happy marriage. My father left her when I got married in 1972, as you may know. I wonder if he blames me for letting her join him too early, so that they were forced to endure their hellish marriage in heaven. Prematurely."

"OK. Let me put your mind at rest. This story wasn't about you at all."

"Then why did you write it?"

"I've no idea. Maybe it was even about my own family. I can't remember. But the important thing is that whether you could have delayed your mother's death or not, I don't know, but I can assure you that whatever your father's situation is now – it has nothing to do with your mother."

I can't believe that I'm coming out with this claptrap – as though his father still has some situation to be in, other than a tired banquet for worms – but Fred looks relieved.

"Really?"

"Really."

"That's good. But then chaos is come again. Unless . . ." – and here he shoots me a hope-filled look – "you can explain to me something about the different worlds he passed through?"

"Sorry?"

"In 'The Giddy career of My Gadd (deceased)'. I understood the Underworld stage – at least, I think I do. That was where he heard the wails of the living and people were getting gifts – though not him, so he had no idea if he was being mourned or not – my poor old father. Then after that I think you were saying that he was promoted – that was the word you used – promoted to the next world, and that seemed to me to be like a soulless Heaven."

"Right." I've just noticed a thick black hair on the carpet. Could be a dog hair. Is this all that's left of Lucy?

"That world didn't make sense to me at all. It seemed so desolate. The people around him were so lost. You remember, they were either sleeping, or they were being passed between angels – never allowed to stop. Sinister, I thought. But the saddest was the character who stumbled around wailing 'I'm here, I'm here. I've come home'. But no-one took any notice of him. I think that disturbed my father. Profoundly disturbed him. He wasn't always a kind man in this world, you see, but I wonder if his promotion . . ."

"Fred." But he is lost in a world - apparently of my making, and I have to repeat his name twice more to get his attention. "Does Mrs Fallowfield - Maddy - experience any of the disruption that your father causes?"

It takes a while to drag him from the soulless heaven, so I repeat the question quickly.

"Oh yes," he said, with quiet vehemence. "All the time. But of course she doesn't see the true picture, Winifred. She thinks I'm the cause of all the problems." He looks at me and adds: "She can't see him. That's the trouble."

"Is he buried in London?" I'm wondering if we can resolve this with a quick trip to a cemetery, where I can come up with some mumbo jumbo and put his (and I mean Fred's) mind at rest.

Fred gives me a look. "Well, he's not - is he?"

"I'm sorry. Yes, you said he died overseas. I'd forgotten."

Fred sighs and holds out his hands for the book. I'm not sure it deserves such reverence, but I play the game, and use both hands to place it in his.

"The Giddy career of Mr Gadd (deceased)," he says. "I know you'll remember once you read it. That's where we're going to find the answers." He fiddles with a pair of glasses, and then he is turning pages so carefully that I fear it will be tomorrow before he finds whatever essay I wrote that he mistakenly believes is germane to his current turmoil. And my eyes fall on my watch, which he is wearing upside down - or right side up for me. What has happened to time? It is quarter to seven, and while I know that the pub should be just around the corner once I'm back on Garratt Lane, I would prefer to have some contingency time.

"Fred, I'm sorry, but I have to go."

"Go where?"

"I'm meeting an old friend." And when Fred's face falls, I add: "an old school friend. He might help me remember things."

"That's a shame. How about tomorrow, Winifred?"

"What's tomorrow?"

"Well, it's . . . well it's tomorrow."

"Ah – tomorrow is Sunday. Yes, OK." I'm at the front door, but when I turn around expecting to see him, there is just the empty hall, as uncluttered as a Petri dish dreaming of some cultural company. Then a cry from the kitchen. I hurry in to see him staring at the open freezer door.

"He's done it again, Winifred."

"OK, Fred. Close it now. I'll see you tomorrow."

Marty and Karen greet me with smiles of recognition. And maybe some relief, as if they weren't sure that I would turn up, though I don't think I'm more than a few minutes late.

Whilst I am pleased to see that they have made an effort for me – they are both sparkling from showers, clothes crisp with ironing – they have chosen to sit inside the crowded once-was-a-bank pub, and the coalescence of conversations is already making me feel nauseous.

"Can we sit outside?" I shout.

I see Karen mouth 'told you' to Marty, and I assume they are agreeing, because they collect their wine glasses and follow me out. There are plenty of tables free, so I sit at the first one; at least the noise of the traffic down Garratt Lane is soft compared to the assault of yacking punters within.

"You're brave," says a young woman. She opens the umbrella above our table and fiddles with a heater set into the post.

"Thanks," says Karen, and the young woman smiles and goes inside.

"Useless service here," says Marty. "She could have hung around. Shall I get a bottle? You happy with red?"

"Just a coke for me."

Their faces fall. "Come on – have a drink," says Marty. "You're not driving, are you?"

"I don't drink. Really, a coke would be fine." He remains hovering, disbelieving. "I'm a Buddhist," I add. Not as powerful as saying you're a Muslim, but I usually find that a declaration of religious constraint shuts people up.

"A Buddhist," says Karen, sounding interested. "What sort?"

"Chan," I say to her, whilst to the indecisive Marty I say "and alcohol gives me a headache."

"Ah," he says. "Can't have you getting a headache." And off he goes.

"Chan? I haven't heard of that," says Karen.

"You've heard of Zen?"

"Oh yes, of course."

"It's the same thing. Chan in Chinese, Zen in Japanese."

"I should have known that. I'm afraid that I'm not religious at all."

"What do you think happens to you when you die?"

"Oh, wow." Her forehead rises with surprise. It's quite an attractive facial movement. "Well, I don't think anyone's asked me that before, but as you've asked, I'm afraid that I think we have no soul. And if you don't have a soul – then you can't have an afterlife. So to answer your question, when we die, we rot."

I like this woman.

By the time Marty has returned, holding a triangle of coke and two glasses of wine, Karen and I have compared notes on travelling in Vietnam, including the family graves buried on the corners of farm land, and embarked on ancestor worship, which she thinks is fascinating. It is as I go to take my coke, that I realise that Fred's problem with his father (deceased) would be interpreted by someone with a traditional oriental mind set as being due to a dereliction of duty: to a lack of ancestor reverence. Superstitious rubbish, of course, but an old Taiwanese person would have thought it the obvious cause of Fred's problems.

"You've just reminded me," says Karen. "The number of times in Wales or Scotland I've seen a modern farmhouse next to the ruins of a stone house. I've always wondered if that was because it was easier to build on an empty plot or because people don't want to disturb the sanctity of their parents' or grandparents' place."

"Ah – ancestor worship in the UK. I like it."

"What are you two going on about?" asks Marty, with a martyred sigh.

"Nothing," says Karen. "Just comparing notes on travelling."

"We were thinking of Croatia this year." He distributes the drinks and sits down. "That's the great thing about the break-up of the Communist states – we've got all these new countries to visit."

"But are they new countries?" asks Karen. "Or old countries regaining their independence?"

"More the latter," I say. "Have you seen that website that shows the borders of Europe changing over the last thousand years?"

"The time lapse one? That's amazing." She looks at Marty.

"Remember? I showed you. Germany didn't appear until – I can't remember when – but late in the day."

"1871." I can see they are impressed, but really it is thanks to Fred Fallowfield and his politically incorrect little ditty: *From pocket kingdoms the Hun, made Deutsche Reich in 1871.* And thanks, of course, to not having a mind cluttered with damp socks.

"Nothing as immutable as change," says Karen. "Europe is a great lesson for that."

"Anyway," says Marty. "As far as I'm concerned it just means more bloody entries to sit through in the Eurovision Song Contest." He gives me a grin. "Not, of course, that we watch it."

"We do," says Karen, cheerfully.

Sadly, with the fetters of a common past, Marty drags the conversation down with a series of "Do you remember . . ." questions. Oh dear. You can always spot an awkward conversation when people start talking about either pets or the past. We have regressed to catch-up. I don't remember Paul (who played volleyball but fell off the kerb and broke his ankle on the way to a trial for the national team), nor Shimmy (who is now in porn films but is in trouble for tax evasion), nor Gavin (who apparently teased me mercilessly for being a swot).

Marty frowns. "You must remember Gavin. He pushed you too far one day. You stabbed him so hard we could all hear your pen hitting bone."

"Did I? Was he OK?"

"Still has a scar on his hand, apparently."

"Good for you," says Karen. "He sounds like a prat." She sips her wine.

Marty spins his wine glass before taking a drink. "Actually,

I think a few of us were a bit mean to you. Jealousy, as you always got top grades. So apologies if I was one of those prats."

"Forgiven. Especially as I don't really remember."

"The class swot?" says Karen, with her forehead-raising expression. "That must have been difficult with these Philistines." She cocks her head towards Marty.

"Yeah, you were pretty bright," says Marty. "That's probably why Gavin kept having a go. He was as thick as a brick. Do you remember when old Crow . . ." he looks at me. "Crow was the headmaster. Remember? He did an assembly on vision, or perspective, or something like that. And he said that a kestrel's eyesight was so good that if there was a newspaper on the ground, it would be able to read the individual letters from a hundred metres up. And then at the end of the day, we had Biology, and Mr Khan said that birds were intelligent. Up pipes Gavin: 'Yes, a kestrel can read a newspaper from a hundred metres in the air'."

"I don't remember that," I say. "But it's funny."

"So who do you see from the old days?" asks Marty.

I decide not to mention Fred. "I did bump into Diana Candle recently . . ." – was it yesterday? – "quite literally. Her mother rolled backwards at a traffic light and hit the car." As soon as I say that, I feel guilty. Did she roll back or did Fred roll forwards?

"You have a car?" asks Marty.

"No, I don't."

"Grand larceny?" asks Karen, with more forehead-raising. It really is attractive.

I laugh. "No. I was a passenger."

Marty hoots. "Diana. I remember her. She had those silly pigtails."

Dublin City Public Libraries
Ringsend
Borrower Receipt

Customer name: Hughes, James

Title: The giddy career of Mr Gadd (deceased
ID: DCPL1000043359
Due: 02-05-18

Total items: 1
Total fines: €1.90
11/04/2018 14:09
Checked out: 1
Overdue: 0
Hold requests: 0
Ready for pickup: 0

Thank you for using the Selfservice System

K1

"And she still does."

"Really? I like a ponytail . . ." – he reaches out to give mine a gentle tug – "but pigtails on a thirty-one year old . . ."

"Oh, I've just had my thirtieth birthday," I say.

"A belated happy birthday," says Karen.

Marty frowns. "You're thirty-one. I'm sure we were the same age."

"Whatever," says Karen.

The conversation takes a subtle turn, and suddenly I feel like I'm being interviewed. Marty says I look fit, and mentions that he does football and that Karen does yoga, before asking me what I do. I say that I walk and hike, and that I would love to swim, if we had swimming pools like the one that I used to frequent in Yilan – in Taiwan – which was emptied each morning and refilled with water from the mountains.

"Wow," says Karen.

Marty says he works in a bank – or an insurance company – I instantly forget, and Karen says she's a therapist – which I'd like to ask more about – except that Marty immediately asks me what I do.

"I'm a translator."

"Translator of . . . ?"

"I translate from Chinese to English."

This gets another Wow from Karen.

"That sounds interesting," says Marty. "Well-paid, I bet. Language of the future and all that."

"No – the reverse. We're competing with Chinese who've been learning English since they were children."

Marty asks if I have a boyfriend, and when I say I don't, he pauses, and asks if I have a girlfriend. I shake my head. They look at each other, and Karen announces that she will get another round of drinks. As soon as she is gone, Marty leans towards me.

"What do you think of Karen?"

"I like her. She's very good-looking. I thought you two were brother and sister when I first saw you."

He frowns. "Yesterday." Then he smiles. "I have a problem, Win, and I wonder if you can help me out. He takes one of my hands. "Karen loves me. But she has special needs."

"Really? She struck me as quite intelligent."

"No – I mean she's bisexual." He leaves a pause and looks at me.

"OK."

"I don't want her to . . ." – he seems to be searching for the right words – ". . . neglect that side of her life. I mean, I don't want her to feel unfulfilled . . ."

"You want me to sleep with her?"

He looks surprised. "Well, only if you're comfortable with that. And to be honest, while I'm hugely accepting of her . . . needs – I would want some parity."

Karen comes back with the three drinks. "I've ordered some tapas," she announces, then looks at me. "I made sure I got some vegetarian, just in case you are."

"You're right, I am."

"I hope you got some meat for me," says Marty.

"Yes," she says, with mock weariness. "I got caveman stuff for you." She casts an eyebrows-raised look at Marty, who I'd forgotten was holding my hand until he releases it to take his drink.

"So would this be a threesome?" I ask, "or to sleep with you separately?"

"Seems like the conversation has moved on a bit," says Karen, sitting down. "So Win . . ."

"I think it will be Winnie soon," murmurs Marty.

"Are you sure about this?" asks Karen. "We'd hate you to feel pressured into it. Do you want to think about it first and let us know?"

"No. Sounds fine."

"And it would be separately," says Karen, firmly – though I think that is aimed more at Marty than me. "I've tried a threesome before . . ."

"Have you?" Marty says, with a frown.

". . . and it is just a right old muddle trying to work out if everyone is getting equal attention. I mean – chaos is come again."

Now both I and Marty are staring at her. Me – because I think synchronicity is mildly interesting, and Marty – well, I don't know what he's thinking.

"Where does that come from?" he asks.

"Othello," says Karen. "I can't actually remember the context. I suppose it means the chaos of jealousy."

"Oh," says Marty. "We had a teacher who used to say that. I don't think he used it like that though." He looks at me. "Fallowfield. He was History. Do you remember him?"

"No," I say, and then when I realise that I am lying, I change it to "maybe", and then when I realise that that is just a softer lie, I change it to, "Yes, actually – I think I do." And then I realise that I am just sliding down a cline of lying intensity.

"He was as mad as a box of frogs, but a brilliant teacher."

"Twosomes," I say. "Let's keep it simple."

"OK," says Marty, and looks at me. "But the really important thing, Winnie, is that there mustn't be attachment. It would just be an arrangement amongst friends."

"Yes, that sounds good." Sounds ideal.

"I mean, seriously," says Marty. "I know it's easy to get attached to people when there's intimacy, but the arrangement will only work if we can keep it light."

"Absolutely. So what are you thinking? Once a week with each of you? I would probably work better with fixed days."

"Oh," they say in unison, and look at each other. Maybe they hadn't thought this far ahead.

"Well, you do football on Tuesdays," says Karen to Marty.

"Yes, but you do yoga then."

"I could change to a Thursday class."

I take out my phone and start typing into my calendar. "So Tuesdays with Karen and Thursdays with Marty."

There is silence. I look up to see them staring at me. "Surely you'll remember that?" says Marty.

"Better if I schedule it. What time? Oh – and where? I think your place is better than mine. My sister tends to drop in. Unannounced and uninvited."

"Seven pm," suggests Karen, and I type it in.

"I'll Facebook you the address," says Marty.

When I've saved the entries, Marty raises his glass. "To complete fulfilment."

Although that is a complete impossibility, and I don't like to toast a false statement, I clink my glass of coke against their wine glasses. "Wonderful," I say, because a waitress has brought the tapas, and I'm hungry.

Chapter Five

HALF THE PROBLEM with tinnitus is not knowing which side of your head a noise falls on. I should have known it would be a difficult night when I turned off the light, and that hateful woman started tearing tissues in my room, and muttering her 'thank God, thank God' mantra. The sensation was so strong that I actually turned on the bedside light, and - of course - the empty room hurled my stupidity back in my face. But it did give me an insight into Fred's state of mind. He doesn't know that Mr Gadd is in his own head. It must be quite unsettling.

For the next part of the night I was back on the ghost train, hurtling through the darkness, with vaudeville acts briefly illuminated off to the side: there was thick Gavin, screaming and holding his hand, and Crow in his black gown wandering the school corridors - his jerky head looking for roadkill. Diana - with her quivering pigtails, triumphant that her gooey 'Till Death Us Do Part' essay was given a high mark by the uxorious and soon to have-a-widowed-wife Turner. And Marty - usually grinning, but with the little flashes of malice that were necessary to retain his alpha male position within his own little group of boys. I am remembering. I don't want to remember. I am remembering.

I really don't see that any of this is helpful. It's certainly not helpful for me, personally, as it means that I now have more damp socks to clutter up my mind. Nor do I see how it is helping Fred.

When I finally give up on the idea of a lie-in, I walk downstairs - stepping over Urs who I assume is putting a new battery in the smoke alarm, and judging by the moans, is giving herself cramp.

"Thanks," I say.

She straightens up looking surprised. "That's OK. Did you do anything last night? You weren't in."

"I went out."

Her back is now so straight that she looks like a meerkat on sentry duty. "Well, I guessed that much. Did you meet anyone?"

"An old school friend."

"Who?" she asks.

"No-one special. Was I into boys or girls when I was younger?"

"What?" She makes a face. "You mean romantically?"

Now I make a face. "God, no. I meant sexually."

"You were into books, actually."

"What?"

"Boys, definitely boys." She snaps shut the smoke alarm, and hits the Test button, and I scarper into the kitchen as the irritating beep-beep-beep assaults the peace of my house.

The rice cooker is on and I wash the spinach that I find in the fridge, and call up to ask Urs whether she fancies a decent breakfast. She appears in the kitchen doorway.

"No thanks. You didn't answer my question."

"Which was?"

"Did you see Diana Candle last night?"

"No." She sent me a Facebook invitation yesterday. Did I respond? I don't think I did.

"So . . ." I can see that Urs is just going to keep asking questions so I jump in with: "do you remember Mr Turner? He taught English."

"Mr Turner. Yes, I remember him. I liked him."

"Did you know he died in a gliding accident?"

"Really? How awful. I didn't know. When was this?"

"I don't know the details. I suppose you could google."

I start to fry the spinach, and when I next turn around she has gone. Whether she has run upstairs to google details of Turner's demise, or whether she has fled the kitchen because my Chinese breakfast is offending her, I don't know. But it gives me some space to eat mindfully. Not that mindfully. It's just occurred to me that whilst I have a guest account set up for Urs to use, if my screensaver hasn't yet kicked in, she will see the selfie picture of Marty and Karen on a beach – both topless – that he sent me this morning.

She comes back, looking sad rather than horrified, so I think it's OK.

"2013," she says. "He was supposed to land at North Weald, but crashed somewhere in Essex. Oh by the way, your mobile went."

"Who was it?" I just know that she'd have answered it.

"Hard to say. He just said, 'Well, that's not Winifred', and hung up. Rather rude I thought." (Rather Fred I think.) "Do you know who it would be? He sounded old. And you hate being called Winifred."

"Yes, just an old friend. So what did you learn about Turner?"

Urs lets out a grunt of exasperation, obviously wanting to

pursue the business of my Old Friend, but fortunately she has a short attention span, so I just need to repeat the question about Turner.

"His glider was called 'Sylvia' apparently – after his wife. Absolutely tragic. She'd gone to the airfield to pick him up."

"Pick up the pieces more like."

"God, you can be hateful," Urs says, and walks out. Shortly after I hear a noise, which I guess is the front door slamming. At least that takes care of evading further questions.

When I go upstairs, I find that my mobile shows Fred's number. I ring him. A female voice answers – presumably Maddy-née-Fallowfield-never-be-Gadd. I toy with the idea of saying, 'Well, that's not Fred' and putting the phone down, but instead ask (politely) if I may speak with him.

"Can I say who's calling?"

"Winifred."

"Are you the girl who had him round on Thursday?"

"I can't remember," I say. Was it Thursday?

Silence. And then "Let me get one thing out in the open now, Winifred. I have power of attorney. Do you know what that means?"

"I certainly do. It's when interfering relatives get their hands on your money."

She ends the call. I ring again.

"What now?" she answers.

"Actually I was returning his call."

"Just who are you?"

"My name is Winifred Rigby. I'm not after his money. I'm an old History student of his, and we're revisiting my essays."

"But why? He retired years ago. Why would you be interested? I can't imagine he was a good teacher."

86

And I'm back in the classroom, sitting in a circle of excited pupils with Fred in the centre. I remember.

"He was a brilliant teacher – the best. He would sit in the centre with us all around. He called it the Lionheart's Den. He dared anyone to try and catch him out with questions. It made everyone revise. Mainly Horrible History, but no matter – no-one could catch him out."

The passion in my own voice surprises me. He knew that Edward II's red hot poker demise would grab the boys, and that Guy Fawkes's shaky signature on his confession as a result of thumbscrews would make us all sigh, and even that the communists in the relatively modern Spanish Civil War fought with lice in their underpants. No subject was too horrible – if it was history. And if a comparatively peaceful period was sharply ended by the nefarious plotting of a wicked uncle – no matter: chaos is come again. Beaming smile. I remember.

Maddy is warming to me, I can tell. A little.

"But I don't think this is about History, Winifred. He's got very confused about his late father. Is that what this is about?"

"Yes, he seems convinced that his father is . . ." – Oh God – what word to use? – ". . . not settled."

Her intake of breath is sharp. "Well, his father is a heap of bones in a heap of earth in China. I would say that he is very settled, as you put it."

Buried in China. My head is pinballing with this new information when I realise that she's talking again.

". . . completely fixated on this stupid little book. As far as I can tell, it's just an old school . . ." And I can hear her putting two and two together. "Oh no – I've just realised."

"Yes. My old English exercise book."

"So these are things you scribbled when you were how old?"

"About fourteen or so I guess."

"About fourteen. So exactly what is in this book that is so significant?"

"I'm not sure. The trouble is that I can't remember why I wrote what I wrote."

"Then, Winifred, I don't wish to denigrate your childhood scribblings, but how could you possibly be helping him? What exactly is the point?"

It takes me a while to formulate a response. I don't know if I can help him. I don't know if I have anything significant to tell him. I don't know if I will remember something useful. All I know is that he is desperate and that I seem to be giving him hope, and however hopeless that hope is, it's what allows some people to get up in the morning and face another day. And when that day is done, and finishes in failure, hope is what makes us get up the next day, and the next. Through all the syllables of recorded time.

But by the time I have converted these thoughts into words and transmitted them down the phone, I realise that Maddy Fallowfield has hung up, because her question was a rhetorical one. And rhetorical questions are ones that people don't like being answered.

I feel a little down after that call. I wish I had some translation work, but a check of the usual websites reveals that no translation agencies are currently demanding my skills. The date on my PC says that it is Saturday today. Three days before I can meet Marty or Karen for sex – I can't remember which one – but no matter. And then I realise that I'm refusing pain, and my mind is seeking distractions. I can't remember who said 'neurosis is refused pain', but they were right. Pathetic.

I go downstairs to make some green tea and find Urs sitting at the table making a list or something. She seems to write a lot of lists.

"I thought you went out," I say.

"No – I was in the bathroom. By the way, what is . . . reality?"

"Heavens. It's a bit hard to put into words. It's a bit like trying to describe a melody without singing it."

"What?"

"OK. It's that moment you first sense something – before language floods in and swamps your perception."

No reaction. I turn and look at her: she's slightly open-mouthed and holding up a post-it note with my writing on.

"I mean what is . . ." she screws up her eyes to look at my post-it, ". . . reyal? Royal? Some sort of tea . . ."

I look at it. "Real tea. I meant green tea."

She rolls her eyes, shakes her head and adds something to her list. "By the way, who were you on the phone to?"

"When?"

"Just now. I didn't hear you say goodbye."

"Oh yeah. That was someone's wife. I didn't say goodbye because she hung up on me."

"Whose wife?" Urs is looking troubled.

I put on the kettle instead of answering. It worries me that Urs's prying ears are bugging my phone conversations.

"Have you been seeing her husband? Is that why she rang?"

"Yes and yes."

Urs bangs down her pen on the table and leans back, and

I can see that she has gone from Troubled to Very Upset. "What have you done, Win?"

"I haven't done anything."

"Are you pregnant?"

"What? Why the hell would I be pregnant?"

Urs sighs, and mutters, "Never mind." She adds another item to her list, and covers it with her hand too late as I cross the kitchen to read it. She has added 'condoms' beneath 'rice' and 'cabbage' and 'green tea'. The mind boggles.

"I'm going to leave you to it," she announces. "I'm taking Mum to Grandad's grave this afternoon."

"Can I come?"

"Why would you want to come?"

"Well – why not?" Because I want another cemetery fix.

"Because . . . well, anyway afterwards we're going to visit Nan in the home. You won't like it."

"No – but you probably don't like it either. You probably feel like it's an obligation – if you're honest."

"Yes. If I'm being honest, it does feel a bit like that." She immediately looks like she wished that she hadn't been so honest and tries to smother her first response. "No, it's fine. It'll be nice to see Nan."

"So I can come?"

I'm halfway through my tea before Urs speaks again. Evidently she has been weighing things up in her mind, though I'm not sure what's so heavy.

"You definitely can't come to the Home."

"Why not?"

"You can come to the cemetery on one condition."

"What?"

"You promise you won't upset Mum."

"I promise that I'll try, but she can get upset whatever I say. Or don't say."

Urs rubs her temples as if she has a headache. "OK, let me be more specific. You can come to the cemetery only if you don't do that sniffy disdain act. You don't lecture Mum on how it's done differently in China or Thailand or wherever. You don't slag off Catholicism or Christianity or anything. You don't mock other people for visiting graves, and, in particular, you don't mock Mum. Right?"

I say "of course", and wonder what on earth goes on inside the strange head of Ursula.

We are silent on the drive to Mum's house - our old house - which seems to take a long time in the south London traffic. In truth, I could have walked much of it faster, though when I mention this to Urs - in a non-complaining, detached and observational sort of way, she just says, 'Don't you start' - after which I shut up. As the crow flies, our houses are not so far apart; indeed, if you are watching the Wimbledon tennis championship on TV and hear a plane over the court, the same plane would be over my little house seconds later. I don't suppose it's a compelling reason for buying a place in Colliers Wood.

I can't remember the last time I came home (as in the Family Home), and I'm not going to ask Urs, whose mood seems rather morose at the moment, and anyway, she's changed the radio to some God-awful station where people are putting forward their inconsequential opinions and shouting down other people's inconsequential opinions, and it seems that this is easier on her ears than my occasional utterances. The timbre of their whingey voices is jarring, and I can look forward to a terrific bout of tinnitus tonight.

When Urs finally pulls into the small drive and stops short of the garage door, she is immediately out of the car and into the house, slamming the front door behind her. I wonder whether to follow her. I do have keys, but feel disinclined to interrupt whatever urgent mission she's on. Instead, I look at the house and try to remember if it looked different when I lived here. I suspect not, though the absence of my father's car gives me a strange little stab of pain. Yes, he taught me to drive, I remember – much to my mother's chagrin, as she felt these things were best left to professionals. I get out of the car and look for the scratch on the garage door. Nope – completely disguised by new paint. The only evidence of my last happy driving lesson with him is a damp sock in my mind. Unless he remembers as well? I must ask him next time I see him.

As I'm getting back in the car, the front door disgorges my mother – smiling sunnily, blonde ponytail bouncing, clutching flowers and a huge bag – as if she had planned a picnic, and Urs, with a nimbus face.

"It's lovely that you've joined us," says Mum, and I remember to smile a cheery smile in return, and to insist that she takes the front seat.

It is hard to hear from the back seat, so I don't know if my mother's incessant chatter is aimed at Urs alone or at both of us. Her words reach me in pulses, like a poorly tuned radio trying to make up its mind which station to settle on. Something about someone on her ward who either fell off scaffolding or was hit by scaffolding, and the effect on his family. Urs mutters something sombrely appropriate and I think Mum answers that it's hard to grieve for someone who isn't dead, at which point they both fall silent, and I can see Urs's eyes checking in her mirror that I'm still in the back of the car. Yup - I'm still here. My mother then turns around and asks me how work is going, and what I've been up to, and I rack my brains for something that doesn't involve Fred or Marty or Karen, who are what I've been up to, or at least with whom I intend to get up to things.

"I bumped into Diana Candle and her mother the other day," I say.

"Yes, Ursula mentioned that. Isn't that lovely? Will you be meeting to catch up?"

Oh God - that again. Have I accepted that Facebook invite? I'm not really keen on cats in clothes. "Not sure. Her mother suggested that as well." I lean forward. "I remembered the time Mrs Candle came round to tell you that I wasn't to mention Death to Diana, and you sent her packing."

I can see my mother trawling her memory banks, and then a jolt of remembrance. She smiles. "Oh yes, you're absolutely right. I couldn't believe it. Something about a gerbil."

"Hamster," I say.

My mother jolts again. "You're right. It was about a hamster." She gives me a beaming smile. "Hopefully Diana knows about death now."

"I think she must. She got hassled by another driver and told him to fuck off and die, so she uses the word when she wants to."

Another jolt. My mother's smile slips before climbing back up her face, whilst Urs's eyes bulge at me in the mirror. Oh fuck - did I use the F-word? Must be more mindful with my speech.

"What do you mean: another driver?" asks Urs, turning around to face me.

"Um . . . eyes on the road please, Ursula," says my mother.

"They were in the car, but stopped when they saw me," I answer, and then wonder if that is a lie. I don't think so. 'See' and 'saw' are often used in a non-literal sense: I see what you mean. I saw the light. It could sort of include two cars colliding.

And now I wonder whether the simple playground see-saw doesn't capture a fundamental truth about the eternal now, in which the present is already the past is already the present, a bit like Eckhart's assertion that a day six days ago or six thousand years ago is as close to us as yesterday.

"You've gone very quiet," says my Mum, and I realise that we're now parking in a residential street. "Everything alright?"

"Fine. Actually I was just wondering where the term 'see-saw' came from."

"Oh." I suppose it is a bit of a conversation stopper, and it's not like I was expecting an erudite answer. But I can see her trying to think of something useful to say. She gives up. Then she is trying to negotiate seatbelt and flowers and basket and getting out of the car.

"Get out and help Mum," orders Urs, and I meekly do just that; I stand patiently by her open door and take the bag that she holds out for me, whilst trying to hold the flowers away, as though I might crush them with my heathen hands.

"Close your own door," says Urs, with – I think after such a short drive – disproportionate weariness.

I shut the door – not harshly – but Urs still does her trademark wince, then I follow them through the streets until we are at the entrance to Wimbledon cemetery. I'm slightly bemused by a sign that reads 'The cemetery is open to residents and non-residents', but try to match Mum's and Urs's purposeful pace upon the sanitised tracks through the grass.

Funny to think of all these supine, rotting bodies at our feet. I wonder if any have been buried prone – a little joke by the undertakers, because of a difficult corpse or a demanding bereaved family. I know there were many cases of prone burials in ancient times all over the world; archaeologists assume it is a negative statement about people who defied the cultural norm or who occupied a lower rung on society's ladder. More recent examples include witches and women accused of voodoo. It occurs to me now that whilst archaeologists assumed that all prone burials – being unusual – must reflect society's opprobrium – they haven't thought of one obvious reason: the 'corpses' weren't always truly dead. Brain death is a recent concept. Funny to think that death has been so plentiful, and still people couldn't always recognise it. Well, not so funny for the poor bugger waking up underground.

"Win. Win!"

I blink in the afternoon sun. Both Urs and Mum are looking back at me.

"What?"

"Why've you stopped?" Urs, impatient.

"Are you OK?" My mother, worried.

"Sorry – I was deep in thought."

"What were you thinking about?"

"I was just wondering if anyone here was buried face . . ."

"You can think and walk, you know," snaps Urs, whilst Mum makes some kind of placatory sound. At least, I think it's meant to placate both of her daughters – not that I need pacifying.

I make an effort to keep up with them. I think I remember Grandad's funeral and his interment in this cemetery, and yet I don't think I came. No – of course I didn't; I had to stay home and look after Dad. And yet I remember Mum and Nan, black-clad gazing down at the coffin, not because I really saw them but because I have conflated my imagining of the occasion with every Hollywood film scene of the bereaved standing around the burial pit. This is why I don't value memories. They are merely narrations dressed up as fact. Ask the witness to a crime to remember the details and he'll say he can't – it was just too long ago. Convince the witness that he's being hypnotised to help him remember, and he'll have more confidence in spouting some details. All still rubbish – but he's now being given permission to narrate his memories. This is all we are: narrators struggling to give ourselves a fixed story. What use is memory? It is sophism dressed up as Self.

"Look," hisses Urs, very close. I don't know how she got that close without me noticing. "Get a move on."

"It's alright, Ursula," says Mum, a little way ahead. "We're not in that much of a rush."

"Yes we are. If we're going to fit in a visit to Nan we have to be gone before they have supper."

"That's true," says Mum.

And Urs is right. I'm thinking too much. From now on, I'll just walk.

I am walking. Walking am I. Walking.

We have stopped. I am standing. Standing.

"Oh, for God's sake, Win. Don't just stand there like a statue."

"She's not really doing anything wrong, Ursula."

I look down at them, both squatting by a well-tended grave. Or at least, I think it looks well-tended, but Urs is plucking at weeds and removing dead flowers. Out of Mum's basket come secateurs and a plastic bag, which she holds open for Urs to drop the weeds into.

"Do you remember when Grandad died?" asks Mum.

I look at the epitaph, in black print on the gravestone.

Grant Hardy
Much loved husband, father, grandfather
Called home 6th July 1996

"Yes, 1996."

"You just read that," snapped Urs. "Mum asked you if you remember."

"Yes, I remember. He went into hospital for . . . what was it? It was something that should have been routine. But it didn't go well."

They are still staring at me. "A by-pass, or something."

"Well done," says Mum.

"Was that at your hospital, Mum?"

"Yes."

"But she wasn't a nurse then," says Urs.

I think. That's right. Mum did some job that didn't involve a uniform. Can't remember what.

"How often do you visit the grave?" I ask.

"Not as often as I should," says Mum. "But I try and get by at least once a month."

"Why?"

Urs glares at me. Mum looks lost for an answer. And so I wander off, looking at gravestones – all relatively recent in this section. No lichen-hugging weathered stones here; just shiny stones with decaying flowers. People 'fell asleep', 'passed on', or were 'called home'. Every gravestone is a lie. Especially the one that says that Grant Hardy was a much loved husband, father, grandfather.

Flowers – in different stages of decay – bear witness to the living relatives' sense of weary obligation to appear to care about the grave.

I don't understand what was wrong with my 'Why' question. If you really believe that the person has gone to heaven, or simply ceased to be – why visit? Unless you believe that part of the soul remains in the grave. And here I'm reminded of a TV program about siblings visiting the graves of young American soldiers whose lives were snuffed out in Afghanistan. They brought cans of beer to leave at the gravesides of their dead brothers. You cannot tell me that they didn't believe that they were somehow in communication with their dead relatives. And America is a much more overtly Christian country than the UK. So how did the soul become dichotomised into Heaven-soul and Grave-soul?

"I don't know why. I suppose it's so that I can tell your Nan that I've been."

My mother has followed me, with Urs not far behind her, carrying a basket and a plastic bag.

"Been where?"

Mum's face clouds over. "Been here."

"Let's go," says Urs, and the two of them do a synchronised pirouette and retrace their steps, their western sides now illuminated in the afternoon sun. A spring breeze is passing through.

I jog to keep up with them, but can only catch the chaff of their conversation.

". . . is why I didn't want her to come," says Urs.

My mother's response is inaudible.

"But she doesn't," responds Urs. "All the time . . . all she's doing . . . looking for clues . . . making up a story."

And this time I do catch my mother's response. "At least she's trying to please us."

They start a more urgent conversation, and this – I think – is about whether we should all go to see Nan in the home, though whether I hear this or whether I am 'making up a story', I don't know.

We are all quiet on the drive. I'm mildly surprised when Urs stops the car outside Mum's house, but I take it that I'm to get out here. Evidently Urs is expecting an argument, because she says "it's for the best."

"Yes, you're right," I say, not having a clue what she means, but agreeing with the statement, because it has just occurred to me that an hour alone in the old house could be very useful. I open my door.

"We'll be back in an hour," says Mum. "Do you have your keys?"

"Yes, no problem." I have them on the same key ring as my own.

I remember to close my car door, and note that they remain on the drive - engine still idling - watching whilst I select the right key and unlock the front door. They really don't trust me.

"Make yourself some tea," my mother calls out the window as I let myself in.

Urs frantically drops her window. "But don't cook anything."

But I have no time for tea or cooking. I do a quick reccy of the downstairs, but cannot tell if much has changed since I - or Dad - left. I can't remember when he left - I was probably in Taiwan at the time, and didn't see much reason to visit the family home when I was forced back to England.

So all I can say is that the layout is familiar, in the sense that it has a hall, a front room opening to dining room, a kitchen and a downstairs toilet.

To be honest, I can look around it and not feel even the slightest throb of resonance. The carpets, walls and soft furnishings seem to whisper an apology for not being an even paler imitation of whatever colour they were trying to hint at. For the first time I notice that the beige (pale beige) carpet in the front room is the same as in my front room. Maybe that's why Urs chose it for me: to remind her of Home when she had made the two mile trek to her 'office' in my Colliers Wood house. Maybe when she covers my breakfast table with balance sheets and double-entry bookkeeping things, she is feeling desperately homesick. I am being facetious, of course, but sometimes I can't help wondering why Urs hangs around my place when she obviously doesn't want to be there.

Anyway, a person is not defined by the colour of their carpets (as I can testify) but by the things that they are happy to have on display, and by the things that they hide away from prying eyes. So, I start a search for my family, which I hope will end with finding me, or to be precise, finding out why I wrote about someone called Gadd whom I didn't know.

My father is no longer in the lounge. 'Zen and the Art of Motorcycle Maintenance' was his bible – but it's nowhere to be seen. I'm sure his Dean Koontz books used to cower on a bookshelf, always outnumbered by Bibles and Catholic guides to living – none of which could have been very definitive, as there were always loads. But now my old mother is absent too: apart from a few modern novels, I can only see books related to nursing and medical matters. What has she done with all the Catholic kitsch? The walls are now bare of Marian pin-ups and figurines of Jesus having open-heart surgery. I can see one mounted photograph of Urs and me as children, smiling – and looking, for once, as if we aren't about to kill each other – but even that is consigned to a second row, behind a jar of pens.

My phone vibrates. Fred – breathless, agitated.

"Winifred? I have to be quick. The bloody woman has just forbidden me from speaking to you and Mr Gadd has ruined a saucepan."

Probably one of the more unconventional conversation openers. "Are you OK, Fred? I did try and ring you back, but I got Maddy."

"I know. I know. Bloody interfering woman."

"Actually, it was useful. She told me that your father died in China."

"Well, I thought you knew that." I hear a noise in the background, and his voice becomes more urgent. "I don't think you should come round today. Not until I've had a chance to get rid of her . . ." – I had picked up a photograph in a gilded frame, but pause now, slightly concerned by a new image of Fred clobbering Maddy with a burnt saucepan and stuffing her body into the cage at the back of his estate car – ". . . but you can probably give the answer over the phone."

I look at the picture of Mum's parents on their wedding day; it must have been a summer's day, judging by the light and colours. Kodak colours. Who would have thought that Kodak would go out of business for failing to change? To keep up with changing trends? To do something with all their early ideas for inventing digital cameras? Why was there no equivalent of Karen in their boardroom shouting, "there is nothing as immutable as change?"

It's interesting that the only photographs that are

unashamedly displayed are this one of Mum's parents on their wedding day and two old black and white ones of her paternal and maternal grandparents, whom I never met, or met and don't remember. But here they all are. Lest we forget.

"Winifred? You have to tell me the answer." Fred. That explains why I'm doing things one-handed. I squeeze the receiver nearer to my ear.

"What was the question?"

"Why is he bothering me?"

We must be on Gadd. "Because you've forgotten him."

"But . . ."

"Do you have any photographs of him? I mean – displayed?"

"No. I . . . Maddy won't like . . ." – a quiet roar of frustration, I think because he can't find the words he needs – ". . . but would he know? I mean if I had photographs displayed – would he know?"

"Sort of. Yes." I think the one on the right is Nan's parents, and the one on the left is Grandad's.

"Is that why Mr Gadd wanted to find the Garden of Remembrance?"

We must be back to my essay. "Yes. Ancestor worship. The Chinese would say he needs to be remembered by his son." God, my Grandad was an ugly bastard – even in his posh wedding suit; he would make a basset hound look ecstatic by comparison.

"Ancestor worship?"

"Yes."

There is a bang, so he's either dropped the phone or keeled over. In case it is the latter, I spend the next minute shouting 'Fred' into my mobile, before giving up and ending the call.

I go upstairs, expecting to find that the Catholic kitsch

has undergone an Ascension to Mum's bedroom, but I find nothing except an ordered female room with a book by Oliver Sacks (neatly bookmarked) beneath one side of the bed. I check Urs's small room - slightly more evidence here of rush and haste - the duvet pulled up unevenly, a couple of scenic photographs hanging on the walls. And a copy of *Fifty Shades of Grey* spread-eagled on the bedside table. That surprises me. When did she last have a boyfriend? I have a vague recollection that she was engaged whilst I was out in Taiwan, but it must have fizzled out by the time I came back, as I never saw any evidence of romance in her life.

I cannot find my father's music room, which is really, really weird. Maybe it was downstairs. I go back down and check each room, and even each cupboard door, in case it leads to Dad's room. Nothing. Just bizarre. The room that was most important to him has vanished.

I give up and go upstairs again, to my room, which does seem a little familiar. I wouldn't go as far as saying that my mother had made it into a shrine for the teenage me, but it is ironic that of the one person in the family who has deliberately moved on - in the whole house, it is only my books which stand undisturbed: history books, horrible history books, dictionaries, an assortment of non-fiction books, some on Chinese culture. Even my early books on Buddhism and Taoism have been left unmolested. There are some items I don't recognise - a powder puff (weird), some lipstick (weirder) - but my books are safe.

Somewhere on these shelves must be a clue to the essays I wrote. But no Mr Gadd leaps out at me. I remember that I was always writing - I wrote so much that my hand used to seize up with cramp - but what I wrote, I can't remember. Would I have kept a diary? Surely not, and yet when something makes me look under the bed, and pull out one of several shallow boxes, the pink spine of a prone book is prominent amongst the slotted notebooks; it is the sort of yucky book with pictures of pink roses on the cover, that just screeches: 'I am a Diary for a Girl' and has the sort of pretend miniature padlock that can be broken with a good yank. I give it a good yank, because I am fucked if I am going to waste time looking for a pretend miniature key to slot into the pretend miniature lock.

I am confident that the contents will have more gravity than the cover. I lie on my side on the bed and start from the first page, where I have helpfully written that I am fourteen, which – if I have to meet the old me – is exactly the age at which I would like an introduction.

It is awful. It is so awful that I have to roll up a ciggie and spend five minutes in the garden, feeling myself unravel. Was this all I was? A silly, fluffy Oh.My.God girl with chubby writing and circles for the dots on 'i's? A thought occurs to me: maybe it's in code? I go back upstairs but fail to see any pattern in the contents; no cipher to unlock a hidden language: I don't like Sandra because she looked at me funny. Danny is gorgeous. I hate Maths. (I thought I loved Maths. I'm sure I was good at it.) Glenda is OK now that she's chucked Tim. And on and on. Interestingly there's no mention of Diana, so she couldn't have figured that strongly in my life. I note an occasional tendency to talk about myself in the third person: Win gets another stunning report. Win is such a swot. But Win hates English. However much I would like to interpret this as an early sign of detachment, it just comes across as pretentious and pompous. But the entry that I find personally wounding is a paragraph that starts: Fallowfield is an idiot – how can you learn History from this old fool?

The book flies from my hands to land in a confused heap on the floor.

"What the hell are you doing?" Urs, shouting, furious.

I half raise myself and stare down. Whoops – I've been lying on the bed with my sneakers on. "It is my bed," I say. Which is only true in a mundane, conventional sense – but that is the level of truth that Urs tends to operate on.

"I mean – why are you reading my diary?"

It's not my diary. Thank God. I fall back on my bed with my arms outstretched, laughing with relief. At which point Urs picks up the diary and brings it down on my face with a force that surprises me. I didn't think the old girl had it in her. It is surprisingly painful. I sit up and look for a tissue, as I suddenly feel like I have a runny nose. Urs stares at me, looking horrified, and my mother – now freeze-framed in the doorway, also looks at me like I've grown two heads.

"How long has this been going on?" she cries as she rushes forward, grabbing tissues from a box.

"What?"

"Nosebleeds."

"I don't know when it started. Just now I think."

For a nurse, she seems surprisingly distressed by my little spatter of blood, though calms down when I explain that I was so surprised by Urs bursting in that I fell off the bed and caught my nose on the side. Oh dear – another fib. Urs is just standing there, more subdued than I have ever seen her.

"At least it's not broken," says Mum. "But maybe you should stay here tonight in Nan's old room."

"My room," I say, and they both look at each other.

Chapter Six

MY HEAD IS growing back. This is a disaster. I can't remember where I am when I wake up, and for a moment I think I'm in my old room in Mum's house and maybe that's the reason I'm disoriented. Then I realise that I'm in my bed, back in my house which means that I should be oriented and headless.

Maybe when I'm standing up it will disappear again. I get up and walk through the house, but my head is still enclosed in an artificial shell – my own little isolated hell. If I don't take immediate action, it is going to grow back completely and undo years of meditation.

I look out of a window and stare at the cherry blossom tree a few houses down. If I try really hard, I can regain the sensation of light pouring through the space my head occupies – the feeling of being at the centre of the universe – but I didn't have to try before. As for my Om, all I can hear is the high-pitched squeal of tinnitus.

I have to get back to Taiwan. I have to leave this behind. No more remembering, no more catching-up, no more Fred Fallowfield. No more bloody Gadd. No more half-baked translation assignments that screw up my eyesight and pay little towards my airfare. I am soon at my PC, searching for schools in Taiwan that need English teachers. My search has barely begun before I become aware of a faint tapping. When I go to the top of the landing I realise that someone is knocking on my front door: polite, not frantic. I go downstairs.

It's Fred. And Maddy. Fred agitated, like a dog on a leash that is desperate to come in. Maddy, smart, in control. She must read my expression, because she immediately asks if this is a bad time.

Of course it's a bad time. My head is growing back. But I just shake my solid head and lead them into the front room, where Maddy immediately sits down on the sofa, and Fred jiggles impatiently in an apparently Gadd-free armchair.

"This is a lovely little house," says Maddy, looking around. Fortunately she has plonked her handbag over the cigarette burn, so that doesn't mar her vision. "Are you OK?"

I was trying to see me through her eyes – usually a good head-cracking exercise – but it isn't working now.

"I'm fine. Can I get you something to drink?"

"A glass of water for both of us, please."

She follows me into the kitchen, and surveys the room, which nudges me off my track so that I forget what I came in for. Fred appears in the doorway, still mute, his discomfort almost vibrating through his suit. I get the impression that he is impatient for something but is under orders to wait for a sign from his wife. He looks hot, so I give him a glass of water.

Maddy is looking at me expectantly, then smiles. "Well, I suppose I did ask for a glass of water for us both."

"Sorry?"

"You're very literal, aren't you? Never mind, I'm not really thirsty." And she carries on looking around.

I wish I could throw my vision over to Maddy – see what she's seeing; a few days ago, I could have done that effortlessly, but now I'm having to force myself to see things through her eyes: she's clocking the washing up liquid and cleaning materials, looking at the surfaces; now she's staring fascinated at the post-it notes over the kitchen door. Most are in English (Clean rice pot / empty tumbler drier / put bins out).

"You're very organised," she says.

"Saves time."

She raises a finger and points to one note. "Why do you write some in Chinese?"

Because I don't particularly want anyone to read a note that says 'shag Karen on Tuesday'. "It partly depends what language I'm thinking in at the time," I reply, which I think counts as an appropriate answer rather than a lie.

"What does that one say?"

"Buy bananas." It actually translates as 'before leaving the house, always drink water, eat a banana and go to the toilet', but I don't think she needs to know that.

"What is this house?" she asks, which baffles me. I find myself translating the question into Chinese in case it makes more sense there, but it doesn't.

"I mean – is it Victorian or Edwardian?"

"Oh. Victorian. 1890."

She nods again. "Ours is Edwardian. Funny to think of all the people who'd have been moving through the same space in years gone by, isn't it?"

"And those still to come, who will wonder how we lived our lives."

She looks surprised. "I've never thought of it like that." The kitchen survey is obviously over. "Would you mind showing me upstairs?"

Fred gives a quiet roar of impatience and sits in the front

room, whilst I lead Maddy upstairs, announcing the name of each room with as much enthusiasm as a socialist butler would muster to intone the names of aristocrats arriving at a manor. "The bedroom." "Another bedroom." "The bathroom." Another fucking Duke.

She looks at each room intently, and I have a sudden panic and wonder if Fred has told her that the house is for sale. No - that would be silly.

"Where do you work?"

I lead her back into my bedroom and banish the screensaver on my PC to reveal a screen with densely packed characters. I had copied them from a Taiwan government website earlier and wanted to go through the article to find out if they would pay airfares for prospective English teachers.

Maddy sits down, looks at the screen and almost recoils in the chair. "Do you need glasses, Winifred?"

"No, why?"

"You use a large font." She rolls the chair a few inches further back from the screen and looks again. "You understand all of that?"

"Pretty much. But these are traditional characters. I must admit that I'm better at the simplified version used in China. I'll show you." I reach past her to change a setting, and immediately the characters become lighter and the page looks less dense. It's quite gratifying that she's so interested. I can't imagine my mother lasting more than a few seconds in front of this computer.

"That certainly looks simpler. So China changed its writing system?"

"That's right. Good old Chairman Mao. You can get fined for using traditional characters in China."

Maddy makes a face. "That sounds awful. What if people didn't want to change?"

"It was a good thing. It helped improve literacy rates in China."

"You know that Fred has dementia, don't you?" She carries on in the same tone as before – as if we were still discussing the merits of the traditional versus modern Chinese script. It takes me a second to jump onto this new track.

"No, I didn't know. I thought he was just . . ."

"Just what?"

"He's just a bit, I don't know – different." I wanted to say he's just a bit old, but while 'old' is an OK term in Chinese culture, it sounds negative in English.

"Mmmm. He is different, all right." She shakes her head, and mutters 'different' again, I think to herself rather than to me. Then she looks up at me. "Fred has the equivalent of a catastrophic brain injury. Do you understand?"

"He doesn't seem all that different from years ago – as far as I remember. He wouldn't have had dementia then, would he?"

"Actually – he did. His fixations were camouflaged by his eccentricities, so he got away with it for a long while. Do you understand what I mean by fixations?"

When I don't answer (because I disagree with her) she huffs, and says "is there a word for fixations in Chinese?"

"Yes, well two words; it sort of back translates as being reluctant to leave something behind."

This gets a mirthless chuckle. "Then it has more of a melancholic charm in Chinese. In English, I would say fixations has a brutal meaning. But the trouble is that when someone like Fred is sure about something, those fixations can be quite persuasive – even to me – who should know better."

She has completely lost me now. "I'm not sure what you mean," I say. "He thinks he's being haunted, and he wants it to stop. That's not a fixation. That's wanting to solve a problem."

"He is fixated on . . . of course Fred thinks you're the Oracle. Apparently we have to put up pictures of his father around the house and pay obeisance." She gives another joyless laugh. "As if he were worth it."

"Gadd? You knew him?"

"Well, I met him. I couldn't see that there was much to him, to be honest. Very distant man. Distant to his wife. Distant to Fred. Completely unengaged with his family. Homosexual, I suspect, and keen to get out of the marriage. I wasn't sorry when he went to China."

"What the hell was he doing in China?"

"His father had just died."

"He went to China because his father had died?"

"He went to China to settle his father's affairs, or to collect his belongings . . ." – she waves a hand dismissively – ". . . I don't know why. Something to do with his father's death. It got him out of attending our wedding, which I suspect was the real reason he went."

"So Fred's grandfather was in China? What was he doing there? Was he a missionary?"

"No. A teacher, I think. Anyway, Fred's father didn't come back. He died there, some years later. Anyway, my question to you is this: where is Mr Gadd?"

"You've just said he died in China."

She lets out a gasp of exasperation. "He was, yes. He died in China. Apparently. But where is he now?"

"Nowhere, if he's dead. He's just in Fred's head."

"Good. Well done. I really thought you were going to come

up with some superstitious rubbish about neglected ghosts."

"No. I don't do superstition."

"Good. So – tell me what causes the disruption in our house? Things on the floor, the oven on with nothing cooking, the freezer door open, the front door open."

"I've no idea."

She sighs. "You don't. Really?" She mutters something I can't hear, then says "why does Fred think this is something to do with his father?"

"I don't know."

I hear Fred shouting something from the bottom of the stairs, but whatever it was, it couldn't have been too alarming, as Maddy is still looking quite comfortable in my office chair.

"Is he all right?" I ask.

"He's . . . all right." She sighs. "But sometimes I wish . . ." She stops. Decisively.

"Sometimes you wish he were dead. Because it's hard to grieve for someone who isn't dead."

Her jaw drops slightly, and it's the first time I've noticed her blink; up to now her stare has been as constant as a basilisk's. But now she's wavering – a little wobbly. "Yes, yes," she murmurs, then adds something I cannot hear, or maybe wasn't meant to hear. Then more loudly: "Fred just shouted up 'Have you asked her yet' – and I haven't. So now I will."

"Ask me what?"

"Your mission . . ." – an unhappy smile nudges her lips – ". . . should you choose to accept it, is to settle a challenge. He wants you to prove – and I mean with evidence – that ancestor worship still exists. Not just exists in some two chicken village somewhere – but is actually prevalent."

"Whereas you want me to prove that it isn't."

She looks at me without answering. I take that as a 'yes'.

"Well, I'm afraid you've lost already. It does exist. It is prevalent."

"In China?"

"Oh, no. I meant in Taiwan. Not in China. Or at least not a mainstream belief. Amongst the peasants, almost certainly, but not amongst the more sophisticated. I wouldn't have thought so."

She almost splutters. "Peasants? That's a bit pejorative, isn't it?"

"To us, yes, but that's the word they would use in translation. The urban-rural divide is massive."

"I see." Her eyebrows have almost gone through the roof. "Well, much as I would cheerfully use any pejorative term to describe Fred's father, he certainly was no peasant." She pauses, then seems to reach a decision. "That's the challenge. If you can prove it is prevalent in China - and not just amongst the *peasants* - then I have told Fred he can build an ancestral shrine or whatever he wants to honour his pathetic father."

"When did he die?"

"1974. Apparently."

"So a British man dies in China in 1974, and his unhappy spirit won't be settled until he has received the correct Chinese rites?"

"Yes, of course it's ridiculous. But - to be fair - Lawrence Gadd was half Chinese."

"What? How?"

"Fred's grandfather - Gideon Gadd, yes, really - married a Chinese woman when he was teaching in China. They had a son - Lawrence Gadd - who was sent to boarding school in England."

"But then, that means that Fred . . ." I stop, because this new information is clashing with my long-held view of Fred as an eccentric, old-school, very British old gentleman.

"He is quarter Chinese, yes. It's not obvious, is it?"

"No, not at all."

"And he had no concept of Chinese identity or interest in China, until someone put the idea in his head."

"Who was that?"

She raises her eyes, as though I should know the answer to that. I hear Fred shouting again from downstairs, and this time Maddy frowns. "He's getting impatient. Look – you know enough for now. Do you accept the challenge?"

"No. Sorry."

Her composure instantly vanishes. "Why not?"

"Because it's stupid."

"You have to," she snapped. "This is your responsibility."

"How is this my responsibility?"

"You put the idea of ancestor worship in his head. Now he's convinced it's what they all do and it's what his father wanted. And when I say convinced, I mean fixated, and believe me, Fred's fixations are bloody hard to live with." 'Bloody hard' is accompanied by two slaps on my desk.

"Maddy, I have no idea how long it would take. It could be a couple of hours – it could be a couple of months. I would need paying."

"Oh." She looks surprised. "I thought you'd be interested, seeing as you're into all this . . . stuff." She nods towards my screen, the contents of which are as far removed from ancestor worship as an English parish council's report on village drains, and I wonder if she is rich on Fred's money, for it doesn't seem to occur to her that translators need to earn a living.

"Forget it," I say. She interrupts with a few "but . . ." noises, so I repeat "forget it" more and more loudly.

"OK, OK," she says. "Let's talk money."

"We can't talk money. If you ask me to translate something, I can give you a price, but you're asking me to do research, and I have no idea what that will cost. Anyway, you need an anthropologist, not a translator. So no. That's final."

She starts hitting my desk again. It is really annoying. I can feel a headache starting, which to be fair, is owing more to my annoyance that she is slapping the desk than to the noise itself.

"Then forget money. There must be something you want. What do you want more than anything else?"

"A plane ticket back to Taiwan." Fuck. That's my secret. I let it out just like that.

"How much does that cost?"

"I don't know. About six hundred quid." In truth, I don't know. I'm out of touch.

"Done. You shall have six hundred pounds. In return for evidence that ancestor worship exists. Or doesn't exist. And I mean evidence. Not just you saying that it does or doesn't."

A ticket back. I could slave for a year over translations (assuming someone bothered to send me some work to translate) and still not raise that amount beneath Urs's radar. I cannot turn this chance down, but I still can't believe it's real. I can see me spending a shedload of time on this and then Maddy denying that we ever had a deal.

"There's a couple of conditions," I say. "First, please don't mention the Taiwan ticket to anyone . . ." – she nods – ". . . and secondly, I need a hundred pounds up front."

"My handbag is downstairs." Maddy is getting up, all sweetness and light now that she thinks we have reached an agreement.

"But you do have to tell me why you're going to so much trouble. I just don't get the logic. Even if ancestor worship existed when Gadd was alive, why would Fred think his father bought into that? Does Fred think his father went native? It just all seems weird."

"As I say, you put the idea in his head. He thinks that his father went out to settle *his* father's affairs, and now Fred thinks he should have done the same for Lawrence bloody Gadd. Filial duty apparently."

"One more question . . ."

Maddy sighs impatiently and rests an arm on the chair. "Last one for now Winifred. I can hear that Fred is getting restless."

I haven't heard any more noise from downstairs, but maybe a wife is more attuned to her husband's agitations. "Last one. Why haven't you asked me to lie to Fred and say that Gadd just wants - I don't know - a park bench somewhere with a plaque to his memory?"

She looks at me, horrified. "Lie?"

"Yes. I wouldn't have gone along with it, but I'm surprised you didn't ask me. You'd save six hundred pounds."

"Right. Yes, I see. Well, I said that Fred's fixations can be persuasive." (Did she say that before she just said it now?) Maddy goes quiet, and looks at the screen. I wonder if that was the only answer I'll get, but then she closes her eyes and speaks so softly that I cannot hear her.

"Sorry?"

She fixes me a look. "You say that a lot." Which I'm sure

is not what she said a second ago, but now I'll never know as she gets up and walks out the room.

I follow her downstairs. We find Fred pacing the front room. He stops when he sees us, and looks from one to other of us.

"It's OK, Fred," says Maddy. "She accepts the challenge."

He beams at me. "Thank-you, Winifred."

"Handbag," she commands, and Fred fetches it from the sofa. She takes out a purse and counts out ten ten pound notes and gives them to me. I wonder if she always carries so much cash or whether she had foreseen this scenario and come prepared. Anyway, it's probably Fred's money she's doling out.

"Well, I'd better get started," I say.

"We need a checkpoint," says Maddy. "How about Friday? Too soon?"

Today is Monday. I should be able to find something by Friday. I nod.

"And don't forget Stonehenge," says Fred.

"Sorry?"

"Have you been keeping up with Stonehenge?"

I have a vision of Stonehenge jogging through the countryside. I don't know what he's going on about.

"Enough," says Maddy. "Don't bring that into it."

As they step out, Fred with a more jaunty step than I've seen before, Maddy looks out at the little front garden and turns back to me.

"Don't forget to put your bins out."

"Why?"

"Because it's written on one of your post-it notes: put the bins out on Tuesday."

"Yes, but today is Monday."

She raises her eyes. "It's Tuesday, Winifred."

How have I lost a day? Oh God – I know how I've lost a day. After Urs whacked my nose, Mum insisted I stay over that night in case I had another 'mysterious' nosebleed. It's completely thrown me. Urs drove me back yesterday morning and scarpered as soon as I had turned the key in the lock. I haven't seen her since. But the date on my PC says it's Monday today. Surely that wouldn't be wrong?

And then I remember that I changed it before I submitted my piece on investment opportunities. Serves me right for being dishonest. Talk about the instant fruits of karma.

Oh God. If it wasn't for Maddy, I would have stood Karen up tonight. I go straight back up to change the date on my PC, then come down again to put the bins out and set two alarm clocks to make sure I leave on time.

Karen looks surprised to see me, which surprises me, as she doesn't look like the sort to forget that she had an appointment on Tuesday or that today is indeed Tuesday. She is wearing smart trousers and a smart but crumpled top, as if she just got in from work.

"You've just missed Marty," she says, as if I had arrived two days early for my appointment with him, and then adds "I have a few chores to do, I'm afraid."

"What chores?"

"I wanted to hoover before you arrived. And I have to give first aid to a goldfish . . ." – she gives her forehead-raising smile – ". . . which isn't as weird as it sounds. And I need a shower."

"I'll hoover. I could do with a mindful task."

"Are you nervous?" she asks.

"Why? Is it not earthed or something?"

She laughs. "I meant about us."

"No." Feeling like I somehow have failed a Mother-and-Urs test, I add "sorry".

"No need to apologise. I guess you don't get nervous about things, do you?"

I could tell her that I don't remember the last time I felt nervous, but instead I just say "Hoover", and she leaves the front room and comes back pushing an upright vacuum cleaner.

"It does seem a bit daft," she says, as she uncoils the lead and plugs it in. "The idea of hoovering was so that you would walk into a tidy flat and think that it was always like that."

I look around. Seems like a tidy flat to me. The front room is nice and light with a fish tank gently bubbling away on a sideboard. The flat is an open plan arrangement, with a dining area and a breakfast bar marking the start of the kitchen. The wall over the fireplace (occupied by a gas fire) has a clock reflected on the wall; not a real clock but one projected, which looks rather smart. I take a step nearer to inspect it, but walk into a vacuum cleaner.

"I really do like hoovering," I say. And I do. Especially with my stupid head growing back, I could do with a quiet mindful task that I can throw myself into. Whilst I run the machine over the carpet, I am vaguely aware of Karen busying herself in the kitchen, but mainly I hoover. I am hoovering. I am. Hoovering.

When I finish, I find Karen sitting on the sofa, watching me intently. There are two mugs on the table in front of her. Her hair looks wet and she is wearing different clothes.

"You really do enjoy it," she says. "Do you always do that ritual before you use the hoover?"

"What ritual?"

"Never mind. I made you some jasmine tea. That OK?"

"My favourite drink, actually."

"I guessed." She watches me as I drink the tea, and I wonder if I am being analysed or therapised or whatever the verb is for whatever a therapist does.

I look up at the bookshelves on either side of the room. There are loads of history books, and not just the glossy coffee table ones, but paperbacks with scuffed covers. I put down my mug and get up to read the spines. There's a couple on Welsh history, but also every period of British history, from the first world war through every feudal dynasty back to the Normans, the Saxons, the Romans through to the Bronze Age. There's a few books with what I assume are Welsh titles.

"Do you speak Welsh?"

"Yes. Though I read it better. I don't get a chance to practise talking much."

"I suppose you wouldn't in London."

"To be honest, I don't get much of a chance to practise it in Wales."

"That's a shame," I say. "Is it true that the Welsh word for the English is Saxon?"

"Yes. Well – Saesneg." She looks at her watch. "Right. Are you ready for goldfish first aid? I have a feeling you'll be better at this than me. You know – goldfish – feng shui." She pronounces it correctly, instead of the 'shooey' mispronunciation I hear from most British people.

Soon I am chasing a very fat goldfish (suffering from dropsy, apparently) with a little net while trying to avoid scooping up its slimmer brethren. Karen moves a smaller fish tank nearer to the main one.

"Is it true that you're supposed to have eight goldfish for feng shui?" she asks, obviously considering me an expert on all things Chinese.

"Probably. Eight is a lucky number in Chinese because supposedly it sounds like 'rich', which means it is pretty stupid in this country really, where eight sounds like . . . eight."

Eventually I manage to corner the plump fellow and lift it out and into what is apparently known as an isolation tank, where it sinks halfway down the tank, like an orange golf ball.

"Expertly done," she says.

I stare at it through the glass, and it seems to look at me with bog-eyed curiosity. I wonder how I look to him. Maybe he just sees eyes. Or maybe it is just aware of pain.

"I suppose I should give it a name," said Karen. "Marty just calls it Fat Bastard."

"That's accurate. It certainly is fat. And I assume its parents weren't married."

"I never thought of that. So all animals are bastards." She stares at it, ruefully. "But I think a less . . . um . . . insulting name would be nice. What's 'fat' in Chinese?"

"Pang."

"Pang is a great name. And sounds genderless, which is good, as I have no idea if it's a he or a she."

"So how are you going to treat it?

"Epsom salts and a drug. It's already in the water. Marty was supposed to help, but he always seems to be running late for something when any goldfish intervention is needed."

"Are you sure it shouldn't go to Fat Club?"

She laughs. "Yes. As in yes I'm sure of the diagnosis. A weakness in goldfish. They can explode if not treated. It's quite horrible for them."

"Oh. No picnic for the other fish then."

"Ugh. Very good, if a bit dark. I didn't mean to rope you into this, actually, but I was running late, and . . ." – she does her forehead-raising look – ". . . you're running a bit early."

"Oh – am I?"

"An hour. Which is fine – quite handy as it turned out." She looks at my empty wrist. "Why didn't anyone get you a watch for your birthday?"

"Because I had a watch then."

"Hmmm." She washes her hands in the kitchen sink. "Do you lose a lot of things?"

Do I lose things? That's tricky. My memories have disappeared, but that is deliberate rather than down to external forces, such as the ECT treatment Fred is convinced I have been subject to. Because our lives are made up of trivial, repetitive tasks. Suppose you could remember in minute detail every time you locked the front door? Or brushed your teeth? Or walked to the tube station? How could this not clog your brain with unhelpful data? But, yes – things disappear. Money has disappeared from my account. My father has disappeared from my family. And unlike freezer doors left open or ovens left cooking nothing – these things aren't down to me.

"It wasn't a criticism," says Karen, and I realise that she has taken my lack of answer for a sulk.

"Sorry, I was trying to think of the answer to your question, which I've now forgotten."

"Never mind. What happened to your watch?"

"My old History teacher came round and walked off wearing it. I didn't like to say 'Stop, Thief!'"

"Oh." She laughs. "I'm sure there's more of a story behind that, but I don't know whether to explore more."

"No – not now. I do forget some things – but I remember why I'm here."

"OK. In that case, maybe we should . . . well, I can imagine Marty turning up early to try and catch us at it."

"We best get on with it then."

I follow her lead, washing my hands at the kitchen sink.

"That is . . ." – she looks at me – ". . . if you're still happy with the arrangement? We don't have to if you've changed your mind."

"No. Let's go. I'll follow you."

She laughs and says "OK", but doesn't move. I take her by the hand and lead her to a hallway with three doors.

"This feels like one of those riddles, where if I choose the wrong door I end up in Hell, but if I choose the right door I end up in Heaven. Presumably the third door is a time portal and throws us out to the street where I first saw you, and we have to go through this all again."

"That wouldn't be so bad," she says. "I'm suddenly feeling a bit nervous."

I reach for the door in the middle, and she nods. We go in.

Chapter Seven

I F YOU TYPE 'Ancestor worship' and 'China' into Google, you get a lot of hits. When you drill down a bit, you find a mixture of erudite articles with references and articles where no sources have been cited. Drill into these a bit more, and you find that the erudite features may have concerned a study into funereal practices in a small Hong Kong village in 1925, and the non-academic articles make statements like 'Ancestor worship is practised in China', with no proof considered worthy of conclusion. Because – I suspect – there isn't any.

The trouble is: people don't like change. Worse than that, people are not interested in knowledge. They are only interested in having their cherished opinions upheld. I lost count of the times in Taiwan when this conversation happened.

Taiwanese person: American?

Me: No, British.

(Taiwanese person would then hug themselves and rock, which I found baffling to begin with).

Taiwanese person (still with arms wrapped round themselves): From London?

Me: Correct. I live in London.

The Taiwanese person would then say *wu* (dance) which sort of went with the rocking motion. It took me a while to realise they meant *wù* as in fog: Britain is so cold you have to hug yourself, and London is foggy. If I said that London wasn't foggy, they didn't believe me, and if I insisted, they got upset. Such a shame that you no longer have fog. So, correction: people don't like change in other people. Sulphur dioxide-laden eye-watering emphysema-causing fog – I'm sure the East Enders miss it.

I decide that the first thing to search for is a national funeral policy, as the Chinese Communist Party probably have stipulations in place, and sure enough I soon find this:

[My rough translation]: 'Cremation is not the only option available that a family can consider. Sea burials are also possible. Land burials are strictly prohibited and any vestige of superstitious behaviour that obstructs funeral reform is illegal'.

OK – but that's just what the authorities say. I remember one time when my father was teaching me to drive; someone had flashed their lights, when I was signalling to turn right. I had hesitated, knowing that the Highway code said that flashing lights were a warning, not an invitation. "Turn," said my father. "She's letting you go." Afterwards I quoted the section on flashing lights to him; knowing me, I probably knew the whole book off by heart. He shook his head in mock disbelief.

"That's what the authorities say, Winnie. For anything, there's always an official set of rules, and the rules that people really follow because they are more natural."

I have to find out what normal Chinese people think is right when it comes to dealing with dead family members.

I also have to find out why I wrote a story about Gadd, or if not Fred's father, why I wrote about a Gadd. Needless to say, I have no memory of it.

Maybe because it never happened. I have no proof that it did.

I ring the Fallowfields. After a lot of ringing, it goes to

a standard BT answer message. I re-dial. Maddy answers, sounding strained. Maybe Gadd has burnt breakfast.

"Do you know what time it is, Winifred?"

"Um . . . no. Sorry."

"It's only just gone six o'clock."

"In the morning?"

"Yes – in the morning."

"I've started the research."

"You're ringing to tell me that?"

"No, I'm ringing to ask you for my exercise book. I need to read that story about Gadd."

"Right. Well after I've gone back to bed and had some more sleep – and then got up at a sensible time, and then wrestled the book off Fred, then – and only then – might I put it in the post."

"One more thing. Where's Mr Gadd buried?"

"Heavens. I don't know. It's on a letter somewhere. Fred's grandfather lived in Tianjin, so I assume it was near there."

"Tianjin. Great." I hang up, only remembering to say Goodbye when the words 'Call ended' appear on my mobile screen.

I wonder what Dad would make of my current mission. I suspect that in the unlikely event that I could get him to focus long enough on the question to understand 'ancestor worship', he would be rather negative: his own family life in the Midlands sounded chaotic, with no male or female relatives to remember with fondness, let alone veneration.

Interestingly, when Karen and I were lying together last night, she had asked about him – not about my mother. I told her how I'd found him, and his current situation – which I had never told anyone about before. Then she asked me how

I'd lost him in the first place. I didn't really know the answer. I said I thought the marriage had broken up owing to religious differences, and then it occurred to me that I don't even know if my parents are divorced. I imagine that he wanted one and my mother refused, so that he had no choice but to walk out with nothing.

"Win. Why is there a hundred pounds on the sofa?"

Oh God. I didn't hear Urs come in, but here she is standing in the doorway, not smiling. I really need to be more mindful about hiding cash.

"And good morning to you."

"I said – why is there a hundred pounds on the sofa?"

"Because that's where I left it. I'll put it somewhere safe later."

"But where did it come from?"

"Maybe I earned it."

"How did you earn it?"

I turn and look at her. I always find her strange, but usually familiar – or at least her strangeness is still within the familial boundaries of irritating but accepted quirks. But now I just see a stranger, looking at me with hostility. It gives me a jolt to realise that if someone in the street looked at me with the same expression, I would be looking around for a weapon, or something I could use for self-defence.

"Why do you hate me so much?"

Urs instantly goes red, develops bog eyes and gulps. Maybe Karen would recommend a bath with Epsom salts. You appear to be suffering from a touch of dropsy, strange sister.

"What a dreadful thing to say, Win. Why on earth would I hate you?"

"I don't know. Sometimes you just look at me like you hate me."

"Oh." She looks quite shaken, one hand suddenly reaching out to lean against the door jamb. "I'm sorry you think that. I certainly don't hate you. Sometimes I just get frustrated."

"Why?"

"Tell me how you got that money. The truth."

"OK. Someone wants me to do some research on ancestor worship in modern China."

She comes in, sits down on my bed and grips the frame. I'm going to have to install grab rails in my room if she carries on like this.

"Really? So – nothing to do with sex?"

"Sex? What on earth has ancestor worship got to do with sex?"

God. This petty obsession with sex, and who's had it off with who? Or maybe that should be 'with whom'. What does it matter?

She just exhales loudly.

Though I suppose the question of whether Catherine of Aragon had it off or didn't have it off with her first husband did completely shift England's axis.

"You know, you should get a boyfriend," I say.

Oh God. I so wish I hadn't said that; her eyes are turning weirdly bulbous – and I realise it's because they are filling with tears.

"I'll make some tea." I dash downstairs. Why can't she just get a boyfriend and get it out of her system and stop being so bloody obsessed with sex? I don't know if the self-denial comes from her own religious beliefs or from concern about what my mother would think, or maybe she's tried to meet

128

someone and failed. Surely she could get a bloke. She's pretty good-looking, in that she looks like a two years' older version of me. Though less serene. There's a nervousness about her that maybe puts off potential suitors.

She should meditate.

I give her five minutes to sort herself out, and eat an apple while I'm waiting. But when I go back upstairs things have taken a downturn, if anything. I can hear her crying – still in my bedroom. I go back down to the kitchen and have a banana, then tiptoe up again. She's still at it. In fact, she seems to be getting worse. From the sound of it, big sobs are happening in my bedroom. I go back down and contemplate eating some cherries, and then realise that I'm eating through the alphabet of fruit. I put the kettle on, musing that I would be stuck on 'D'. I can't think of a fruit that begins with 'D'.

I take her a mug of English breakfast tea, pausing outside the door to check that it is safe. Seems to be quiet in there now. When I go in she is blowing her nose and looking red-eyed.

"Thanks," she sniffs, when I give her the mug. "Sorry about that. I'm not sure where it came from."

"That's OK." I sit down at my PC and sign in again to banish the screensaver. I check my emails, where I see that one enquiry I made to a language school in Taiwan, (unfortunately it uses 'Pedant English School' for its anglicised name) has responded with some information about teaching.

I am just changing the font to large when I hear a sniff behind me and remember that Urs is still sitting on my bed, and if she sees the screen, it will be obvious what I'm up to. I quickly click a link to the Chinese version of the website and idly read the characters. Hopefully if she looks up she won't notice the bright orange and green colours and the blessed, ecstatic expressions of Taiwanese pupils that collectively scream 'come and be happy teaching at our school'.

The 'Pedant English School' was established in *Mínguó* 2004 – so last year. I remember when I first when to Taiwan (with my inevitably Christian-centric mindset) it confused me to walk into a bank and see a date displayed of 12 years earlier. I'm idly amused that when China became a republic in 1912 it continued the imperial system of using the emperors' era name and year of reign, but just substituted the word 'republic' for Qing or Tang or whatever. The Chinese communist party changed to the Gregorian calendar in 1949, leaving Taiwan to retain its traditional dating system. China – a great example of letting go of the past.

"Ah. D is for date."

"What?" says Urs.

"I was trying to think of a fruit beginning with 'D'. I've just remembered that date is a fruit."

"Is that really what you've been thinking about?"

Her tone sounds weird, so I swivel around to look at her. She's giving me that hostile stare again.

"Well, I just . . ."

"While I've been sitting here crying you've been thinking about fruit?"

"Well, not just fr . . ."

"You didn't think to ask me why I got upset?"

"Sorry." She doesn't answer, so presumably I'm meant to say something else. "OK. Why did you get upset?"

"Never mind. You really don't give a damn about anyone else but yourself, do you?"

"That's not true, I . . ."

"It's all planet bloody Win, isn't it? There's just no compassion in you now."

I could tell her that she is muddling up being dispassionate with not being compassionate.

"I feel compassion towards Dad," I say simply. "I do try and help him."

"Bit late now for anyone to help him."

"Hardly. He sells the Big Issue."

"Yeah – right." She shakes her head and then looks at me with red eyes, but no longer with tears. "It's all in your stupid mashed-up head, Win."

"I'm going for a walk." I get up.

"Off to see Dad I suppose?"

"Yes, I am actually." I didn't have plans to see Dad today, but I will go now and blow two pounds fifty on a magazine just to prove to myself that I'm compassionate. "Shall I give him your regards?"

She lets out an exasperated sigh. "I've put some things in your rucksack, Win. It's not meant to encourage you, by the way."

"OK. Thanks." God knows what I'll find in my rucksack later. Maybe a box of oats to balance my dangerously eastern rice diet.

"Take a jacket. It's quite cool out there."

"Will do." I walk into the kitchen and have a banana and some water.

I walk to Tooting Broadway, I walk to Tooting Bec. I get little replays of Urs crying on my bed, but I try to let them go. I concentrate on each step. I try to soften my senses so that I don't get stuck on the sounds of cars hooting or the bright colours of saris on sale. I am walking. I am walking. But Urs's little episode seeps back as surely as mould forms on grout. She gave no reason for her emotional storm other than to imply that it was somehow my fault. But the trigger was something like boyfriends or sex or love.

I bunch up with other pedestrians on a pavement, waiting for the traffic lights to turn red.

The man next to me laughs and says, "I don't know."

"What don't you know?" I ask him.

He raises his eyes and looks at me, smiling, but in a quizzical sort of way. I don't recognise him. He's good-looking, dressed in a smart tracksuit. I think older than me, which rules out school or college, but not by much, which rules out teacher. Maybe he was involved with the church in Wimbledon years ago, but he is black, and while I can remember there were a few young black women at the Catholic church, I don't remember young black men.

"I don't know why she hasn't got a boyfriend," he says. Then he laughs and jogs across the road and I realise that the light has gone red and a green man is flashing.

I don't cross. It occurs to me that I'm not in the right frame of mind to see Dad. The last thing he needs is to have a confused daughter turn up who is distracted by the baffling behaviour of his other daughter, who can't even be bothered to pass on a civil message to him. Damn Ursula. This has thrown me.

I turn back. I will just keep on walking. I will clear my mind. If Urs sits in a corner of my head, sobbing and carrying on, she will soon get bored and fade away. Heel down, transfer to ball of foot, push off the toes. Other foot: heel down, transfer to ball of foot, push off the toes. Again and again. I

132

can sense my mind letting go of the thoughts, like a cat losing interest in a toy. I am lost in walking. I am walking. Walking.

Where am I? I am stopped. I have stopped in front of a large-ish house in a long quiet road with other large houses. Or maybe it would be better described as a boulevard or an avenue. I am somewhere in surburban London where substantial trees deliver protective shade to all beneath and the cars parked at the sides of the road are paintballed with bird poo. The nearest one to me is a silver Volvo, and I can see that the next driver will have to get out a scrubbing brush, or maybe just guess what's on the left-hand side of the road when they are driving.

"Winnie? Is that you?"

There's an oldish woman kneeling on some sort of pad in the garden, taking shears to a bush that has apparently got too big for its roots. Or at least I think that's what she was doing: she's dropped the shears and the bush is still so huge that it could hide a troop of burglars. She makes some squeaking sounds and pushes herself to her feet, an action which takes a couple of attempts.

"It is Winnie, isn't it?"

I agree that it is and she gives me a smile.

"I'm afraid if you've come to see Diana . . . well – it's just me right now."

Now I recognise Mrs Candle. She looks different when she's gardening from when she's stopped at green traffic lights. Or maybe she looks older than I expected.

"To be honest, I was just taking a walk. I sort of lost track of where I was."

"Well, come in, come in." She starts to bend down to

retrieve the shears then gives up and leaves them on the grass.

"Did you find that poor man's dog?"

Of course: we pretended to lose a dog that was already lost, and Fred pretended to have a fit or a heart attack. Funny that she only remembers the dog.

"I'm afraid not."

She makes some distressed sounds, and I follow her through the front door - copying her in leaving my shoes on a mat in the hall - and into the kitchen.

"But that is the trouble with pets," she says, filling the kettle with water and needing several goes to place it on its base. "One way or another, they never last very long, do they?"

I almost say that Di's hamsters seemed to go on forever, but instead I shake my head and look sad.

"Sit down, sit down." She motions me to a single high-backed chair by a cut-down breakfast bar and lets out a little explosion of frustration when she sees me moving a pile of opened mail from the chair to the counter. Or at least I stack the papers on top of things which look like they're on top of things which may touch the breakfast bar; in truth, the surfaces of this kitchen are rather occupied. I try and make sense of the clutter. The shelves on the kitchen wall are given over to what I think you'd call 'novelty teapots' - presumably the novelty being that you would never dream of brewing tea in something shaped like a chicken or a red postbox. The invasion of teapots has pushed out the recipe books which are stacked on the counters, along with an accumulation of the detritus of modern living - letters, bills, folders . . . things.

"It's awful, isn't it?" says Mrs Candle, and when I look up at her looking at me, I realise that she has been doing my head-hopping exercise.

"No, it's fine."

"It isn't fine, it's . . ." – her voice has the hint of a crack – "I will get round to clearing it up, but we've had a bit of an accident."

She gives a bitter laugh and looks out the kitchen window, and I half-stand up to get a view of a rather unkempt lawn and a garden shed that has been ambushed by some sort of creeper. I'm a little surprised, as I imagined the Candles would have had a sanitised garden with crew-cut grass and plum-line garden beds. I know that there was always order here. Once. A long time ago.

"Your garden's nice." I have no opinion on it, but I'm hoping if I say something nice that she won't start crying, because the slight jerkiness of her body and the catch in her voice makes me think that something is going to blow, and I'm still a little shaken by Urs's loss of control yesterday. Or whenever it was.

With arms crossed, Mrs Candle stays facing the garden, but I sense her eyes take in nothing outside. She's either quiet because she is trying to control herself or she's forgotten I'm here. Which is fine. Someone must have died or something serious happened to merit this distress. It cannot really be about a cluttered kitchen: otherwise you'd just hire a man with a van and pay him to take it away.

"Is Di . . .?" I hesitate, because I want to ask if Di is dead, but that would mean that she'd have died since she sent me the Facebook invitation, which was sometime very recently.

"Di is . . .," and she stops, so I'm no nearer to knowing. Anyway, I'm being silly. I remember now that Di's parents were much older than mine. She called herself a miracle baby.

"Is Mr Candle . . .?"

"At work. He only had a couple of days off. He hasn't been much use, to be honest."

"Right."

I wonder what the accident was. I can't remember if the Volvo was crumpled at the back, because I was too taken by the bird poo at the front. Whatever the accident entailed, it has left Mrs Candle in some sort of stupor, for the kettle clicks off and she hasn't noticed. I'm quite thirsty.

"Could I have some water please?"

"Of course." She gets me a glass. "So what are you doing now, Winnie?"

Drinking a glass of tap water. She can see that. Does she mean what have I done today or what do I plan to do later?

"I mean job-wise."

"Oh, right. I'm a translator."

Usually people then inquire which language, but she asks, "have you moved out of home?"

"Well, yes. I'm thirty. I got my own place years ago."

"Just thirty?" She stares out of the window again. "I thought you were slightly older than Diana." A definite crack. Di-ana.

What on earth has happened here? Maybe a pet's died? She mentioned that pets don't last very long.

"Do you still keep hamsters?" I ask.

She looks confused, but at least gives a little chuckle. "No, Winnie. We haven't had hamsters since Diana was a little girl. To be honest, I think that my husband and I liked the hamsters more than Diana."

A rather surprising admission, but I guess it explains why Diana is an only child.

"Would you like to see Diana's old room?"

Why would I want to see a bedroom? I think saying, "I would rather have an ice-pick through my skull", would be a little tactless, so I just say "OK."

As I follow her out of the kitchen, she says over her shoulder "You probably remember where it is."

"I have a really bad memory. I'm afraid I don't remember this house at all."

And I really don't. The kitchen is a cluttered kitchen. The hall is a hall. I suspect the front room will look like a front room.

She stops, then turns to look at me. "But you were around here all the time. I think you preferred this house to your own."

"Oh. Sorry."

"Don't apologise. We were quite pleased to have you, Winnie. You were just happy to study, as far as I could make out. I'm not sure Diana would have done as well in her exams if it hadn't been for you." She frowns at me. "How can you not remember?"

"To be honest, Mrs Candle, I've had so many things happen to me after I left home, that it's rather pushed out my earlier memories."

"What sort of things? Did you have . . ." – she pauses – ". . . it must have been very difficult with your father. That got worse, didn't it?"

"No – not really. Things got better for me." I decide not to tell her that learning about Buddhism was the best thing that could have happened to me and that I had *satori* up a mountain. I suspect that a woman who didn't want her child to understand the death of pets is hardly going to embrace the death of Self.

"But you remembered your way to the house."

She's right. "I guess I did. I was on autopilot to be honest."

It takes her a while to get up the stairs – something she apologises for, halfway up.

"Arthritis. I have more bad days than good, now."

"Sorry to hear that. You should get a bungalow."

She stops for a long time ahead of me, hanging onto the banister. Then she continues up. "You're right. We should."

When she finally hefts herself up onto the landing (which I don't recognise – but yes, it looks like a landing), she pauses before pushing open a door, and that is when I realise that Di must be dead.

The first thing I see is a giant poster of the Spice Girls above Di's bed, for she desperately wanted to be Scary Spice when she was a teenager. (Unfortunately, there wasn't a Silly Spice). When I obey Mrs Candle's 'go in first' nod, I have a flashback.

Diana and myself having a mock fight with the ridiculously pink and fussy cushions that lie on the pink and frilly duvet that covers the bed in front of me now. Her silly little teddies are still in a row just beneath the pillows, and I may have thrown one across the room during the fight. I can't remember how 'mock' the fight was, or even its cause or its outcome.

I tilt my head to read the spines of the books on the shelves. I recognize some from the teenage years: books about girls who ended up with magic powers and could communicate with animals or fairies and who were suddenly pivotal to saving the world from a disaster and who had to accomplish the task before start of term back at the boarding school their uninterested parents banished them to. I don't think I was too impressed with these.

I can't see that anything in this room is much different from when Diana was a teenager.

It is a shrine.

There are wall-mounted cork boards covered in photos, and I instinctively move closer to peer at them.

"You were always dressed in black back then," says Mrs Candle.

That must mean I'm in here somewhere. There are so many photos of Di in later life - I guess from sixth form and college - that it takes me a while to understand Di's unique system of chronology, which doesn't progress from left to right in terms of her journey through life. In fact, the photos seem to be deliberately mixed up: her young teenage years interspersed with her older years, so that she doesn't appear to age - or at least - not permanently.

It takes a while to find me. There are three pictures of Di and myself dressed up as if for an evening out; Di looking plump, pig-tailed and made-up, me looking . . .

"Oh. I was a Goth. I'd forgotten." I laugh. It seems obvious now. I probably did it to irritate my mother.

Mrs Candle edges along the side of the bed to peer at the photographs. "Oh yes," she says, with a hint of weary recall. "As far as I could tell, you liked to look as dead as possible. Still - look at yourself now."

I wonder if she means that I should cross over to the white alcove and peer at myself in the plaster floral-rimmed mirror, but she isn't looking in that direction.

I spot myself in a few other photos. I am guessing we are now in our mid-teens. We just look like teenagers having fun. We never seem to be doing anything interesting, other than standing with arms around each other and looking a bit pissed.

Why have I been brought into this room?

"Is Di OK?" I think this is more sensitive than 'Has Di died in the last few weeks and have you returned this room to her teenage years as a shrine to that stage when youngsters are happy to perch on the edge of adulthood in perpetuity'? Which is weird, because surely when someone dies you leave their room as it is, in case they were to walk back into their lives.

Mrs Candle gives me a level stare and then nods at the room. "What do you think?"

"What happened?" Because now I think she must be dead.

"Exactly. Nothing happened." Mrs Candle looks around – though I suspect this is for my benefit as she must be so familiar with the room. "She won't let us change it."

"No – it has changed." I look at one of the book-bearing shelves. "She had a couple of tea-pots there."

"The collection grew until it took over our kitchen. It was your fault."

"My fault?"

A bitter laugh. "I'm joking. You brought her one back from Venice at the same time as an Aunt gave her a silly chicken-shaped teapot. Unfortunately, it started a bit of a craze."

"Sorry. I don't remember that. Anyway, why don't you just shove them in here if you don't like it? I mean – the teapots. She can't be reading those books anymore. You could just chuck them."

"No – we could not just *chuck them* as you put it," says Mrs Candle. "She wants her room left exactly as it is."

I'm not sure how to describe the sound I make. It was an involuntary laugh – I suppose more of disbelief than humour. "But it's not her room any more. It's your house, isn't it? I mean she's moved out – hasn't she?"

"Di rents a place in Clapham," says Mrs Candle. "But she visits at least every week."

"That's nice." She called her Di; a first, I'm sure.

"Isn't it?" says Mrs Candle, mechanically. "But maybe it's time she moved on a little bit. Reconnected with some friends."

I sense that she is looking at me but I have just spotted another photo in the 'pissed teenagers' series – and in this photo I can see that I have painted (with nail varnish?) 'GADD' on my face.

"I wonder what that meant."

"What what meant?"

"G-A-D-D. In this photo it's painted on my face."

Mrs Candle looks uninterested, and is no longer close enough to see the details of the photograph I'm pointing to. "No idea," she says. "Ah, but of course Diana might know. You could ask her." And a sentence that started out dully ends with a hopeful inflection.

"Why do you want me to reconnect with Diana?" I ask her.

She goes rather vague. "I just thought it might be nice if you met and caught up. You must have lots of news to give her."

"Sure. We've been Facebooking each other." (Diana has sent me a Friend request and I have actively ignored it. So I don't think I've lied to Mrs Candle.)

Mrs Candle gives no reaction to this. In fact, I think the visit's over, as she turns and makes her way slowly down the stairs.

I stop on the landing and look at the closed doors. "Would you mind if I used your bathroom?"

Mrs Candle pauses on the stairs. "Of course. But be careful.

As I say, we've had a bit of a disaster. The copper piping's wearing out in all these houses. It's so thin now that . . . well, just mind how you go."

When I push open the right door I can see that there has been quite a flood by the toilet. There is a shiny section of pipe leading to the toilet, but the lino in the bathroom has been ripped up and tiles near the floor seem to be raising themselves as if to jump off the wall. So that was the disaster. No deaths. I have a moment of unmindfulness after I've washed my hands, and trip when I turn. I recover, of course, but I can see that someone who is unsteady on her feet would face quite a challenge.

I find Mrs Candle sitting in the front room (which looks like a front room). She has eschewed the sofas and armchairs to sit in a chair that looks sensible rather than comfortable, and which almost faces the TV, though that is switched off at the moment.

"I'd better be off."

Mrs Candle twists her upper body to see me, which is a feature I've seen in some senior religious teachers, who would throw their whole bodies into facing something, rather than make do with a superficial turn of the head, but I see that she is doing it because she cannot turn her head.

"Where would you like to go?" I ask, and then realise that I've given her no context. "I mean, if you were going to . . ."

"South coast," she says. "Hove, or Worthing, or anywhere down there. We could easily afford it if we sold this place."

"Then sell."

"Anyway. Where are you going back to? Do you need directions?"

"Should be OK. I'm in Colliers Wood."

"OK. So you know you just turn right when you're out of the house, and right when you reach Merton High Street?"

"Yes, thanks."

I say "Goodbye", then I am walking. Walking.

I try to make sense of the last hour or so. How did I end up at that house and what is wrong with Mrs Candle (apart from arthritis, a flooded bathroom and a really odious teapot collection)? I try very hard to remember why 'GADD' was painted on my face. I wonder why Diana's bedroom has been returned to how it was when she was a teenager. Or maybe it never changed.

Damn. I wish I had taken that photograph. I could have shown it to Urs and asked if she knew what 'GADD' meant. I have a feeling Mrs Candle would have let me borrow it. In fact, I suspect Mrs Candle would have let me take all the contents of the room plus leg it with the teapot collection. I'm not sure she likes her house any more.

Obviously you can't blame unmindful walking on someone's collection of teapots or teenage-fixed bedroom, but they certainly were contributing factors to my turning left when I reached Merton High street. I don't know when I realised that I was automatically heading for Wimbledon. Strangely enough, I am not walking towards Mum's house (which would have meant more of a left turn) but towards Wimbledon station.

Where was I going – if not my old home?

God knows. I turn back and head for Colliers Wood. I seem to be doing a lot of walking these days.

Chapter Eight

I HAVE POST. Urs tells me this as she hurriedly gathers together her paperwork at the sight of my wok. I have been working for a couple of hours already, and I'm hungry. I fancy broccoli today, and fortunately there's loads in the fridge. I wash some and start trimming it on a board and slicing tofu into cubes.

"It's a strange shape," she says, then adds, "the envelope." She is feeling an A4 brown envelope on the corner of the table.

Did I send off for information to the Taiwan Pedantry school, or whatever it was called? No, I didn't. Safe. I know she's curious.

"Can you open it?" She immediately tears it open. Maybe it's a cheque for the investment piece.

I'm frying my food when I realise that there is silence from the table. Urs is staring at an exercise book, leafing through the pages, turning to the front cover, leafing through again.

"It's an exercise book," she says. "I think it's yours. Like from school or something."

"Oh great."

"You're not surprised that you've just received an old exercise book through the post? There's no letter or anything with it."

"Not surprised. I asked someone to send it."

"Is this Mr Turner's writing?"

"Don't know. If it's in red ink and says something sarcastic then it is." I turn off the hob. I would prefer gas but Urs was insistent on an electric cooker. My rice cooker has switched itself to 'keep warm' mode. I love my rice cooker. Not even Mr Gadd could burn the rice in one of these things.

"When I set a story title of 'A promotion that goes wrong', I don't expect a career in the afterlife, Winifred."

"Sorry?"

"That's what it says here. In red, so I guess it's Mr Turner. Strange to think that he's dead now." She turns back a few pages. "The giddy career of Mr Gadd deceased."

"Great, can you leave it open at that page?" So I did write something about a Mr Gadd.

She is reading my essay. It must be absorbing, because when I bring my bowl to the other end of the table and sit down, she doesn't scarper. Usually she's fleeing to the front room at the first sign of the wok let alone the chopsticks. She is frowning. With every page turn, she frowns more heavily.

I assume she's reached the end when she shakes her head.

"What?"

She looks at me. "You and your bloody change."

"Sorry?" I'm visualising coins, which makes no sense.

She slaps the book. "Acceptance of change. You ram it down people's throats."

"It's a basic truth."

"Yeah, well that's the irony, Win. You . . ." and she stops, so I will never know what the irony is.

"Whatever I wrote there I wrote over fifteen years ago."

She gives an explosion of exasperation. "Oh – whatever. But why has someone sent you this?"

I'm eating. I don't reply.

"Win! What's going on?"

God – I wish I could just eat mindfully and in peace. I finish my mouthful. "Nothing's going on. Someone had my old exercise book and I was curious to see what I'd written, so I asked for it back."

"Who?"

"Do you know who Gadd is?"

"Yes," She nods towards my book. "He's a character in a weird essay of yours. Hang on – you asked me if I knew someone called Gadd. What was it now . . . Fred Gadd, wasn't it?"

"But did I ever mention someone called Gadd when I was younger?"

"No. Not to me anyway, but as you were over at Diana's at every opportunity – well, I hardly saw you."

And therein lies a mystery: nothing I have seen or heard about Di makes me think that she would have been my soulmate.

"Why was I always over there?"

"Maybe Dad freaked you out."

"Dad never freaked me out."

"Yes, he did. He freaked us all out sometimes."

"He just liked listening to his music." I say this without having to rack my brains, for I remember that he did have strange moods, usually presaged by David Bowie's tinny voice invading every room, despite emanating from a record player in a little box room with the door shut firmly against the outside world. It didn't freak me out. I just thought it was a bit loud. Then there would be silence. And after that Dad would either lie down or disappear out the house and temporarily out of our lives.

I don't fully understand the physics of it, but if I think of us as energy, with an Ego that defines 'my' bundle of energy as separate to 'your' bundle of energy, then our bundles vibrate at different frequencies as we age; you could take this further and say that reliving any memory is bad, as you are physically incapable of accommodating the recall without consequences. An adult listening to the music played in their youth and being revisited by the teenage feeling they had then, might interpret the resulting physical agitation as increased vigour, but what they are really feeling is their sub-atomic particles in a state of distress. Dad should never have played songs from his teenage years – it could only have made things worse.

". . . sweet to slayed. Are you alright?"

"Sorry?" I realise that my chopsticks are frozen in the air and that I have a mouthful of unchewed broccoli.

Urs gives a heavy sigh. "I said that it was a relief when he wasn't playing bloody Bowie songs. I preferred Sweet to Slade."

"Oh right. Yes, I think same here. Actually no – I think I liked Slade more. Oh, I can't remember which was which now. It's not like Dad came out and announced each song before he played it."

Urs leans forward. "Yes, but usually the chorus was the title. Do you remember any?" I shake my head. "Fox on the run? Blockbuster? Far, far away?"

"Far, far away. I remember that one. He played that one a lot."

Urs gives me a wan smile and lets me finish my cold broccoli in peace. I wash up and head upstairs. She shouts something at me when I reach my room. But I can't be bothered to shout 'What?' back at her. For I am about to look into Gadd.

I don't know why I chose to have Gadd painted on my

face, but I would have done it for a reason. It would have had significance for me. Also it has significance for Fred. Or maybe it is a coincidence and we are chasing a brace of Gadds.

I google it, and learn that Gadd comes from 'goad' as in the verb (to annoy something to stimulate a response) and is also a noun (as in a spiked stick to drive cattle). I am a little dismayed to read that Gadd may have been given as a nickname to a persistent and irritating person, and rather hope that Fred's ancestor herded cattle. My fantasy that my choice of the name (to adorn my face and essays) will be revealed on learning the origin of the surname remains a fantasy.

I know – thank-you, Fred – that surnames were only created during medieval times to make it easier to collect poll tax. One suspects that the dishing out of surnames was done rather hastily, so that faced with four Freds in one village, one of whom made barrels, one of whom came from Yeovil, one of whom was a paradigm of virtue and one of whom had no distinguishing characteristics other than being a complete prat – you might end up with Fred Cooper, Fred Yeovil, Fred Goodfellow, and Fred Gadd.

It occurs to me that in a sense, if we had no surnames, we'd have no ancestors. Obviously we'd have genetic ancestors, but we wouldn't have traceable ancestors – which are the only sort people are interested in, rather than the amazing little bundles of DNA that are our link all the way back to primeval soup. Ancestor worship would be impossible and people would be forced to live their lives in the present without the artificial constructs of family.

"You forgot this," says Urs. She is in the doorway holding out my exercise book.

"Thanks. Can you just put it on the bed?"

She frisbees it onto my bed. "I'm going over to Mum's."

"OK."

She's right: it wasn't just Bowie. Dad played loads of 70s stuff. I do remember Slade. A song called 'Far, far away'. It wasn't bad as I remember – strangely wistful. Just played a little loudly so that it didn't sound at all 'far, far away'.

"You up to anything tonight?" asks Urs.

"No, just a quiet night."

"Reading your weird story?"

"Yeah, probably. I'd like to know what it was about."

"It's obvious what it's about."

And with that she is gone. If I believed that she had some insight into my reason for writing it, I would rush after her, even beg her to come back and explain it to me. But I don't believe her. I'm really keen to read the essay, but I have just come across an article by an angry Chinese Christian priest (based in Hong Kong), who not only denounces ancestor worship as superstitious nonsense, but draws the parallels with Catholicism's veneration of saints. I see what he means; both look for the intercession of the dead to benefit our lives – I'll remember you if you remember me. Can't wait to introduce that topic into the next conversation with my mother. I imagine that an accusation of ancestor worship would be akin to me melting down her gold jewellery and presenting her with a golden calf.

By late afternoon I have a raging headache and am looking forward to sex with Marty. I think I've been spending too much time in front of the screen, so I intend to make use of the bus trip by staring as far into the distance as possible. I will also sit mindfully on the bus and hopefully my head will shatter into a million pieces and I can get back to where I was.

Things get off to a bad start when – having retrieved my Oyster card from my rucksack and waved it past the ticket sensor next to the driver – the sensor stays silent and the light doesn't go green. I wave it past the sensor again with the same zero result.

"Isn't it working?" I ask the driver, who – now that I look up – is sporting an odd expression.

"I think you'll find it works better with a bus pass."

That is when I look down and see that I am holding a condom. I delve into that section of my rucksack again and pull out a handful of condoms, useless in their shrink-wrapped packets – or at least useless for bus travel. More delving and I find my pass and now get a beep and a green light.

"Looks like you're going to have a good night." At least I think that's what the driver says.

When I sit down and look through my rucksack, I find about a dozen of the things in the section that I reserve exclusively for my Oyster card. I know my handwriting is bad, but I cannot think of anything on my shopping list that Urs could have mistaken for 'condoms'; baffling bloody woman.

My head now feels like someone has rammed a child-size halo around it. I stare out the windows and try and focus on distant objects: chimney pots, the registration numbers of cars a distance away, anything to counter my eye strain. It has started to drizzle, which is smudging the details on which I am trying to concentrate.

When we go past St George's Hospital, I see my mother's white car drive out, at least I think it's my mother's car – I can't remember her registration number – but I can make out the blonde ponytail. I look away quickly. There will be all sorts of questions if she sees me.

I wonder what she did with my money. It wasn't a fortune – about six thousand pounds if I remember right – but it was my entire savings. I try to sit mindfully, and gaze mindfully and even recite (in my head) a Buddhist sutra on Loving Kindness, but when I get to the line, 'Just as a mother would protect her only child with her life, even so let one cultivate a boundless love towards all beings', I remember that an earlier translation said 'Just as a mother would protect her only son . . .', which always made me picture her daughters playing in the traffic whilst she adoringly cradled some male brat. Six thousand pounds. The Bank said that I had paid it to some charity I had never heard of: Saint something or other. I think it is a safe assumption that my mother donated my entire savings to a Catholic charity to stop me from getting a plane back to Taiwan.

I'm afraid that by the time I get off at Garratt Lane my resentment and anger have fuelled the headache, so that my Loving Kindness mantra might as well have been a meditation on Raging Hatred.

Marty is delighted to see me. He is showered and wearing shorts and a T-shirt and seems to be half-way through a glass of white wine, with a second empty glass lined up.

"I'm under strict instructions to offer you something non-alcoholic," he says. "Though frankly, I think this white wine would count – if you care to try it."

"Jasmine tea, please."

He gives a mock sigh and goes into the kitchen, whilst I wander over to the goldfish tanks lying side by side. Two days of Epsom salts don't appear to have made a dent in Goldie Pang's sphericality, though I notice that the fish looks no more startled or distressed than its un-annexed companions.

If Goldie Pang were a human – particularly a female – there would be no end of 'I've gotten so fat – I used to be so slim' laments. Clearly, we could learn a lot from goldfish about living in the now.

And caterpillars. I remember now that I was once on the top deck of a bus when I was at some flakey teenage stage of life. I don't remember where I was going to or why, but I remember that I was unhappy about whatever situation I was in, and wished it could be different. The branches of a tall tree brushed the windows of the top deck, and that is when I noticed that the curling yellow London-polluted leaves of the tree had holes in. Holes meant that caterpillars were munching them. It meant that caterpillars were fulfilling their existence, with neither regrets for their inner-city disadvantaged state, nor wishes that they lived on a tree in the middle of an arable field, feasting on healthy green leaves. The effect on me was like a mini-enlightenment. Bless the Lord for dappled things and urban caterpillars.

"That's Fat Bastard," says Marty, appearing quietly beside me. "He has dropsy. Apparently. Karen's the expert."

"Are they her fish then?"

"I suppose they are. She rescued them from her father's pond. He was going to fill it in and she wanted to save them." He puts on a dreadful Welsh accent. "Children could fall in the pond, see? We don't want that. People might blame me and say Jones The Garage drowns children."

"So Karen is Karen Jones?"

"Karen Gwendolyn Jones. Mind you, they are all called Jones, aren't they?"

"Well, they would be if they're from the same family."

"No – I mean the Welsh."

"Not all of them. Some are named after saints. Others have patronymic names, like . . ."

"You haven't changed," he says, laughing. "Speaking of fathers, is yours still on the scene?"

I try and think of a truthful answer as to whether Dad is 'on the scene', as Marty puts it. "Yes and no."

"You . . . er – haven't mentioned me to him, have you?"

"I don't think he remembers you."

"Oh. Good. Let's keep it that way."

He sits down on the sofa and I notice that he's made me tea, though left the teabag in. His legs are very muscular, and he must catch me looking at them, because he says 'football'.

"Very nice," I say, and he chuckles.

"I try and keep fit. And if I may say so, you're not looking bad. What's your sport?"

"I don't really have one. I suppose I walk quite a lot."

"Yes, I think you said. Anyway, you're very slim."

"Rice diet."

He starts talking about his caveman diet, which as far as I can tell involves a shed-load of meat and a loud disdain for anyone who eats bread.

"My fat levels have gone down to eight percent."

"Is that good?"

"It's bloody brilliant. You know I bumped into Shimmy yesterday. He has really let himself go. I asked him how the porn films are going and he said that the work had dried up. I'm not surprised – the fat bastard – I can't imagine him sustaining a hard-on." He puts down his empty glass. "Speaking of which . . ."

"I'm ready." The tea is too strong and my headache hasn't gone away.

"I was hoping for some details from Karen about what you two got up to, but she's gone all silent on me." He gives me a hopeful grin.

"Nice try, but a futile try. Tuesdays are Tuesdays, and Thursdays are Thursdays."

"Oh Win. You always were a tease."

I can't believe that's true, but let him lead the way, as though I've never been to the Heaven door before.

He's not bad, in fact he is bloody good, and just as well he remembered the condom business, because I would have forgotten it, despite the packets that Urs has so thoughtfully furnished my rucksack with. There's little faffing round on foreplay, which suits me fine tonight. Afterwards, my headache is a bit better, but not completely gone. I take advantage of the lull, (whilst Marty lies on his back, panting and blaspheming), to squeeze a meridian between the thumb and forefinger of my left hand; it's usually pretty effective at reducing headaches, though has been up against a blacksmith's forge of head banging tonight.

Marty rolls back on his stomach and looks at me. "Good to go again?"

"Why not?"

He grabs my left hand and pins it on the pillow, then says, "Oops . . . almost forgot", and extricates and rolls on a condom with his free hand. I imagine it's quite a skill, and I start wondering if it has any other application in daily life. Something in the kitchen, maybe? I really can't think of one.

Condom engaged, my left hand pinned – almost but not quite in the right spot – he looks down at me grinning. Unlike Karen, who had just left a soft lamp on in the corner, Marty has opted for the lights full on.

"Do you remember the last time we did this?" he asks.

"Yes." Obviously. It was about five minutes ago.

"It was good fun, wasn't it?" And he's off again.

At the end of the evening, my headache is barely a memory. Much better than taking the pills. Unfortunately I still have a head, but I can't expect Marty to sort out that problem.

He insists on a long hug before I step out the door.

"I'll see you next week," I say, a little alarmed to receive the sort of bear hug you might give someone who is emigrating to Australia.

"Hope I can wait that long."

It is on the upper deck of the bus home that I remember another Bowie song that my father played obsessively, and sang obsessively. From the Man Who Sold the World to the Man Who Sold the Big Issue: the quite forgettable career of Mr Rigby (Undeceased).

When I walk home from the bus stop I have a strange feeling that I'm being followed, and I turn around, suddenly aware that Urs's curiosity might have extended to stalking me. But there is no-one bar the figure of a man leaning against the dark window of an Indian restaurant that never seems to attract the punters. Of course there is no Urs.

Accept the winds of change like a bamboo bowing to the wind rather than a plane tree standing tall in arboreal defiance. I have tried telling Urs that resistance to change is useless, but still she stands, face to the wind, preferring to believe our father is dead than different.

Chapter Nine

THE GIDDY CAREER of Mr Gadd (Deceased)

Mr Gadd's last memory should have been a gentle slipping away, borne aloft on the cloud of wailing grief of those who had venerated his corporeal presence to the extent that separation evinced a pain as acute as appendicitis. Instead, his demise was accompanied only by the sound of his own breath and heartbeat.

His only comfort – as he lay passively in a vessel that rocked on the gentle waves of the subterranean Stygian waters – was that he would be remembered and that his lofty achievements in life would be communicated to those who could raise him to his former heights with the minimum of delay.

He was dismayed to find that his first posting was to the very lowest of the low; not only was this netherworld a common clearing bank of human souls, but he was at a significant disadvantage to some of his new colleagues, for not only was their listless waiting serenaded with the grief-soaked crying that poured out of Earth by those who remembered them, but their mourners were sending gifts. Mr Gadd watched, fascinated, as a wisp of smoke would appear before one soul and then reconstitute itself into a mobile phone or a car or a packet of cigarettes. His envy was tinged with schadenfreude, for the lucky individual's rapture at being so blessed by his mourners' generosity soon dissipated when he or she discovered that there was no cellular signal, no roads, and no shortage of 'No Smoking' signs in the Underworld.

Still, he bitterly reflected, the giving of useless presents was a common enough phenomenon in life, and if it was the thought that counts, clearly no-one was thinking of him. Surely they knew he had died?

Unseen judges must have passed a silent sentence, for Mr Gadd soon found himself promoted to a higher realm, where all was white. Mr Gadd was hopeful that his fortunes were on the rise, but disappointment soon flooded in as he discovered that not only had no-one heard of him, but that, on being introduced to Mr Gadd, people instantly forgot his name. Whilst this world initially seemed an improvement on the Underworld, in that people were able to move freely, a miasma of grief clung to everyone. This was because all were in denial of their status. Now that they were beyond the aural reach of their mourners' howling, souls drifted around in lonely distress, resistant to their separation from the mortal coil. Some could do no more than sleep, as though the effort of living out their new existence was too heavy a burden to bear. Others wandered ceaselessly, crying out an individual mantra.

"Where are his arms?" shouted one, over and over again, though Gadd could see no armless subject of this man's distress.

Another repeated endlessly "I'm here, I'm here. I've come home." But no-one took any notice.

Mr Gadd was cheered when he saw a host of angels swoop down into this bleached-out world. But all they did was surround one poor soul and jostle him between them, as if he were a toy with no more than a passing interest for each individual angel.

Mr Gadd's final promotion was to a giddyingly higher world more familiar than the previous two. True, it was a wasteland colonised only by buddleia, but it reminded him of Harlow, and his new colleagues were recognisably human and in their own clothes. He learnt – though he knew not how – that this land was called the Garden of Forgetfulness. He tried to ask people if there was a Garden of Remembrance, but people squinted at him mutely, seemingly too dazzled by his appearance to brave a conversation with him.

He somehow learnt that a trio of the most esteemed residents would be allowed to return to Earth for one solar day. He begged to be allowed to join them, but he knew (though no-one said) that these three were privileged precisely because their deeds in life were remembered. Mr Gadd argued that of these three – Keir Hardy, Cicely Saunders and Fenner Brockway – he had heard of Keir Hardy and for sure he had been a great man, but the others were hardly household names. When this cut no ice with the celestial being responsible for the earthly excursion, Mr Gadd tried a different tack; he argued that even Judas was let out of Hell for one day each year, so surely he was as deserving. "Yes, but Judas is remembered," he was told.

The solar day passed in a blink of the eye in the Garden of Forgetfulness, for no sooner had the trio disappeared than they returned, though none in high spirits. All souls – Mr Gadd included – crowded around them, desperate for news from the Homeland. Even the perpetually-sleeping beings roused themselves briefly to hear the trio's pronouncements.

"They learn in me," said Fenner Brockway.

"They live in me," said Keir Hardy.

"They die in me," said Cicely Saunders.

"So you're remembered?" cried one soul.

The trio looked at each other, a heavy glance that spelt mutual disappointment.

"We are just noises to those left," said Keir. "Just sounds

uttered by empty shells, as removed from us as a memory brought out at a family party concerning a family member who has no memory of the event."

Mr Gadd knew this could not be true. There were rumours of the existence of a Garden of Remembrance and a Garden of Revival. But he had reached the top of his career path. There was nowhere else to go for the unsettled.

The sad thing was that – unbeknownst to Mr Gadd – back on earth, people thought of him and felt very grieved. The sadder thing was that – unbeknownst to them – they were not grieving for the loss of him as he was, but for the loss of themselves as they were when they thought they knew him as he was.

For the first time, I picture Turner sitting, red pen in hand, giving one of Urs's head shakes as he tries to make sense of what I've written. The content doesn't even make complete sense to me. Turner didn't stand a chance.

I feel a little sorry for him now, and I wonder at what point he knew he was going to die. Did he see the ground rushing towards him? Was there the briefest sensation of the impact and the flimsy glider folding in around him? Was his last thought that his wife would be a widow? Or regret that he'd given up smoking unnecessarily? (He was a particular misery that term).

Every instant is transformation. It just usually happens too slowly for most people to be aware, so they only think in terms of 'life events'. I sense the ground rushing towards me all the time; it is liberating. It is why some monks liked to meditate in graveyards.

As for the netherworld in my essay, and the description of presents sent to the dead, it reminds me of Chinese Ghost month in Taiwan – the seventh lunar month – and always my favourite time in Taiwan. People would burn fake money – ghost money – in braziers, and leave gifts of fruit and fags at shrines. Older folk would refuse to have operations or do anything in which a bad outcome was possible (such as swimming). I loved it. It was like a whole month of an old-fashioned Samhain (or Halloween) in which wandering ghosts could bother the living and lay claim to all they envied (such as warm bodies with beating hearts). 'Trick or Treat' doesn't quite do it for me.

My phone has a single text from Karen and two from Marty.

I read Marty's first: 'Really enjoyed last night. You're pretty good!' followed by 'Everything alright? If you need to talk about it, let me know'.

Talk about what? I can't remember starting a conversation that wasn't finished. In fact, we didn't really talk that much and it wasn't what I was there for. I text back: 'All fine. See you next Thursday'.

The text from Karen reads: 'Thanks for a wonderful evening, W. By the way, Goldie Pang is still unexploded.'

I can tell that she doesn't like my name. She avoided using it last night, apart from when she had to get my attention, and she paused each time before saying 'Win' or 'Winnie'. Now she's trying 'W', which is not an endearing, soft-sounding letter in any language, I imagine, apart from maybe Welsh. Let's cwtch up on the sofa. I might try that on Karen next time; impress her with one of the few Welsh words I know.

I text back 'Last night was great.'

A few minutes later, a text: 'Ouch'.

That confuses me. I text back 'Why ouch? Did I hurt you?'

After a few more minutes my phone pings. 'I'm glad to

hear you had a good time with Marty. I hope you enjoyed Tuesday too'.

I am baffled. Then I check again and see that she sent the text on Wednesday. My computer says it's Friday. I must get better at checking my phone each day. I lost Wednesday with my little promenade around south-west London and Di's bedroom and yesterday – of course, I was with Marty.

I text back: 'Sorry. I meant Tuesday. It was great'.

Instantly I get back 'Phew. By the way, did you and Marty go out last night?'

Does she think we were shagging al fresco? In urban Earlsfield? 'No, we stayed in. Why?'

'Not a problem if you did, W. He wasn't in when I got back and was a bit cagey when he finally got back. I was just being nosey.'

'No. I left him in your flat. By the way, your fish now has a nicer name than I do. Perhaps you can find me a name you like.'

Instantly I receive a response: 'Working on it. Kxx'

I put down the phone and re-read about the giddy career of Mr Gadd. It resonates a bit, but that's probably more because I've just read it than because I remember writing it. Why did I write it? Why did I choose a Mr Gadd?

I know I was a bit different from my peers. I know at fourteen I was probably already familiar with the death cultures of a range of societies. I know it interested me, and if I had to be at an extreme end of the teenage spectrum of bizarreness, I am pleased that I was at the morbid end rather than the Spice Girl O.M.G. end.

The description of the oriental afterlife-world sounds accurate: I mean accurate in terms of what I know about people's beliefs, of course. It is quite possible that I read up on that as a teenager.

But Gadd still eludes me, even though I once painted it on my face. Oh dear. I have ignored Diana's Facebook requests because I don't particularly want to see pictures of cats in sunglasses playing a banjo, but such are the sacrifices I make to help Fred. I accept her request.

Yesterday Diana was caught in the rain and had a pizza with 'naughty pepperoni'.

I briefly entertain the notion of putting something on my own blank Homepage which reads 'Last night Win shagged an old boyfriend then came home for some kick ass spinach'.

Of course I don't. I really despair of things like Facebook which serve only to help the misguided maintain the illusion that they are real.

I read about Diana's existence. She describes herself as 'obsessed with teapots', and seems to belong to a couple of groups of people similarly fascinated. Apparently she went to the School of Hard Knocks, followed by the University of Real Life, and now works in the Real World. There is no mention of a relationship, but apart from the inevitable cat pictures, there are many, many photographs of Diana existing and embracing other smiling people who are also existing. Apparently.

By the time I have read this, she must have noticed that I'm online, for a little Chat window has appeared:

Di: Hi Win!!

Me: Hi Diana. Do y . . .

Di: Hiii! Mum said you'd been round.

Me: Yes. Do you know what GADD means?

Di: What did you think of my bedroom. Bring back memories!?

(She is a ferociously fast typist. I barely type a few words before her next message comes along and derails mine.)

Me: (No) Yes. Do you rem . . .

Di: Remember my teapot collection? It really grew. It had to move downstairs.

Me: It had to be moved downstairs.

Di: Sorry??

Me: It can't have moved itself. You must have moved it downstairs. Into the kitchen.

Di: Yes. Anyway, I'm still collecting!

Me: So I see. Do you know what GADD means?

Di: Oh my God – YES.

Me: Great. What does it mean?

Di: You once painted it on your face.

Me: Yes. But why?

Di: You were a strange girl!!

Me: Do you know what it means?

Di: You tell me.

Me: (*God Almighty give me patience*) I can't remember. I hoped that you knew.

Di: You're asking the wrong person, Win!

Me: Who should I be asking?

Di: The boys in the band.

Me: What band?

Di: GADD!!!

Me: There was a band called GADD?

Di: Yes, yes, yes. Do you remember Marty Wilcox? From school. O.M.G. You went out with him!! You must remember.

Me: A little. I don't remember the band, though.

Di: He played guitar.

(Oh God – he did. I have a vague recollection of him singing and playing.)

Me: Thanks, Diana. I'll FB him and ask him about the band name.

Di: Do you remember your father chasing him off? It was hilarious.

(I hesitate a long time before typing the next bit, for I fear that the answer will offend me.)

Me: Did Marty 'break my heart'?

Di: (A laughing emoticon appears, followed – shortly – by some text) Winnie. You? What heart!!? You only liked books!! And bloody history!!!

There is a noise downstairs which may or may not be someone at the door. Saved. Or maybe it's a burglar trying to make off with the TV (in which case good luck to him, as Urs tells me that since our last bathroom flood, the TV only condescends to switch on intermittently). I type in 'got to go – someone at front door', and close down the session.

The Fallowfields are on my doorstep. Friday already.

"You were expecting us, weren't you?" says Maddy, on the doorstep, with Fred behind her.

"Yes," I lie, and lead them into the front room. I'm not as prepared as I'd like to be, but I think what I've found so far will have Maddy whooping for joy and Fred very depressed. He is moving slowly today, and with some uncertainty; I feel bad about what I have to say. I settle them in the front room and offer tea. Maddy declines on behalf of Fred's kidneys. I offer her a tea and Fred a herbal tea, which he waves away, impatiently.

"We'll both have herbal tea," says Maddy. "And I do mean two separate mugs, Winifred."

She follows me into the kitchen and looks at me filling the kettle. I wonder if she is after a preview of my findings, but once I've switched the kettle on, she turns away to read my post-it notes. I see her looking at the ones written in Chinese and then shaking her head. Then she looks at the ones in English.

"You have nice writing, Winifred."

"You must tell my sister. She says my notes in English are as difficult to decipher as the ones in Chinese."

Now she's watching me again. I am doing nothing more exotic than pouring water over ginger tea bags in two separate mugs, but I feel her gaze; Karen was the same the other night – she seems to find me fascinating.

"Do you always do that with the kettle?"

"Do what?"

She laughs. "I suppose it's a sign of respect."

I have no idea what she's going on about. If filling the kettle with water and switching it on is a sign of respect, then yes – I respect the kettle.

She carries the two herbal teas into the front room, where Fred is fidgeting, I guess keen to hear what I have to say.

"Do you need to use the loo, Fred?" says Maddy, with more than an edge of impatience.

Fred pauses, before shaking his head.

"Go on," she snaps. "We're not going to start without you."

Fred levers himself up and shuffles out. Maddy sidles along the sofa and sits down at the far end. I see her notice the cigarette burn and frown.

"You're much younger than him," I say.

"I was his student."

"You were at the same school?"

"This was at university. He had to leave, unfortunately – there were some accusations about bias." Maddy narrows her eyes. "I still got a First, though. Which I think rather disproves the partiality theory."

"I see."

"Do you? Would you believe that a university lecturer had to re-train for the privilege of teaching youngsters like yourself?"

"Then we were lucky to have him. He was the best teacher."

I cannot read Maddy's change of expression. From staring intensely at me, she blinks and looks down. "Yes, he was, wasn't he?" But I don't think she is asking a question.

We sit in silence until the sound of Fred's labouring descent down the stairs becomes evident. Some time seems to pass before he reaches the bottom and appears in the doorway, steadying himself with a hand on the jamb. Then he surveys the few feet between the doorway and the free end of the sofa as if planning how to traverse a flat rock face. I am filled with sadness. I fully accept old age, but the speed of his deterioration is hard to witness without pity. He was climbing a tree just a few days ago.

I am getting soft. Not only has my head grown back, but it has grown back soft. When they are gone I will meditate on impermanence. There is a dead shrew in the front garden by the bin, maybe the victim of a little feline nocturnal entertainment. Last week his body was wet and plump and supine; I meant to check on his progress yesterday but forgot. It will be a good image to use.

"Come on, Fred," says Maddy gently. Whilst he gingerly reaches out for the arm of the sofa, I see her jerk her head as though distracted. "Who's that?" she asks me.

"Who's what?" Then I hear a jangle of keys and Urs is in the doorway, staring at the scene and trying to make sense of my company.

"Hello," she says, I think to all of us. She throws her keys on the table and gives me a strange look.

"Hello," says Maddy, politely. "I'm guessing you're Winifred's sister, as you two look so similar."

I can see Urs bristle, though I don't know why. "I'm Ursula. Winnie's older sister. I live here. And I look after her affairs."

I have a momentary stab of panic that Urs knows about my arrangement with Marty and Karen, but I deduce she must mean she keeps my books, or at least she would if I actually declared all my earnings to her. Maybe it's because she suspects that I am up to some illicit work that she now plonks herself down on the armchair. Fred looks irritated, but whether that is because she has just squished Mr Gadd or because – like me – he thinks she's intruding on a private matter, I don't know.

I give Maddy a hard look which I hope she will correctly interpret as 'please don't mention the air flight to Taiwan', which is quite a complex message to deliver by a look. She looks a little startled, so heaven knows what she thinks I've tried to communicate.

"Why don't you sit down, Win?" she says. But there is nowhere left to sit unless I perch myself on the far end of the sofa and deliver my findings with a cricked neck.

I kneel on the carpet opposite the sofa and put my mug on the table between. Instantly Urs is up and manoeuvring a coaster under my mug. She settles back down in the armchair, looking from me to Fred, who seems oblivious to her presence, for he is staring at me, expectantly.

"Mr Fallowfield?" says Urs, imbuing 'Fallowfield' with so many tones that I can literally see the notes on an invisible stave in the air in front of me. We ignore her.

Fred looks very unsettled, sitting so near the front of the sofa that I fear he will fall off. "Come on, Winifred – what have you found?"

"Officially there is no ancestor worship in China."

Maddy and Fred (and Urs) look at me in silence.

"I've translated a few articles from the official Chinese department that looks after funerals, and they are consistent: ancestor worship is an overhang of feudal imperialism and . . ."

"They actually say that?" asks Maddy. "Imperial feudalism?"

"Yes, it's a straightforward translation. Ancestor worship is seen as a vestige of feudal imperialism – in other words – it is seen as 'old' or 'previous'."

"Mr Fallowfield?" says Urs again. He ignores her. I'm not even sure he remembers she's in the room.

"The Communist party really pushed cremation in the urban areas, but this clashed with people's instincts regarding the proper way to treat their ancestors. So in the 1950s the Communists realized that they would have to have a complete overhaul of funerals: if they didn't change the elements that fed into the ritual side, then they would never be able to change the practical matter of how to dispose of the body."

I wish my audience were just the Fallowfields. In the periphery of my vision, Urs's face is like a gormless white balloon, fidgeting on its string.

"So they insisted that from then on funerals had to be conducted in public buildings rather than at the home of the deceased; burning paper offerings was banned. Instead of a complicated set of rules about what mourners should wear, people were only allowed to put on a black armband. Mourners weren't allowed to go overboard on displaying grief – so no more prostration and wailing. And most important of all, responsibility for conducting the funeral was removed from the family and placed in the hands of the deceased's employers. So the body is whisked away to a crematorium and cannot become the focus for superstitious beliefs."

"So what if families really, really want to bury their dead?" asks Maddy.

"If it was somewhere where cremation is mandatory then . . . tough. The authorities will exhume illegally buried corpses and cremate them. And fine the families."

"Ugh," says Maddy.

"Well, you've got to see it from the communists' point of view. Too many people, too little land. They don't want people cluttering up good arable land with corpses. And you can't argue with their rules. Poor people used to bankrupt themselves arranging ostentatious funerals so that their deceased family member would know that they were being remembered properly."

"It's still horrendous," says Maddy. "You cannot ride roughshod over people's instincts like that. And digging up corpses: it's inhuman. Disgusting."

"I have to disagree," I say. "Beliefs eventually change to follow the law. And anyway, there have been cases of elderly people being murdered so that the family could substitute the body for cremation whilst quietly burying their own loved ones. They think that murder of a stranger is justified so that their family can follow their instincts, as you put it."

Fred is clutching the arm of the sofa so hard that he's in danger of tearing the fabric away from the frame.

"What would they have done with a body buried in Tianjin in 1974?"

"A foreigner's body," Maddy adds, softly.

Jesus wept. They could have used Gadd's skull in the Dead-Foreigner-Head-Hurling championship for all I know.

"I don't know. At least the Cultural Revolution would have been over by then, which is when fanatical young Red Guards plundered graves and exhumed some bodies."

"So he could still be in a grave?" asks Fred.

"Who?" says Urs. We ignore her.

"I don't know," I say. Which is almost as truthful as saying that pressure for land would have almost certainly meant that Gadd's body would have been exhumed and cremated or just ground up for fertilizer.

"I can't believe these people would have dug up bodies," says Maddy. "What sort of people are they?"

"They are people like us. There was a case in Wales when I was young, of a wife burying her husband on her land. She did it all legally, but when she later moved and a neighbour told the new owners that there was a 'body' on their land, they freaked out. They hired a JCB to dig up the ground. When they did find the body they had it exhumed and cremated – and legally his widow could not stop them."

"You know an awful lot about death," says Maddy – I think with admiration.

"She was obsessed with it," says Urs, without any admiration.

Both of them are wrong. They have heard me talk about funeral culture, not death. We cannot discuss death without talking about the illusion of life, and now is not the time.

"Have I answered your . . . challenge?" I ask Maddy.

"What challenge?" asks Urs. No one answers.

I expect Maddy to look triumphant and Fred to look glum, but they are both looking glum. Fred's arm now hangs limply over the end of the sofa. I notice that Urs is staring at it. It is an arm, nothing more or less. What is she looking at? And why did she say she lived here? She spends at least half her time with our mother.

I look again at Maddy, who is biting her lip. Maybe she's thinking that this wasn't worth six hundred quid, and I think I'd have to agree. Now she and Fred look at each other, and I have the strange impression that I am seeing the inner workings of a marriage. It is as though a grandfather clock were opened and one could see the cogs and pendulum working together.

"It hasn't answered the question," says Fred to her. "Why put the effort into banning something if it doesn't exist? You cannot condemn in a vacuum."

"Well, you could," says Maddy. "It's like the straw man in politics. If a politician said 'we don't accept that bananas have to be straight', it doesn't mean that the EU have insisted on straight bananas, it just means that the politician has created an artificial enemy to show off his own standpoint."

"You only need those machinations in a democracy where you have to convince a gaggle of credulous voters that your set of mythologies is more potent than the opposition's set of mythologies. In a one-party state you don't have to bother creating straw men."

Maddy shakes her head. "Even a one-party state is vulnerable to revolution – in fact particularly vulnerable. When was the last revolution to affect a democracy? And don't give me Chile or Thailand."

"I accept that," said Fred. "But this is still not proof."

They stare at each other, then turn their heads towards me in unison. For the first time I can see why they married.

"Winifred," said Maddy. "You've given us the official stance on ancestor worship . . ."

"Now give us the unofficial one," says Fred.

"The unofficial but *mainstream* one," says Maddy. "Think you can do that?"

"I don't know how. Everything's official in China."

"You'll think of something," says Fred.

"With proof," says Maddy.

Urs stays seated when they leave and ignores Maddy's "Goodbye, Ursula", which is understandable, as she has been blanked throughout the meeting. I see them to the front door, where Maddy pauses and opens her handbag to extricate money held by a paper clip.

"The next instalment," she says quietly.

"Thanks for not doing that in front of . . ." I tilt my head in the direction of the front room.

Maddy nods and takes Fred's arm, as if he can't be trusted to reach the car unaided.

She pauses at the end of the path. "You have a dead mouse by your bins."

"I think it's a shrew."

I shut the door and return to my spot on the carpet in the front room. I can tell Urs is not in a good mood, but I can't be bothered to fathom the reason. I am too confused by Maddy's response. This was her chance to close the door on Fred's fantasy of settling Gadd's restless spirit and denouncing it as the mumbo jumbo it is. Maybe she just has a sense of fair play.

"Was that the old man you said came around?"

I'd almost forgotten Urs was there. "Yes."

"And he was Mr Fallowfield?"

"He still is."

"He didn't acknowledge me at all," says Urs, as though this casts doubt on his identity.

I can see that she is brooding. I sit quietly waiting for the questions to start. Ancestor worship, disturbed graves and absent Mr Gadds. If she asks, I will explain. I don't think it can do any harm, and she does act very oddly when her curiosity is not satisfied.

"He's wearing your watch."

"Yes."

"What do you mean - *yes*? Why did you give him your watch?"

"I didn't. He picked it up by accident."

"I see. And you didn't think to ask him for it back?"

"No, I didn't."

"Why not?" A definite querulous edge to her voice now.

"Because it was my watch, but now it's his watch."

"How can it be his watch if you didn't give it to him?"

"It was only my watch when I had it. Things have changed. He's got it now."

"So just like that you don't have a watch anymore?"

"Yes, the circumstances that made it my watch have changed. It's no big deal."

"No big deal?"

I cannot understand why she is so upset.

"So if I took the watch off him it would be mine?"

"Yes, I suppose so."

She gets up and gives me a very unfriendly look. "Well, then I might just do that the next time I see him."

"You could, but why? You're wearing one now. Do you need two?"

"Why? Because that watch was a present. I gave it to you." And she storms out. I assume right out, because I hear the front door slam. I think she's quite upset.

After a while, I go out and walk fast and hard and then realise that I'm on the way to the Candles' house. I stop and come back home.

I spend a long time sitting on a cushion meditating on a dead shrew, visualising its stages of decomposition until it has slimed and shrivelled its way into its constituents of Earth, Water, Fire and Air. Then I visualise my mother, undergoing the same process, then Urs, and then me. I start to decompose Marty and Karen but stop. It is weak of me, I know, but I will allow myself this one indulgence: I will maintain the illusion of Marty and Karen, because it is more sexy than putrescent corpses.

After all of this, I feel calmer, but I sometimes wish that Urs would get out of my life.

Chapter Ten

I POST THE question 'Do Chinese people still believe in ancestor worship?' on a China-hosted website for people wishing to improve their English or Chinese. As I usually use the forum to discuss the definition of economic terms like 'arbitrage', this is a bit of a departure from the norm.

Horace: What time is it in UK?

(I look at the time on my PC, which says 02:00, and draw back the curtain to see the street outside in darkness.)

Me: It is morning, 2 am. Do Chinese people still believe in ancestor worship?

When I get no response, I post the question in Chinese. Still no response. Then he starts to type something. Then he gets rid of it and starts typing again. This happens a couple of times. Eventually:

Horace: No.

Me: No-one believes in ancestor worship?

Horace: Only old people who are confused, maybe old ignorant peasants.

Me: OK. Thank you.

I wait a few seconds for Horace's habitual 'No problem', but it doesn't appear.

Maybe I should go to bed. I feel awake and cannot

remember if I've slept already or not. Urs is fairly rigid about routines, but I don't think she came back yesterday.

I brush my teeth and lie down, still wide awake. After I've turned off the light, I hear that bloody woman tearing tissues in my room. I switch on the light and lie back in bed with a pillow over my eyes. When I no longer hear the tearing tissues, I get up and turn off the light. In the new darkness of my room, a light is pulsing. And that is when I notice a message flashing on my PC. Idiot. I forgot to shut it down and the forum is still up.

Horace: Why do UK people believe they can go to Heaven by car? Rich people drive car, poor people ride horse.

It is timed a good 30 minutes after my previous response. God knows how Horace has got the idea that the British think that heaven is just a drive or a canter away. Maybe some mischievous westerner told him that for a joke. I make a note of it to puzzle over in the morning and shut down the PC. Then I lie down again. I will try counting backwards from 100 in Chinese. I don't think it ever works.

My phone goes and I answer it, hoping it's not Urs. It's Marty. In the middle of the bloody night. I wonder if he or Karen has had an accident.

"Hi Win, just checking you're OK." Maybe he thinks I've had an accident.

"I'm fine. Are you both OK?"

"Yes. We're fine."

There's a pause, so I go to the window to see if it is still dark. It's a sunny day. I turn off the light and return to the window. It must be morning – not too early. I can see one or two people in the street wandering about. Is it Saturday or Sunday?

"Then why are you ringing?"

Marty doesn't answer. There's a neighbour a few doors down – I don't know his name – but he strims his postage stamp front garden on a Saturday and washes his car on a Sunday. I go to the side of the window and peer along a few houses, and see him start his strimmer, so that a high whine breaks through my tinnitus. Must be Saturday. The man once told me that he gets surrounded by bees when he strims, so he wonders if the frequency of the strimmer is the same as whatever sound bees make during the Pollen Dance. I can only imagine huge disappointment in the local order of Hymenoptera beings as they arrive in this near greenless street, having expected the Chelsea Flower Show.

"I just thought it was a bit unfair that you don't have anyone to talk it over with, whereas if Karen and I need to talk we have each other."

I had forgotten Marty was there, and the funny thing is that if I put the phone close to my ear the sound of strimming gets louder and if I hold it away I just have the low whine buffered by a double-glazed window.

"Hello, Win. Are you not talking because you're upset?"

I'm not talking because I've just spotted Marty on the pavement at the far side of the Pollen Dance man. I don't think that can be coincidence. I'm sure I didn't give him the address, so this is all a bit weird.

"No, why would I be upset?"

"Well, just . . . anything you want to talk about?"

Yes, I want to ask you why you are in my bloody street. "Actually there is, I . . ."

"Want me to come round?"

"No need. I want to ask you about GADD."

"My old band?"

I don't remember it being his band as such, but we'll let that go. "The name of the band. Why did you call yourselves GADD?"

"Hang on. The washing machine's on." I can see him walk further up the street, mobile clasped to his ear. The noise of the strimmer recedes a little. "You thought of the name, actually."

"Did I? Do you know what it meant?"

He laughs. "You should be asking yourself, really. I asked you if it stood for anything. You said - hang on, let's have a think. Yeah, you said 'God and Devil Duet'. I think that's what you said. We just liked the sound of 'GADD', so we stuck with that."

"I don't suppose I explained what it meant?"

"I'm not sure it meant anything. I think you just thought of the word then made that up when we asked what it stood for."

God and Devil Duet doesn't tickle any damp socks, but it sounds a pretty obvious thing to come up with in a hurry. I wouldn't have bought into the simplistic Good versus Evil themes that dog every era - from the Bible to the tales of King Arthur to Star Wars to Harry Potter. I would have known that duality was a false concept. So first there was the word, and it was GADD.

"Would it help if I brought round some old songs? I've got them on CD somewhere. Or I could play them to you if you have a guitar lying around?"

"No, that's very kind," I say, thinking that it sounds like an opportunity for self-indulgent strumming. "I'll see you Thursday."

"Oh." He sounds disappointed. "Can you wait that long?"

"Yes, anyway I see Karen in a few days, then you. Time will pass."

He says "oh" again, and doesn't have time to respond to my "goodbye" before I end the call and watch him cast a look up at the house. He seems to be hampered by indecision. He pockets his mobile, looks at his watch. Looks up at the house. Looks at his watch again. Eventually he trudges off.

I ring Karen, who answers after a few rings, and sounds surprised – but pleased – to hear from me.

"I have a moral problem," I say.

"OK . . ." I know she is doing that forehead-raising expression. "Fire away."

"If someone gave you a watch as a present but then someone else who was a bit confused accidentally picked it up and started wearing it, would the person who gave you a present be right to feel upset?"

"Right. So this is your old history teacher and . . ."

"I told you that?"

"You did. And who gave you the watch?"

"My sister. She came round when Fred was here and she saw he had my watch. She seemed quite emotional."

"OK. And what does she do for a living?"

"She keeps books."

"She's a collector?"

"No, I mean she's a bookkeeper."

I can hear her laugh. "Slight difference. That sounds as boring as hell."

"Yes," I say.

"And quite a lonely job, I guess."

"I guess so. She certainly works alone, from home."

"So let's say that she finds her job as lonely and as boring as we think it is. But she spends a few lonely, boring hours making the money needed to buy you a watch, as opposed to buying something for herself." Pause. "Are you there, Win?"

"So you think I've been a bit of a prat, then?"

"I think you've been a bit insensitive."

I sigh. "OK, I'd better see old Fred and get it back. Thank you. Is this therapy session gratis?"

"I'll collect my payment off you on Tuesday."

"OK." I think she's joking. "By the way, is Marty there?"

"No – he's out running. Bit of a first, actually, him running around without a ball to kick."

"Right. OK – see you Tuesday."

As soon as I end the call I try Fred and Maddy. Maddy answers, which is what I hoped for. I explain my predicament about the watch.

"I wondered where he got that from." She sighs. "Why didn't you ask for it back yesterday?"

"What difference does a day make?"

Maddy seems to pause before answering. "If you'd asked for it back yesterday then we could have handed it over in your front room. Now I have to get in the car and spend an hour in Saturday traffic to get to you."

"I'll come to you."

"You don't have a car, though, do you Winifred? So you'll have to spend an hour and a half on a bus in Saturday traffic because my husband has walked off with your watch."

"But I could have asked for it yesterday. So I'll come to you."

"No, it's all right. Permit me my little bouts of martyrdom, Winifred."

"OK. Sorry."

"As you keep saying. Look, can it wait until this evening? The traffic will be lighter, and I'll need a break by then."

"A break from what?"

"I'll see you later."

I'm feeling out of sorts. I try meditating, but for some reason I am bothered by the thought of Urs suddenly materialising in my room. I hate the way she does that. Maybe I could do with going on a retreat for a week; even if it's just in the UK, at least I wouldn't have to worry about family members rocking up – or at least – not if I don't tell them where I'm going. I spend some time googling Buddhist retreats. They are hellishly expensive.

Retreat. It's a calming word. Funny that it has negative connotations in Chinese: it implies hiding from the police. Or in my case, hiding from my family.

I am hungry, and surprised to see that it is dark outside. I have wasted the day. When I come back upstairs, after having something to eat, I puzzle over a note that must have fallen beneath my desk: '2.40 am: Horace asks why we think people go to Heaven by car or horse'. I had forgotten the forum.

I read it several times, but it is no less baffling, so I give up and try to think of another way of asking the Chinese about ancestor worship. My two main tutors at university came from Taiwan and Singapore. The Taiwanese lady *Lu Yao* came from a traditional family. Having been told that her father was dying she arranged her affairs in the UK as soon as possible and got on a plane. Too late, sadly. By the time her plane touched down in Taipei her father had died. To do penance for not being there for his last breath, she had to travel to a neighbouring village, and *crawl* home from there, kowtowing until her forehead was bruised. God knows what state her hands and knees were in. This is what she told my class, and I know she would not lie.

If I ask her whether ancestor worship is still the norm, she will almost certainly say yes, because ancestor worship is an extension of filial piety, and it would be inconceivable to her that it wouldn't exist. But that is Taiwan, not China.

I go back on the forum. I don't expect an answer, as now it will be about 4 am in China. In fact, it will be 4 am all over China, whether the sun is rising in Shanghai or is a distant dream in Chengdu. We agonise enough over whether a uniform time is more unfair to children in the highlands of Scotland or in the south downs of England. The Chinese just make a decision without moithering over it.

Me: Horace, are you there?

Horace: Hello.

(If Horace is a real individual then he must be living on amphetamines and wearing nappies.)

Me: Hello Horace, previously you said that the British people think they can go to Heaven by car or horse. I am curious as to who told you this?

Horace: Sorry I am a little tired today. When did I say this?

Me: 02:40 UK time today. 10:40 your time.

(Ten minutes go by before I see him type.)

Harold: This is a British funeral. Drive car, ride horse, ride motorbike to heaven.

Me: Who told you that?

Horace: Nobody told me. I have looked at your funeral company websites.

(Of course! Why didn't I think of that? Genius. I can look at Chinese websites.)

Me: OK, thank you for your help.

Horace: No problem.

I google UK funeral companies and choose a few at random, paging through them quickly. I try to imagine coming to these sites with no preconception of what a British funeral involves. A pattern emerges fairly quickly: the images of fields, paths, trees, autumn, dappled sunlight are ubiquitous. As also are pictures of coffins ranging from standard up through a range of luxury, until the deceased can recline in a state of great comfort in a solid oak coffin with panelled sides and a luxurious satin suite. And then there are the modes of transport: hearses, motorbikes with a sidecar adapted to take coffins, or horse-drawn carriages with black-plumed horses (though I've read that this last mode of transport fell out of favour a little following the funeral of the Kray twins).

There are no pictures of churches, crematoria, services or cemeteries. Which makes sense, as these aren't things that funeral companies have any choice in, nor are they customisable products. If I came to these websites with no prior knowledge, I would think that the funeral was based around a coffin and transporting that coffin 'somewhere'. I can see where Horace is coming from.

I've only once helped choose a coffin – or at least by help, I mean I tagged along and watched my mother and grandmother disagree over which one was appropriate for my grandfather. Actually, they had disagreed on which funeral company was appropriate – my mother suggesting that we "at least stick our heads in the Co-op" and my Grandmother insisting that we go to 'F Gibbs & Sons' – a good, solid family firm, who had the most elaborate shop frontage on the high street. As wife of the deceased, Nan won the argument and this seemed to force her into a waspish pattern of behaviour. When a suited man with the appropriate gravitas brought them a catalogue of coffins, Nan pointedly turned to the expensive end – and then dithered between the Dorchester and the Winchester model. I remember itching to leaf through the catalogue to see what they came up with for the cheapest model (the 'Manchester'?), but I could hardly make a lunge for it between Nan and Mum's stiff upper torsos. The Winchester was the top of the range. Although the suited, grave man had sat like a stone statue whilst my mother exclaimed "that seems like an awful lot", he did gently point out that the oak Dorchester had a satin quilted interior, whereas the Winchester was a beautiful, hard mahogany lined with cream, hand-brushed, crushed velvet, I think the implication being that the higher price was justified by the greater number of adjectives.

"I mean, they both seem like an awful lot," said my mother. She was not a mean woman, and her parents were loaded (Nan presumably now doubly-loaded), but, like my Dad, my mother hated being ripped off. I was eleven or twelve, and an interested observer of this hitherto-unseen Nan-Mother dynamic. Plus I was in a funeral company shop for the first time, which I remember seemed to be more about a hushed atmosphere in an empty space than wall to wall coffins and reliquaries and death masks – or whatever else my young imagination had entertained me with.

Nan chose the Winchester, and was already on second name terms with the suited man, whom she addressed as "Mr

Gibbs", though my mother said later that she couldn't recall him introducing himself as such. The subject turned to memorials and gravestones, and I got bored and wandered off to look around. I had been intrigued by an unremarkable piece of white A4 paper sellotaped to a white wall which I struggled to read until my nose was three inches away from it: F Gibbs & Sons was owned by 'Dynasty PLC' or 'Diligently PLC' – or something like that – which was headquartered in the US. Nan was almost certainly not talking to Mr Gibbs, who was probably in retirement, mourning the buy-up of his family firm.

I didn't actually go to Grandad's funeral, though Urs got to go. (Fortunately, there were various aunts and uncles on my mother's side who died and whose funerals I was able to attend, otherwise I would be a funeral virgin). I remember a few arguments between my parents leading up to the day, strange pieces of conversation that reached my ears whenever their argument left the sanctity of the parental bedroom to continue in liminal zones such as the landing or hall. I suspect Dad was following her around the house.

Dad: I want to come and support my wife.

Mum: . . . support me more by staying at home.

Dad: Is this about my father? . . . years ago . . .

Mum: . . . can't take the risk. What if . . .

I was used as the excuse. Mum said I was too young to go to a funeral and that he must stay at home and look after me. I think I was more miffed at the transparent falseness of the excuse than at not being able to go: I don't recall if I was truly disappointed. Mum and Urs left, and Dad prowled around the house, unable to settle. Eventually he went into the tiny box room and music – Bowie? – blared through the house. He went downhill from there.

Urs and I compared notes later. Mum and Nan were quarrelling in the car on the way to church; Urs said that Nan seemed more focused on Dad's absence than on the ceremony that lay ahead. Mum said "leave it" a couple of times, then in the face of continual needling from Nan said that she hadn't wanted her husband to come because he had reacted badly when his own father had died and she didn't know what his reaction would be at this funeral. This provoked more needling until Mum said – in a whisper that was supposed to lie outside Urs's hearing – that he had gone to view his own father's body a few months before, and had come over 'all strange'. Nan wanted details. Urs reported to me that Mum had then told her to "shut up" – a deliciously inappropriate thing to say to her own mother; how I wished that I had witnessed that.

I have my mobile pressed to my ear, though I can't remember hearing it ring, or dialling a number. I am thinking that it is strange that Urs and I had more sensible conversations at fourteen and twelve than we have now. Maybe I just rang her to talk about it.

"Urs," I say now. "I was just thinking of Grandad's funeral. Do you remember?"

There is no reaction down the phone, though I sense that I am connected to someone.

"Who's that?" I try.

"Win, it's Mum. Are you OK?" She is sounding flustered or worried or something.

"I'm fine. Did I ring you or did you ring me?"

"I rang you, because Urs is very upset."

"Ah, I was hoping it was her, actually."

"Were you going to apologise?"

Apologise for what? "No, I was just going to ask her about Grand . . . about your father's funeral. I just remembered it."

"It's good that you . . . no Win, you've got it wrong. I mean you can't remember it because you weren't there."

"I know I wasn't there. I just wanted to ask her . . . I suppose I should be asking you. What happened when Dad went to see his father's body?"

"What on earth has brought this on?"

What has brought this on? I look up and see that the PC screen is showing a website of a funeral company.

"I was just thinking of funerals. I'm researching something on funeral culture."

"Is this something to do with . . . ancestor worship?" She says it as she might say 'paedophilia'.

"Yes."

"And an old teacher is paying you to do this research?"

"Yes. Chinese funeral culture."

There is such a long pause that I wonder if she has nodded off or dropped the phone, but then I hear a noise that could be a sigh. "Well, I suppose it won't hurt you to know. Your Dad's long gone after all. You do know he had some problems? Some minor mental health issues? Well, not that minor in the end."

"Yes, of course I know. He was a bit - confused."

Another pause. "Yes - euphemism of the year. No wonder. Your father really didn't have the best start in life. His mother had been sectioned. He hadn't seen his father in years. When he was told that his father had died, he went to view the body, and I suppose he had mixed emotions."

"Like what - exactly?"

"Why do you want to know - after all this time?"

I play my Get Out of Jail card. "I want to remember."

"OK." Another pause. "Well, I bitterly, bitterly regret not going with him. I should have insisted. I thought it would be closure for him, and that he would need a private moment, but . . ."

"So what happened?"

"I'm sure that nothing actually happened."

"OK, so what did Dad think happened?"

"He was left alone with the body, and he said that he thought his father's lips were moving. Your Dad got nearer, wondering if the doctors had made a mistake. And his father's eyes opened and he started rebuking your father, saying he was a useless son."

"Oh."

"Obviously, none of that was real."

"Yes. Understood."

"And he was a very good father, when he was well." Pause. "Your Dad, I mean, not his father, of course."

"Yes, I know."

"You two got on very well. Like partners in crime, sometimes. It must be a big hole in your life – yes, you more than Urs, I think – not having him around."

I don't have holes in my life. In fact it's a very weird concept. I'm not even sure how to visualise that. I translate it into Chinese in my head, but the translation is a straightforward one, word for word, so it doesn't help. A hole in your life, as if life were a solid groundmass with a nice meteorite depression.

"It's completely natural that you're upset."

"Sorry?"

"About your father."

"Oh yes. Yes, it is a bit sad seeing him now."

Pause. "What do you mean – seeing him now?"

Whoops. I don't want to get into this. With Mum, always deflect a question with a question. "What was his job? I mean, before."

"He was a social worker. Remember? Probably not a great job for him. Very stressful sometimes." Pause. "What did you mean – seeing him now? Did you just mean it's a bit hard to remember him?"

I scout around for a truthful answer. "It is hard to remember him as he was."

"Right." A long pause. "OK, I suppose I'd better let you get on with whatever you're doing. That's ancestor worship, right?"

Something has been bugging me for the last few seconds. A noise or a vibration. I take the phone with me downstairs, and sure enough I can see a figure on the other side of the door.

"Right Win?"

"Sorry?"

"Oh, never mind." My mother's voice, sounding tired. "Oh – I almost forgot why I was ringing. I want you to speak to Urs. She's really upset."

"What about?"

"Don't you know?"

I open the front door, and Maddy stands there with a smile that I think would be described as 'ironic', though I don't really know what an ironic smile looks like, but it feels like the right word. She is dangling my watch in one hand.

"Ah, the watch."

"Yes," says my Mum, who still seems to be on the phone. "Good. You remembered."

Chapter Eleven

I LOOK OUT to see if the man who strims his garden on a Saturday and washes his car on a Sunday is strimming or washing, but he is neither. However, there is water in the road around his car, so it must be Sunday. I may have overslept. Last night was a late one. I decided to translate the website of a Taiwanese funeral company first to understand what a traditional Chinese funeral would entail (without the restrictions of the Communist Party) and found it very challenging. I can see that it lays out funeral procedure very clearly and so I should just be able to translate this to get what I need, but translation skills alone are not enough – I need some background knowledge. I remember contacting *Lu Yao* – my old Taiwanese tutor – for help, and I'm hoping now that I emailed her rather than rang her, because I suspect that this was way past midnight.

I fire up the PC, partly to check the time, and then realise that I'm wearing my watch, which tells me that it is eleven. I'm feeling jaded. When I go downstairs to make breakfast, I find that I forgot to set the rice cooker on last night, and there's only some limp pak choi in the fridge. I have also been rather lax with my post-it notes these last few days, so whilst I am waiting for the water to boil for my noodles, I write out some reminders: spinach, cabbage, rice, broccoli. The old staples. It occurs to me that I haven't had any protein for a while, so I also scramble the solitary remaining egg and add 'eggs' to the list.

I'm still feeling weird after my green tea and riceless breakfast, so I meditate for half an hour. It helps a bit. I have such a longing to go back to Taiwan and feel normal again that I momentarily know what it must be like for a refugee or an exile. I could jack in the ancestor worship mission and get back to looking for teaching jobs. It is so tempting. Then again Maddy came to see me yesterday – I think it was yesterday – and tells me that Fred has taken a real downturn; he is barely able to sleep at night, and his daytime dozes are so deep that he awakes disorientated and confused as to whether it is day or night. She hinted that there is some urgency to my research. I am not trusting my short-term memory at the moment, so I wrote all of this down, including the year that Gadd went to Tianjin to sort out his father's affairs: 1972. And when he died: 1974. No doubt my father thought it was a good year for music.

I google '1974' and 'music' and recognise many of the names from my Dad's playlist: Bowie (of course), Rolling Stones, Marc Bolan, Slade, The Sweet. Any Rolling Stones song meant a good day – particularly if Dad was accompanying it on air guitar. Gary Glitter and Alvin Stardust tickle a damp sock, but I think were rarely heard in the house. However, Terry Jacks's Seasons in the Sun gives me a slight chill. If Dad ever put that on, then it was never the once; it could be played three times, five times, ten times in a row. It always presaged a day without Dad (in any meaningful sense), for if he was ever seen slipping between rooms, he was as insubstantial as a wraith, and as present as a revenant; should you ever stand in front of him and look into his eyes – I think I did it once or twice – it was like looking at someone who had travelled forward in time to find himself in a place he didn't know, with people he didn't recognise (who were rapidly darting off into their own rooms), and trapped inside a body that wasn't quite his. Mum would sometimes just hug him, or if the weather was OK, she would lead him into the garden to do some repetitive task, like pulling out bindweed. He would sit on the ground pulling out shoots for hours, it seemed. With that, Dad would very gradually return to the present. Mum must have been unique amongst English wives in saying, "God bless bindweed."

I fear I have been a little harsh on Diana. I saw a Facebook message from her with another invitation to 'meet for a catch up' and 'reminicse' (sic), and even the suggestion that we meet at her home for old time's sake (by which she must mean her parents' home and her ghastly teenage bedroom) – and – complete bloody horror – she still has some perfume from her teenage years which will 'take us back' (like some sort of sickly, flowery time machine).

I came to that message straight after my memory of Dad and 'Seasons In the Sun' so I fear my reaction was a little emotional:

'Just forget it, Di. We can never go back. Just grow up and go forward for fuck's sake'.

We can just about cope with lifting old memories from the murky sea bottoms of our minds, for they will have been adapted for our current selves – barnacled with later thoughts, painted with layers of words, each layer the produce of our level of language attainment at the time, rather than the thing that was buried at the time. But playing old music, revisiting old smells – these are more dangerous because they bypass language; they reawaken vibrations that our bodies can no longer handle.

Hanging onto perfume you wore as a teenager. For fuck's sake.

I have an email from *Lu Yao* and am relieved to see that it is in response to an emailed query of mine, so hopefully I didn't ring her in the early hours. I came across a summary of actions needed for a funeral in a Taiwanese funeral company website, and whilst I could translate them directly, the translated version didn't make complete sense. This is what I sent her last night, along with – I'm relieved to see – a polite note explaining that I have been asked to contrast funeral culture between the western and eastern worlds (which for some reason I thought would sound more scholarly than saying that I was interested in ancestor worship), and that I need some help with understanding the first and last phrases in the following list:

守鋪關貓	→ 擇日辦理死亡登記	→ 報喪
→ 買棺	→ 哭路頭奔喪	
Guard bed, lock-up cat	→ choose day to sort out registering death	→ announce the death
→ buy coffin	→ cry on the journey home for the funeral of elder	

If I were doing a translation of this, I would be worrying over how to translate the brevity which so characterises Chinese writing into something in English which retained the original's lean charm but still made sense. I may still have to do something like this; I need to agree with Maddy exactly what form (and how polished) this 'proof' that ancestor worship exists or doesn't exist should take.

I have a sweet response from *Lu Yao*:

Hello Winnie. How interesting that you do this! You can ask me anything anytime. Guard bed, lock-up cat: this step refers to the superstition that if a cat jumps across the corpse, the deceased will sit up; therefore, any cats should be locked away.

Cry on the journey home for the funeral of elder: this step refers to traditional families, when children who are travelling back home after a parent has died should cry (or even crawl) on the approach to the house. When receiving visitors who come to pay their respects, children of the deceased should crawl from the house to greet them.

As I say, ask me anything.

Lu Yao

Lu Yao is unusual in being from both a traditional family and being OK to talk about this stuff. It took me a long while to accept that there really is some truth in the notion of a superstitious oriental mindset, as opposed to an empirical occidental one. When I first went backpacking to Vietnam, I thought that the western notions of the 'otherness' of the Far East were largely an attempt to render the latter exotic to 'talk up' the novelty of visiting such places, which in reality globalisation has rendered largely familiar to us. Certainly, travel guidebooks for far-eastern countries generally devote texts to advising the hapless western traveller on how to avoid offending the superstitious nature of Orientals: for example, not standing chopsticks vertically in rice bowls, owing to their resemblance to incense sticks burning at a funeral. When other travellers destined for China and Malaysia and I compared guidebooks, we realised that all contained identical sections on 'mad taxi drivers', and concluded that either the companies producing these books were incredibly lazy, or (as I myself suspected), this was evidence of an invented Far East.

Then I ended up in Taiwan and noticed that the lifts of some small hotels offered no fourth floor, because the word for four (sì) sounds too close to death. But who can be smug about this? My mother was not overtly superstitious, but Nan's anecdotes of early life in a convent school confirmed that in living memory Catholicism was so saturated with the fear of upsetting God that every activity dripped superstition.

I've still got the Facebook page open, and another little message pops up from Diana: 'How about it? I'm going home now'.

I'm just thinking that she's either very forgiving or very obtuse, but realise that I hadn't pressed Send, so she didn't see my 'for fuck's sake' message. Maybe it is relief that makes me type 'OK. Walking now. See you there.' Then I add: 'Which home?'

Diana: Mum and Dad's.

Why am I going? Guilt over a message she never saw? Because a walk might clear the slight headache that has started? I don't really know.

It is only when I'm into Merton High Street that I realise that I'm hungry and haven't had lunch. I go into a convenience store to buy a banana or anything that I can have quickly and then remember that I'm supposed to be buying something else. In the end, I pretty much buy every non-wilting fruit and vegetable I can see, plus eggs, plus packets of noodles, plus a packet of polenta (which I've never tried, but whilst I'm here . . .), and lentils and anything else that takes my fancy. The one thing I forget to buy is something to eat now, so that by the time I reach the Candles' house (carrying two bags and with a rucksack like a camel's hump), I'm definitely feeling a little light-headed.

"My dear," exclaims Mrs Candle, when she opens the door and sees my bags. "Are you moving in?"

There's some delighted squealing as Diana skips down the stairs, but whatever extravagant hug she had planned when she reached the bottom is thwarted by a barricade of bags and a hastily set down rucksack.

"I did some shopping on the way over," I explain to Mrs Candle.

"Why didn't you do it on the way back, so that there would be less to lug?"

"I don't know. I suppose I was worried I would forget on the way home."

Mr Candle, looking balder and more rotund than I remember, comes out of the front room, holding a newspaper, and tilts his specs to half-mast to get a look at me.

"Winnie! You haven't changed."

"Thank you," I say. "I think. Neither have you."

We all chuckle at the polite untruthfulness of this, except Diana, who is fidgeting like a child being kept from a toy. "Let's take tea up to the room."

"You have to make it first," says her mother.

"Well, have a catch-up with us first," says her father and I follow him into the front room.

When we are all arranged in armchairs - Diana finally condescending to sit down - Mr Candle says "I hear you've been travelling."

"I did a bit of backpacking after university, and ended up in Taiwan."

"Working?"

"Yes, teaching English. I also got a bit of translation work. And I stayed in a monastery for part of it, which was fun."

Mrs Candle raises her eyes. "What other young person would call a monastery 'fun'?"

The parent Candles make quite a fuss of me. Diana joins in with the occasional tease about me being a swot at school, but really it is her parents who ask me what life was like in Taiwan. In the end, it is Mr Candle who goes out and makes tea, and brings in cake, which they seem to enjoy watching me scoff.

"I used to think your mother didn't feed you enough," says Mrs Candle, cheerfully. "But I suspect you're not feeding yourself properly now."

I guess we are catching up, and it's not so bad. I rather feel at home here, and I remember that I was always welcomed. Mrs Candle - I notice - seems to have more energy than when I saw her last, though she has to drink tea by bringing her face down to a cup held low, as though the action of lifting it to her lips is a feat beyond her.

"Dare I ask how your Dad is?" she says.

"Not great, to be honest. Sometimes I'm not even sure if he really recognises me."

They greet this news with sympathetic noises but - I notice

- without surprise. I tell them how I found him on a google map, and that he lives in a hostel.

"Your poor mother," says Mrs Candle. "And poor you and your sister, of course. I think you were very loyal, but we still picked up that things were quite difficult sometimes."

I remember to ask about the state of the bathroom (now "almost completely fixed") and pose questions about Diana's current situation, which she answers carelessly. She works in Admin for a small company of solicitors and shares a house in Clapham with three others; she is dismissive of both work and living arrangements.

"What are your plans?" I ask.

There is a pause, which I sense is awkward, whilst we all look at Diana, and I see a fleeting scowl, before she ripostes, "well, what are *your* plans?"

"I need to save a bit of money first. But then I'm back to Taiwan."

"But you've done Taiwan," snaps Diana, whilst her mother gives her a sharp look. "For how long this time?"

"Well, forever, I suppose. Mind you, it takes a long time to establish residency there." In fact, it takes five continuous years, so that being dragged back to the UK after four years has dealt me a major blow. I will have to start all over again.

"You must really like it," says Mrs Candle.

"I feel more at home there."

"I could certainly do with a change from London," she says.

"This isn't really London, Mum."

"This is London," says Mrs Candle. "Terraced housing and endless traffic."

"Did you say you were interested in Sussex?" I ask. "I think it was the south coast?"

"That's the plan," says Mr Candle. "I could have retired this year, but I carried on – don't know why really. If we bought a bungalow in Hove, I think we could . . ."

"Oh God," says Diana. "Who wants to live in a bungalow?"

"Well, me for one," says Mrs Candle, "and your father for another."

Suddenly the Candle parents are gushing about their new planned life. The South Downs are lovely, they would love to live in a place with its own plot instead of being cheek by jowl with neighbours; they want to get up in a place with light flooding through the windows, and to hear the sound of seagulls in the morning.

"We have seagulls in London," says Diana.

I think it must be time to go, and say so.

"With all that shopping to carry," says Mrs Candle, dismayed. "Ian – couldn't we give . . ." and Mr Candle is already rising to his feet.

If it was just them, I would gladly accept a lift. But then Diana will know where I live, and I'm not sure where that will go. I thank them but insist that I walk.

"To be honest, I spend so many hours in front of the PC, it's a relief to get some exercise."

There are a few 'are you sures?' and 'it would be no troubles', but then both settle back into their armchairs. Diana shows me to the door, where I pick up my shopping and rucksack.

"Sorry they hogged the conversation," she says. "Next time."

"That's fine. Actually, it was really nice to see them."

"Yes, but there's loads of stuff I wanted to chat about."

"Well, you could walk with me part way and take the tube from Colliers Wood station."

She makes a face. "They like me to stay the night."

I am replaying some of the conversations in my head when I reach Merton High Street and find myself turning left for Wimbledon rather than right for Colliers Wood. I hate to admit it, but old habits die hard.

Chapter Twelve

I WAKE UP with my head on a hard surface. I have no idea what time it is, or where my watch is, which I wouldn't see anyway, as it is dark, apart from a strange light in the corner of the room. Once I've worked out that the light is from the open fridge, everything falls into place. I turn on the kitchen light and see that the kitchen clock says quarter past seven, which throws me, because it is dark outside. I close the fridge door, relieved that at least I seem to have packed it full of shopping. But what day is it? Have I stood Karen up?

I worked late – I know that. There is a scrap of paper in front of me that reads:

1 × 7 (grieving sons), 2 × 7 (daughters-in-law), 3 × 7 (daughters), 4 × 7 (sons-in-law), 5 × 7 (inner grandsons/daughter), 6 × 7 (outer grandsons/daughters), 7 × 7 (grieving sons).

God knows what it means.

I have got to get my act together. I have no Mr Gadd to blame. I had routine when I was in the monastery in Taiwan. This is what I'm lacking. I write myself two sets of post-it notes: one set for the kitchen and one for the bedroom. From now on I will get up at 7 am, and meditate first thing, and be in bed by 11:30 pm, with no exceptions.

I go upstairs and find that my PC says that it is 4 am on

Tuesday. I set the alarm clock to wake me in three hours' time and fall into a dreamless sleep.

When the alarm goes off, I want to hurl it at the wall, but I get up. I meditate for an hour. I find my watch in the bathroom and put it on. Downstairs, the rice cooker isn't on, so I add a post-it note to the noticeboard (put rice cooker on at 11:15 pm) and notice that I have to put the bins out today. No time like the present: I change the bin liners in the bathroom and kitchen, throw the bags in the bin and push it out. I have noodles and spinach for breakfast. I can't remember what I did yesterday, but hopefully my recent documents on the PC will reveal all.

While I'm eating breakfast, Urs walks in – carrying a bag of shopping – and responds to my "hello" with an unfriendly grunt.

"Haven't seen you for a few days," I try. I can't actually remember how many days it's been, but more than a couple, I'm sure.

"Yeah. Well I'm only here because Mum was worried you'd be starving." She doesn't look at me but goes to the fridge. She says something, but seems to be addressing the closed fridge door.

"Did you hear what I said?"

I pincer some spinach. "Sorry – no. I didn't realise you were talking to me."

She says very loudly in an over-enunciat-ed and spaced out way, so that I can visualise huge words written in the air with hyphens in between: "Mum-wants-you-to-stay-at-hers-to-give-me-some-respite."

"I don't want to stay there. Respite from what?"

"Respite from . . ." – she opens the fridge door with a

flourish that has it banging on the adjacent kitchen unit and stares inside. "Who bought all this stuff?"

"Well, me, of course."

She starts to wedge her shopping in amongst the vegetables there, unpacking and re-packing the fridge until it all fits in.

"Mum rang you yesterday, and on Sunday. She was worried that something had happened to you." When I stay quiet, she adds, "so where were you?", with squashed-face annoyance.

"I'd probably gone out on a walk."

"You can't have probably gone out for a walk. Either you went on a walk or you didn't."

"I went for a walk."

"On both days?"

"Probably." I can't remember. I went to see the Candles – I know that. I probably did a walk yesterday as well, to take a break from the screen.

She is still watching me, as if waiting. Waiting for me to finish breakfast, maybe. I will do that in my own time.

She lets out a quiet roar of frustration. "It's like dragging teeth."

Then she looks at the noticeboard and sees my notes in Chinese. To her it will just look like '7:00 blah blah', '11:15 blah blah', '11:30 blah blah'.

Then she looks at me.

"You've got your watch."

"Yes, I asked Maddy for it back."

"Is that Mr Fallowfield's wife?"

"Yes. Is something wrong, Urs?"

"Why would something be wrong?"

"I don't know. You just seem a bit . . . unhappy."

"No. Nothing's wrong."

"Do you want some tea? I think there's water in the pot."

"No."

I give up, wash up my bowl, and take my tea upstairs. The last thing I see in the kitchen is Urs going to the bin with a liner in her hand and freezing when she sees that it's already been changed.

Once upstairs, I hear a high-pitched whine downstairs, which I take to be the hoover. I can't remember the last time I hoovered. From now on I will hoover on Tuesdays, before I change the bin liners. I make up a timetable on the computer, showing what I'm doing and at what time on each day of the week. Of course I do it in Chinese, because of Tuesday and Thursday nights. Then I print out two copies, and sellotape one on the wall above the computer.

What did I do yesterday? I wrote up a document describing what a westerner would observe if they were present at a Taiwanese funeral, assuming that the deceased was male and died of natural causes after a long life, leaving behind a widow and children:

The western observer might notice that the relationship between a representative of the funeral company and the family might start even before the relative had died; if the relative was in hospital, the company might make much effort to bring him home to die. It wouldn't be obvious to the westerner which part of the proceedings could be designated as 'the funeral', as the stage between the death and the actual burial of the body would seem to involve a number of processes, including informing neighbours by wailing or displaying banners outside the door; the living room being transformed into a 'mourning hall' by the funeral company; displaying of the body, whilst being 'guarded' by the deceased's children standing either side; guests arriving to pay respects by bowing and holding incense sticks; preparation of the coffin with coloured cloths and what would appear to be gifts for the 'other side' (for example, shoes); nailing and sealing of the coffin; outpourings of voluble grief by family members (particularly by the eldest son's wife); and chanting of scriptures by a monk – who may be accompanied by professional mourners and loud wind and percussion instruments. The religious nature of the funeral would not be clear – it could be Buddhist or Daoist or some combination. The family's involvement in proceedings would be led by the eldest son. Money – genuine or fake – might be burnt in a brazier, along with paper models of anything that might be useful in another life, such as cars, houses, mobile phones. A geomancer might be engaged to suggest a date for the conveyance of the body to the gravesite, which would entail taking the coffin inside a flower-bedecked truck. In the funeral procession, family members would wear clothes of differing materials and colours to reflect their genealogical proximity to the deceased, and non-relatives would have patches of coloured cloth or red thread attached to their clothes to ward off any negativity from being close to death. During the procession, wind and percussion instruments would be played, firecrackers might be let off and offerings of money or incense given, should the procession have to cross over water. Financial gifts brought by relatives and friends would be recorded by the funeral company in a 'funeral book'. Non-family members would be given sweets and coins before their departure, again to ward off any negativity. Starting before and continuing beyond this stage (which the British observer would have assumed was 'the funeral') a ritual called 'doing the sevens' is performed, whereby – in its fullest form – forty-nine days is divided into seven blocks of seven days, with one relative giving offerings and prayers during each block of seven days, starting and finishing with the son(s). The urn containing some of the deceased's ashes would be brought back to the house (with a ceremony intended to invite the deceased's spirit back home) and placed in the room or part of a room which is permanently designated as the Ancestral Hall or Ancestral Shrine. A memorial tablet for the spirit of the deceased is set to the side of those for previous generations of ancestors, and can be left at an angle; this represents that the deceased is not yet on an equal footing with those of the ancestors. After one hundred days there may (optionally) be another ritual similar to 'doing the sevens'. After a designated period – and following a reminder from the funeral company, the urn would be placed near the urns of previous ancestors, and the deceased's name inscribed below previous forebears on wooden ancestral tablets, with the character for Host inscribed – but without the top dot (王). To 'fix' the deceased's spirit to the tablet, a ceremony would take place during which a dot would be added (originally using blood from the eldest son's middle finger for ink) to complete the character for Host (主). ('Host' means the ancestral tablet that would 'seat' the soul, as opposed to the Catholic Host: the bread of Eucharist, meaning 'sacrifice'). Offerings of food and paper money would be made regularly by the family to the deceased (and other ancestors), particularly on set days of the lunar month, and on major festival days – notably Qing Ming ('tomb-sweeping day', a day when people maintain their family graves and honour their ancestors, which is a national holiday in Taiwan and China). The western observer would puzzle as to where the deceased's soul is believed to be. In the tomb that is swept?

In the home's ancestral tablet? In the 'Otherworld' where they were meant to receive the money, car, mobile phone that were burnt for them? Or somehow in all three places?

A few things leap out. The urgent need to bring the person home (if they were dying in a hospital) is hardly unique to the Taiwanese. The culture just across the Irish Sea is similar, where home deaths are preferred; if that is not possible, the deceased may be driven past his or her former home 'to get a last view of it' – something to which I also found a reference in one Taiwanese funeral company's website. Timing would be tricky here, I imagine, though not as challenging as the ancient Roman custom of the eldest son trying to inhale his father's dying breath.

The 'doing the sevens' ritual is interesting when it is broken down into its blocks:

the first 7 days performed by grieving sons

the second 7 days performed by daughters-in-law

the third 7 days performed by daughters

the fourth 7 days performed by sons-in-law

the fifth 7 days performed by grandsons, granddaughters by the sons

the sixth 7 days performed by grandsons/granddaughters by the daughters

the final 7 days once again – grieving sons

It is no surprise that in a traditional Taiwanese ceremony the son will take precedence over the daughter, but for the daughter-in-law to take precedence over the daughter would jar with the British mindset, maybe with the whole western mindset, if there is such a thing. Most people would take a dim view – I think – of having to pay more attention to their in-laws than to their own parents. But the clue is in the literal translation of the daughter's children: outer-grandson, outer-granddaughter. For these children, if the deceased were the maternal grandfather – he would have been known as 'outer-grandfather', while their father's father would simply be grandfather, i.e., 'inner'. Such is the status of women in these ceremonies that once married they are outside the family, and belong to the family they marry into. Whilst her own parents will in time become 'outer grandparents', the daughter-in-law will now gain precedence over her in-laws' natural daughters.

If China found it hard to impose the one-birth policy, I can imagine how much harder it would be for Taiwan: doing the sevens would have to be downsized to doing the threes or fours.

I think I rang *Lu Yao* for help on this. Sure enough, I can see that I called her just after 10 pm. I know she would have been too nice to protest, but time-wise that is pushing it. I start a list of rules: (1) DO NOT RING ANYONE AFTER 9 PM (2) CLOSE FRIDGE DOOR. I will add more as I think of them. I cannot hear the hoover whine downstairs any more, but no doubt Urs is still down there, doing something. She has taken the other bedroom, but doesn't seem to use it much for bed, let alone as an office.

The next thing that leaps out is that the funeral procedures indicate that there are three parts to the deceased's spirit: one that remains with the grave, one that resides in the ancestral tablet, and one that may have incarnations in a range of worlds, depending on how his/her previous life was judged and – for 'him' in particular – on the intercessions of his descendants. Western beliefs may accommodate a range of options for the deceased's spirit, including Christian notions of heaven or hell, reincarnation, or that it dies with the body – finito / game over / the end. Multiple destinations are not considered; or at least not officially: unofficially, people like my mother tend to favour burial plots, as though their 'loved ones' will somehow be aware of the attention.

Finally, I pretty much had it right when I wrote about Mr Gadd's career path. The deceased does have something of a career trajectory. Of the part that reincarnates in other worlds, depending on his performance on Earth and the help of his descendants, there is clearly a progression. And for the spirit that comes home, quite some time must pass (and attention to ritual) before he can be promoted and join the ancestors' private club.

If this were the website of a Chinese funeral company, I could more or less hand it over to the Fallowfields and say that Fred is right about ancestor worship, and watch with interest as to what they want to do next to sort out the unsettled Mr Gadd. And collect the balance of my six hundred pounds fee. If only.

My headache has kicked in early, so to take a break from the screen I print out a copy of the document, scrawl 'This is what a traditional Chinese funeral in Taiwan involves' on the top and walk to the nearest post-box. At least this will reassure the Fallowfields that I'm on the case.

When I return, I start searching for websites of Chinese funeral companies. I've barely come up with a list of two before Urs darkens the doorway with a face that suggests no improvement on her previous mood.

"Have you had the cheque yet? For that investment thing?"
I think. "No, not yet."
"Maybe they didn't think it was good enough."

"It was fine. I'll leave it for a couple more weeks before I chase."

"The light's gone in the front room. I'll buy some more bulbs."

"OK, great."

"I'm going now."

"OK. Bye."

And she's gone; presumably back to the family house.

The bus has just turned into Garratt Lane when I get a text from Karen. 'Marty is being a prat and not leaving for football. Can you delay arrival until I've got rid of him?' I respond with 'No problem. Text me when free', and get off the bus. I might as well use the time walking.

By the time I've reached the top of the lane, there is still no text from Karen, so I walk down Skullbrook Road and try and remember where Fred lives. There is no helpful brown estate in any of the driveways, but number eight looks familiar. I don't know why, but I go up to the front door, from where I can hear the beep-beep of a fire alarm within. Concerned, I stick my fingers through the letter-box flap and peer through the slot: I can see the kitchen ahead. I can't see any flames, but the air has a heavy look about it. An unmistakable smell escapes through the slot towards me. I let the flap fall and I withdraw, satisfied that there is no fire. Mr Gadd has clearly burnt the toast.

As I am walking back down Skullbrook Road, I get another text: 'coast clear, can you come?' I text back 'on way' and powerwalk to Karen's flat. The journey from the Fallowfields to Karen and Marty's flat is easy now – it's shaped like a sideways 'Z', with Garratt Lane forming the middle line of the 'Z'. She greets me with a hug, but is fuming, which makes her Welsh accent more Welsh. Funny how people's accents get more pronounced when they're emotional. Dad used to get more Brummie.

"I am so sorry about that. Marty's been an absolute pain in the backside. He made out he was feeling ill and couldn't go to football."

"Is he ill?"

"No, definitely not. I know when he's lying. I assume he wants to see us together. It was only when I said that I would ring you to cancel today and Thursday that he suddenly felt well enough to go to his practice. With a lot of whingeing and wimping."

She has already made me a mug of jasmine tea, which I drink straight down, as I'm thirsty after all my walking. I check on Goldie Pang, who – to my untrained eye – is looking less like a satsuma and more like a fish.

"Are you annoyed?" asks Karen. "I feel like we've messed you round."

"No, I'm fine. I don't expect everything to run smoothly."

"I just hoped Marty behaved himself on Thursday."

"Um . . . I think you'll have to define what you mean by 'behaved himself.'"

Karen laughs. "What must you think of us?"

"I think you're both OK."

She does her forehead-raising expression. "But I'm still fed up with him. I feel like he's short-changed our session."

"And I need a shower," I say. "I did a bit of walking around."

"Of course. Poor . . . Win."

"So you haven't thought of a name for me yet?"

"Working on it."

As time is short, I suggest that we both have a shower, and she pauses but agrees. Afterwards, when we are towelling each other down, she says that it was a first for her, then says, "How about you?"

"I've had loads of showers."

She gives me a playful whip with the towel and then looks concerned. "Are you joking – or are you really that literal?"

"I was joking. Really. Though you're not the first person to call me 'literal'." I wonder if Maddy has come back to a smoke-filled house and given poor Fred hell for Gadd's latest culinary gaff. "Can toasters catch fire?" I ask. "I mean like, a real fire, not just burning the toast."

"Yes, of course they can."

"Bugger. Can they?"

"Yes – it's a major cause of house fires."

"Karen. Sorry. I need to run."

"Where?" She looks bereft. I don't know why. We've had sex. Vertical sex, but still sex.

"Run to someone's house to check it's not on fire."

"Where?"

"In the kitchen."

"Where's the house?"

"A few minutes from here." I am pulling on clothes, looking for socks.

"I'll come with you."

"Oh. OK."

We run out the flat, down the stairs and across Garratt Lane. I was worried that she would slow me down, but she is keeping up OK, and thankfully is not asking me silly questions. I should have checked the route on my phone first, and we get lost, as I've got my 'Z' the wrong way round in my head. Karen asks me where we are going and says that she knows Skullbrook road. When we get to number eight, Skullbrook road, I notice the brown Volvo in the drive, and pull up abruptly.

"Is this it?" asks Karen.

"Yes. His wife's home. I think we're OK." In fact, the house hasn't burnt down, and just looks like a normal house in a normal street.

We are out of breath, panting.

"Let's walk around," says Karen. "Cool down a bit."

We have reached halfway up the street before Karen says, "Do you want to tell me what's going on – or is it a secret?"

"How long have you got?"

Karen checks her watch and makes a face. "Marty will be home in a minute." She frowns and seems to be making a decision. "Sod it. I can go out when I want. I want to hear this story."

We go to the was-a-bank-now-a-gastropub where I met them for drinks, and I accept her preference of a table inside, just in case we're seen from the street, but she doesn't specify who might see us. There are not many punters tonight and I have no problem hearing Karen. I sit down at a table and shortly she comes back with cokes for us both and a glass of wine for herself.

"Do you mind?"

"Mind what?"

"Me having wine."

"Of course not."

"OK. Spill. And I do mean talk rather than throw your coke everywhere."

"I'm not that literal – really."

"Yes, you are. Anyone else would have known that was a joke. Now: talk."

And so I tell her about Fred turning up on my doorstep, about the late Mr Gadd, and about the essay that he thinks I wrote about his father. I tell her about the commission, about ancestor worship, about the Fallowfields. I tell her about my lack of memory and explain about getting locked in a cemetery on the evening we first met. I think I tell her everything. At no time does she interrupt or do anything other than stare at me with blue spotlights.

When I'm finished, she does her forehead-raising expression and I wish it was the start of the evening and that we still would get to go to bed together. But it's the end of the evening, and I realise now that she'll think I'm completely weird and that maybe she and Marty should have found someone else to have sex with.

She spends a long time staring into her empty glass. It occurs to me that I should maybe buy her one so I go to the bar and order another and hopefully hide the condom in my hand before rummaging again in my rucksack for my purse.

When I get back with the wine, she looks surprised and says 'sod it' (again) before thanking me.

"Ancestor worship was in this country as well, wasn't it?"

"I'm afraid I don't know," I say, and curse myself. I should know these things.

"Have you been keeping up with Stonehenge?"

I laugh. "That's what Fred said to me. I didn't know what he meant."

"I can't remember exactly, but I think that there's more evidence now that it was a place to hold ancestors rather than a purely astronomical site. There's evidence of different stages of funeral customs, for example, bodies being buried and then the bones reburied elsewhere."

"A career path for the dead."

"Like your essay."

"Yes. I wish I knew what I was going on about."

"You really can't remember?"

I shake my head. "I was fourteen or thereabouts." I watch her thinking. She is either deciding what to say or has thought of what to say but doesn't know how to say it.

"Marty was in a band called Gadd."

"He's told you about that?"

She rolls her eyes. "Never stops. If he's telling the truth, then they were brilliant, particularly him, and they were on the brink of making it when - I don't know - he hasn't really got an answer for the dark forces at work that - apparently - jinxed them."

And now I do have an image of them playing at a school music night: Marty strutting around the stage. I can't remember the names of the other boys.

"I probably do have an answer for that. They were only about fifteen years old. None of them really knew how to play. Their equipment was pretty rubbish. And we were coming up to exams, so their parents probably told them to stop mucking around and study."

Karen laughs. I join in but then stop.

"What's wrong?"

"I've just realised that my essay on Gadd predated the band by one or two years."

"Oh yes." She pauses. "Well maybe it's still relevant. Maybe it was a buzzword in the school."

"Maybe. I'll ask him on Thursday."

It may be my imagination, but I think that Karen's face clouds over momentarily. Then she looks at her watch and does a sort of 'I'm late' yelp. I look at my watch and grimace.

"You've also got to get back?" she asks.

"I have to be in bed by half-eleven."

She frowns. "Is that for a medical reason?"

"No - I'm trying to stick to a routine. When I'm on a project, things can go a little haywire. I end up working through the night."

"At least you've got your watch back."

"Yes."

"Was your sister pleased?"

"Actually, no. She wasn't."

"It was still the right thing to do. Anyway, I have a favour to ask."

"Yes, whatever."

"You don't know what it is yet." She shakes her head with a smile. "Next Tuesday, cook a Chinese meal for me and stay over. Marty won't be back that night. He's got a couple of days off on some corporate jolly."

"Isn't that breaking the rules?"

"He broke the rules tonight. Anyway, I don't think our rules specified that you had to be out by a certain time." When I hesitate, she adds "if you feel uncomfortable, forget it."

"No, that's fine. But there's one important thing."

She looks at me. "Yes, I know. The only rule is that no-one gets attached."

"I meant - do you have a wok?"

"Oh, yes I do. We do. Two actually. Was that the only important thing?"

"Yes. Well I suppose there's one other important thing." She is staring at me intensely. "You find me a new name."

"Oh that. Yes, OK. Deal."

We leave, hug at the bus stop and I insist she goes home rather than wait for my bus. She hurries off. I think she's worried about something.

Chapter Thirteen

I HAVE LESS than a week to learn how to cook a Chinese
meal that Karen thinks is authentic. Obviously I can throw
a few vegetables into a wok and do an egg-fried rice and cook
an authentic meal (providing I'm left alone and not expected to talk about the weather or whatever), but I know that
unless I include dumplings or stuffed bread, she won't think
it's authentic.

I will pay more attention to what I cook for myself in
the evenings, but really I need a trial run with a guinea-pig.
I could invite Diana around for a meal, I suppose, but the
woman is starting to alarm me a little. It's not just the pictures
of very pissed-off looking cats dressed up as Star Wars characters and being spun around on upturned dustbin lids (which
I assume are meant to resemble starships) that are now posted
on my page, but also some rather strange messages about her
parents being too foolish and old to move at their age. Plus a
horror story of a bungalow which fell into a sinkhole (though
nowhere near Sussex). Plus a link to a New Age article about
being happy with what you have. Plus a link to another article
(with a "you'll understand this, Win") which is supposedly
a 'Buddhist' exhortation to accept your current situation in
life rather than assuming that the grass is greener elsewhere
– which logically would mean that a Buddhist should starve
to death rather than get something out the fridge when they
feel hungry.

I don't know what I'm supposed to do with this information. So I ignore it, and try and limit my time on Facebook to mere nanoseconds in case I get messaged.

I ring my mother, which I guess must be a first, because she says, "Who's that?" a couple of times before accepting that it really is her younger daughter.

"Are you OK, Winnie? Do you want me to send Ursula over?"

"I'm fine. I just wondered if you were busy on Saturday. I want to come over and cook you a meal."

"A meal?"

"Yes, a meal for you and Urs."

"Did you say you'll cook it round here? Rather than me come to you?"

"Yes. Because it will be nice for you to be cooked for in your own home." (And because I need to practise cooking in someone else's kitchen).

"That sounds lovely, Winnie. A family meal then." She really sounds happy. "What time?"

"Oh, don't know. Eat at eightish?"

"Oh damn - hang on. I'm working Saturday. I don't suppose there's any chance you could do Friday?"

That gives me less time to practise. "Yes, could do Friday." I write it down on two post-it notes with my free hand.

"I suppose we need to check if Urs is free," says Mum. (It hadn't occurred to me that Urs would be doing something). "But to be honest, I think she usually is with me or with you on Fridays."

"OK, so I will cook a meal for you and Urs on Friday at yours. I'll come around earlier, of course, to cook, but to eat at eight."

"Perfect."

Urs's reaction is less positive when she rings me five minutes later. "Mum's just said you'll be cooking. Will it be Chinese muck?"

"It will be a Chinese meal."

"Hmmm. Why?"

"Why will it be a Chinese meal?"

"No, I mean why are you cooking us a meal at all?" When I don't answer – because I'm trying to think of an answer that won't sound like I'd rather poison my family than Karen – she snaps, "What will be in it?"

"Nice things."

"It's not going to be all Buddhist stuff?"

"It's just going to be a simple family meal."

"Marvellous," she says. "A strange meal for a strange family."

That seems to be the end of the conversation, though I am left pondering what she meant by that last line. She's right really: a family meal needs a family. I go out and walk as far as Balham before the rain soaks through my sweatshirt and I catch a tube to Borough; I spend the tube journey dreaming up inducements.

As soon as I see Dad I can tell that it's not been a good day: in addition to the Big Issue magazines in his outstretched hand, there is a huge wodge in the bag behind him, and it is now raining heavily, which means that London's finest can't be bothered to pause on the threshold of the station to search for change. I buy a magazine straightaway.

"Thanks, Ponytail."

His eyes barely graze my presence before they slide away to the rain outside.

"How's the hostel?" I ask, and then I think the question is as nonsensical as asking, "What is this house?", so I add, "the hostel that you live in." When he still looks blank, I try, "Do you like the hostel that you live in?"

He nods. "Yes." After a pause, he adds, "We can keep dogs."

"Do you have a dog?" I've never seen one with him.

Elongated pause. "No, but if I did have a dog, I could keep it."

"We never had a dog, did we?"

He frowns. "No."

I have a list of inducements in my head: if he comes next Friday, I will buy him alcohol / he will have a meal / I will blow all of Maddy's second instalment on a taxi to and from the hostel. Now I play with the idea of offering him a dog. I bet more people would buy the Big Issue if he had a dog curled up at his feet. Especially if it was a dog that looked perpetually sad, like a retired greyhound – or maybe a really scruffy little mongrel half-wrapped up in an old blanket. But what if he couldn't feed the dog? Or if it got lost like Fred's black Labrador, Lucy, which I keep meaning to ask Maddy about, but keep forgetting.

Someone has stopped to buy the Big Issue. A youngish man in a rain-patched suit is rifling through change from his pocket. Dad must recognise him, because he grins.

"Bloody miserable weather," says the man, handing over some coins, and accepting a magazine at the same time.

"Cats and dogs today," says Dad. His Brummie accent seems slighter than I remember.

"And this suit is supposed to be dry-clean only." The man gives Dad a rueful smile, before saying, "See you, Jeff", and disappearing into the station's throat.

My father's name is Harry. That was my own joke in church: "Our Father which art in heaven. Harold be thy name."

"Do you call yourself Jeff now?" I ask.

He nods.

"Oh. Right. Do you like Chinese food?"

Dad frowns. "To eat?"

"Yes, Chinese food – to eat."

"I don't really know."

"No, I suppose we didn't have it at home, did we?"

No response.

"I want you to come home on Friday. I'm cooking a Chinese meal."

"Home?"

"In Wimbledon. Remember? I'll come and get you, then we'll go home together. We won't stay too long. You can have a drink." What did he drink? I can't remember. Beer, I think. "We'll have a nice meal, and then I'll send you back in a taxi."

This has been the longest time he has actually looked at me. Actually looked at my face. He is blinking, but I think he is, sort of, waking up. Then he looks away. "I used to . . . Wimbledon?"

"Yes. Our old home in South Wimbledon. And you re-member Urs?"

"Us?"

"No, Urs. Ursula. You used to call her . . ." – oh, what did he call her? I don't think he liked her name – ". . . U. You used to call her U, and you called me 'double U', which I thought was funny."

But which has totally confused him now. I was so sure that the mention of Wimbledon had tickled something in his brain,

222

but after that he is just hearing 'blah blah blah'. His cloudy blue eyes are almost swimming with incomprehension. I have been an idiot and overloaded him.

"Look, you don't have to call us anything. You can carry on calling me Ponytail. But will you come to Wimbledon for a nice meal? Not now. I mean on Friday. Friday evening."

"Maybe."

"OK. I'll see you tomorrow. I'll come and talk to you again tomorrow. OK?"

"OK."

That's quite enough for today. It's still raining outside, and I'm feeling chilled in my soaked top, so I catch the tube all the way home, which means just a ten minute walk from the station.

It is Thursday, according to my PC. I have meditated, and put on my watch. Last night I chose three dishes from the Internet: I will do steamed dumplings stuffed with vegetables and for Urs and Mum, steamed buns stuffed with pork and prawns. And then just a simple vegetable side dish with cabbage. I'll buy the buns in advance rather than make them.

I've printed out the instructions and lie back on my bed now, re-reading them. I visualise myself going through the steps for each dish. I can't see an issue so long as I can buy pre-made dumpling wrappers and steamed bread. It will be a bit like serving a British meal with haggis and laver bread and toad-in-the-hole at the same time. But no worries – so long as other people think it's authentic.

Urs must have sneaked in and out, because there are a few boxes of light bulbs on the kitchen table, and a note from her:

Win – DO NOT change light bulb. I will do it when I come back.

Are you really cooking on Friday? Do I need to get some ingredients?

Shall I get a back-up meal?

Good reminder, actually. I hadn't planned when to buy the ingredients. I'll do it on the way back from seeing Dad later. I have printed off what I need:

VEGETABLE DUMPLINGS

spinach	pak choi	shitake mushrooms	bamboo shoots
bean sprouts	coriander	red chilli	wonton wrappers
cornflour	hot and sour sauce	vegetable oil	

MEAT-FILLED STEAMED BUNS

spring onions	ginger	soy sauce	rice wine
vegetable oil	pork	prawns	

VEGETABLE DISH

garlic	red chilli	3 spring onions	red onion
mange-tout	shitake mushrooms	green cabbage	water chestnuts

I spend the next couple of hours going over the recipes and the preparation steps. I tried typing out the tasks needed in time order, but I lost track of which of the dishes each task was for. Then I tried colour-coding the font, so that the dumplings were in black, the steamed buns in blue, and the mange-tout dish in green, but I found I couldn't read the text apart from the recipe for the dumplings. So now I've created a sort of bar chart with all the tasks for the dishes colour-coded and then re-arranged in sequence. I need to know how long the cooking tasks should last. I try annotating the times – adding a bubble that says three minutes to the 'fry garlic' task, but I know I will have problems reading that later. It seems to me that most of the fry/simmer/steam tasks are done in multiples of three minutes, e.g., 'fry for three minutes' or 'fry for six minutes', so I divide the horizontal axis into blocks of three minutes, and fatten the bars to show the number of time blocks they must occupy. The buns must be steamed for between fifteen and twenty minutes, so I allocate eighteen minutes to this.

I lie on the bed with the print-outs in my hand and try and visualise myself doing each step.

Having gone through the preparation twice, I visualise bringing it to the table. I will provide chopsticks as an option, but will ask Urs to lay a normal table; it will give her something to do and the more tasks I give her to do the less time she will spend trying to ask me questions when I cook. In fact, it would be good to give her some of the chopping up tasks, as hopefully it will engage her sufficiently to shut her up. I mark 'U' on the tasks on the bar chart that Urs could do.

Once again, I visualise bringing the meal to the table: Mum and Urs have their usual places. That leaves the space on the table nearest the door free, which I think is right for Dad, as he will need to know that he can escape at any time: make a bolt for it if Mum asks whether he's found God, or lost God, or whatever. I must say that Dad is a bit of a dark blob in my mind. I wonder what he eats with now? Is it all hand food and mugs of soup or will he still be able to use a knife and fork? I'd better ask Urs to lay a spoon in his place as well.

It is not raining, so I walk all the way to Clapham Common before getting on the tube. Dad is expressionless when he sees me, but he does at least say, "Hello Ponytail".

"Hi Dad. I'm just reminding you about Friday. That's tomorrow."

"Friday?"

"Yes, tomorrow. We're going back to the old house in Wimbledon to have a meal with the family. And afterwards I will send you back to the hostel in a taxi."

He is nodding a little, but I sense there is some conflict, understandably so.

"How much is a taxi?" he asks.

"I'm paying for the taxi."

He sells a copy of the magazine to someone who calls him 'Jeff' and then turns back to me. "I can't afford a taxi."

"Don't worry. I'm paying for the taxi. The important thing is that you'll come and have a meal with us on Friday."

He seems to be thinking about it. "I'm not sure I can come for the meal."

"OK. Well, no pressure. Why don't you come with me just to say Hello, and if you don't want to eat the meal, I'll send you back in a taxi immediately."

More furrowed forehead expressions. I'm not going to rush him, so I take a step back and just open my awareness of the pavement in front of the station, which actually belies the contours of the slightest hill underneath. Tarmac does disguise the land beneath; of course, the land should be sloping down-wards towards the Thames.

"Could I just come and look through the window?" Dad has stepped back to be parallel with me.

"Sorry?"

"I could just look through the window, couldn't I? I could see if . . . everyone's all right?"

"Yes, if that's all you feel able to do, that's fine. Though of course you might want to stay for the meal. Or just have a drink, or just a steamed bun."

"I could just come and look through the window."

"OK, you can just look through the window. I'm not going to have time to come back tomorrow during the day to remind you. Shall I meet you here or at the hostel at half-past five?"

"Here."

"OK. Here. Half-past five. I've written the time down."

I give him a post-it note, which he looks at. "What does that say?"

"It says 'half-past five'."

He nods Goodbye – I think, so I return to the tube, but forget to get out at Tooting to go to the market, so I end up retracing part of the journey by foot before returning home with heavy bags. I need to buy a bigger fridge.

What was I thinking? I can't even remember if my mother has curtains or blinds, and whether she closes them at night. If Dad decides to remain outside and look through the window, the chance of Urs and Mum just seeing a face at the window and freaking out is pretty likely. They won't recognise him, because they won't expect to see him, and will probably call the police. If the police turn up before my father has run off

– and probably straight into traffic on Kingston Road – then he will freak out, as he was never that comfortable with the police or any representative of authority when he was a family man, let alone someone who lives in a hostel without a dog.

What the fuck was I thinking of?

"I hope that was a groan of pleasure?"

I realise that Marty has stopped moving, and is looking at me, worried.

"Yes, it was."

"I'm not hurting you, am I?"

"No, no. Carry on." I was just about to say that I was miles away, but I manage not to.

"Karen says I'm too rough sometimes."

"No, you're fine." God – he is still not moving. He is normally like a metronome – which I like – but now he is more like a stopped clock. "Exactly as you were. Don't change anything."

He grins. "That good? OK."

Afterwards, Marty seems reluctant to do anything but carry on lying entwined in bed, but eventually he props himself up on an elbow and looks at me.

"You seem a bit . . . worried about something. Is there anything you want to talk about?"

"I'm sorry. I have a few family issues. The sex was great."

"Family issues?"

"It's nothing. A little problem with my father."

"So you've told him?"

"Told him? Well, he's coming around to see my mother on Friday. Tomorrow. At least I think he is."

He freezes. "Wow. That's a bit . . . I mean I understand, but – we did say no emotional attachment."

I'm confused. "We said no emotional attachment between me and you and Karen. Family is different, obviously."

Now he's looking confused. "So you've told him? About us?"

"What? No, of course not. I don't mention sex to my father. Or any of my family."

Marty thinks about this. "No, of course not. Though of course it's not just sex, is it?"

"No, obviously, there's lots of things that shouldn't be discussed with families."

I get up and start dressing, and Marty slowly does the same.

"I've dug out some old GADD recordings. Don't suppose you're in the mood to hear them now?"

My head is in cooking mode and Dad mode. I don't want to think about Gadd for a few days.

"Next time," I say and he nods.

Chapter Fourteen

"**I**'M GOING OVER to Mum's now," says Urs. "Is there anything you want me to take over for tonight?"

I don't believe it. I have spent so much time planning the cooking that I forgot the logistics. It isn't just the food that needs to be taken, but also the rice cooker and two woks, because I know my mother's house will be a wokless house. Otherwise I would have to cart those over to meet Dad and then to South Wimbledon. Thank God Urs has mentioned it.

"That would be great," I say.

She watches me put everything on the table. I clean the rice cooker – still warm from my breakfast – and double wash both woks. The ingredients are already bagged up with coloured labels to show which dish they are for. I put these on the table as well. Urs inspects them.

"You don't need two bottles of vegetable oil," says Urs. "And do you need two packets of spring onions?"

"Yes, less confusing. OK – we can leave one bottle of vegetable oil here."

"Do you want me to take this now or wait until I come back for you?"

"Now please. Don't come back for me. I'll make my own way."

She gives me a look. "Really?"

"Yes, really. I'll be there at 6:30 and start cooking." I put one copy of the bar chart in with the ingredients. I have another copy in my rucksack so that I can re-read it on the way.

"If you're sure. And what's the chart?"

"It's the recipes."

"It looks like a bar chart." She takes it out and studies it. Then she turns away, and refuses my offer to help her load the car. "No. Least I can do."

I go up to my room, but watch her as she loads the car, making sure that I see both woks and the rice cooker are loaded into the back seat, plus all the bags of food. Once she's in the driver's seat, she blows her nose. I do hope she doesn't cry when she sees Dad tonight. I don't think we want tears.

I have already written down a few things that he can ask her about: her bookkeeping, a long weekend she spent in Europe last year. I can't actually remember where or when she went, but if he says something like "I hear you went to Europe last year," that should be enough of a trigger.

I have really struggled to think of some conversations he could have with Mum. I can't think of any nursing topics or church topics or anything that would support a lighthearted conversation. I have googled obituaries, but apart from Alvin Stardust – who died a couple of years ago – I can't find anything that might have common currency. Well, I'm sure David Bowie would, but I have an inkling that Dad will just fall apart if we talk about Bowie in the past tense.

I've spent so much time going through the cooking plans that I think I could do with a break. I set an alarm to go off at 3:30 pm (when I will have a shower) and another to go off at 4:15 pm (when I must leave the house to see Dad).

I start looking through the website of a Chinese company with a name that translates to 'Crane Dragon Springs'; this one is unusual in that it administers a large memorial park and seems to allow burials, though whether just of ashes or also coffins I haven't yet fathomed. Whilst there is an admonishment that 'feudal superstitious rituals are severely prohibited', the site pushes *feng shui* to an extreme, extolling the benefits of its location of forest-covered mountains and 'natural water', though whether this means a lake or river isn't stated.

I read some more to try and figure out what sort of water it's referring to, but the only description is 'natural water' - in fact there are several references to the park having 'natural water'. It is a feature of translation that one shouldn't just ignore information that seems superfluous; I could assume from this that artificially created water features are the norm in Chinese landscapes. Or I could assume that they are pushing the description of 'natural water' because it isn't natural at all.

When I was looking through the Taiwanese websites, I came across a couple of references to 'lawful graves' - something that would look jarringly superfluous in an English translation, because we don't have a concept of 'unlawful graves'. But the inclusion of the 'lawful' adjective indicates that there has been a problem of people being buried in unlawful sites.

In a similar vein, I came across this advice on helping the bereaved offered by a UK funeral house: 'Don't worry if your friend cries or even if you cry yourself - it's a normal reaction'. A Chinese translator rendering this from English into Chinese might consider this behaviour too obvious to mention, when in fact it might reveal that crying in front of another person is not the default behaviour in the UK.

I make a note to myself and underline it: never overlook the obvious. Then my alarm goes off and it's time for my shower.

I have mixed feelings when I reach ground level and see Dad waiting outside Borough station: relief that he has kept to the arrangement and apprehension over how the evening ahead will pan out. He has made an effort in that he has on an old jacket over a shirt and seems to have combed his hair.

"Great – hi Dad."

"Ponytail."

He looks terrified. I had originally planned to take a taxi both ways, but it occurs to me that he hasn't used public transport for a long while, and this is an opportunity for him to be normal again. Also, I suspect that he'll be less at ease in a taxi. I have borrowed Urs's Oyster card, and topped it up with twenty quid.

"Take this. This is your Oyster card. Put it somewhere safe. We're going on the tube. OK?"

He nods and follows me into the station and the lift. At least it's just straight down the Northern Line to South Wimbledon, so no worries about changing lines and my losing him. One thing I hadn't allowed for was rush hour, so my vision of us sitting side by side on a quiet tube, and my planting some conversation ideas in him is replaced by us rail-hanging mutely amidst a stack of bodies. This doesn't seem to bother him too much. Or to be more accurate, he looks no more terrified in the tube than he did on the street.

But as the train drops southwards – Clapham South, Balham, Tooting Bec – sweat appears above his lips.

"I'm just going to look through the window at them and go."

"That's fine, Dad. See how you feel when you get there."

If the worst comes to the worst and I hear a scream, I will explain the situation to Urs and my mother. Surely they will be OK about that. Oops – I'd almost forgotten the exit strategy. I didn't want to be seen handing over cash to him in case he later got targeted by a mugger.

"Dad. It's very important that you remember this." I seem to have his attention. "The Oyster card in your pocket has forty quid in the flap. No – don't take it out. I don't want you to lose it. Have you got that? The Oyster card has more than enough money to get you home, but there's also forty pounds in cash. If you need to take a taxi back to the hostel, you have money."

He is nodding. I hope he's got that.

When we reach Colliers Wood, I say "I live near here", but I get no reaction. One more stop.

When we get off the tube at South Wimbledon, his pace slows further, so that the ticket barriers ahead seem like a visual trick, not getting nearer. But eventually we are there. He shuffles to the exit and looks out at the traffic-stricken road. I'm not sure how familiar the station would be to him – I think he usually drove to work, depending on where his clients were. He steps forward and looks left and right, almost like an animal sniffing the air for a scent. He turns left down Kingston Road without waiting for me. I have to put on a bit of a spurt to catch up. The house is only a ten-minute walk from here, but I had been worried he would find it too far, thinking that his level of fitness may not be great. However, he is walking, if not fast, certainly with purpose. I'm wondering if this evening might not be better than I'd dared hope.

Suddenly he crosses the road and takes a right turn northwards towards Wimbledon.

"Dad – not that way." The lights are red and he catches me unawares. I run after him, just as the lights are turning amber. "Dad. We need to go back." But he is a man on a mission: either he's ignoring me or he's forgotten me. Or he's doing a runner.

He turns right and slows down, looking at the houses. (I can't imagine what the houses here cost – more than Mum's house, that's for sure.) I touch his sleeve.

"Dad, we've just gone a little bit wrong. We need to go . . ."

"That one," he says, though I'm not sure if he is talking to me. He steps onto the driveway of a large detached house with a garage at the side. His feet crunch across the gravel, but then he sidesteps onto a tiny piece of grass on the left. I halt on the street and hiss "Dad" a couple of times, which he ignores. There are lights on inside; I think a TV screen, blobs of people, maybe sitting on a sofa. Dad edges along the patch of lawn, over to the window and looks in. No-one screams, but his head is craning for a better view. Trying to avoid the gravel, I edge my way along the right side of the garden. I reach the garage door, and beckon to Dad with another hiss. This time he looks over at me. I assume that anyone looking out of the window won't be able to see anything directly in front of the garage door, so I sidle along it as if negotiating a precipice. When I get to the end of the door, I beckon with my hand, which must be what sets off the security light. It completely throws me, and for a second I cannot remember where I am or what I'm doing. Then the front door opens and a male voice shouts "Oi" and my father turns and legs it out of the garden, followed by me.

After I have put a length of street between me and the house, I decide that walking at a normal pace would look less suspicious. There's no sign of Dad. I retrace my steps to the house, where it seems the whole family is now standing out front, but not bothering to venture into the street. I walk past. I scan all the immediate streets. Nothing. Dad has disappeared. I have a vain hope that he has remembered the way to my mother's home – which seems unlikely after this aberration – and decide that there is nothing else I can do now but go there myself.

Except that I am lost. I try to get back to Kingston Road – which should be south – but I don't know where south is. I wander around for a while. Eventually I ask a woman walking her dog to point me in the right direction.

I don't arrive until 7 o'clock. Needless to say, there's no Dad waiting for me, just my mother and Urs standing in the open doorway. I wonder if they were startled by a face at the window, but it seems they were just looking out for me.

"Where have you been?" asks Urs. "I assumed you'd be cooking by now."

"Sorry, I'm late."

"Never mind," says Mum, placatingly. "You're here now."

"Yes, sorry. I'd better start cooking straightaway."

They seem flummoxed. They don't know whether to join me in the kitchen or to stay in the living room.

"Where do you want us to be, dear?"

"Probably out here. If I need help in the kitchen, I'll shout."

I go into the kitchen. I know that I'm not in the best frame of mind. I have no idea if my father knows where he is. I have no idea if he can find his way back to the hostel. I don't know if he'll remember that he has an Oyster card with cash tucked in the pocket, or if he will be groping around completely disorientated.

But I'm here to cook a meal. I close my eyes and try to

focus on the task ahead. I wash my hands, concentrating on rubbing the liquid soap over them, then concentrating on rinsing it off.

I lay out all the ingredients and start working along my bar chart. I could ask Urs to come and do some of the chopping, but I've just realised that if she helps, it will throw out the relative times of the other tasks.

After a while Urs comes in, and turns off a tap. "I'm not nagging, Win, but it's quarter to nine."

"I'm almost there. Can you lay the places?"

"Done that."

"Um . . . have some – I don't know – wine."

"We're both trolleyed already."

"OK, give me ten minutes."

At ten past nine I start taking dishes through, and they seem bemused when I ask them to change places.

"Does it matter where we sit?" asks Urs.

I suppose it doesn't. It's just not what I'd visualised. However, Mum quickly rearranges the places and we sit down.

"Can we start?" asks Urs. "Are we waiting for anything?"

"I assumed one of you would want to say Grace."

They seem surprised, but Mum puts her hands together and simply says "Thank-you Win for taking the trouble to cook us this meal", and that's it.

"Wow," says Mum after a mouthful. "This is very nice. It's really authentic, isn't it?"

"Actually, it *is* really nice," says Urs. "Love the dumplings, but I especially like the buns."

"Great," I say. I need a non-vegetarian's perspective.

Mum asks me who I've been seeing and what I've been doing. I had already prepared some anecdotes about the Candles, and how I know Mr and Mrs Candle want to move to a bungalow in Sussex because they are tired of London and Mrs Candle's arthritis is quite bad but Diana seems to be somehow keeping them there. It proves to be a rich topic, and when they have run out of comments to make about Diana and her parents, I throw in her teapot collection – for which I am apparently responsible – and that uses up another ten minutes. Then I mention Diana's posts on Facebook and we start on a Facebook conversation which is good for the rest of the meal. I cooked for four but the serving dishes are almost empty. I know it's a success when Urs says she would be very happy for me to cook this again.

We collectively scrape out bowls and load the dishwasher. They have coffee and I have tea.

"You're staying over, aren't you?" says Mum.

"Oh," I hadn't really thought about it. I look at Urs, whom I had assumed would be driving us both back to my house.

"Don't look at me," she says. "I've drunk far too much to drive."

"And it's too late to be walking around," says Mum. "Stay in your room. Your old room."

"My room?"

She and Urs swap a look. "Yes. Your old room. Obviously."

After I've done my teeth I lie back in the bed, and look at the books arranged on the shelf. I turn out the light, and wonder where Dad is and how he is. I have a flashback to sidling along that garage door – a flashback so intense that I can almost feel the metal contours beneath my hands and see the green door as it flashed into colour under the security light.

Obviously this is not my room. And I'm not sure this is our house.

238

Chapter Fifteen

"WHERE DID WE used to live? Before this house?" I ask.

My mother rests her spoon in a bowl of muesli that looks like it could be used as pebble dashing. "Not far from here. Tadstone Road. Do you remember it?"

"Maybe. Vaguely. The houses there must cost a bomb."

"Yes. We were very lucky."

"So how did you end up here? And why don't I remember us moving?"

There is that look of guarded hope in her face. "You don't remember it because you were in Taiwan. Your father lost his job, and you weren't here and Urs was hardly at home; it seemed a bit silly to hang onto a four bedroom house."

"Where was Urs?"

"Where you are now. Living with . . ." she stops.

"In Colliers Wood?"

"Yes – where she is now. With you. So you see, we could hardly justify a big house just for two of us."

"And why did Dad lose his job?"

"He was finding it very stressful. He was struggling."

"Oh. I didn't know this."

"It's no secret," says Mum. "I didn't know you didn't know. We'd have told you."

"So that room upstairs really isn't my room?"

Pause. "Of course it's your room. In this house, it's always been your room." When I look at her, she blinks.

Mum says that they are off to visit Nan today. Urs – who has yet to surface – will apparently give me a lift back to South Wimbledon station and will bring on my rice cooker and woks later tonight.

"I can't remember the last time I saw Nan," I say, more because it has just occurred to me than because I have any desire to see her. She was Catholic with a capital C; strange to think that 'catholic' with a small 'c' means broadminded, as that she certainly wasn't. "Years ago, I think."

I can see my mother get edgy. "She's really gone downhill. You wouldn't want to see her."

"Have I seen her since I came back from Taiwan?"

"No. And she wouldn't recognise you."

"So she has dementia or something?"

There's a little pause before my mother answers "yes".

"Does she recognise you and Urs?"

A longer pause. "Hard to tell sometimes."

"Where is this Home?"

"In Surrey. You haven't had any breakfast, Win."

"Where in Surrey?"

"It's quite far away. Is Urs still not up?"

They drop me off opposite the station, with effusive thanks for my cooking last night, though Urs says she has a hangover (as if it were my fault) and Mum makes me promise that I'll have something to eat as soon as I get home, and I promise I will.

But I don't go home. There is a mini-cab office opposite the station and a free car outside. I get in the back seat.

"Hey?" says the driver, turning around and looking at me.

"Can you follow a car?" I ask. "That white car ahead?"

He looks confused. "Are you chasing them?"

"I need to find out where they're going."

"No, no. You've got to go to the office first." He nods towards the building and I get out. The traffic lights have gone green and amidst a blast of car horns, Urs has worked her way into the right-hand lane and gone south.

I give up and get on the tube. I stay on the tube to Borough station.

Dad's not there. I can't remember where the hostel is, otherwise I would go there and ask if he turned up last night. I don't really know what to do. So I head for home. There is a torn bit of paper sellotaped to the door: COME ROUND TO NO. 16.

I knock on the door of No. 16 and Strimmer/Wash Car man opens the door and gives a sort of 'A-ha' noise of recognition, reaching to his side and then handing over my keys.

"Left in the door. Again."

"Thanks. I left in a bit of a hurry last night. I don't even remember if I locked it."

He puts his hand to his forehead. "That's a little irrelevant, isn't it?"

The first thing I do after I come through the door is head upstairs and find my list of Rules. I add: 3) WHEN GOING OUT, LOCK DOOR AND TAKE KEYS. Then I come downstairs and find the front door open. So I close it. I feel pretty pathetic about having to go upstairs and add to the list: 4) WHEN COMING IN CLOSE DOOR.

I know I've had a lot on my mind, but I have got to sort out this lack of mindfulness.

My mobile is on the kitchen table: One missed call from Marty, two from the Fallowfield's landline. I ring them and both Maddy and Fred answer simultaneously.

"Put it down, Fred," says Maddy. "I've got it in the hall."

"Well I've got it in the bedroom," Fred yells into the mouthpiece. "You put your one down. I want to talk to her."

"No. You're just going start talking about ghosts and other nonsense."

"This house *is* full of ghosts. You said so yourself. You heard Lucy scratching at the door."

"I wish I'd never mentioned it." Maddy gives an exasperated roar. "Winifred. I'll leave him to talk to you. But I'm coming around, OK?"

I'm confused, but just say "OK", and instantly there is a click.

"Has she gone?" asks Fred.

"I guess."

"Good. I've so much to ask you, Winifred. Hang on, I've written it down. No – can't remember where. Damn. It was something to do with the thing you wrote."

"About the traditional Chinese funeral?"

"No. The other thing. Your piece on the career of Mr Gadd. She said she sent it to you."

"Oh. My essay. Yes, I've read it."

"Ah, good girl. I wanted to ask you about the Garden of Forgetfulness."

"Sorry?"

"You made it sound like there were a number of heavens – which I believe fits into the Buddhist concept of multiple,

242

impermanent heavens, but then you mention angels. It's the jostling that worries me, Winifred. My father was clearly very upset to see the angels jostling that poor man. Why were they doing that?"

"Er . . ."

"I thought maybe he had done something bad but not bad enough to preclude getting into a heaven, so it was a benign punishment."

"Yes, that's it." God knows what I really meant.

"And the poem is making more sense now."

"Poem?"

"At the close of day, there is only the wisp of smoke to mark the death of dreams,

survey your fallow fields."

"Ah, yes." Fuck knows.

"You were quite right of course. It's come back to me that he was cremated, not buried. Even worse, I'm afraid that I barely mourned his passing. When of course he himself grieved the loss of our roots."

"Roots?"

"I neglected the East, Winifred. And now that I've been reading up on Confucian beliefs, I know that he would have abhorred cremation. The body had to be kept intact. If you destroy the body, you destroy the relationship between the current family and their ancestors. That's why the worse thing an enemy could do would be to dig up your ancestor and burn the body – your family would be cursed forever."

"Yes, but you're not Chinese, Fred."

"Of course I'm Chinese, Winifred."

"A quarter Chinese. That's three-quarters not Chinese." In my mind, Fred is the archetypal English old man; I don't know

243

what sort of school he went to, but I suspect it was one which had playing fields that weren't covered in houses. I imagine he went to an Oxbridge university and became an eccentric years before his time owing to his passion for history, and didn't even get bullied for it.

He goes on about why he is Chinese. And on. I tune out. At some point, I wonder if I really did close the front door. When I open it to make sure I had closed it, Maddy is walking up the path.

"Sorry Fred. I have a visitor."

Maddy makes the tea while I slump on a sofa. I can't remember if I've eaten today.

"I had to get out the house," she says, as she brings in the mugs. "Sometimes I just drive around."

"Oh?"

"He really does believe that your essay is the word of Gadd."

"Yes. Sorry."

She sighs. "And this from one of the most intelligent men I've ever known. You know, I once challenged him to learn Sanskrit – which should have been almost impossible for a man in his fifties. It took him a few years, but he did it – he can read Sanskrit. People consult him on it – even now." She looks down at the table. "But he has this blind spot when it comes to his bloody father. And to you."

"I take it that you don't experience anything weird?"

She rolls her eyes. "Weird things happening? Definitely. It's almost like having a poltergeist in the house – a septuagenarian poltergeist. I can leave a room tidy and minutes later I will walk back in to find it trashed. Drawers gaping open, paper and books all over the carpet. And Fred denying that he was the culprit."

"Oh. That does sound a bit odd."

"Not really. Fred gets fixated on looking for things. When his mother died – that was quite a few years ago – we found a few things when we cleared out her house; not much really, but a few letters his father had written her from China, plus an official letter – half in Chinese – informing her of Gadd's death in 1974. We threw most of it away – apart from the Death letter, but Fred has forgotten and is convinced that somewhere in the house is a bundle of letters from his father."

"So Gadd went there to collect his father's body or ashes, but he never came home?"

"That's right. China got a brace of dead Gadds."

"Oh. And Gadd's mother?"

"Fred's grandmother died years before – somewhere in China. I don't think Fred ever met her."

"So just to be really clear, Grandfather Gadd died in 1972, father Gadd goes out to collect his body or get his ashes, or something, but never comes back. Instead he stays out there and dies in 1974 – when he must have been relatively young."

"Early fifties. Pretty young by our standards. And then twenty-five years later a schoolgirl in south London writes about him after his death." Another eye roll. "And you really can't remember why you wrote it? I mean, is there the slimmest chance that he mentioned his father to you in a lesson, and you – for whatever reason – put it in an essay?"

"No. It seems that the name Gadd did mean something to me, but I just don't know what. Fred's lessons were pure history. I can't imagine him ever talking about something personal."

She rubs her temples. "It would really help if you could remember, Winifred. I'm sure there's a simple explanation that isn't supernatural."

"Yes. It won't be supernatural."

"Glad to hear it." She looks down at her skirt and picks off a hair. "Oh dear. Still finding them."

"What happened to Lucy?" I ask.

"We lost her in Wales," says Maddy. "We were on holiday. Last year. That was the start of it all."

"The start of what?"

"Anyway," she says. "Back to the matter in hand. Thanks for the piece about the traditional Chinese funeral. Shame it was about Taiwan. What's your next course of action, Winifred?"

"I've started to translate some Chinese funeral company websites. I just need to find one that mentions similar procedures."

"Any hint of traditional practices?"

"Not so far. You'll be pleased to know that one of them explicitly says something like feudal superstitious practices won't be tolerated."

"Pleased?" She makes a strange noise. A bitter chuckle maybe. "Keep looking. Fred is convinced you'll prove that ancestor worship is prevalent now. And that as soon as you prove it we will go to China to pick up Gadd's ashes."

"What? Do you know where his ashes are?"

"No."

"Then how would we find them?"

"Apparently, you will lead us to them."

"What?"

She smiles. "And I have to put a time limit on this. So let's say two weeks for you to prove ancestor worship exists."

"Or prove it doesn't exist."

Her smile turns metallic. "No pressure Winifred. But if you don't mind me pointing out – you started this."

Maddy pauses in the hallway. "I have something for you. If you don't want it, throw it away." She opens her handbag and takes out some beautiful yellow-gold paper. "We found it amongst Fred's mother's things. I'm sure it isn't Chinese, but it looks sort of Chinese-y. I hung onto it because it looks so pretty, but we need to declutter."

"Thanks. It looks lovely."

Chapter Sixteen

ME: HELLO HORACE.

Horace: Hi, I am here.

Me: I asked you about ancestor worship previously.

Horace: There is now no ancestor worship.

Me: Yes, I know. But it is true that previously people thought that if someone died, his family must remember him often, otherwise he would become a restless ghost. Does anyone still have this belief?

(Long pause)

Horace: Old people sometimes have old thoughts. They get easily very confused.

Me: Do you believe in ghosts Horace?

Horace: There are now no ghosts.

Me: Do you worry that when you die no-one will remember you?

Horace: Because my son will remember me I do not worry.

Then the session disappears and when I retry the link I get 'Page not found'.

It crosses East and West – this belief that the dead had to be remembered by the living to improve their lot in the afterlife. We see it in almost every church built before the twentieth century: names of the rich families inscribed in stone on the church walls or on the church floor, if they were rich enough to secure burial within the church. Remember my soul. Remember me. And the Catholic version of 'doing the sevens': obsequies performed for the departed souls on the week, and month and first year after death. The rich could pay for the parishioners to say prayers for their souls, the poor could be remembered by having their name added to the Bede-roll, which was recited each year.

The equivalent of Chinese Ghost Month was All Soul's Day, a catch all-who-may-have-fallen-through-the-net service, so that all dead souls could be at peace.

And so the bizarre belief that although one's soul went on to Purgatory and from thence (hopefully) to Heaven, the dead wished to retain their presence in the community of the living – in their local community. And so the twain do meet: people clearly thought that their spirit existed in two places. Though if Christians really thought their afterlife consisted of a single soul's progression to Heaven (with the intercession of the living), what sort of omniscient God did these people imagine, if He needed constant reminding of the deceased person's name?

And now I'm thinking that we have a third repository for the spirit: the Internet. The messages posted on online memorials go way beyond the 'Rest In Peace' ones on notes attached to flowers left at the scene of an accident. After the Malaysian Airlines plane (flight MH370) disappeared, a friend posted messages to one of the missing passengers 'You can read this, right? You know how much we miss you'.

"Oh, for God's sake," says Urs. "They are bloody everywhere."

How does she do that? Never any warning – she's just suddenly there. Here.

"Who are everywhere?"

"Not who – *what?*"

I've obviously done something wrong. The only thing I can think of is the condoms, which I took out of the rucksack and put – well, it wouldn't have been everywhere: a kitchen drawer I'd have thought. Somewhere tidy. I was fed up of trying to use them as currency.

"You've even got one here." She reaches over me and flicks a piece of yellow-gold paper which I have suspended from a red cord above my computer. "I suppose you spent a fortune on this – whatever it is. Is it calligraphy?"

I have merely cut the stationery Maddy gave me into strips and drawn out some characters using felt pen. It cost me nothing but a couple of pounds for the red braid. I only tried calligraphy a couple of times in Taiwan – with proper brushes rather than felt pen – and it was relaxing. But it isn't having the same effect on Urs, as her face is an unrelaxed red.

"No answer, so I'll ask again: why are they everywhere? By the front door, in the kitchen, in the bathroom. It's all so . . ." – she wrinkles her nose – ". . . it's so *Chinese.*"

"It makes me happy."

I get a grunt in response.

"What do they say?"

"Nothing much."

"Nothing much." There is a pause. "And still no cheque for that investment piece, I see."

"No, I don't think we got any post today."

"Well, we wouldn't have today because it's Sunday. But it could have come yesterday. And it didn't."

"These things take time."

"I'm not being funny, Win, but do you think you need a second opinion?"

I turn around to see where she is. She has withdrawn to the doorway, as if my dangling mini-banner on a red thread were a ticking bomb. Heaven knows what she thinks it says.

"A second opinion on what?"

"On the quality of your translation."

"No. It was a good translation." I turn back. She mutters something I can't hear.

"Win!"

I turn around again. She's still in the doorway. "I said, do you know where my Oyster card is? I can't find it."

Of course: Dad's got it – it could be anywhere. "No idea. Can you take mine for now? It's in my rucksack."

Which reminds me. Dad.

He is there. Thank God, he is there. Standing in a duffel coat with a bag of Big Issues at his feet and his Big Issue vendor's tag hanging beneath his neck. I don't normally see him from the front, but then I don't normally walk all the way from my house to Borough station. I had a mind flutter at Balham when I went to catch the tube for the rest of the journey and remembered that Urs had taken my card.

"Dad?"

"Ponytail." His face is expressionless: there's not even a hint of happiness at seeing me.

"You were right, Dad. The house that you went to. I found out from Mum that we lived there. Before I went to Taiwan."

Nothing. I've done it again. Thrown too much information at him. I try again.

"You got back safely then."

He nods, but carries on looking around for potential magazine buyers.

"I'm sorry about Friday."

We stand in silence, and I can't think of any conversation to make.

I find myself fiddling with a piece of red braid around my wrist, which I'd put there for a reason. Something . . . something . . .

A young man stops nearby, patting down pockets. I sense my father is aware of him - expectant. But the young man doesn't produce change from a pocket, just an Oyster card. He heads towards the ticket barriers.

"Dad, do you still have the Oyster card?" Nothing. "Is it back at the hostel? Remember? I gave you a card with some money in."

"I don't have any money." This is said quite defensively.

"I'm not worried about the money, it's the card I need. It's not mine - it belongs to Urs. Ursula."

"Ursula." He frowns.

"Remember Ursula? She's two years older than me."

I get a violent headshake in return and don't bother to say Goodbye; it's time to walk home.

I spend a lot of the journey wondering what to do, before realising that Urs doesn't have to get her old card back. An Oyster card is an Oyster card; it has no memory of who it belonged to. I go into a shop and buy another Oyster card and load some money on. Then I carry on walking, and only realise at Balham that I could use the card to catch a tube the rest of the way. Seems silly to bother now. So I keep walking. Win is walking. I don't care if anyone forgets my name when I'm dead. They can forget my name now if they like. I hate the name. I am walking. Walking am I.

It is late afternoon when I return, and I spend some time looking through websites of Chinese funeral companies. I've decided to concentrate on three: one in Liaoning Province in north east China, one in Sichuan province, and one in Anhui.

All of them are similar in their basic format, with tabs for mourning halls (different room furnishings and embellishments are offered), suggestions for elegiac poems for the dead, outlines of memorial procedures, and always prominent mention of the deceased's place of work. Interestingly, all have prolix text under a tab marked History or Former Customs; I don't spend much time reading the text for them, but concentrate on the tabs for current services.

I do a quick search for 祖先 (ancestor) in the main tabs on the website. It produces nothing. I try 封建 (feudal) and instantly get matches. This one from the Anhui company is typical: "In the area of the grave it is strictly forbidden to let off firecrackers and indulge in feudal superstitious practices. It is strictly forbidden to burn paper and other sacrificial offerings".

It isn't looking good for Fred. Nor is it looking good for Gadd, if indeed he were a restless spirit that needs settling through the remembrance of his son.

I wonder about my own father and whether it is worth persevering. I really thought that our trip to Wimbledon would have stayed with him, especially as he found our old house, but it seems to have switched off more lights in his brain than it switched on.

I stop when I get a headache, and try to plan my week ahead. I will be cooking the meal for Karen on Tuesday. I could buy the ingredients beforehand and take them in my rucksack. Or I could find out if there are any shops selling Chinese food in the area and she could watch me buying what I need. That would look very cool. I need to do a reccy. Except that I will eat first because I've written myself a note to say that I should.

Earlsfield at night is starting to look familiar – like I'm on home ground. A few streets to my right is Fred and Maddy's (and Gadd running amok) and a few streets to my left is Karen and Marty's (and an unexploded goldfish). It has turned into a warm evening. Little groups of people are walking around, and seem happy. What month are we in? My birthday was recent, which means that March was recent, so I think we are in April. It worries me that I am getting hung up on things like this. March doesn't exist. April doesn't exist. Whether it is seasonably warm or unseasonably warm is neither here nor there. It is warm. I am warm. I have a vague recollection that 'warm' in Czech means gay, and is not a friendly word. It annoys me that my thoughts are playing Chinese whispers in my head, but at least the metaphor reminds me of why I am here. Somewhere here is a shop that sells Chinese food, because I googled it.

I find it and go in, the smell of raw meat just a shadow of the sweet, rotting smell of so many 7IIs in Taiwan: a smell I found quite comforting. I walk around it several times; they have everything I need: dumpling wrappers and frozen buns that I can steam alive on Tuesday. Just as I leave, the male proprietor intercepts me at the doorway.

"What the problem?" he says. He looks suspicious. Maybe he thought I'd pocketed something.

I tell him in Chinese that there is no problem and that I just wanted to see what his shop sells, because I will be cooking a meal in a couple of days. He looks confused, but maybe he doesn't speak Mandarin. I shouldn't assume that all Chinese people do. Even Chairman Mao couldn't speak it well.

Now I need to make sure that I know the way from Karen's flat. I plot the route on my phone and follow it to the flat. Ten minutes, but I make a note to allow fifteen on the journey back because we'll be carrying food, which could slow us down. So when I get to Karen's I need to try and get her out of the flat as soon as possible, allow ten minutes to reach the shop, five minutes to pick up what we need (as I have taken a photo of the relevant shelves), and fifteen minutes to return. I need to allow an hour for cooking, and probably ten minutes of chit-chat before I start cooking, so if I initially arrive at 7 pm, the earliest we will be eating is 8.45 pm. Even with eating, washing-up and more chit-chat, we should make it to bed before 11.30 pm.

Now I need to make sure I know the way from Karen's flat to the Chinese shop, as my schedule will be wrecked if I lose the way. Tomorrow is Monday and I will spend much of the day planning the meals and neglecting ancestor worship. I wonder what Maddy and Fred are doing right now. I wonder what sort of marriage it is when one spouse challenges the other to learn Sanskrit from scratch at the age of fifty. It's not exactly a language that you can do an immersion course in.

"Win? What are you doing here?"

I hadn't really clocked the two people coming towards me,

but here are Marty and Karen. Where am I? Garratt Lane now – thank heavens. Not in their street. That would look odd. It looks odd now, I guess, for whilst they look happy to see me, their smiles are strained with surprise.

"Hi Marty, Karen."

They are looking at me expectantly, and I hunt around for something that isn't a lie. "My old history teacher lives in the area." I say, before remembering that he was Marty's teacher too. "Fallowfield. Do you remember him?"

"Of course I do, "says Marty. "I asked you the same question a couple of weeks ago." He screws up his face. "I remember you were Fallowfield's star pupil – but – you mean you've actually kept in touch with him since school?"

"No, not since school. It's more of a recent re-acquaintance."

"You were visiting Fred?" asks Karen. And then I see her wince. She wishes she hadn't asked the question, because she suspects I haven't been visiting Fred and thinks she has put me on the spot.

"Yes." Not a lie. She used the past tense. Or the past participle – I can't remember. It doesn't really exist in Chinese.

"How do you know his name?" Marty asks her, and they stare at each other. There is something awkward between them, though I can't exactly put my finger on it."I mentioned him to Karen," I say. "If he didn't live in the area, I would never have met you two."

"Ah," says Marty, cheerfully. "Then Gadd bless Fred."

"Do you want to come in for coffee or something?" says Karen.

"No thanks. I've had a long day."

There is another awkward moment which I try to make less awkward by giving each in turn a kiss and then heading off for the bus-stop. And I feel annoyed with myself for blundering towards them in such a daydream that I didn't even register who they were until Marty called my name. But maybe that was because the first time I saw them they were walking arm-in-arm, whereas the two silhouettes walking towards me this evening were walking apart, as though no longer the couple they were.

Chapter Seventeen

KAREN HAS DECIDED that she will come up with a new name for me in the short walk from the Chinese shop to the flat, based on what she sees – a bit like the old joke about the young Red Indian called *TwoDogsFucking*. Our purchases are swinging in plastic bags. I have no sense of whether the walk is taking ten minutes or fifteen minutes, but I don't care.

"Garden."

"*Huayuan*."

"Oh God, no. Um . . . Rose "

"*Meigui*."

"Too Chinese."

"So you want to know the Chinese word for an English word, but you don't want it to sound Chinese? Do you think this strategy might be flawed?"

"Shut up. It will work. Bamboo."

"*Zhu*."

"Fence."

"*Li*."

"So . . . bamboo fence would be . . ."

"*Zhuli*, I guess."

She stops on the pavement, and I wonder if we are lost. I've been too wrapped up in her unique game of I Spy to notice the names of the streets.

"That's it, then. Julie. Do you mind being Julie?"

"Great. Julie I am."

We start walking again. "You're very easygoing," she says. "What other names have you got?"

"Only my Catholic name of Eleanor."

"Eleanor Rigby. You're kidding. Were your parents Beatles fans?"

"No, too young. My father was more into 70s stuff, particularly David Bowie."

"So now you're Julie Eleanor Rigby."

"Guess I am. Though I think I only like the Julie part."

Karen studies my 'recipe bar chart' but makes no comment. Then she picks up the little yellow-gold banner that I had put with the recipe to remind me to give it to her.

"It's for you. Your Chinese name in traditional characters. *Ka ren Ga wen du lin Jiang. Jiang* was the closest I could find to Jones."

"Wow. How did you know my full name?"

"Marty once mentioned it. Is it correct? I didn't write down what he said at the time."

"Yes. Perfect." She looks around the room. "Now – where to hide it?"

"Why do you need to hide it?"

She looks at me for a while before answering. "Marty gets very jealous."

"I can do his name as well. He can have one of his own."

"I'm not sure he'll appreciate it, to be honest." She looks at her books, running her fingertips along the spines. "I'll hide it under History. In fact, let's go for Welsh History. Anything you give me will go under Glendower. You've heard of him?"

"Of course. Owen Glendower." Is she expecting me to write more for her?

She gives her forehead-raising smile. "I'm not sure there's any 'of course' about it, but I suppose you aren't typical, Julie."

Eek. My timetable. I hadn't factored in all this chatting. I look up at the projected clock. She notices.

"Anything wrong?"

"No. Julie is going to say Hello to Goldie Pang and then start cooking."

We both crouch down and peer into the isolation tank. Goldie Pang is swimming around more gracefully than I remember.

"If he or she carries on like that, we'll have to get a little Fishy WeightWatchers sash for him or her."

Karen laughs. "Yes. He or she is doing well. Isn't it annoying that there isn't a singular pronoun in English? How about Chinese?"

"Sort of. *Ta*. He and She have a different Chinese character, but they're pronounced the same. That's why you quite often hear Chinese people using he or she the wrong way round, because they have just grabbed the first English pronoun they can think of. How about Welsh?"

She makes a face. "No. Very gender-oriented, is Welsh."

"Then we should revert to Anglo-Saxon: *Whych* for He or She." She has pulled down a notepad from the History shelf and a pen hovers over a page.

"How do you spell *Whych*?"

"W-H-Y-C-H. Do you write everything down?"

"Everything interesting. It drives Marty mad. I don't know any Anglo-Saxon." She giggles. "Apart from the rubbish you lot use now."

She offers to help me and doesn't seem surprised when I ask her to stay out of the kitchen. She pours a glass of wine and watches me from the sofa. She has left out everything I could want – a selection of knives, chopping boards, two woks, pots, a steamer. I close my eyes briefly and get in the right frame of mind for cooking. I realise my omission very quickly. I've brought rice, but not my rice cooker. How could I forget my rice cooker? I know if I do rice the convention-al way it will throw out the relative times of everything else.

"Can you take care of the rice? I forgot my rice cooker."

"Sure – how long will the whole meal take?"

"An hour."

After I have spent some time chopping vegetables Karen comes in and gets the rice ready. She doesn't get in the way, but leaves the rice simmering and checks it a couple of times, then returns to the sofa to watch me.

I have got this down to under an hour.

"This is wonderful. I've never had steamed bread. Why aren't you having any?"

"They're filled with pork and prawns."

"Wow, that's very nice of you, but next time veggie stuff is fine. I'm really enjoying this, but I don't want you to make sacrifices for me."

I get more compliments, including "I don't know how you cook in someone else's kitchen – it would freak me out", which I take particular pleasure in, without sharing that I took a photo of the kitchen last Thursday and spent virtually all of yesterday neglecting ancestor worship in favour of visualising every aspect of food preparation.

After dinner, we wash up and talk about everything: History (she loves Neolithic onwards, apart from the Romans), Marty ("he's probably throwing up right now"), her work ("some people use the fact that they need therapy as an excuse for bad behaviour") and my work (I say, "I seem to be set a task to keep looking until I find a particular answer, and to do it in two weeks").

"So what happens if you do find that ancestor worship exists?"

"Then we go to China to find Mr Gadd's ashes and bring them back for Fred to build an ancestral shrine, I guess."

This elicits some extreme forehead raising. "So a foreigner goes to China in 1974 – could they do that then – for a start? And you have to find his ashes, and . . . it's crazy, Julie."

"I know. Actually, it was 1972 when Gadd went out, and he died in 1974, so he was somehow living there for two years."

"I don't know much about Chinese history, but I can't imagine that foreigners could just swan out to China and live there for a couple of years."

"I know. The whole thing is mad. Even if Gadd was half Chinese – apparently his mother was Chinese – the idea of him going out there to settle his father's affairs is just about conceivable – but the idea of him being allowed to stay there is hard to imagine."

"Unless he wasn't allowed to leave."

"That's possible." Actually, I hadn't thought of that. Maybe Gadd was desperate to get back home.

"Could he even speak Chinese?"

"I don't know. Doubt it. He was born in China, though,

before being sent to England for schooling – so maybe he was somehow registered as being Chinese."

"And you're going to China with them?"

"I think that's the plan. If I find the evidence that Gadd needs the appropriate rituals performed."

She finishes her wine and rubs a finger around the rim. "I think – if I were in your position – I would be tempted to say that I've found that ancestor worship is a complete fiction and that Fred needs therapy to settle *his* spirit."

"I know. But it also sounds like you're trying to drum up trade."

This earns me a mock slap. "I take it he has been tested for dementia?"

"It's been mentioned. But I can't remember if Maddy said he has it or that he doesn't have it."

Karen looks at me. "It's pretty relevant, you know."

"I guess. I'd have written it down at home. I think he's just a bit eccentric. She said that he learnt Sanskrit from scratch when he was quite old."

"Impressive. That doesn't sound like dementia, then."

We go to bed on sweetly smelling sheets – "Of course I changed the bed – I don't want any reminder of Marty tonight" – have fantastic sex and are done by half-eleven. It feels weird not to be dashing home, but it's OK, even if I forgot my toothbrush; Karen seems to have prepared for this and has given me a spare one. I can't remember the last time I spent a whole night with someone.

When I wake up, she is turned towards me, but still sleeping. I don't want to wake her, so have a short session of lying-down meditation, which Sleep always treats as an enemy to be overcome. I vanquish sleep by visualising Buddhas radiating different colours. I sometimes neglect the devotional side of Buddhism, but it is the best way to stir up some energy, something that many western Buddhists - working alone and from a text book - don't get. I would like to say that I was never one of the westerners who arrived in Taiwan with the hope of practising 'real' Buddhism and then found the devotional Buddhism in the orient looking remarkably similar in form to the Christianity that had been rejected back at home. But I would be lying. At least I was never as arrogant as one young man I met who insisted that the orientals can't be practising Buddhism 'properly', because they seemed to be worshipping the Buddha rather than concentrating on *koans*. We are blinded by what we already know. Then I realise that my thoughts have drifted and I might as well get up.

The muffled noise of traffic suggests that it is a working day, and the world outside is going about its business. I wonder if she has forgotten to set an alarm - maybe she has work to go to. Should I wake her?

I decide that the correct way to wake someone you've spent the night with is to make tea, and manage to get lost on the way to the kitchen before remembering that it is further along the front room, which I've already been into once. While I'm waiting for the kettle to boil I spot my rucksack and check my phone. There's two missed calls from Marty and one from Urs. Urs has also texted me: 'Where are you? Are you OK?' and a missed call from my mother. I text Urs: 'I'm fine. With a friend'. Marty has also left a message. What an earth does he want? We will see each other on Thursday. Which must be tomorrow. What can't wait until then? I won't bother to listen to his message now.

Karen is sitting up in bed when I return. She looks relieved to see me.

"I thought you'd done a runner."

"No. I went to make . . . hang on."

I go back to the kitchen and return with two mugs of tea.

"Do you have to go to work today?"

She gives a laugh and looks sort of embarrassed. "Nope. I deliberately kept today free. Just in case."

"In case of what?"

She rolls her eyes and smiles, before answering me in a string of Welsh, which she then refuses to translate.

"Do I have to learn Welsh?" I ask.

"Might do. Depends how long you plan on being around."

We sit up in bed and plan a Museum of Languages, which you could site anywhere in the UK. A place with maps of the World. Where someone can press a location, and choose a year and hear a recording of what that language sounds like or sounded like. Karen has added the option of a Migration button where you can see how the language migrated over the world, and an Evolution button to hear a recording of what its predecessors might have sounded like. I have suggested a standard option for *language isolates* like Basque, which has sent her scurrying out of bed to get her notebook.

"I can see I'm going to need to keep this closer to hand."

She is ambivalent about her work, in that she thinks she doesn't have enough time with people referred to her by the NHS, but that she has too much time with her private clients who want to prolong therapy as an excuse to not change. She gets on with her parents and has an older brother. She thought she wanted children until she became an aunt. She finds males and females attractive, but has found women too needy for a steady relationship, then laughs and says that men are equally demanding. She is proficient in French and listens to French podcasts between clients. She is passionate about Welsh and thinks it should return to being the main language in England. She doesn't believe in God but loves churches. She doesn't like keeping goldfish but felt she had to rescue them, and her anxiety dreams are not about missing exams but about the fish tank exploding and her fish flopping around the carpet, drowning in air. She would like to have studied History but couldn't see a career in it.

"You could still study it. There must be distance learning programs."

She makes a face. "Where would I study quietly? Marty practises guitar whenever I even open a book."

After breakfast, she wants to show me her flat, which confuses me, but I pick up my rucksack and we get a train to Wandsworth.

We are standing beneath a smart block of flats with a park nearby and the Battersea skyline ahead. She points.

"That one. On the third floor."

"Why do you have two flats?"

"Marty and I are renting the one in Earlsfield. This one's mine, but I'm renting it out to a couple, and Marty has a house in Wapping, which he rents out to some rich banker. It was just meant to be for a year while we figured out if we can live together, but I suppose we never got round to changing anything."

And now she wants to see where I live, but I've lost track of where we are.

"Is Wimbledon any good?" she asks.

"Yes, we could get a bus from there."

I follow her to East Putney station and we chug along, looking into people's gardens from up on high.

"You didn't tell me your anxiety dream," she says. "Even you must occasionally have a nightmare."

"Even me?" I think hard. There is the permanent feeling of something wrong – though not something I felt in Taiwan. It's just the common feeling of unease – the Buddhist *dukka* which westerners translate as 'suffering', but which really means a chariot with a wonky wheel, jarring the rider. I feel constantly jarred.

"Do you want me to repeat the question, or are you still thinking about it? Recurring nightmares?"

"It's not really a nightmare, because I'm awake. If I'm feeling out of sorts when I go to bed, when I turn the light out, there's a woman in the room tearing tissues."

"Tearing tissues?"

"That's what it sounds like. And sometimes she says 'Thank God' over and over again."

"And have you always had this . . . experience?"

"No. Only when I came back to this country a year or so ago. I really don't belong here at all." I smile as I say it, but her reaction is to pat my knee as if I need comforting. Which I don't.

When we get off at Wimbledon, I decide that Karen might as well have the full Rigby backstory.

"I'll show you where I grew up – in the conventional sense. There's two houses."

We walk down the Broadway and I start to tell her about my wretched (and failed) plan to get my father round for dinner on Friday. I lose track halfway through, when I realise that if I'm not careful she will know that the family meal was really about me practising my Chinese cooking, and so I finish off rather abruptly with a one-liner about how my father led me to our old house and scarpered.

Her pace slows, and when I turn back to check on her, she is looking appalled.

"What?"

"What do you mean – what? There was so much in that, I don't even know where to start asking questions. So your mother and sister think he's dead, and you were going to just have him show up at the house, except that he took you to a house that you don't remember living in?"

"Well – I remember it now."

She does her forehead-raising gesture, but this time, without the smile. When we get to the house, I point out the green garage door I drove into, the upstairs bedroom on the right, which was my parents' room and the one on the left – which was where Urs slept.

"So your room was at the back?"

"Yes, and there was a study, which my mother had turned into a bit of a shrine, and there was a funny little room downstairs behind the garage where my father played his records."

"Records?"

"Vinyl. It was all pretty scratched and old. Seventies stuff."

"Who was the shrine to?"

"Mary."

"You had another sister?"

"As in the mother of Jesus, you heathen."

She laughs. "Oh right. I was completely on the wrong track."

"Can I help you?"

The front door has opened, but not fully. A middle-aged woman stands side-on in the half-open space, holding on to the door as if anticipating that Karen and I will sprint across the drive and force entry with our shoulders.

"Sorry for loitering," Karen calls out, cheerfully. "My friend was just showing me where she used to live."

The woman takes some keys and comes out, closing the door behind her. She seems quite unrelaxed.

"Really? You were one of the Rigbys? I don't remember seeing you."

"No, I was abroad when my parents moved house."

"They stayed local, didn't they? Where did they go to?"

My mind is blank. I cannot remember the street name of the 'new' house. I was there just a few days ago, but no street leaps to mind. "Yes, they stayed in Wimbledon," I say, but I can see suspicion in her face. I am failing a test.

"We'd better get on," says Karen softly and lays a hand on my arm.

But the woman has locked eyes with me. "How did you find the back garden?"

Oh fuck – what does she mean by this? It must be some sort of trick question, because the answer is surely in the question. Maybe it's something to do with Dad's room.

"All the windows at the back of the house look out on the garden, apart from the funny little room behind the garage."

"Actually, I meant in terms of gardening. How did you find the garden?"

"I wasn't into gardening, I'm afraid."

I have failed the test. The woman is turning away. The garden was a bloody garden. My mother planted flowers, helped by a young Urs, and my father did the weeding. God Bless Bindweed. Karen is gently pulling me away.

"Have you managed to sort out the bindweed?" I call out.

I have said the shibboleth. The woman turns back, this time with a bit of a smile on her face. "Hateful stuff. We had to put gravel over it in the end."

"Ah, sorry."

She laughs. "Not your fault, I'm sure. And I've got to ask, did your family bury several dinner services out there?"

We did have a dinner service. I remember my mother's dismay unwrapping it one Christmas – from her parents of course – and saying 'oh no, this must have cost a fortune'. I can't imagine her burying it in the garden, though.

"I mean, I've never come across so many pieces of plates."

"Oh, I see. No, those was there before. I think you find pieces of china in every old garden in every country. I don't know why."

"Bone china has bone ash," says Karen. "The phosphates were good for the soil."

The woman laughs. "The bindweed certainly thrived on it." She pauses to have a think then nods towards the garage. "Actually, we have something of yours, I think, or your parents'. I can't say what state they're in, but it seemed a shame to throw them away."

She unlocks the garage, which – like every typical English garage – contains everything but the car. "Come in, come in."

Karen and I follow her, sidling in between stacked

furniture, lawnmowers and tins of paint with wonky lids and legs of magnolia down the sides.

"They're a bit heavy, so if you don't want them I can just throw them away."

She picks up a plastic bag and grimaces when passing it to me. "And another." Karen holds out a hand, which drops beneath the weight of a second bag. I look inside.

"My Dad's old records. Wow. I wonder why he left them."

The woman straightens up and we sidle out of the garage and into the light.

"He probably did mean to take them. How is he, by the way? He didn't seem very . . . very *well* either time we came to see the house."

"He's not too bad, thanks."

"He's still got a record player?"

"I think so. Probably in the new garage, though."

We all laugh – I guess at our shared understanding of garages – and say goodbyes.

"That was weird," says Karen, once we are well away from the house. "To begin with, I thought she was going to set the dogs on us."

"Sorry. Welcome to my world." I stop and look around. We are in one of those areas you get in London's outer tube zones: urban disguised as suburban with a hint of the rural past just beyond view. I don't know where we are.

"Do we need a compass?" asks Karen, carefully placing her plastic bag on the kerb; her fingers have gone white.

"Yes. We need an ancient Chinese compass that points south."

"What? All compasses point north, don't they?"

I pretend to tut. "Typical Northern and Western-centric

arrogance. The ancient compass used lodestone, which always points south. And which is where we need to go now."

"Lodestone? Put the bag down for a second. I can see there's no blood in your fingers. Are we going to your home?"

There is a strange noise in my ears. We've just been to my house. Where are we going now? I have such a clear image of my home, high off the ground, with a water purifier in the kitchen and the coolest stone tiles that are so inviting in the humid heat that I sometimes just lie on them – but I have Dad's old records with me, which is the sort of extraneous clutter that would wreck my apartment. I can't be taking them to Dad because he doesn't live in a house now and therefore he has no record player.

"Julie – come back, come back."

"I haven't gone anywhere."

"Yes you have. You've gone quiet and you're ignoring everything I say."

"Oh. Sorry. To be honest, I've forgotten where we're going."

"You were going to show me another house. You said we needed to go south."

I have no idea how to get to Mum's house from here. I know it's nearby, but I just can't connect it to here. I don't want to go there, anyway.

"Do you mind if we skip that house and just go back to where I live now?"

"Fine by me. Do you remember where you live now?"

South. Of course. The Candles' house is south. I start walking.

"Bag!"

I retrieve the bag of records and remember to turn left at

the bottom towards South Wimbledon tube rather than right towards the Candles.

"It's just one stop."

We get on the tube and Karen takes out a couple of singles from the plastic bag and looks at them.

"Wow – I can't remember the last time I saw a real record." She smiles as she looks through them, then frowns. "Don't know this lot. Have you heard of Wishbone Ash?"

"No Easy Road?"

"Well done. How about Python Lee Jackson?"

"In a Broken Dream?"

She looks at the label and her eyebrows rise. "Yes. I guess this stuff is familiar to you."

Along with Seasons In the Sun, that is one song I never want to hear again. Rod Stewart sounding like he is on the point of cutting his own throat with a broken wine glass. I'm relieved when she looks at me and puts them back in the bag, and the Colliers Wood roundel flashes past the windows and eventually stabilises. We get off.

"It's just a ten-minute walk," I tell her.

When we turn into my road, Karen is telling me how she failed her first driving test in Wales by stopping the car (after carefully checking her mirror and pulling in) to free up a plastic bag that had blown onto the windscreen – and by some freak chance – getting stuck on a wiper.

"What's wrong with that?"

"I didn't put the handbrake on. And we were on a bit of an incline, so I had to watch the car and the driving instructor getting smaller and smaller. I caught up with them in the end, but I was too out of breath to argue when he said I'd failed."

"He sounds a bit pedantic. I drove into the garage once."

"Well, what was wrong with that?"

"It wasn't open."

"That's the house we saw earlier? There was a bit on the left-hand side which had no paint."

"You're observant."

She laughs. "Actually, you told me about the garage when we were outside the house."

We are facing a fence and some railway tracks.

"Over the bridge?" she asks.

I am puzzled. The bridge isn't normally here, though there is one at the end of my road. "Walked too far, sorry." We walk back up the street. Number twelve."

"Now I know what's wrong with you."

I will ask her what she means by that in a minute, but not until we are in the house. We are at my front door and Urs's car is outside.

"Right. Urs is in."

"Urs?"

"Ursula – my sister."

Karen grabs my right wrist. "Good – you've got it on."

"She can be a little odd. And best not call me Julie in front of her."

"OK." She taps her head. "Must call Julie Win. Must call Julie Win." Then grins. "Ready."

Chapter Eighteen

ALMOST AS SOON as I open the door, Urs is filling
the hall with hysteria. "No bloody call. No bloody . . ."
She stops when she sees Karen. "Oh. Did you bring her back?"

I can see that Karen has no idea how to answer this, and
I'm not surprised. "Urs, this is Karen. She can't have brought
me back because she doesn't live here. I've brought her back."

"I'm not always sure *you* live here," says Urs, then she and
Karen stand in the hallway looking at each other.

Karen sticks out a hand, which Urs eventually shakes
before turning back to me.

"Glad to see you're OK. Why don't you make some tea?"

I look at Karen, who grins, I guess at the sight of me being
bossed around. "Jasmine tea, please."

"We do have normal tea as well," says Urs.

"Jasmine is fine."

"Will do," I say, and quickly take the bag of records off
Karen before she follows Urs into the front room. I run upstairs. In my bedroom, I slide the two bags as far as possible
under the bed, then go down to the kitchen, where I make two
jasmine teas plus 'a normal one' for Urs. When I take in the
mugs, I hover in the doorway because I have just heard Urs
say, "You know what's wrong with her, do you?"

I remember Karen saying that she knew what was wrong
with me as we were coming into the house, so I'm curious
to hear how she will answer this now. She answers, "There's

nothing wrong with her, she's just different", and Urs's grunt of disagreement is just tailing off as I round the corner and see them both start in their respective seats. Karen pushes coasters into easy reach before Urs has had a chance to do her normal desperate tombola performance, and I sense that a little bout of martyrdom has been thwarted.

"Thanks," says Karen. "You've quite got me into this jasmine tea business."

She moves along the sofa so that I can sit next to her, whilst Urs sits marooned in the armchair.

"So how did you two meet? Exactly?"

Karen and I look at each other.

"I live near your old history teacher, don't I? I think you had just visited him," says Karen.

"Mr Fallowfield? I might have guessed that he would be involved somehow."

I ignore that pointless comment, and look at Karen. "Yes, I'd been to see Fred and then I stopped to ask you for directions."

"That's it?" asks Urs, after a pause. "That's really how you met? I can't remember the last time I made friends with someone who gave me directions."

"We both like History," says Karen, with a smile. "And languages." I don't know how she knows not to mention Marty, but she just seems to know instinctively what to say and what to leave out.

"And are you also a Chairman Mao fan?"

"What?" says Karen, frowning. "No, of course not - one of the most evil men to set foot on the planet."

I don't know why I start talking about it, but I say that when Chairman Mao died, there began one of the biggest non-refugee domestic migrations of all time. Everyone had to travel to their home towns for the funeral. A teacher of mine described being on a train so packed that when anyone had to use the toilet they had to be 'crowd-surfed' to the cubicle and crowd-surfed back to their original position.

"Well – you two seem to have different opinions," says Urs. "If Karen thinks he's evil and you think he's wonderful."

"Do you?" says Karen, looking at me with a hint of a frown.

"No, I don't." I look at Urs. "Where do you get these ideas from?"

She scowls at me. "I thought you did. All things oriental are wonderful."

"No. I'm not that keen on genocidal tyrants. Mao is up there with Stalin and Hitler."

"And Pol Pot," adds Karen. "Though in terms of dead people . . ." – she frowns – "I'll have to look it up. I think Mao gets the gold medal."

"He would," I say. "More people died as a result of Mao's activities than Stalin's and Hitler's combined."

Karen gives me her forehead-raising smile. "I won't bother to look it up, then."

I've almost finished my tea and want to take Karen upstairs to see my room, but Urs seems to have locked on to her.

"If Chairman Mao was such a bad man, why do the Chinese revere him?"

"We can't assume they all do."

"Yes they do. All those pictures of him everywhere. Tiananmen Square or wherever it is."

"But that doesn't mean anything," says Karen. "That's like saying the Tibetans don't revere the Dalai Lama because they don't put up pictures of him."

"Maybe they don't."

"Or maybe they do but are thrown into prison for eight years if they're caught with a photograph."

"So you're into human rights, then?" asks Urs, making it sound like a highly dodgy hobby.

"Yes I am, actually. Aren't you?"

I suppose it's nice that they're getting on – sort of – but I'm bored. I spot my tobacco and lighter on the high shelf – placed on top of an old speaker of Dad's. (I suspect Urs thinks that putting my smoking paraphernalia above my eyeline means I will forget to smoke.) I get up and go out into the yard and make a rollie.

Why do we have two big old speakers on the wall? They came with Dad's old CD player which replaced the record player (the fate of which I can't recall), but I can't remember the last time we played any of the CDs. There's a pile of them on a shelf in there. Urs once put on a Best of Bowie one, which started with 'The Man who Sold the World', but she turned it off pretty quickly, which I get. If you listen to things that you heard when you were young, you start to vibrate at the same energy levels you had back then, and your body can no longer cope with them. I wonder what would happen to Dad if I gave him an iPod with his old music on. That could be the most powerful way of bringing him back; he would literally have to resonate with his former self.

What about 'In a Broken Dream'? That would be as bad as it gets.

It's a terrible idea: like pushing someone off a cliff to remind them that they suffered from vertigo.

I go back in and take my place beside Karen. They still seem to be going on about Mao.

"You can hardly assume that," Karen is saying. "All you can say is that they mythologised him. Every country likes to mythologise its leaders. It becomes part of the fabric of the country's identity. Look at Putin. Some Russians really believe that animals recognise he has special powers."

"I don't see how that works. You can't say someone has achieved something if they haven't done it. They'd get caught out."

Karen looks at me. "We're talking about how leaders get mythologised by having achievements attributed to them."

"Oh, right," I say. "In that case, I don't think mythologising is so much about overstating people's achievements so much as leaving out the information that would counter the myth."

Urs frowns. "Like who?"

"Chairman Mao, for one. How about Edward Jenner? He pioneered the smallpox vaccine. Was he a good man?"

"Obviously."

"He never sought money for it and ended up financially disadvantaged. Still a good man?"

"Definitely."

"He also deliberately infected his gardener's small son with cowpox and then repeatedly tried to infect him with smallpox to prove the theory that one prevented the other."

"With his father's consent?" asks Karen.

"Possibly not. He was just a poor labourer without a bean."

"Oh," says Urs.

"The question now is do both of you feel like your own identity has been compromised through the puncturing of a myth?"

Karen smiles. "Yes. A little."

"Truth is a function of time."

Karen frowns. "I suppose it is. A function of time if you mean that we learn more information over time. Is that your own saying?"

"No. It comes from *Zen and the Art of Motorcycle Maintenance*."

"Oh God," says Urs, darkly. "That bloody book."

"I should read that," says Karen. "It's hard enough keeping up with you."

Urs waves a dismissive hand, as if swatting away an inconvenient fly. "So how is Fallowfield and the crazy Mr Gadd?" She looks at Karen. "You've heard this daft story, I take it, Karen? Hauntings and ancestor worship and God knows what else."

Karen gives her best forehead-raising smile. "Yes. Fascinating."

"And you're not working today?"

Karen smiles ever more sweetly. "No. How about you? I'm told you're a bookkeeper."

"Yes, I am. My work is flexible."

I turn to Karen. "Do you want to see my office?"

"Sure. Nice to meet you, Urs." Karen gives Urs another smile.

"Likewise," says Urs, expressionless. "Win – don't leave the mugs here."

Karen takes the mugs into the kitchen then follows me to my bedroom, where she gives a theatrical sigh and lies on the bed, whilst I swivel the chair around to look at her.

"Sorry. She can be a bit heavy, can't she?"

Karen laughs, then props herself up to look at me. "I didn't know you smoked."

"Not very much. I was bored, to be honest. I mean it's

good that you two were talking together and it didn't involve me."

"Oh Julie. That was *all* about you." She lies back. "Urs doesn't trust me. Everyone normally trusts me." She makes a face. "Almost everyone."

"I wouldn't take it personally. She doesn't trust anyone I meet now."

"I wonder why she's so protective."

"She's just paranoid that I'll be led astray and will run off to the Orient. Hang on – I'll show you how her mind works." I open the rucksack and rootle around for the condoms.

"Why would someone . . . oh never mind. So you can only have friends from the past?"

Urs certainly seemed happy at the thought of me 'catching up' with Diana. I nod.

Karen is frowning. "So Marty would be OK, if she knew he was an old school friend?"

"Oh no. She's remembers Marty as being bad news. Don't know why."

"Marty tells me that you two were madly in love but your father broke it up."

"He said that? I don't remember it quite the same way."

"Of course he was quick to add that I was the only one for him now."

"Good." Why do I have my hand in my rucksack? My phone starts singing, so I pull it out.

"Talk of the devil." I don't answer it, but hold it until it stops ringing.

"What? That's Marty?"

"Yes. I don't know why – he keeps ringing me."

"Does he? Has he left a message?"

I look at it again. "Not this time. He left a message this morning, or maybe it was last night."

"Saying what?"

"Don't know. I haven't listened to it."

She sits up, looking annoyed. "That is definitely breaking the rules. Marty and I have been through this. We can Facebook you because we can see what each other has written, but he said that phone calls were out, and I agreed." She motions for the phone. "Can I listen to the message?"

"Sure." I play it and hand the phone to her.

She winces. "Yes, must have been last night. He's sounds completely pissed." She listens some more and then shakes her head and hands the phone back to me. "I really don't know what to make of that."

"Make of what?"

"He thinks you need to talk. He says he knows that when we bumped into you on Monday that it wasn't a coincidence."

"Oh."

"Is that true? Or would you rather not tell me why you were in Garratt Lane that night?"

I think back. Why was I there? It was the night before I cooked Karen the meal. Ah yes.

"I wanted to find out how long it took to walk from your flat to the Chinese shop and back. And I wanted to make sure I could find it."

"Why?"

I can't think of anything else to add. After a while she gets up and wraps her arms around me.

"Never mind. Sorry I put you on the spot. You answered the question fine."

I wonder what time it is and glance at the computer. I

haven't turned it on. Then I notice my watch. "Half-past one. What do you want to do with the rest of your day off?"

"I want to see the Celts exhibition at the British Museum. That suit you?"

"Sounds good."

"But I'm starving. Aren't you?"

We go downstairs and I make a super-quick meal of vegetables and noodles. I did offer to feed Urs, but she shook her head and silently moved her books and papers from the kitchen table to the front room.

"Better tell her where you're going," says Karen, so we go into the front room and tell Urs that we're off to the British Museum.

"To see the exhibition about the Celts," says Karen.

"Oh." Urs looks up at Karen. "Congratulations on persuading Win to see something that isn't Chinese." To me she says, "I don't suppose you've found my Oyster card?"

"Keep mine," I say. "I've bought another."

At the doorway, Karen strokes the yellow-gold banner that hangs by the door. "Beautiful. Is this you again? What does it say?"

"Do you want to guess?"

"Mmm. It could be something inspiring. Something like 'Be mindful in your every endeavour' or 'Every step takes me closer to God'". She looks at me. "No. Thought not. Will you tell me?"

"Nope. You'll have to learn Chinese."

When I shut the front door behind us and start to lock it, she stops me. "Do you normally lock your sister in the house?"

"Oh. Habit."

We get the Northern line up to Tottenham Court Road

and walk to the museum from there. Karen seems to know the way, though – out of the blue – she says, "Promise me you won't do that again? I mean trying to spring your father on your family", and I say, "OK, sorry", and wonder where her mind is if not on the stately Bloomsbury houses that watch over the street. Once at the exhibition, she seems absorbed whenever I remember to look at her. We stare at gold torcs and feasting bowls and I try to hop into the heads of the wearers and feasters.

"I've finally met my match," says Karen, once we've sat down for peppermint tea (in my case) and Welsh Breakfast tea (which I can't believe I actually ordered – parrot-fashion – at the counter before seeing Karen laugh and put her head in her hands).

"How so?"

"You spend even longer than me looking at things. You know – we were in there for two hours?"

"But looking at them is all we have, isn't it? Well, I suppose you can say whether something is made of gold or silver, and roughly when it was made, but that's it. You can't say it's something Celtic. That's just meaningless."

"Yes. Modern romanticism. I agree."

"It's worse than that, isn't it? If you have to invent a past to invent the present."

"Not sure you can invent the present," says Karen. "You can invent the past to try and explain the present. And you can invent a future to try and make the present significant. Like the Third Reich. It was never realised – thankfully – but it was an invented future."

I try and think about this and there is something about Fred that is nibbling at my mind – an invented Chinese past to explain the present, or to explain Gadd's apparent presence, but the roaring in my head has started again. I would like to give into it and see where it takes me, but not in a busy café in a busy museum.

"What happened there?" she asks.

"Nothing. I'm just thinking too much. What's the day today?"

"Well yesterday was Tuesday and you cooked a meal for me."

"So today is Wednesday and tomorrow is Thursday."

She puts down her cup. "Yes. Speaking of which – I must get back before Marty returns with a pantomime hangover."

"I guess I'll be seeing him tomorrow night. Did today happen?"

"What? Oh – I see what you mean." She seems to spend a while in thought. "No, I'm afraid today didn't happen. Which is annoying, because I can rearrange my schedules to have every Wednesday off, if you're free to do something in the day. But it would be wrong of me to ask you to keep secrets."

"Actually, I'm very good at keeping secrets. I've got no-one to tell them to."

"But it would still be wrong of me to ask."

"And what did you mean when you said you knew what was wrong with me?"

"I shouldn't have said that. There's nothing wrong with you, Julie."

"Urs thinks there's plenty wrong with me."

"Hmm."

"What's wrong with me? Tell me or say goodbye to Tuesdays."

"Right – you're serious." She sits back and looks at me. "OK. Here it is: you have no autopilot. I don't know if you were born like that, or had a bang on the head, or even a stroke, or are just too involved in higher thoughts – but you have no autopilot."

I am pondering this autopilot theme on the tube after we've said Goodbye at Tottenham Court Road. I'm not sure what she means, because as far as I can tell autopilot is a negative thing, so lacking it should be positive. Doing things on autopilot means acting without mindfulness. Autopilot is something pilots switch on which means they only engage with flying for a few minutes on a long-distance flight so that they react too slowly when the autopilot hits an unexpected set of circumstances and says the autopilot equivalent of "could do with a bit of help here if you don't mind". Autopilot means switching off.

There is a strange whirring sound and the feel of a breeze on my face. The whirring sound reminds me of a time when I was walking back home from the Candles' house one evening and got chased by a stag beetle, flying at a crazy angle and silhouetted against the evening sky. I remember it followed me until I hit Merton Road.

I seem to be outside the Candles' house now. There is no stag beetle, and how could there be? It is April and the stag beetles have not yet quite awoken. The whirring sound comes from the wind filling a plastic bag in a near leafless diseased tree – as though the tree had hoisted its own sail in an attempt to leave London behind.

Clearly I sailed past my tube stop. Unmindful to an extreme.

I look up at the Candles' house, strangely inviting, like an Advent calendar. Why do I keep coming back here? Was this really home from home?

It seems silly to thank a plastic bag for shaking me out of my reverie. So instead I extend feelings of *metta* towards the tree and towards any creatures living within its diseased body. And I intend to walk home mindfully, but soon I am wondering if *metta* is the Pali or Sanskrit word for Loving Kindness, and remember that it is Pali (as are most of the Buddhist words I know) and then I wonder if old Fred, whose intellectual capacity was such that he learnt Sanskrit in his fifties, would know the Sanskrit equivalent of *metta*. And once again I am at the end of a road facing the fence-separated railway line and a bridge that will lead me further away from where I live.

"You're very quiet," says Urs, when she comes into the kitchen.

This strikes me as an odd thing to say, because until she came into the kitchen, there would have been no-one to talk to. Surely it would have been more worrying if I hadn't been quiet. "And you're back a bit later than I expected."

"I was miles away." Which I realise answers both of her statements. In fact I was pondering why I have a very strong autopilot when it comes to getting me to the Candles' house, and a really rubbish autopilot when it comes to getting back here.

"How was the exhibition?"

I am confused: was it yesterday or today we went? I have got to sort out this Time problem. I grab a pen and scribble the character for Time. She is still watching me. She has a book in one hand, so I guess she was reading next door.

"It was a good exhibition."

"Why was it good?"

"It was as much about an invented past as the actual exhibits."

She puts her book on the table and sits down. "I'm not sure what I think of that Karen woman."

"She's not that Karen woman – she's a friend. She said you didn't trust her."

"Did she? Very clever of her."

"What do you mean?"

Urs looks down. "She certainly finds you interesting."

"Well, that's good isn't it?"

"I'm not sure it is good, Win."

"Why not good?"

"She's a therapist. And she finds you interesting."

"What's wrong with that? I'm a translator and I find her interesting."

"Never mind. I'm just saying be careful what you share with her."

"Right." I am tempted to goad Urs by saying that I already share a bed with Karen on Tuesday nights, but if I do that, apart from crossing Urs's morality threshold, she might ask why just on Tuesdays and then I'll have to say that I share a bed with Marty on Thursday evenings as Karen and Marty are an item, and it's really not worth the thrill of shocking her.

I must be in bed before half-eleven. I get up and head for the door. But I've been told off before for not saying Goodnight first, so I hunt around for something to close the day with. She does like reading.

"What's the book?"

She tilts the book so that I can see the cover. "Take Six Girls. It's about the . . ."

"Mitford sisters. I know. OK, goodnight."

"You just go through the motions, don't you, Win?"

"Sorry?"

"Never mind. Goodnight." She sighs and opens her book.

Chapter Nineteen

THERE IS THE problem of an invented past and there is the problem of people needing to give their present lives some legitimacy through a link to the past – invented or real.

I suppose it's co-incidence that the two most caustic books about the American funeral trade involved the Mitford sisters. Evelyn Waugh dedicated his satire (The Loved one) to Nancy Mitford, but it was her sister, Jessica Mitford, who completely blew the lid off the industry. Married to a union activist (Bob Treuhaft), it was his despair at seeing widows of deceased union members fleeced by funeral companies which led her to research the practices of the American funeral industry. Their book (The American Way of Death) was a pretty shocking exposé of the means funeral companies would use to encourage the grieving families to splash out on their loved one's departure: they created a bogus 'traditional' American funeral, involving expensive products and techniques such as embalming, for which there was neither tradition nor necessity, unless a body had to be transported for long distances. You could call it an invented past.

The UK funeral company websites that I've looked at don't appear to push sham traditions, but they all stress that they are small family firms with continuity of service. The images on the websites often have sepia-tinted photographs of the shop front. Of course there is a view that the UK's industrial revolution spawned such a rapid change from a rural landscape to dark, smoke-belching satanic mills that the British psyche will never catch up with itself, but be forever in mourning for a lost pastoral paradise.

I notice that the Taiwanese websites, on the other hand, don't stress tradition for the simple reason - I think - that they have no need to: despite occupation by the Japanese, there has been no cultural break with the past to create a mindset that is forever harking back to bygone times. If that were the case, then I would expect to find that China - with the most fractured link to its past - would be the one most desperately laying emphasis on traditions, but I have found no evidence of this. Fred is only convinced I will because he wishes it to be so.

It could be that the Chinese really do accept change; if so, they should be stuck on pedestals for the world to admire.

"OK, how about this one? Bet you'll remember this."

Marty is strumming away on an electro-acoustic guitar in which the electrical bits inside have apparently come loose so that there's a rattle every time he swings the neck, which he has stopped doing after his first wine glass went flying. White wine, fortunately. He is also singing. Judging by the chorus, the song is called 'Hear drums that Judas', though he is singing the name as 'Ju-dis'. I sip jasmine tea ("You've got Karen into buying this shit") and think about China.

If I find something that warrants the Chinese expedition I assume that Maddy will be paying my fare, so I could get a relatively cheap flight onto Taiwan afterwards. The 'Pedant English School' is based in the Jiufen area, which isn't so far from Taipei. It isn't an area that I know, but it sounds as if it has mountains and opportunities for hiking. Maybe my head will disappear again when I'm back on a mountain in Taiwan. In fact, I know it will.

And if I find that funerals in China are perfunctory 'burn them and chuck away the ashes' affairs, would we still try to discover some ceremonial gesture to satisfy Fred's need to demonstrate filial piety? I can't see Maddy shelling out hundreds of pounds for us to pick up a handful of soil or whatever that just might come from the approximate area where Gadd's ashes may have been dumped.

"So – remember that one?"

The guitar is now mute and Marty is looking at me.

"It's certainly familiar. What was it called?"

"'Eardrums that You Dissed'. It is catchy, isn't it? I really think we could have got somewhere with that one."

"Actually the chorus sounds like Ballroom Blitz. The Sweet."

He frowns. "It can't do. I wrote the music and I've never heard of that. Are you sure?"

I dig my phone from my rucksack and search for the song. Marty looks bored throughout the rather camp build-up and disheartened when the Ballroom Blitz chorus starts.

"Bollocks."

"Sorry." I stop it and put the phone away.

"It's not plagiarism if I didn't hear the original."

"I think it is, legally."

"We were good, though – weren't we?"

"Who?"

"Gadd."

"Oh yeah. Not bad." I have no idea what I thought of them – probably not much. If we don't hurry up we are not going to fit in two sessions, or at least not before Karen comes back.

Marty gets up and leans his guitar in a corner but then settles back on the sofa and pats the place next to him.

"Come and sit over here."

I move next to him and he puts an arm around me. "What time does Karen come back?"

"Ten. Don't worry about her for now. I wanted to say something."

"OK."

"You know, you can ring me when I'm at work. I guessed you haven't rung back because you're worried that she'll see the calls on my phone, but it's fine – really. She never looks at my phone."

"Why?"

"I suppose she trusts me."

"No, I mean why would I want to ring you at work?"

"Well – because it's during the day. She's not around."

"OK." I still don't know why I would ring him at work, but time really is passing. I think we'll have to forget two shags and settle for one.

"Win, I feel like you're having to hold back on something. I mean that rubbish about being in the area to see Fallowfield. That wasn't true, was it?"

"Not entirely, no. But Fallowfield does live in the area."

He sighs. "That's not really the point, though, is it? I thought as much. Do you think we should talk about it?"

Questions. Questions. Everything he says seems to end with an expectation that I should plug the sentence with my own words. I am getting bored of this. "No, not now. I think we should go to bed."

"OK, fair enough."

He insists on giving me a massage before sex, which should be very welcome after my day hunched in front of the PC, but I keep having a vision of Karen coming in and I don't know how that scene would pan out. It would be untidy, if nothing else.

The sex lasts a long time – he seems much slower than usual, but it's nice enough. Afterwards, he seems in no rush to let me go, and I have to gently extricate myself. He sits up and watches me dress.

"It's not enough, is it?"

"No, that was nice. Once is fine. Quality not quantity."

He laughs, but he's not smiling.

Once out on the street, I head for Garratt Lane. I am tempted to keep walking to Skullbrook Road. I have the journey etched on my mind now, though it pays to stay mindful.

They kept saying China. Not a town in China, not even a province, but China. I want that official death notification letter. If there is nothing in the contents that say where Gadd was cremated then it doesn't matter what I find out, because we're not going to find any trace of Gadd, or the soil in which he was scattered – which is probably covered in concrete anyway by now – and I would have to say vaguely, "It was round here . . . ish", followed by, "thanks for the trip over here, but now I'm off", leaving Maddy with an unhappy Fred, haunted for the rest of his life.

I recognise the figure coming towards me and I think she recognises me. I try to hop into her head, but then all I see is a figure with a rucksack coming towards me.

"Julie." She gives me a quite a tight hug.

"Hi Karen. Do you think it's too late for me to go round to the Fallowfields now?"

She releases me. "What? Now? God, yes. Of course it's too late. Much too late."

She sighs and walks off without a goodbye or a backward glance.

"See you Tuesday," I call after her, but get no response. I will ring the Fallowfields when I'm waiting at the bus stop. I know I have a rule somewhere about the latest time to ring someone but I can't remember what the threshold is. I'm sure I'm OK at the moment. I need to ask Maddy for Gadd's death letter, and to check with her whether they really know where the ashes are or whether they have some bizarre notion that I will be able to discern their location through my non-existent connection with Gadd.

I am in bed by half-eleven, and am not sure if the image of Karen walking away from me with her head down is a memory or a half-dream. Though of course they might as well be the same thing.

The Chinese websites feature a variety of euphemisms for death, from 'leaving the world' to the optimistic 'reborn in paradise'. Part of this is owing to the natural abhorrence the Chinese have for repetition, so that asking Chinese students to translate into English a page of dialogue will result in a plethora of verbs (he stated, she asked, he opined, she questioned) and they seem horrified when told to replace the lot with 'he said' and 'she said'. But I also think that part of the variation reflects the belief that the deceased is undergoing change, in the sense of a journey rather than decomposition; even the word for coffin changes depending on whether it is empty or contains the deceased corpse, though the meaning of the latter hints more at containing the spirit than the remains. Career-wise, obviously corpses have more opportunities if they are Chinese than British. All our stiffs get is progression from 'John Smith has died' to 'the late John Smith', until Mr Smith fades from our memories, and he is no longer even late.

When I go downstairs to make breakfast I find Urs and my mother sitting at the kitchen table, my mother in uniform, which is always a worry, as it means she has made a special detour on her way to the hospital. Steam is coming out of my rice cooker, so at least her special detour wasn't to screw up my breakfast.

"Morning, how are you?"

"Good." I open the fridge and find spinach and cabbage, which I don't remember buying.

"Thanks, Urs."

"For what?"

"Shopping."

"Heavens. That's a first."

"No, you do quite a bit of the shopping." This gets no response, and when I turn to look at them they are just staring at each other. I've wondered sometimes if they have some sort of telepathic ability that I've not inherited. I suppose I was always closer to Dad. Sometimes I knew what he was feeling – though that was connected more with the music he was playing than any telepathic ability.

"You've got a letter," says Urs. "Not posted – put through the door."

I take the A5 envelope she is holding out and open it. There's a handwritten note, which says 'Winifred, please DO NOT ring after 10pm. It frightens Fred and wakes me up. We are early sleepers. Or at least I am. Fred wanders about the house for much of the night. Things are not too good. This is the note that Fred's mother received. It is the original. Please, please DO NOT lose it.' Inside there is an open envelope with a faded address in Surrey, typed on what appears to be a rudimentary typewriter. The stamp on the envelope bears the Queen's head, which confuses me because I expected the envelope to have been posted from China. I extract the folded paper from inside it. It states simply: 'LAWRENCE GADD DIED 1974 Heart arresting. Cremated Lululongping, Shanxi province 1974 May 19.' There is some faded text in traditional Chinese at the bottom of the paper – in red – which I can't read in this light. I'll examine it later. I throw away the A5 envelope that bears the single word 'Winifred' and put Maddy's note and the death notification into the Surrey envelope, and wonder where is the safest place to put it.

"What is it?" asks Mum.

"Nothing."

"So I can throw it away, then?" says Urs impatiently, tugging the envelope out of my hands.

"No, absolutely not. It belongs to the Fallowfields." I move to snatch it from her, but Urs takes a step backwards. She looks at the envelope, wide-eyed.

"Where the hell did this come from?"

"Maddy must have put it through the door. It's nothing."

"What is it?" says Mum again.

Urs shows her the envelope, and now my mother's eyes widen with something like horror. She takes the envelope from Urs and seems to tap it, shaking her head at Urs. She mouths a word at Urs. It looks like 'Go into sense'. Urs evidently makes more sense of it than I can, for she nods and takes the envelope back. "I'll stick it by your computer, Win."

"Thanks." I know she'll read it but what the hell. Anyway, it was something about the envelope itself that attracted attention. I try and remember 'Go into sense' for later. Maybe I can glean the meaning.

"I think I saw you yesterday," says Mum, once we're alone in the kitchen. "Sitting on a bus in Blackshaw Road."

"Could have been."

"So were you going somewhere nice?"

I must have been on my way to Marty's – or on the way back – depending what my mother's definition of yesterday is. "Just visiting someone."

"Urs tells me you've got a new friend. Was it her you were meeting?"

Her must be Karen. "No. Someone else. Though actually I did bump into her, yes." Spinach or cabbage? Cabbage for a change. I'll stir fry it with some sesame oil.

"She's a therapist?"

"Who? Karen? Yes, that's her job."

"Urs says you two met in the street."

Must get more sesame oil. I add it to the shopping list post-it.

"Urs says you went to an exhibition together."

God, this is really messing with my preparation. "Do you want some breakfast Mum?" Maybe she'll go and sit next door.

"No thanks, Win. And are you seeing Diana?"

Di-Di-Diana. Yes, there have been attempts to contact. As well as the recent missed phone call from Marty (he rang while I meditated), plus a slightly odd text from Karen ('I have to go to Wales today. Not sure when I'll be back but I won't see you Tuesday'), I seem to be getting daily Facebook pokes from Diana, which I think are meant to be a follow-up on an invitation to go around to her parents' on Saturday for Sunday afternoon tea, but with an insistence that we spend some time in her bedroom rather than downstairs with the 'old dears'.

"I said, have you got any plans to see Diana?"

"Might do. It's quite nice to see her parents."

"Win, that oil is looking awfully hot."

"Well, you keep asking me questions."

"Oh yes. Sorry. I'll get out of your way." She gets up and at last I have the kitchen to myself.

When I've finished my breakfast, Urs comes into the kitchen carrying her work. She makes a face and seems to be waving away something invisible. She used to do this when I smoked in the kitchen – before I was banished to the yard.

"What?"

"Cabbage. I think I prefer it when you cook spinach in the morning."

"OK."

"You will wash up, won't you?"

"Just about to."

I take my mug, bowl and chopsticks to the sink, but haven't even had a chance to turn on the hot water tap before there's an explosion of exasperation behind me, and I realise that Urs is watching me.

"Why does everything have to be a ritual with you? A bloody pointless ritual."

I can't be bothered to answer. An ignorant observer will call an activity performed by someone else a ritual because they don't understand the motivation behind it. The question is whether the person observed knows why they are doing what they are doing. If they know exactly why they are doing what they are doing and are confident that the result they will get is different from the result they would have got without the activity, then it's not a ritual any more than studying for an exam you want to pass is a ritual. At some point, salting aubergines before cooking was a sensible step in food preparation but when it was no longer necessary (because less salty aubergines were cultivated) it became a better-do-it-just-in-case activity (which is surely the same thing as superstition), and finally a pointless ritual.

Nothing I do is a ritual. I just can't be arsed to explain myself to Urs.

"So are you going to wash up or what?"

"Yes, in a minute." Actually I fancy a rollie now. I take my mobile from the table. I can imagine Marty ringing again and don't want Urs to pick it up, which I think she would do. I go into the front room, where I find that my mother is still here, talking on her mobile with one hand cradling her head. I retrieve my tobacco and papers from on top of the speaker and listen to her while I roll a fag. She's making strange sounds – not conversation – more a series of little sighs and 'oh dear's, and then, "Yes, that's exactly what happened to us. All that attention when they're in hospital, but as soon as they're back home you feel like you're on your own."

I let myself out through the French doors, close them behind me, and light up. Funny that I never think of just coming out here to sit. The garden's a postage stamp; Urs paid someone to give it a low-maintenance makeover, and the plants that border the paved area get by with no maintenance whatsoever. I am enjoying the space and the sound of traffic when my phone rings. Marty. Why does he keep calling me?

"Hi Marty."

"Win. Do you fancy meeting up this weekend?

"Why?"

"Karen's going to Wales for a few days, so I'm free. I thought we could meet and do something different."

"Why is she going to Wales? I mean, why so suddenly?"

There's a pause. "Well, it's bad news. Her father has been ill for a while. He died last night."

"Oh. That is bad news. Is she OK?"

"She's fine. I mean . . . upset obviously, but – you know – it's been a long time coming."

"What has?"

"His death. It's been touch and go for a long time."

I can't figure out what these words mean. Death has been a long time coming but it's been touch and go.

"Win? Still there?"

"So, are you not going to Wales?"

"I would, obviously, if it would help. But it's quite a close family. I would just get in the way."

"So she's going to the funeral?"

"Yes."

"But you're not going?" I can't quite get my head around this.

"No. As I say, I would love to go, well, I wouldn't love to go, obviously, but I would love to support her, but she doesn't need me there. Whereas I suspect you do."

I do what? Marty is speaking gobbledygook.

"Let's start again," he says.

"OK. Good idea."

"Would you like to spend the weekend with me?"

When is the weekend? I think I saw him last night, which makes today Friday. "You mean tomorrow?"

"Yes, we can go out for a meal or something."

"Will Karen mind?"

There's a funny splutter from his end of the phone. "She'll be in Wales, won't she?"

I don't know the answer to that question. 'M4' creeps into my mind. How do you get two whales in a mini?

"So what do you say Win?"

"I'm not sure."

"Come on. Silly us both spending the weekend alone. You're up for it?"

"No. Sorry, Marty, I've got a cracking headache." I end the call. It was a bit of a lie, but I feel like I could get a headache if I thought about it.

When I go back inside, Urs has joined Mum who is now off the phone. They both look very grave. Mum breaks off from whatever she was saying to look surprised to see me.

"What were you doing out there?"

"Just smoking."

She looks pained. "After breakfast?"

I don't know what to say to this. I would have thought that 99% of cigarettes smoked in the world would be smoked after breakfast and only 1% before breakfast. Instead, I say, "Who was on the phone?"

She sighs. "I don't suppose you remember Margaret? We used to know her from the church. She had a son a bit younger than you."

I shake my head.

"Never mind – it was a long time ago."

"So what's happened to him? The son."

"He got attacked by some yobs."

"I can't believe they got off," says Urs. "Or as good as."

302

"Is he dead?" I ask.

"As good as," says Urs again.

They look at each other and then they look at me.

"I'm going to do some work." I head upstairs.

I look at the envelope that Urs has left beside my PC. The type is faded black but with a tier of red ink – I assume something to do with an old style typewriter ribbon. Probably not unusual in its time. The address reads simply:

Mrs Lillian Gadd
The Old Vicarage
45 King's Road
Sutton
Surrey
SM1 1NY

The $10 stamp has a younger-looking Queen and is labelled Hong Kong. I can't see anything remarkable in a stamp that's over forty years old and posted from a (then) British colony. I don't even know if a philatelist's heart would skip a beat at the prospect of owning one. I suppose it's weird that a letter posted in China would have a Hong Kong stamp, but maybe that was how mail was routed from China to the UK in those days. It isn't something that Urs would have picked up on.

I write down 'Go into sense'. I mouth it a few times. Nothing comes. I give up.

I should be tackling more Chinese websites, but I feel unsettled. It isn't the envelope. I'm sure it isn't Gadd's death notice. I think it is something to do with Karen – and her dead Dad. I think I should ring her, but I don't know the right thing to say. I'm rather with the Chinese on this one in that I wouldn't naturally say I'm sorry, as it would sound as if I'd done him in myself. They would say something like, 'I hope you can restrain your grief and adapt smoothly to the change'. The sentiment seems sensible, but I've been told by Urs not to say it as it doesn't translate well. I write down 'say SORRY', and underline it. Then I ring Karen.

She answers after a few seconds.

"I'm sorry to hear about your father."

"Oh. Julie. Thank-you. How did you know?"

"Marty told me."

"Oh," she says again. I think she's surprised. "That's sweet of him."

"Is he with you?"

"No, he's at work."

"How are you getting to Wales?"

"I'll take a train from Paddington. I just need to sort out some things. I'm trying to rearrange clients. It's a bit frantic to be honest."

"Sorry."

"No, no, it's really nice that you've rung. My train's not until quarter past twelve, anyway."

"Where do you catch the train to?"

"Newport."

"OK. I'll leave you to it." I end the call and then wonder if I said Goodbye. I can't really ring her up again and say it.

I need to be a bit more mindful.

Chapter Twenty

IT LOOKS SO easy on the tube map. Northern line up to Elephant and Castle. Bakerloo line. Just keep going north. It's not that easy in the end, but I still arrive in Paddington with an hour and a quarter to spare. It takes me a while to figure out which train she must be catching. I spend a long time at one of the ticket machines before giving up and heading for the ticket office.

Eighty odd quid for a return. I had no idea train tickets were so expensive.

I have been standing at the ticket barriers for a long time before she appears. She looks harassed, though that may be owing to the heavy looking holdall she has slung over one shoulder. And of course because her father is dead. I think I sort of know what that feels like, even though Dad isn't dead. As good as. Karen is heading my way, yet still she doesn't recognise me, but I guess we only see what our brains expect to see, which evidently isn't me, because she only really sees me when I call her name. I can't read her face, though Surprise definitely figures.

"Julie? What are you doing here?"

"Seeing you."

"That's so . . ." I don't know what it's so, because she looks up at the platform screen and winces. "I've got to run, I'm afraid."

I put my ticket in the barrier and go through. She doesn't follow me but stands open-mouthed on the other side.

"You can't come with me, Julie."

"Sorry?" I don't understand why she's not following me.

"You can't come with me to Wales."

I look at the train indicator. There is a list of stations. I can't read it from here.

"I'm only going as far as the first station, then I'll come back."

She looks relieved and comes through the barrier. "Sorry, I didn't mean that I didn't want you to come to Wales, I just meant . . ." she trails off, which means she either meant it or doesn't know what she meant.

"It's OK. I wouldn't have just turned up in Wales. Obviously."

"No, of course not. I was being silly. It's just that I saw you dressed in black and panicked. Really silly, because you'd have known the funeral wasn't for a few days."

"You choose which carriage."

We walk through the train and she stops at an empty table in a sparsely populated area and squashes her holdall into the rack above. I do the same with my rucksack.

"What have you got in there? It looks heavy."

"No, nothing much."

We each take a window seat.

"This is so sweet of you."

"Oh. Not really. It just seemed appropriate."

She laughs. "I shall stick with sweet. To be fair, Marty did offer to come with me, but I know it will be a bit of a strain on my mother having non-family stay."

"You didn't mention that your father was ill. You asked me about my father."

"Because I was interested. And because – to be honest – my father has been ill for so long, I can hardly remember him not being ill." She closes her eyes for a few seconds. "The strange thing is – as soon as my mother rang me with the news – I started remembering him as he was."

"What did you remember?"

"Mainly just being in the garden with him. He designed a model railway that went all around it, through tunnels, around the pond, over the pond. It was completely mad, because it couldn't be left outside; it took us about two hours to put together, and almost as long to dismantle it, but there was a golden hour or so after it was built when we could have two trains going around, appearing from behind bushes, bemusing the cats. The aim was to try and get the trains to cross the bridge over the pond at the same time."

Her fingers have been playing with her ticket so constantly that it will be frayed by the time it gets inspected.

"Sounds like fun."

"It was more than fun, actually. When I look back, it almost seems mystical. I can't explain it." She almost tears her ticket, so I pluck it out of her hands and put it on the table.

"Was it just you and him, or your brother too?"

"No, Malcolm was never into it. Strange. You'd have thought he would have been more into trains than me, but he just didn't get it at all. If it wasn't on a screen he couldn't see the fun of it. And my mother thought we were mad to be out in the cold all that time. She couldn't get her head round why we would spend so much time setting up and dismantling just for a little bit of fun in the middle – as she put it. But half the fun was –" she frowns – "I want to say mantling it . . ."

"Assembling."

"Assembling it. It was partly the anticipation of the golden hour, and partly – I don't know really – just putting it together seemed fun enough."

The train is slowing down. She looks out and some of the joy seems to go out of her. "What a shame. Reading already."

I look up at the train indicator in the carriage, but the words are zipping off to the left too quickly. "I'll get off at the next one."

"Didcot?"

"Yes. Is that in England or Wales?"

I hadn't seen the forehead-raising gesture for a while, but she does it now. "Still very much on the English side. But I don't want you getting in trouble."

"Trouble?"

"For going beyond your ticket."

"I won't get into trouble." If she wants company all the way to Newport, I won't get into trouble. I wonder what I did with my ticket, and then realise that I must have put it on the table, where it became the object of some rather frenzied attention from Karen's hands. I can't see if it says 'Newport', but I cover it with my hand anyway. People are getting on and filling the seats near us, but no-one joins us at the table. The train departs.

"I can't get over how sweet this is of you."

"It's nothing. Where's your ticket, by the way?"

Her hand flies to a top pocket and squeezes it. "Got it." She looks down at the table, clearly confused. Mine is under my palm.

"And what happened to the trains? I mean the model ones."

"I grew out of it. I got busy. We did give it one last go

308

when I was about twelve, but the magic had gone out of it. Poor Dad."

"Why did he fill in the pond?"

"That was years later. I was at uni. It was really sad. Apparently he fell in one day – which he tried to make sound funny – but I suspect it wasn't. Mum said he got caught up in the duck weed. Not long after he went out and found the fish floating on the surface. Golden Orfe, ghost carp, all belly-up. It was so sudden that he even wondered if someone had poisoned the water, but then my mother admitted that she had tried to tidy up the pond, as she put it, by pulling up a lot of the weed. She was mortified."

"That killed the fish?"

"Yes, apart from a few goldfish. You should never stir up the muck underneath."

"This from a therapist?"

She laughs. "I hadn't thought of that. But now you mention it – no, I don't think you should. Everything settles over time for a reason. I would never trust anyone's motives for wanting to drag up the past."

"I couldn't agree more."

"OK, if we're going from duckweed to psychology I'll have a whinge about some of the people who come to see me. It's as if they're determined to find themselves in their past rather than deal with their problem in the present, which is too much like hard work for them."

"People can't find their identity in the present. And they certainly can't find it in the future – which is their death – so they're only left with their past, which they can invent to their heart's content."

She sits back. "Oh. You and your invented pasts."

"Then we end up with invented group pasts – a golden age back in the mists of time which we just need to rediscover. Or which will send us back a Messiah, or a newly-woken Merlin."

"Wow. How did we get to that from ponds?"

"OK, back to ponds. Filling it in sounds a bit extreme. Like your Dad was breaking with the past completely."

"I think it was practical rather than symbolic. They planned to move to a bungalow before his health got too bad, and they thought filling in the pond would make the house more saleable. In the end they never actually moved, so the garden became more like a memorial. Really sad. The frogs were coming back for years afterwards."

"And you took the goldfish?"

"It was crazy. I don't know why I did it. Malcolm had to drive me back to London via the back roads with me holding a bucket between my feet and pleading with him to drive more slowly." She winces and gets out her phone. "Marty will forget to feed them. The trouble is that when he remembers, he just tips the food in without measuring it. I gave up having pot plants because they all drowned." She taps into her phone whilst slowly mouthing the text: 'Marty. Please feed the fish a few flakes twice a day. No more'."

"Do you want me to go round there and check?"

She looks at me and pauses before answering. "I suppose you could do. In fact it's very nice of you to offer. I suspect he'd be delighted. He'll probably jump on you, in fact. I get the impression that there's something not resolved from when you were going out together before."

"Really? I don't think we were that serious. I'm sure it was no big deal." I don't have the slightest notion how I felt about him.

"Well, I think he's got a bit of a thing about you now. Actually, we both have."

I wonder whether to mention that he rings a lot. Or that he once turned up in the street. Or that he wanted me to stay this weekend. I'm not sure it would be helpful.

"Sorry – have I embarrassed you, Julie?"

"No, not at all. Is this Didcot already?" The train has stopped, but I can't see any station signs or anything but fields and hedges.

Karen leans forward and looks out. "Not yet. I'm afraid you're stuck with me for a bit longer."

"That's OK."

"What are the birds over there?" I follow where she's looking, but can only see small brown things flitting in the leaves. They're just sparrows," she says, then grimaces. "What a thing to say. Just sparrows. I don't know if they're tree sparrows or hedge sparrows or house sparrows."

"They don't have names for us."

She laughs. "They might do. How do you know?"

"They are what they are, whatever you call them. We kill something as soon as we give it a name."

The forehead-raising expression again. "Hmm. I guess Buddhists make lousy ornithologists. What I meant was I shouldn't be so dismissive. A sparrow should be as worthy as a sparrowhawk."

I would like to grab what she said and play with it for longer. Just got to remember it. Sparrow. Sparrow.

The train starts moving again.

"Anyway, I'm sure you're right," she says. "What's in a name? Speaking of which, you really don't mind being called Julie?"

"No, it's a great name. And it also means I have a ready-made

Chinese name for when I go back to Taiwan. It was impossible to find the Chinese equivalent of Winifred."

"What do you mean, going back to Taiwan?"

"That's the plan. The ideal thing would be if I can travel to China with the Fallowfields and then I'll go on to Taiwan and teach English."

"How long for?"

"Well, forever."

I've said something wrong. Her body language has changed. I repeat what I just said in my mind. Teaching English. Taiwan. I can't find anything wrong in what I said.

"But why? Why do you want to go back?"

"It's not a question of want, it's a question of need. It's where I feel at my best. I don't really feel at home here. It's hard to explain."

She looks like she's going to cry. I really don't know why. It can't be what I just said. I think I've mentioned Taiwan before, but I can't be sure. Actually I can't even remember if I've emailed the 'Pedant English School'. I need to check my Sent box when I get back. I look out of the window. There are still green fields but now houses as well. We are slowing down. I guess this is journey's end. Of course I could go on to the next station, but I sense I'm not being very useful to Karen. I try to think of something to resurrect her from whatever pit she's fallen into.

"What did you mean when you said it was mystical?"

She sniffs. "Sorry?"

"The golden hour. The trains in the garden. You said it was a mystical experience. What exactly did you mean?"

"Oh." She frowns. She thinks. At least she's stopped looking like she's going to cry. "I suppose I just meant that time stopped. The garden was the whole world and the golden hour could have been ten minutes or ten hours. I guess we were completely absorbed."

"Wow. A whole world in a grain of sand."

"Sorry?"

"What an amazing experience to have shared with your father."

The sudden screech of brakes brings us to a rocking halt. 'Didcot', say the platform signs. I lean across and kiss her, then get my rucksack from above.

"Will I see you again?" she asks.

"Well, yes." What a weird thing to say. Just as I am wondering what I did with my ticket, she picks it off the table, and holds it out for me, fortunately without looking at it. "You were right – you didn't get caught."

I take it from her hand, and say "obviously", before hurrying off the train. I hadn't researched this station at all but I stop a man who looks as if he's going to London (he is carrying a briefcase) and he tells me that London trains go from platforms two and five and the one that comes first gets to London later than the one that leaves afterwards. I ask him the question again and he just points to some steps. Then I remember that I should probably have waved to Karen before her train pulled out, but it's too late now.

Chapter Twenty-one

S HE IS RIGHT: sparrows might have names for us. In fact they might have different names for us, because they would see a human on a tractor as a different species from a human on a train or one walking with a dog across fields. We have some bird books in the front room, and because the drawings in one don't really help me distinguish between a tree sparrow and a house sparrow, I open another. Then it occurs to me that they would be easier to distinguish by song, so I head upstairs and google bird songs. They are quite different, and all familiar: even the shyer hedge sparrow's song rings a bell, though we aren't hedge-heavy in my neck of the woods.

I guess Karen will be at the family home now and hopefully has completely forgotten about me. I wonder if her mother is grief-stricken or relieved that it's finally over and she can move on. Maybe there will be more grief in the garden, with frogs chasing the ghosts of ponds.

I can hear Urs calling me above the shrilling of the dunnock. I kill the birdsong and check – yes, she's still calling me, and rather stridently.

"What?" I call back, when I'm halfway down the stairs.

"Come in here and bloody well tidy up."

In Here seems to be the front room, where Urs is leaning on the back of the armchair as though she needs support.

"What?"

"If you take a book off the shelf just bloody well put it away afterwards. They're not even on the bloody table – why does everything have to be on the floor?"

The carpet is indeed strewn with books; I must have pulled down a few to get to the two I wanted. She's right. Unmindful. Though I don't understand why it warrants the near-tears act.

"Sorry." I put them away and find her sitting at the kitchen table with her chin in her hands.

"Are you having a bad day?" I ask. She just looks at me. "I'll take that as a yes."

"It's a bit like noise pollution, Win. When you have a neighbour who plays music loudly all the time you become over-sensitive, so the smallest sound sets you off. Do you understand me?"

"I think so." Not really. We have neighbours whose music occasionally creeps through the Victorian walls, but they never play stuff beyond the early evening. I sense this is about me. I fetch a few post-it notes and place them in front of her.

"Write down everything I do that annoys you."

She puts her hands over her face and looks at me through spread fingers. "You really want to know?"

"I really want to know." I'm not sure I'm that interested, but Karen tells me a lot of people's frustration can be mitigated by simply recording their gripes and looking interested. And maybe it will be useful to see what she comes up with; it will save me trying to head-hop, which always needs a bloody big jump with Urs.

"Then I need something bigger than post-it notes."

I find an A4 notepad and put it in front of her and watch her, but she seems to freeze after picking up the pen.

"Bugger off. I can't do it while you're watching me."

I bugger off and spend some time looking at google maps, trying to locate Lululongping. I can't find it, and Shanxi province is huge. I try searching using Chinese characters: I try every phonetic permutation I can think of but with no hits. Presumably it is too small to register. I wonder how Fred's grandparents ended up there. Did they move voluntarily? Or were they forced out to the sticks as part of the communist revolution? They could have been sent away as part of a re-education programme for intellectuals. Maybe they had to work the land as punishment for Fred's grandfather being a teacher and therefore bourgeois.

When I come downstairs for a drink I find Urs at the table, rubbing her right wrist and staring at a single piece of A4 paper with a few lines of writing. She looks as though she has been crying.

"I'll do you some tea."

She nods and rubs her eyes. "You've forgotten already." This is said so quietly that I would have missed it if I hadn't been looking at her. I don't think she expects a response.

As soon as I've handed her a mug she mumbles something and goes into the front room. I sit down at the table with my jasmine tea and study the lines she has written. There's not much:

THINGS THAT ANNOY ME ABOUT WIN.
1. I wish you would see your actions through:
    a. Turn off taps you've turned on
    b. Close doors you've opened
    c. Put away books that you've taken out.
2. I wish you weren't so bloody pompous.
3. I wish you would stop going on about bloody Taiwan.

That's it? That cannot be it. I look in the bin. Sure enough, there are some sheets rolled into a scroll and pushed vertically down one corner of the bin; fortunately, I missed them when I chucked the teabags away. I pull out the scroll and go upstairs.

THINGS ABOUT WIN THAT ANNOY ME
1. She cannot see a single action through. She cannot turn off a tap she has turned on, close a door that she has opened, or put away anything that she has taken out.
2. Items under 1. would be easier to put up with if she wasn't so deluded and arrogant as to call herself 'mindful'.
3. She doesn't notice that every time she has a shower I have to mop the floor afterwards.
4. She puts dirty washing in the washing machine on top of just-washed clothes and adds wet clothes on top of dry clothes in the tumbler drier.
5. She is incapable of looking ahead. If she isn't cold now she won't take a coat, even though it will be cold later. Ditto rain and raincoat.

There's more, but I am really struggling with her handwriting. Urs's script seems demented at the best of times, but today she has surpassed herself: it resembles the web spewed out of a spider on caffeine. I turn to the last item on the last page:

32. Because of Win, we have had to lie to Nan.

Funny that she's used the third person rather than referring to me directly. So there are thirty-two things about me that annoy Urs, though I can hardly see what it is about me that makes them have to lie to Nan. Because of my existence they have to lie? Rather than because I (allegedly) don't turn taps off or shut doors?

Still, I hope it made Urs feel better. Which was why I suggested it. Maybe I should show the list to Karen so she can carry out a remote diagnosis of whatever is wrong with my sister. Still – I will make more of an effort to turn off taps, shut doors and carry coats, if that will earn me a peaceful life.

"I'm going out."

Urs is in my room. How does she do that? "Sorry?"

"I'm going out. Off to see a client."

Bugger. Where did I put her '32 things that annoy me list'? On top of the printer. Hopefully she won't notice. She comes over and then recoils.

"Oh God, not more of them."

I am merely felt-penning some characters onto cut-up strips of yellow-gold paper. Amateur calligraphy. Hardly a crisis.

"It relaxes me."

"Why do you need relaxation? You don't have any stress in your life."

"Karen thinks they're pretty."

"Well, go and live with her, then." She walks out.

I throw myself into shaping my characters, pour myself into every stroke; gradually Urs's negative energy is gone, and there is nothing between me and the writing. My phone is buzzing, I don't know how long it's been doing that. I finish the character I'm on before looking. Karen.

"You got back OK Julie?"

"Yes. No problem." No problem until I reached Paddington, but I got home in the end.

"I've made a decision."

There's a pause, so I just say "Yes?" and when no more is forthcoming, I add, "What decision?"

"I'm leaving Marty. I've had enough."

"Enough of what?"

"Enough of lots of things."

I don't know what to say to that, so after a while I just say "things?"

"Today really brought it home to me. I've been with him for several years. I've been with you – well, I've *known* you for several weeks. And yet you're the one who bothers to turn up at the station. He could have done that. I know he's not that busy at the moment – and he's got loads of holiday left."

I don't think I would have described this morning as a holiday. I make a couple of 'ah' and 'mmm' noises to show that I'm thinking about what she's said. I rather think this will affect my Tuesdays and Thursdays – and their Tuesdays and Thursdays, unless the opportunity of doing twice-weekly yoga or football is an adequate substitute for sex with me.

"He's just so needy. And the one time I need him, he's quite hands-off."

"He probably believed you when you said not to come to Wales."

She sighs. "True. I am being a little unfair. But he still could have done something spontaneous – just like you did."

Spontaneous. I must try that word on Urs next time she berates me for acting impulsively and not thinking through the consequences.

Karen is still talking about Marty, and still isn't convinced he'll feed the fish properly. I've lost the thread of the conversation, so I try and turn my attention back to her words. She is talking about leaving him, planning to time it so she can go back to her Wandsworth flat when the current tenants move out. I suppose this will affect a lot of things; in fact, the more I think about the implications, the more scattered my thoughts become. Thought-hogging is normally so unwelcome and yet now I'm trying to hold steady my thoughts before they wriggle away like slippery fish. What was the bigger picture? Karen's in Wales. She went back because her father had died. Her mother is still there. The funeral is not today but presumably they will be preparing for it and the house will be sombre. Karen may have to comfort her mother.

"How's your mother?"

Karen sighs. "You're right. I'm being a bit self-obsessed." (Did I say that? I'm sure I didn't say she was self-obsessed). "Mum's not too bad – thanks for asking. Sad, obviously. But you know I think she's quite relieved that he's finally gone. Both of us feel like we've done our grieving a long time ago."

"It's hard to grieve for someone who isn't dead."

"That's so true." She pauses. "Do you mean it's difficult to grieve for someone before they're dead or that it's hard to grieve for someone who's still alive but not as you remember them?"

"Um . . . both I guess. And how's your –" I know there's another one. Sister or brother. Brother. Like Marty but not Marty. "How is Malcolm?"

"He's on his way. He'll be OK. He wasn't as close to Dad as I was."

There is a pause, as decorum demands we should be talking about death matters, but I've run out of relatives to ask about.

"Julie, you haven't reacted at all to what I said."

"Which bit?"

"Me leaving Marty. After four years."

"I guess relationships are like people. We have a shelf life."

"Oh. Does that go for you and me as well?"

"Well, yes. Of course."

There is a strange noise down the phone, and I realise it is the sound of Karen crying when the line goes dead.

I sit there trying to remember what she said and what I said, and why what I said could have started her off crying. I feel like a translator faced with a piece of text that is untranslatable without the cultural background that lies beyond the text itself. The consequence was that I upset Karen, but I can't find anything in the conversation that led up to it.

I think back to all the times we've been together, but I don't think there's much background there. As far as Karen is concerned, I am wonderful. She has said several times that she likes my company. Loves it, I think she said once. She listens intently to everything I say, and asks questions if I don't say anything, just so she can hear me say something. She watches me intently, too, even if I'm only making us tea or doing housework.

It was something to do with my answer to her question, which I can't remember now, but was something to do with 'shelf life'. Maybe she thought I was saying that if they split up I wouldn't want to see her again. But I do. I like our Tuesdays. It shapes my week.

I text her back and say 'Sorry, I just meant that we're all going to die.'

After a few minutes, a text comes back. 'That's so you. Anyway, should be me saying sorry. I'm being a prat and putting too much pressure on you. You haven't said or done anything wrong. I would be in love anyway'.

What the hell does that mean? In love with who?

Surely not me. Oh fuck. No, no, no. I text back 'With me?'

Immediate response: 'Yes, with you – idiot. Who else?'

'Why?'

There is a long pause before I get a response. 'I think it was your coming to the station that clinched it.'

Talk about unintended consequences. I went to the station because – actually I don't know why I went. It just felt appropriate at the time. If I'd foreseen the consequence, I would never have gone. The road to hell indeed. Like all the roads to hell in China that I can think of, and all the unintended consequences. Under the one-birth policy families got rid of their daughters because they wanted their sons to carry on the line, but then the line stopped dead because the sons have no-one to marry.

I've just got a text from Karen saying 'Sorry, have I scared you?' and I have to run back through the text exchange to remind myself where we are. She thinks she's in love. I text back 'Don't know', which is not strictly true, as the answer is Yes, that has scared me.

I get propositioned all the time. Karen isn't the first to get fixated. The more I try to be dispassionate, the more fixated people get, as though through intimacy they can unravel me and find the secret to life. I don't understand it – but it's definitely a pattern. If only these people knew that if they unravelled me they would find nothing in the middle, then maybe they would spend their time on more useful quests – like finding the emptiness within themselves. I suppose I expected Karen to have some insight into the whole 'in love' illusion. She is pissed off with Marty and balancing that negative energy by projecting positive feelings onto an imagined me. Plus her father has died, which means her own mortality is more evident. What else is 'in love' but a distraction from our ever-closer date with Death? It will only upset her when she finds that there is nothing to me.

My eyes fall on Urs's 'Things that annoy me' list.

I pick up the list again. Do I really put dirty washing on top of clean and wet washing on top of dry? If it were true then it would be very irritating – I imagine. I scan through, looking for a short one that won't tax my patience to decipher. Here we are:

13. She cannot love.

Perfect. Rubbish, but perfect. Surely this would put anyone off me. I ring Marty. He sounds pleased. "I knew you'd come round." This rather throws me, as I haven't mentioned coming round yet. "OK. What time shall I come?"

"Now. We'll get a take-away."

"OK. Give me an hour or so."

I have a shower and make a big effort to avoid splashing the floor – just in case that bit is true. I return to my room and put the 32 Things-list in my rucksack. When I come downstairs, Urs is watching TV, so I make a point of saying that I'll be with a friend and I'm not sure what time I'll be back.

"Are you seeing the therapist?"

"Karen? No. She's in Wales."

"Best place for her." Or at least I think that's what Urs says.

"Her father died."

"Oh. I'm sorry to hear that." She looks like she's going to say something else, but instead turns back to the screen. She looks unhappy. It is Friday night – she should be out somewhere with friends or lovers or someone. I find myself feeling sorry for her, and the image of her sitting in a despondent heap watching a quiz show with people desperately trying to be funny stays with me for much of the bus trip.

As for love, no, I can't love – not in that sense of loving someone outside the boundaries of me – and neither can anyone else. Even mothers can only love their children as extensions of their own self.

Chapter Twenty-two

MARTY GIVES ME an elongated bear hug at the door, then releases me and slides back, still holding my arms. He looks down and examines my wrists, giving a delighted grin, as though my arms are the best arms he's ever seen.

"This is brilliant. And you'll stay the night?"

"Oh. OK." I really hadn't planned on that, but luckily I still have my toothbrush in my rucksack from my aborted Wales trip.

"I'm starving. Indian? Chinese?"

"Chinese."

I search for something remotely vegetarian on the menu he shows me and choose a dofu dish and a side of broccoli.

"You should ring up and talk to them in chinky-chonk."

"No - they'll talk Cantonese."

"Shame. I bet you'd have sounded sexy."

He must be the first person on the planet to think that the Chinese language is sexy. One westerner I bumped into in Taiwan described the language as sounding like someone with a low pain threshold having root canal treatment.

Marty seems so happy to see me - quite unaware that I know something about his future that he doesn't. Why is Karen walking away from him? I'm sure she said that he offered to go to the funeral and she turned him down. Maybe we can come up with a new version of Tuesdays and Thursdays when they've sorted themselves out. I wonder if they will still share this flat when they've split up. They could do that if she can't move into her flat immediately. There are two bedrooms, though one seems much smaller than the one we usually have sex in. I guess that might be a bone of contention.

"Right," he says. "I'm going to order in boring old English, and then you can tell me what changed your mind."

"Changed my mind?"

"The reason you came here tonight."

In my rucksack there's a note with my reasons on. I have no need to look at it because I know I have written 'Fish' and 'History'.

"Have you fed the fish?"

He screws up his face. "Oh fuck. She texted me this morning as well. Mind you – we can just toss in some of your broccoli. She gives it to them sometimes."

"From a Chinese takeaway?"

He laughs. "Come to think of it – no. Just plain stuff. But you can give them any old crap, really."

"I'll feed them, then."

"Those little orange bastards get more attention than me, you know. Go on then – there's some flakes by the tank."

I ignore his urgings to "go on – chuck it in" whilst he watches me sprinkle some flakes onto the surface of the main tank and onto that of Goldie Pang's smaller residence. The fish rise up to gobble them. I wonder if they have memories of their life in a huge pond. Probably not; still less any knowledge of the human tragedies that brought them to this artificial space.

"I'll be honest. I just don't see the point in them." Marty has encircled my waist and rests his chin over my right shoulder.

"Not in a tank, I agree."

"Their only party trick is being able to swim whilst pooing. I do have this fantasy about introducing an eel into the tank. There's some clips on YouTube of eels catching live fish in tanks."

"You'd like the zoo in Taipei, then. I remember some of the snake tanks had live mice in, all huddling together, waiting to be picked off."

He laughs. "Well, it's nature, isn't it?"

"In a tank?"

"Maybe not. Right – I'll order the food."

I mentally tick off Fish. History is next. Marty gets on the phone, and runs through the order whilst I go to the bookshelf. I leaf through Owen Glendower, and make a show of examining others on Welsh history. There are so many lovely books here.

"You and history."

"Sorry?"

He is sitting on the sofa watching me. I assume he has ordered, as the phone sits snugly in its cradle. "Everyone knew that Fallowfield liked you. Mind you, I think all the teachers liked you."

"Turner didn't."

He wrinkles up his nose. "Turner? Oh yeah. English. Greasy hair. You know he died in a plane crash or something?"

"Glider crash."

"Gliding. I wouldn't mind trying that. We should give it a go."

"What about Karen?" Almost as soon as I say this I remember their days are numbered.

"No – I don't think she'd be up for it. She'd be quite happy to stay at home every night and read books." He pauses. "You know, there are loads of things I'd do if we weren't together."

"What things?"

"Oh. I'd love to get back into a band, for one. I'd love to get a motorbike."

"What's stopping you?"

"She wouldn't like it. I quite fancy working in Australia for a bit. She definitely wouldn't like that."

"Why don't you start with the motorbike and the band?"

He gets up. "Wine? Or no – you'll want that funny tea."

When the doorbell goes, Marty is halfway through a bottle of white and a story about how the cousin of a drummer in a well-known band (that I hadn't heard of or have forgotten) wanted Gadd to be a supporting act.

"Really? I don't remember that. I'm sure you'd have said."

"We'd split by then. Or should I say your father split us up." He looks at me and then looks startled; maybe I gave him a glare. "Anyway," he says quickly, "of course it went tits up, because Shimmy's mother said he had to give up playing. Shame – we'd have been made." He gets up abruptly; it must have been to answer the door, though I heard no knock or bell; he comes back with two bags that are bursting with food smells.

"Didn't you say that Shimmy was in porn films?"

"That's right. Though I really can't think why anyone would pay to see his fat white bottom humping." He giggles. "His sense of rhythm was bad enough on drums."

"So his mother wanted him to give up the band to concentrate on his studies?"

"Ha. I see where you're going with this. I don't think she

knows exactly what he does now – though it is a career of sorts."

The rest of the evening passes in a bit of a blur. The food is welcome enough, though unfortunately I wasn't quick enough to stop Marty from throwing soy sauce over my broccoli, which now tastes like lumpy seawater. He is chatting away, but I rather tune out of the conversation. There is a scene playing in my head where Maddy and Fred and I arrive at a location in Shanxi province (still to be identified) and they are both staring at me, as though I will magic up Gadd's ashes from the concrete jungle of a Chinese utilitarian town. My attention returns to the here-and-now whenever Marty mentions Karen, which he seems to do a lot, though always in the context of everything she is stopping him from doing.

I insist on washing up before we go to bed, partly to have something mindful to do, and partly to get rid of the islands of broccoli in the brown Dead Sea on my plate, which he keeps threatening to drop on top of Goldie Pang. I remember seeing the clip on YouTube of the squid that danced when soy sauce was poured onto it and figure if the salt content has that effect on a dead squid, I hate to think of what would happen to a live goldfish. Too late. Marty says, "Fatty will love this", and drops a big sprig of broccoli into the isolation tank.

"Oh. He normally loves it."

Goldie Pang is swimming frantically in the opposite direction to this intruder, which doesn't count for much in such a small tank. I pick up Karen's little net from beside the tank and corner the plump fish immediately and drop it into the main tank. I don't think it looks as fat as it did before, though it would still be signed off work with 'a touch of dropsy'.

"Oops. Karen will be mad." He giggles. "And I'm going

to have to say that I did it, otherwise she'll know you came around tonight."

"Whatever." I wash up.

Just when I think we can brush teeth and go to bed, Marty pours himself another glass of wine and motions to me to sit with him on the sofa. I glance up at their projected clock: ten past eleven. We need to allow at least ten minutes to brush our teeth and get ready for bed. Unfortunately, Marty's body language on the sofa is sprawling and languorous; he seems in no rush.

"It's time we had a talk," he says.

"OK. But I could do with an early night."

"Every time I want to get serious, you shy away Win."

"What?"

"Come on. Sit down." When I sit down, he starts stroking my left arm. "I know you're holding back." When I don't answer, he turns over my left wrist and points.

"I haven't seen girls do that since school."

I have a small 'M' written there. I had thought it was inconspicuous to all but me, but it turns out that Marty has spotted it and I had forgotten it.

"You want to tell me what the 'M' means?"

"Not really." M is for mindfulness. I was really a little horrified by Urs's accusations of my lack of it, and was wondering about getting it tattooed as a constant reminder. I wrote it with a biro as an interim reminder. This must have been after my shower, unless I can add 'unmindful washing technique' to my list of shortcomings.

"Look, we're alone. You can be honest about how you feel."

"About what?"

"There you go again. About us. You're holding back on something."

I really have no idea what he's going on about. Yes, I hid some papers in Owen Glendower, but I don't think he saw me do it – I was quick. "I'm not holding back on anything."

"But you've written M on your wrist."

"Oh, I see. You think it's to do with you."

"Er, ye-es."

"No, really it's just a coincidence."

He gives me a pained look, and mouths 'coincidence'. It looks like Urs's 'go into sense'. Coincidence – that's what she was saying. But what was it in relation to? Aagh – slippery fish. It was something this morning. Something important. A letter – an envelope. I need to get back to look at the envelope. "I have to get back."

"What? Now?"

It is almost eleven-twenty, according to the not-real clock above the not-real fireplace. In truth, I wouldn't mind sex before I go, but, sex or no sex, being late would mean a transgression of my half-eleven rule.

"I have to go early in the morning. I can stay tonight if we go to bed now."

He sighs. "OK. But you can't keep running away from it."

I can't be bothered to ask him what he thinks I'm running away from, because it will just delay our teeth-brushing. At least we manage to get to bed before half-eleven, if not to sleep.

I am running through endless, cropless, barren fields trying to find an address on an envelope, but when I look again, the address has morphed into a single word: COINCIDENCE.

Straightway I know that this is the sleep paralysis that Fred describes, but the knowledge doesn't help me escape. I remember this from childhood. It took me a long while to accept that fighting to wake up does nothing to free myself from the paralysis. I relax into it. Gradually my body condescends to release me from sleep.

I scoured the Internet yesterday (was it yesterday?) for pictures of Lululongping, but found nothing. Either it doesn't exist or it's too small or it's been renamed – probably swallowed up by a new conurbation.

What did Urs and Mum think was a coincidence? I need to find that envelope. It was by my computer, but when I look around the room now, I see no computer. I'm annoyed to find Marty in my bed, and then realise that I'm in his bed. He is still sleeping when I sidle out. I put on my clothes and pick up my rucksack from the front room. Goldie Pang looks fine: s/he's back with his or her mates, and a rotting sprig of broccoli has a tank to itself.

I feel I should write a thank-you note to Marty, but I don't know what to say: 'Thanks for the sex' sounds a bit stark. I find a pen, replenish the 'M' on my wrist, and leave 'Thanks for the meal' on a notepad in the kitchen. I pull the front door behind me and make sure it is engaged before I walk to the bus stop – the route so familiar I hardly have to think about it now.

Chapter Twenty-three

I T I S S T I L L early when I reach home, but Urs is up and Doing Things. I meditate for half an hour and spend half an hour on visualisation: I open doors and close doors I open, turn on taps then turn them off again, take out books then put them back on the shelf from whence they came. I check that the washing machine is empty before I put clothes in and do the same for the tumbler drier. I can't remember when mindfulness took such an effort, but that of course is the point. It is a bit like westerners whingeing that it is meditation that makes their minds wander, rather than acknowledging it is meditation that gives them the opportunity to notice that their minds are constantly wandering.

Then I go downstairs, make breakfast and offer Urs tea, which she turns down. She seems quite purposeful.

"What are you up to today?"

She pauses – broom suspended above a crouching kitchen floor. "We're going to the cemetery and then on to see Nan."

"Oh. Seems a bit early."

"Yes, well done. It is earlier than normal. Mum's got a friend coming over this afternoon." She gives me a look and adds, "Margaret", which means nothing to me, but I nod as if it does. Sometimes Urs gets quite irritated if I don't appear to recognise a name I've never heard of.

"How is Margaret?" I ask. A friend from the church, maybe.

"Heartbroken. As you can imagine."

"Yes, I expect so." Must be someone whose husband has walked out, or maybe died.

"She tried playing him old songs to see if he remembered any, but he doesn't react."

"Right." Maybe her husband has had a stroke or is in a coma. "I've got some of Dad's old records upstairs, if that helps."

She freezes. "What do you mean?"

In truth before I said that, I'd forgotten the records I brought back with Karen. What did I do with them? I haven't seen them around my room. Unless I've put them under my bed, which is where I tend to put things I don't want Urs or Mum to see. Aaagh. What an idiot I am. Unmindful speech indeed. Too late for subterfuge now. The only option is truth.

"I've come into possession of his records. From our old house."

"In Tadstone Road?"

"Yes, the big house."

She is looking at me very intensely. I suspect she thinks I've broken in and pinched the new owner's vinyl collection.

"You remember it?"

"Our house? Yes, of course I remember it."

"OK. So how – exactly – have you come into possession of Dad's records?"

"I was showing Karen where we used to live and when I told the woman who lives there now that I used to live there she gave me some records. She'd been keeping them in the garage, as she didn't like to throw them out."

She stares at me for a while. "How is Karen?"

"She's in Wales."

"Yes, I know that. But you said her father died. I wondered if you were in contact."

"I spoke to her . . . yesterday." I think yesterday. "She was OK. So would the records help your friend?"

She resumes her brushing. "Thank you. It's nice of you to offer. But I don't think Margaret's son is going to be helped by listening to old 70s records. Even if they had a record player, which they probably don't."

"No, I suppose not. I don't want to throw them away, though, in case Dad is ever in a position to want them back."

The brush stops again. "And just remind me what position he's in now?"

"He lives in a hostel and sells the Big Issue."

"Right." The brush starts again. She's been punishing the same spot for ages.

"You don't believe me, do you? You can't accept that he's been reduced to that."

Urs finally moves to another spot of floor to bother. "On the contrary. I can't imagine he would have been elevated to that."

"What do you mean?"

"I mean, if there was the slightest possibility that he is still alive, he wouldn't be organised enough to sell anything."

"People do change, you know."

"So you keep saying. It's like a mantra."

I wash up while she sweeps around me, then go upstairs. My phone shows a missed call from Marty and a weird message from him saying that he understands why I rushed off, which he doesn't. I toy with the idea of ringing Karen for an update, but I can't really imagine what can have changed: presumably her father is still dead and she and her mother are still sad and relieved.

I dashed home for a reason. It was something to do with 'Go into sense' or 'Coincidence'. Ah, the envelope that Maddy sent. I find it on my desk.

Mrs Lillian Gadd
The Old Vicarage
45 King's Road
Sutton
Surrey
SN8 1NY

I wonder what Fred's mother made of the news of Lawrence Gadd's death. If Fred had moved out to the nuptial home with Maddy, maybe Lillian Gadd rattled around the big house (I assume vicarages are big) alone and haunted by the death of a husband far away. Maybe she was Sad and Relieved. Maybe she was heartbroken. Maybe she didn't care: I think Fred said that the marriage wasn't happy.

Did she try and get the body sent home? I ring the Fallowfields and get Maddy.

"Did Fred's mother try and have Gadd's body sent back to England?"

"And good morning to you, Winifred."

"Morning, Maddy. Did Fred's mother try and get Gadd's body back?"

"The letter said he was cremated." Her voice has an edge to it, though I don't know if the cause is me or something at her end. I guess it's at her end, as she breaks off now to shout "Stop that, Fred".

"Sorry, I forgot it said cremated. So I suppose the question is whether she tried to get his ashes back."

"To do what with? Stick in an ashtray?"

"I don't know. To scatter somewhere?" I'm a little alarmed by Maddy's tone. I've heard her sound angry before, but not so facetious.

"She got the letter months later. I don't know whether she tried to make enquiries – I can't imagine that Lillian would have known where to start, frankly. She wasn't the most . . ." she breaks off. "Fred! Leave it." She gives a roar of a sigh down the phone and then in a quieter voice says, "If I didn't remember him as he used to be, I think I would have murdered him by now."

"Sorry."

"Not as sorry as I am. Would you believe that one of the country's leading experts on Sanskrit would be examining every ornament looking for a message from his father?"

I can hear Fred make some retort.

"I got that wrong, apparently," she says. "Fred is looking for a Chinese ornament that his father sent him from China."

"What's wrong with that? That doesn't sound so unreasonable."

"Except his father never sent him so much as a postcard. In the two years he was in China I don't think he sent Fred's mother a damn thing, apart from two notes saying that the weather was too hot. Fred's dreamt it, and he's finding it very hard to distinguish between dreams and reality."

"Sorry."

"I'm beginning to wonder if it isn't too late."

"What do you mean?"

She speaks more quietly. "Have you found anything yet?"

"On ancestor worship?"

"No. On the price of rubber in New Guinea. Yes, I mean ancestor worship."

"Not really. References to filial piety. Feng shui. Some websites mention *Qing Ming Jie* – that's the national tomb-sweeping day."

"What's that? A spring-clean of cemeteries?"

"It's a fixed day each year when people maintain their family graves and honour their ancestors."

"Isn't that . . . surely that is evidence of ancestor worship?"

"I mean, that's what it used to be. The Communists banned it in 1949, to discourage outward manifestations of kinship, then they realised that it could be subverted, so they re-introduced it as a holiday and re-packaged it as a day for celebrating revolutionary heroes, thus encouraging people to visit particular graves rather than family ones."

"Bloody communists."

"Do you want me to pretend I've found something?", I ask. "We could tell Fred – I don't know – we could tell him that his father was cremated in Beijing and his ashes were scattered in whatever river runs through it."

"No, I do not want you to *pretend* you've found something. That's not the way we work."

"OK, OK."

"Are you really trying, Winifred?"

My initial reaction is to tell her to fuck off, but I realise that the rush of energy I feel is more to do with guilt. I haven't been trying these last few days: I've been distracted by Marty and Karen and sparrows and God knows what.

"Do you need more money – is that it?"

"Oh. To be honest, I can't remember how much you've given me already."

"Then I can't imagine how you do your job. I've given you two hundred pounds. Four hundred still to come. And a return ticket to China if you find that it makes sense to go there."

"I won't need a return."

"What?"

"Never mind. I'll get back to it now."

I put the phone down. I won't take Maddy's aggression personally. I think it's just that she is unhappy.

I spend the rest of the day translating the contents of some tabs on the Junfeng Funeral Company website, and summarising my findings:

Funeral Supplies: photographs include ornate boxes for ashes, tomb stones, brightly coloured funeral clothes in traditional style.

Traditional Funeral Customs: pages of irrelevant information. I scan through quickly and see references to 'kite flying', and swings and God knows what other extraneous material.

Choosing the Date of the Funeral: interestingly, amongst the mention of ensuring a date when managers from the deceased's *danwei* (work unit) can attend, there is a reference to using a *feng shui* expert to come up with an auspicious date; evidently *feng shui* doesn't count as superstition, or at least not any more.

Modern Ceremony: places more emphasis on colleagues than family.

Anniversaries: Describes memorial activities for family to perform on anniversaries and dates such as Qing Ming; they seem fairly prosaic, though: cleaning the memorial tablet (above the buried ashes, presumably). And the obligatory note that indulging in 'superstitious practices is not permitted'.

Information on Memorial Park: describes how many

Chinese acres are covered in water and extols its *feng shui* location.

Of ancestor worship: nothing. That has taken me three hours. I don't think Maddy will be interested in China's history regarding kites and swings. Fred would gnash his teeth. And Gadd (bless his ashes) won't give a damn. I am intrigued that *feng shui* seems so acceptable when I am sure it was once denounced as superstitious nonsense by the Chinese Communist Party, which would have denounced anything it couldn't control, but when I trawl the Internet I find a eulogising article on Chairman Mao ("he only picked up a pen, never a gun") which says that he studied *feng shui* diligently; so maybe it gained acceptance.

I am getting nowhere, and despite what Maddy says – I am trying.

I do what I should have done earlier and email the Pedant English school. I outline my previous teaching experience and emphasise that I am comfortably accustomed to life in Taiwan. I won't ask about airfare yet, but hopefully they will pay.

Then I wonder why I don't apply to my old school in Yilan. Except my mind is blank – I just cannot remember the name. Ridiculous – it's just gone.

And then my eye falls once more on the envelope containing notice of Gadd's death.

I examine it a few times and try and see what Urs saw that shook her. But I can see nothing on the envelope that shrieks 'COINCIDENCE'. I'm sure the name of Fred's mother couldn't have meant anything to them, so it must be the address.

I try searching on the postcode and get a lot of hits for

properties sold or for sale in King's Road. On the second page I see Oak Tree Care Home. Could that be it? The day when Mum and Urs dropped me off after the Chinese meal, they turned right at South Wimbledon. They could easily have been going to Sutton. Is that where Nan is? So not as far into deep, dark Surrey as my mother wanted me to believe.

My instinct is to immediately plan a route there and go and see Nan. I don't *want* to see her, but I'm rather getting the feeling that Mum and Urs don't want me to have any contact with her and I can't think why not.

I go down to make some tea and find the house empty. Urs said she was going somewhere. I think it was to see Nan, so today is not the day for me to visit. I write myself a 'Visit Nan (see address on envelope)' post-it note in Chinese.

What to do now? I can't face another Chinese website. It occurs to me that whatever happens, I will need my passport. I'm sure I've seen it recently: I have a strong impression of holding it in my hands and doing something with it, but I can't remember what. Maybe I dreamt that.

I turn my room upside-down looking for it. Nothing. I look through the files downstairs where Urs keeps bills and just about every official piece of paper that personally I would throw away. Nothing. It occurs to me that Urs has hidden the passport, but I haven't given her any reason to think I want to use it, so I'm not sure why she would do this. Then again, she may have spotted the Pedant English School website on my PC during one of her infuriating Ninja entrances into my room – in which case she would very likely have hidden it.

I ransack Urs's room. She keeps files of my accounts and her own accounts on a shelf, so I go through them, but find nothing (apart from the invoice for the translation piece on investments, on which she has stuck a note saying 'Still unpaid!'). There is also a diary hidden in a folder marked 'Past Tax Returns'. I don't open it. I'm not interested.

I wonder where to look next before I remember to put everything back the way it was in Urs's room.

So if my passport is not here, then where?

Energised by anger, I take the tube to South Wimbledon station and walk to Mum's house. Her car is there with a red one: hopefully Mum is entertaining someone and won't notice me. The garage door is unlocked, perhaps in the vain hope that someone will steal all the things that my mother can't bring herself to throw away.

There is a corner where Dad's things are stacked: the Black and Decker stand, all his old tools, solid, metallic and with a hint of a bygone age. I think Dad eschewed modern tools for older ones, and he kept an eye on the local papers for the occasional adverts in which widows would offer 'tools to a good home' for nothing or next to nothing. An old zip-up bag releases a smell of oil as soon as I pull the zip back a few inches. It's full of tools, including a couple I remember he used to design a device to stop doors banging on the walls (or was it to keep them open?). His best design was for the kitchen, a little set of tracks to deliver pots and pans mechanically, I suppose a bit like the sushi-go-round in a Japanese restaurant, only these tracks were at chest level (on an adult) and made of real wood with deep grooves (similar to the ancient grooved roads found in China for carts). I suppose it was a bit like the little railway system that Karen used to put together with her father – except that Mum got to be in charge of the railway and was always under pressure to use as many pots and pans as possible, to maximise the number of times Urs and I could each fetch down what she needed.

I can see one big spirit level near the top of the pile (they fascinated me when I was young), and there should be two more, but I won't look for them. I could rummage around and pull out more memories, but I can already sense that the smell of oil is making my molecules vibrate at a frequency that is now alien to them. I zip up the bag, feeling rather sad. I don't know how long after they moved to this house that his episodes became more joined-up, but I have a feeling that his tools may never have been used once they moved here. Such a shame. I remember wondering why there always seemed to be something that needed doing around the old house on rainy days. Mum seemed to have a never-ending list of requirements and now I wonder if this was a bit like her Bindweed strategy: God Bless DIY.

Paint pots, a wallpapering table, plant pots, accessories for either the current or a bygone lawn mower.

Why am I here?

Beneath the replenished 'M' on my hand I have written 护照, but I can see nowhere sensible that someone would hide a passport. All the same, I look in and under anything that could hide one.

I let myself into the house. From the kitchen window I see that Mum is with a woman in the garden. They are sitting in deckchairs and talking; whatever the subject is, it is a serious one, for neither of them is smiling or laughing. It's a good time to search Mum's room.

I seem to go through it in minutes. I have a new respect for my mother; not only do I not find the Christian kitsch that I expected, there is no other clutter to search through, either.

There's an Oliver Sacks book by her bed which looks familiar, but there's no paperwork in the drawers, apart from an address book. I leaf through it quickly. I don't recognise some of the names, but I can see that under 'M' for 'Mum' she has the Oak Tree Care Home in King's Road, Sutton. That confirms my 'Coincidence' theory. On a whim, I try my name, and find c/o Hope School, Tainan, Taiwan, now with a big cross through it. So that was the name I couldn't think of earlier. (How could I have forgotten Hope? I need to remember that as an alternative to the Pedant English school). Under 'U' there is 'Urs (& Steven)', with my current address. Who is Steven? What was he doing in my house? What was Urs doing there? Had I agreed she could stay there while I was in Taiwan?

I check Urs's room, which has just a few books on a shelf. I seem to remember that she was reading a dodgy one, but nothing leaps out at me from the spines. I really don't know why she comes here – there isn't room enough to swing a catechism, but maybe I'm so irritating that she has to get away a couple of nights a week to a house where the doors are closed and the taps turned off. I could go through the small collection of clothes she keeps in the closet, but I really can't imagine that my passport is hiding in a pocket. That only leaves 'my' room. I walk in.

"Hello?" My mother's voice.

I appear on the landing, trying to look innocent. "Hi Mum. I was just looking for one of my old books."

"You didn't close the front door properly."

"Aagh. What an idiot – I'm really sorry."

She is looking a little startled – I think at my pained expression. What is the point of doing all this visualisation if I go and fuck it up?

344

"It's OK," she says. "You almost closed it. It just hadn't engaged."

"I still fucked it up, though."

She is looking up at me with a strange expression. "Don't worry. You'll know for next time. Come and say hello to Margaret while I make some tea."

"OK. Do I know her?"

"Well, she'll remember you – just keep her company for a couple of minutes please. You can tell her about – I don't know – something about Chinese culture."

"OK."

"If you can, try not to swear, though."

"OK. I don't normally."

I come downstairs and join the woman in the deckchair. I don't recognise her. Her hair is sort of reddish and the dark bags under her eyes make her look ill, but she smiles when she sees me.

"Winifred! Aren't you looking good?"

"What did I look like before?"

She gives an embarrassed laugh. "Well – younger, I suppose. You probably don't remember me?"

"Um . . . from church?"

"Yes, yes – that's right. Though your mother tells me you're a Buddhist now."

"I've been one for years. I don't think she approves."

She frowns. "I don't think she . . . well – I can't remember the last time I heard on the news that Buddhists had declared jihad on the non-Buddhist world, or declared war on other Buddhists or . . . no – your mother certainly doesn't disapprove."

"Oh." My mother is obviously more tolerant of me in front

345

of other people. "I'm sure she'd prefer it if I went back to church, even so."

"Why on earth would she prefer that? She doesn't go herself." She is silent for a while before she murmurs something.

What?

"Oh. I didn't know that. When did she stop going?"

"When . . . a year or so ago." She looks down and closes her eyes briefly. "Yes, over a year ago. Anyway – I've always wanted to ask a Buddhist a question."

"OK." Usually it's some weird misunderstanding about reincarnation.

"How do you feel about . . . how shall I put it? It seems to be a religion that's used to accessorise people's homes. You know, Buddha statues in the garden and in people's front rooms. I suppose I'm asking how you feel about it being hijacked by New Agers."

This wasn't the question I was expecting. While I'm rethinking my answer I notice her face do that little slump, just like Urs's face does. "Sorry," she mumbles. "It was a complicated question. Never mind."

"No, it was a good question." Fuck. Something about accessories? "Can you ask it again?"

"It wasn't important. I just wondered why non-Buddhists have Buddhist statues." I tell her that it is no different from China in the early days of Buddhism.

"I can't remember if it was the Wu or Jin dynasty or both, but anyway, in about 200 years AD they didn't really understand Buddhism, so they thought the Buddha was a lucky symbol and they'd put figurines around the house as auspicious emblems." Why has Mum stopped going to church? But

346

of course that doesn't mean she's stopped being a Catholic, it just means that . . . she has to work some weekend shifts, maybe that's why she hasn't been.

"So you're saying it's gone full circle?" Margaret is now wearing my mother's expression of hopeful expectancy. Which throws me. "Or do you mean that there have always been people who didn't understand it so have projected exotic ideals on to it."

"The latter. Exotic, yes." Mum is coming out with a plate with slices of cake on it and three mugs. I find myself looking at her, as if trying to fathom her degree of Catholicism, but there are only so many ways in which one can carry cake and tea. I excuse myself.

"Take your tea."

The mugs all seem to contain the same milky tea, so I take one at random and go inside to tip it away. Through the kitchen window I see Mum settle into the deckchair I've just vacated. The red-haired woman is talking animatedly to Mum – about me, I think, and Mum is responding less enthusiastically. And then Margaret settles back into a chair with a sigh and says, "She gives me hope." At least, I think that's what she says. And then she covers a face with one hand, rocks forward and I think she is crying.

I might as well leave now, except I think I should say goodbye to Mum and I don't want to approach her while the woman is in that state. I will give it a few minutes. I look around the kitchen. There are two shelves on a wall. The books on the lower one look like recipe books, but the higher shelf has a mixture of recipe books and folders with labels: Utilities, Guarantees & Instr. Manuals, Car. And a black spine with no label. My mother is a labelley sort of person. I find a footstool under the kitchen table and take down the black folder. It is stuffed with papers from the hospital, test results – the sort of information I would have thought a nurse shouldn't remove from her workplace. Behind a divider I see some information about Oak Tree Care Home, and an exchange of letters which are about Nan moving there.

Out of the window I can see Mum sitting in the same place, but with her hands bent on the armrests as though she intends to lever herself up just as soon as politeness permits. I try to close the folder, but there is a wodge of papers that need to be coaxed around the rings of the binder. A form grabs my attention: a Court of Protection application form, filled in with my mother's handwriting and with my name, WINIFRED ELEANOR RIGBY, printed under 'Full name of the person to whom the application relates'.

I thought so. If I had time to look, I would find again the piece of paper that proved she's disposed of my funds to a Catholic charity – I should have taken a copy when I first saw it.

My mother's seat in the garden is now empty. I force the folder into its slim slot on the shelf and kick the foot stand under the kitchen table so it makes a bang just as Mum walks into the kitchen.

"What was that?" she asks.

"Nothing. I'm off, Mum. I didn't want to come out while . . . Er . . ."

"Margaret?"

"Margaret. I didn't want to come and say goodbye while she was crying."

"That's sweet of you. Yes, she's in a dreadful state."

"I'm sorry." I need to get out of here before I lose my

temper with Mum. What did I do with my rucksack? It's not in here and I never go anywhere without it.

"Still – I think it did her good to see you. Your rucksack is in the garden, if that's what you're looking for."

"Ah, I'll get it."

I say Goodbye to Margaret and leave. Mum comes into the hall to give me a hug, but I suspect she is really looking to see if I shut the door properly.

"Are you OK?" she asks. "You seem to be a little down now."

"Sometimes I wish I had more money." I watch her face for some semblance of guilt. Hard to say if there is any; she definitely looks sad and serious, maybe sympathetic. All of those could be facets of guilt. But my dislike of her right now is a little mollified by the Margaret woman in the garden: she has come around for comfort and obviously thinks Mum is the one to give it. I suppose it must be a nursing skill. She probably has to deal with gibbering patients and blubbing families every day.

There must be a way of getting that court of protection order overturned. I should be able to challenge it.

I see 护照 written on my hand. God knows where my passport is.

Chapter Twenty-four

I AM STANDING outside The Old Vicarage, which is in a sunny tree-lined street with church bells being pulled nearby, calling in the faithful. It is a substantial building whose dark bricks seem to mourn their divorce from the church. Or maybe I'm being fanciful – the thought of Fred growing up here (assuming he spent his formative years with mother-Lillian and father-Lawrence Gadd in this house) is strangely disquieting. I cannot imagine him as a young man – though presumably he was my age when he swept a student off her feet and got sacked from university. But once he must have been younger still, a boy with a father whom I suspect was a stern patrician with no time for children. Looking at this house, I can scarcely believe that Gadd was half Chinese. This house shouts 'Jerusalem', not 'China'.

I want to ask Fred when he started feeling Chinese. You can feed children any old rubbish to give them a backstory: a white lie about an Irish ancestor, or a Scottish laird ten generations back. Like the Germans who became Americanophiles because they were told their absent fathers were US servicemen, only to find out later that their mothers had been raped by Russian soldiers.

I think Maddy said that Fred had never met his Chinese grandmother, but maybe she figured in his imagination, along with all the images people of Fred's generation had about

China: a land of braided ponytails and Chinese hats and misty-headed mountains.

But I am procrastinating. The Oak Tree Care Home is a few yards away and I'm feeling strangely ingénue about this visit. Do they have visiting times? Maybe the oldies get bussed off to church and won't be back for a while.

I ring the bell and the door is opened by a woman who looks cheerful but harassed. I expected someone in a nurse's uniform, but she is wearing a sort of plump smock, and is middle-aged in a way that is older than my mother's middle age. I suppose my mother's blonde pony-tail makes her look younger.

"Hello?" She seems to ask it as a question.

"Hello. I'm here to see my grandmother."

"Yes of course. Um . . . and she is?"

"Mrs Rigby."

"Oh." She is frowning. "I don't think we have anyone with that name."

I don't know my grandmother's name. I try to think of my mother's maiden name – blank. I try to think of the name on my grandfather's gravestone. Blank.

"We do have someone of that name who visits her mother."

"That's my mother. I've completely forgotten my Nan's name. I'm afraid I've never visited before."

I can see she looks uncertain. She wants to be helpful – she is a sympathetic woman – but she is being careful. Maybe they get gold-diggers turning up pretending to be long-lost relatives, preying on dementia-muddled old people.

"Can you give me a bit more? I'm really sorry but we have to be careful."

"My sister – Ursula Rigby – comes with my mother to visit."

She looks at me. She's wavering. "You do look like her granddaughter."

"There's two of us. Two granddaughters. I don't know if she's free – I thought she might be at Mass."

Recognition. The woman smiles at me. "We take her to evening Mass sometimes. Let me tell her you're here. What's your name?"

"Winifred Rigby."

"Come in. Will you just wait here for a second? I'll let her know she's got another visitor."

I come in and she shuts the door. She leaves me in the hall, on a red swirly carpet. There is the smell of a bygone breakfast – eggs and bacon.

It's a good few minutes before she comes back, and I can tell that something is not right. Her forehead is creased.

"Winifred Rigby?"

"Yes. Ursula's sister."

She looks at me as though she is expecting to see something else. Whatever she's looking for, she doesn't find it, because the creases increase.

"She seems to think . . . she does have a granddaughter by that name, but she's surprised that you'd visit. Very surprised that you're here on your own."

"Oh. I guess I've been very neglectful. Quite honestly, I can't remember the last time I saw her. I was abroad for a few years."

"In Thailand?"

"In Taiwan."

"Oh, I see."

"Is she very . . ." - I want to say demented, but I look for a softer option - "Is she very confused? My mother told me that she has dementia."

"Oh no. She's very switched on. Absolutely. She's got her fair share of problems relating to old-age. I must warn you that she can be a little grumpy, but she's all there."

I am following her along the red swirly carpet when she stops so suddenly that I almost collide. "Would you mind telling me why you have decided to visit now? I believe you've been ill?"

Ill. What a joke. I didn't go on about my *satori* because it is a personal thing, but I had to give Mum some explanation as to why I wasn't quite the same daughter she remembered and now she's hanging on to that as if one day I'll 'get better'. "I'm fine now."

"Yes. Yes." She has started moving again. We are going down a corridor. Still the red swirly carpet, and cream swirly wallpaper that is so in 3D that I can imagine it being a repository of arcane knowledge for braille-readers. In fact, bumpy wallpaper could be a database for the blind.

She stops again, a few feet from a half-opened door, and talks so quietly that I can't catch what she's saying. I move closer.

". . . like it here, but I'm afraid she's quite resentful. She would much rather be back at home."

"Right."

She pushes the door open fully, and ups the volume and brightness of her voice.

"Here's Winifred."

The old woman sitting in this light and neat room stares at me without smiling, which is how I know it is Nan, who

353

always had a natural tendency towards disapproval and a dislike of joy in others. She is staring at me hard now, and I think I recognise her face.

The Care Home woman seems uncertain, but pulls out another chair for me. "Winifred, when you leave, would you mind just checking out with me first?"

"Sure."

"Right. I'll leave you to it." She is still hovering. "Would you like some tea, Mary?"

"No."

"Winifred?"

"No, thanks."

"OK." She doesn't quite close the door, but she pulls it a little, so that we get a hint of private space.

"Hi Nan." She is staring at me so hard that I feel like I've done something wrong. I search my mind for the last time I met her. I can't recall exactly, but it was a general family occasion – some time before I went off to university – or certainly before I finished my degree. I don't remember Dad being there. Family occasions with my mother's family – of course there weren't any with my father's relations – didn't often include my father. My grandparents made no effort to be warm towards him; I remember an occasion early in my childhood when they were so openly unpleasant that my mother invented a migraine and cut short the visit. Dad disappeared to play music – *Nantucket Sleighride* pops into my mind, though it could have been anything – and the next day was a Bindweed day.

I have just remembered how much I hate my Nan. My poor father had enough stacked against him already. I can't remember or maybe I never knew the reason for their hostility – I either guessed or overheard that his atheism was one reason and his non-white collar job (as they regarded social work) was another. My mother's father had been in senior management, and being well off seemed to be a minimum requirement for a son-in-law's acceptance into the Hardy family. Hardy. It's come back just like that. What an imperfect database our minds are: amazing storage with a capricious indexing system. How did that help us when we were mammoth-hunting troglodytes?

"So how come you're walking?" says Nan.

I don't know what to make of the question. "Sorry?"

"When did you get out of bed?"

"I get up at seven to meditate." Oops – don't use the M-word, use the C-word. "I get up at seven and do half-an-hour of contemplation each morning."

Her stare is unflinching. "I don't believe you're my granddaughter."

"I'm sorry. I'm not surprised. I haven't visited for years. It just occurred to me it was about time."

"Where do you live?"

"I have my own house in south London. Urs – Ursula – stays there a few nights a week."

Some weird expression has just taken over her face. "What about Elizabeth?"

"Who? Oh – Mum? Well she has her own house."

"On her own?"

"Yes. Urs stays there, I don't know – half the time maybe."

She seems to freeze – apart from her lips, which are fluttering slightly, like a butterfly at the end of its life. I don't know whether this is normal in old people. Certainly this isn't a normal conversation by my reckoning. I look around her room. It is spartan and neat – attractively uncluttered. Of course there's a crucifix and rosary beads hanging over her bed, but I find that strangely comforting; I dislike the woman but at least she's consistent.

"We bought that house."

"Sorry? Where Mum lives?"

"As good as."

"Sorry – I don't follow."

"We bought them the big house. So when they sold it and moved into that little one – it was with our money. So it's our house. My house."

"Oh – that was nice of you."

"That's my room, you're living in. My room."

"I live somewhere else, Nan – I have a little house in Colliers Wood – not in Wimbledon."

"Then who is living in my room?"

"I don't know which room you mean Nan."

"In my house. Who is in my room?"

"No-one."

She has started breathing heavily. Her lips are fluttering for a while before anything comes out. "Does Elizabeth have another husband now?"

"No. Well, if she does she's hiding him very well. I've never seen another man." My mother should have another man, actually. She's a nurse, not a nun. There's clearly no chance of her and Dad ever getting together again. Not that I know if they are divorced.

"Nan – do you know if my parents ever got divorced? I've never liked to ask Mum."

"Death saves us from divorce." This is snarled at me – literally snarled. I can think of nothing to say, nothing to lighten the atmosphere in this room, the walls of which are now closing in on me, and seem barely sturdy enough to withstand the waves of her aggression.

"When did they let you out?"

"Out of where?"

"Out of hospital?"

"I don't understand what you mean, Nan. I don't think I've ever really been in hospital. Not more than a few nights at most."

She is gulping air. She will give herself wind. "Are you going back to Thailand?"

"Tai . . . Yes, as soon as I get the money for an air-fare." Maybe she will give me the money. She clearly doesn't like me, and if that extends to helping rid the country of my presence, then I will quite happily take any sub.

"Is my room empty, then?" The breathing is getting quicker. She seems distressed.

"No, Nan. If I go back to . . . Thailand, *my* room in *my* house will be empty."

"Your house is my house."

"No it isn't." I have had enough. She is mad – in both senses of the word.

"They sold the big house and bought the little house." She is almost bouncing on her chair now, still with the gulpy breathing. "I bet they used my money to buy the other house for Ursula."

"OK, Nan, I'm going to go now."

"It's my house. My room."

"OK, Nan. I'm sorry I seem to have bothered you, but I won't bother you again." I get up. I go, pulling the door into the same half-closed position that the care woman left it in.

My own breathing is unsettled. I watch it until it settles into a steady rhythm. I look left and right. Red swirly carpets and cream Braille wallpaper in both directions. A 50:50 chance of getting out of jail. But the nice woman wanted me to do something first. To find her and say I was going.

It occurs to me that I should check on Nan first. It wouldn't be good if I sign out with the carer and leave Nan having a cardiac arrest in her room. I'll just quietly push open the door and make sure she hasn't keeled over. I hope she doesn't notice me. I push open the door slowly. There is the sound of tearing tissues. For a moment I wonder if I'm asleep and dreaming or awake in a nightmare. I know this sound.

I push open the door. The crucifix on the wall is swaying on its chain. My Nan sits on her chair with her eyes closed and her fingers nudging beads. Her lips are moving. Now I recognise it. She is saying the Rosary – whispering it – it sounds like tearing tissues. Similar, but I think not the same as the woman who sometimes tears tissues in my room. I don't understand.

I pull the door to again and stand outside, but this time I cannot settle my breathing.

"Are you OK?" It is the nice woman, who's a few feet away on my left and staring at me with great concern.

"Yes, I think so. I'm sorry – she seems to be very angry."

She moves forward and touches my arm – I think it is meant to be a comforting gesture. "Don't worry too much. She is a naturally angry woman."

"Is that a symptom of dementia?"

She smiles and frowns simultaneously. "Not in her case. She doesn't have dementia – she's just an angry woman."

"Ah."

"Are you OK?"

"Yes. Thank-you. But I don't think I'll visit again. Sorry."

She stands back and gestures with her left hand, which I guess is to show me the way to go. "Don't feel guilty. Some relatives seem wrecked after visiting. You have to look after yourself."

"Yes. Thank-you."

For some reason, I thought it would be dark outside – I was expecting crepuscular gloom with bats flying around and people with grotesque faces catching the light under street lamps – but I walk out into a sun-warmed leafy road. I am completely disorientated and ask the first person I see to point the way to Sutton Common station. I want to get a bus back to South Wimbledon, but I have found that people seem to give directions to train stations more clearly than to bus-stops, so it is best to start with that.

I just cannot still my mind. It is turning around like a cement mixer. I choose – a deliberate choice – to go to the Candles, rather than directly home. Mrs Candle welcomes me in with a smile and no hint of reluctance, but she is wearing an apron, which means she must be in the middle of something messy.

"I'll only stay for a minute. I just wondered if I could ask your advice."

"Of course. Actually, you'll make Ian's day."

Again the same welcome. Mr Candle is hoovering the front room, and gives me his glasses-at-half-mast appraisal before grinning. "Excellent. Come in here – I'll use you as an excuse to stop."

I am thirsty, but respond to Mrs Candle's invitation to

have water by insisting I get it myself. She had lowered herself into an armchair with such relief that I would feel like a beast making her get up again. In the kitchen I find a leg off some poor animal – lamb, I think – marinating in red and brown sauce and vegetables out, maybe waiting to be peeled.

After two glasses of water, I refill a third and join them in the front room.

"Diana will be around later," says Mrs Candle.

"In time for lunch," says Mr Candle.

"OK, I'll be quick."

"You hardly have to rush away because she's coming."

"OK, but I'll ask you something before she gets here. I've just been to visit my grandmother, and now I'm in a dilemma."

I narrate the chain of events at the nursing home, in exact detail, for it is imprinted on my memory, or at least the emotional gist of it is imprinted on my memory; already I am getting replays of the red swirly carpets and cream wallpaper telescoping away either side of me whilst the sound of tearing tissues fills the corridor. Of course it didn't happen like that – but that's how memory works, even mine.

The Candles listen patiently, gravely. Mr Candle wants to know what state Nan's room was in and nods when I say that the Matron or whatever she was seemed sure that Nan didn't have dementia. I don't mention the tearing tissues.

"That doesn't sound like much of a thank-you for visiting," says Mrs Candle. "You're quite upset, aren't you?"

"I'm a bit thrown. I felt like I was being accused of something, but I couldn't figure out what."

"I suppose it could have been true. You were in – how shall I put it? I never actually saw inside, but Diana said it was quite a big house – and in Wimbledon."

Oh, yes. I think Diana came a few times to Tadstone Road. I don't remember Dad having any bad episodes in front of her - quite the reverse - he was easy-going with teenagers, but she thought him 'un-Dad-like' with his denims and loud music and I could tell she was uncomfortable. Then one time she swore she'd "caught him doing something weird with his hands" on the landing, and looked blank when I tried to explain 'air guitar' to her. After that, Diana insisted that I go to hers. Admittedly, it was easier to get homework done at her parents' house. The Candles are looking at me.

"Sorry - did you ask me something? I lost the thread."

"Never mind - you're upset. I just meant your parents lived in quite an expensive house." Mrs Candle is trying to be careful, I can see. "I suppose I'm saying that I was curious how they could afford it. Your father was - a social worker, was it? And I never knew what your mother did."

"I can't remember what she did before she became a nurse. She had a part-time job somewhere." A shop? I can't remember. I just knew that whatever it was she tried to make sure she was home when Urs and I came back from school.

"Yes, part-time. So . . ." She lets her confusion hang there.

"So your grandmother - or grandparents - could have given them money towards the house," says Mr Candle. "You would have to ask your mother if you really wanted to know." I must look stupidly blank, because he adds, "I'm just guessing, but in your grandmother's mind, if she thinks she paid for the house - it sounds like she thinks she should be living there rather than stuck in a home."

"Oh - I see. That should be between Mum and her, then - I don't know why she took it out on me, as if I was responsible."

"True. Can't help you there, I'm afraid," he says.

"Stay for lunch," says Mrs Candle. "It will be nice for Diana, and for us."

I feel very odd. My head is as hard and enclosed as an ostrich egg. I need a task.

"OK, thanks. But can I do something? I feel as if I need to do something." Rather stupidly, I shake my hands, as though they will get up to mischief if they aren't usefully employed.

They laugh, although I don't think I've said anything amusing.

"Oh, Winnie," says Mrs Candle, examining her own hands as if they belong to someone else. "There's lots you can do."

There's potatoes and carrots to peel. Mrs Candle fusses around me in the kitchen, as if I were exploited child labour, but eventually she relaxes. The teapot collection is distracting me with its assortment of ceramic colours. I change position so that I have my back to it.

"All right?" she asks.

"Fine. Let me know if you ever want to lose the teapots."

There is a sharp intake of breath, followed by a laugh. "I would love to lose the teapots. What are you suggesting?"

"eBay?"

"Oh. No – I couldn't do that to Diana."

"OK." I am peeling. Peeling am I. Peeling. When Diana arrives, accompanied by some squealing when she sees me, I have finished peeling everything and am about to offer to mow the lawn, but time has run out.

"Why didn't you say you were coming?"

"I didn't know I was. I just sort of ended up here."

"Winnie's had a bit of an unpleasant experience with her grandmother," says Mrs Candle. When the lamb and vegetables are dispatched to the oven for roasting, Diana insists we go to her room, which is chair-less, so that we both have to sit on the bed.

She wants to know who I am seeing, who I'm having sex with, and what I was doing with Mr Fallowfield on the day we bumped into each other.

I lie and say that I'm not having sex with anyone. I ask her who she's seeing and who she is having sex with, but she doesn't seem to be doing much of either; in fact she's cagey about whether she's ever had sex with a man.

"How about with a woman?"

She screws up her face. "Ugh, no – that's just gross."

We are running out of conversation. She talks about school, releasing a string of names and what their owners are doing now. I don't recognise any of them except Marty. Diana thinks he was a 'loser'.

"So come on – you and Mr Fallowfield. What's all that about?"

"I'm doing some research for him."

"You? What sort of research could you do?"

"I'm translating Chinese websites – trying to find proof of ancestor worship."

"Oh. Do you remember Mr Turner? He was my favourite teacher. He died in a plane crash."

What did we have in common? Why did we spend any time together? She is like a pretend person, conjured up for some online game where nothing happens. It is a relief when Mrs Candle calls us for dinner, and asks me to take the roasting dish out of the oven, as it's heavy.

I have the smallest amount of lamb that I can get away with without looking rude. The Candles laugh when I choose the seat by the window.

"Old habits," says Mr Candle.

"So how are the plans for Taiwan going?" Mrs Candle asks.

"I've applied for an English teaching job north of Taipei. I'm pretty hopeful." Fuck. I think I probably used simplified Chinese script on my email application instead of traditional Chinese. Bugger, bugger. "I just need to find my passport. God knows what I've done with it."

"Why don't you get a job in London?" says Diana. "There's loads of foreigners here."

"Yes, but it isn't Taiwan."

She says nothing for ages, leaving me to respond to her parents' questions about Taiwanese culture. I am telling them about a bizarre sight I once witnessed: a funeral cortege going through the fields, with the traditional 'buzzy' instruments to frighten away the spirits, and people in hooded garments – but led by a female cheerleader twirling a baton and wearing the skimpiest yellow shorts. It seems an outrageous transgression of all that we would expect from a traditional funeral in any culture. I confess that I have never been able to find out what lay behind the incongruity.

"Maybe the deceased was a fan of baseball or American football," suggests Mr Candle.

"I guess. That's what Taiwanese friends suggested."

"Can we stop talking about Death, please," says Diana. "It's just so gloomy."

"We're all going to die sometime," says her mother.

"I know – but we don't have to keep going on about it."

"We're hardly going on about it, dear."

"How are your plans for Brighton doing?" I ask, which elicits a strange squeak from Diana.

"Hove," say her parents in unison.

"I don't retire until next year," says Mr Candle.

"You could start looking for places now." I get a kick under the table – Diana is sitting opposite me – and I respond with a little tap on her shins. Hardly enough to write home about, but she somehow inhales a carrot.

We all stop eating while we watch her trying to sort herself out.

Mrs Candle flutters around her daughter, not knowing whether to bang her on the back or move in with the Heimlich. Mr Candle looks concerned but stays in his seat.

"Let's just give her some space first," he says. "See if she can do it herself."

It's hard to say if Diana is coping. She's certainly quite panicked, but not blue yet. Mrs Candle turns to me. "Winnie – please. Get a glass of water."

I fetch water from the kitchen, but Diana shows no interest in it and really seems to be struggling for breath. Mum has told me and Urs that the Heimlich manoeuvre is regarded as a last resort these days: something to do with over-enthusiastic first-aiders breaking people's ribs – but I can't remember if the preferred method of banging between the shoulder blades means putting the person across my knee, or if that is just for choking children. I really don't want to put Diana across my knee.

In the end I execute a very imperfect Heimlich; it's really hard to do when someone is sitting in a chair. My sudden bear hug, with arms around the chair as well as Diana, causes something orange to fly out and fall just short of my own plate. After all the fuss I was expecting a whole carrot, but it's the tiniest orange shred.

There is lots of fluttering by Mrs Candle and 'oh dears'

from Mr Candle. It takes Diana quite a while to recapture her breath. I am rubbing the inside of my upper arms, which got a little mashed by the backrest of her chair.

It's pretty much Meal Over. Poor Mrs Candle – all that effort – and we only got about halfway through. I am being effusively thanked ("Thank God you were here, Winnie"), though not by Diana, who is regarding me with baleful eyes and a dribbly nose.

Mrs Candle refuses my offer to wash up. I leave to the soundtrack of Diana wailing that she thinks she has at least one broken rib. I am walking down a pavement that looks like a corridor and everything seems swirly. Someone is calling my name. I stop and look back. I am in a normal sun-dappled street, with Mr Candle hurrying after me, holding my rucksack.

"Thanks. Sorry, I forgot it."

"No, I'm sorry, Winnie," he says. He is panting a little. "For what was meant to be a relaxing meal, it got quite fraught. I don't know why Diana is so . . ."

"It's OK. Never mind."

"But you came around for advice, and I don't really think we gave you any. So, for what it's worth, I wanted to say to you that I think you need to warn your mother that you went to visit your grandmother."

"Oh, why?" I really don't want to have that conversation.

"I think – obviously don't know – but I wonder if your mother has been entirely truthful to your grandmother."

"Oh?"

"You mentioned that your grandmother asked you when you got out of hospital."

"Yes. I don't know what that was about."

"No. No." He looks at me above his glasses. "Old people can be quite demanding."

"Yes."

"My mother – towards the end of her life – wanted to come and live with us."

"I don't remember seeing her."

"Well you wouldn't have. I said no; I used Diana as an excuse. I said it would distract her from exams to have someone else around the house."

"OK. A white lie."

"We do tend to use our children to provide excuses sometimes."

"I wasn't even living there at the time. I was in Taiwan."

"I think you'll have to ask your mother what she's told your grandmother." He gives me a sad smile. "These things don't work very well unless everyone is in on it."

I nod. I think this may be the last time I see him or Mrs Candle. I don't really know how to say Goodbye to this man. A handshake is too formal, a hug too informal. He reaches out and pats my shoulder and then turns back for his house.

I feel a sense of loss watching him walking away, though I don't know why. Maybe because he was always such a calm presence.

Because of Win, we have had to lie to Nan.

What Urs should have written was 'Because of Nan, we have had to lie to Win'.

Chapter Twenty-five

TRUTH IS A function of time.

I wonder if Dad remembers Zen and the Art of Motorcycle Maintenance? I wonder if he knows that Chris (the author's son who shared the road trip, and was pivotal to his later understanding of his breakdown) is now dead, the victim of a fatal mugging? And now his father gone too.

My right shin is still quite sore and every time I touch it to remind myself that it hurts I have an image of Diana dribbling. That's the least of my problems. My mind is all over the place this morning – like a mass of freshly-salted slugs. I know that I heard the woman tearing tissues in my room last night, though even that illusion has changed and I heard Catholic prayers whispered over me, 'Thank God' being the only distinct words. Finally I turned on the light, not to prove there was no-one there, but because I thought if I made a list of everything on my mind I could get to sleep. I read it now:

1. Tell Mum I visited Nan and ask her what lie they told about me.

2. Tearing tissues (*No action next to this, so I don't know why I wrote it*).

3. Try to remember where I last saw my passport.

4. Try and get Power of Attorney overturned (ask Mum outright?). *I know the form said 'Court of Protection' but I assume it's the same thing.*

5. Look for alternatives to the Pedant English school. Old school maybe? Hope.
6. Funeral – text something nice to Karen.
7. Remember Gadd: hypnosis? Will Maddy pay?
8. Ancestor fucking worship (I *must have been a little wound up last night – I am not normally a swearer*).
9. Sort out Marty (*I checked my phone last thing yesterday: 4 missed calls from him and 1 voicemail message saying that today is the last chance to see him before Karen is back. Also 1 from Maddy, but at least she won't be trying to entice me round for sex*).
10. Ring Maddy.
11. Did Gadd ever go to China?

I have no recollection of writing the last one. What did I mean?

I text Karen: 'Thinking of you. I hope the day goes smoothly. Jx'

I get a text back: 'Thanks. On way to church soon. House already filling up with distant relatives dressed like blackbirds. Missing you. Back tomorrow. Kx'

That was the easiest one on the list. The next one is Marty. I decide that the best way to 'sort' him is to ignore him; his interest/lust will soon wither, like an un-watered plant. I can tick that off the list. The next is Mum. I get no answer at home, so ring her mobile. As usual, it seems to take her a couple of 'Who's thats?' to establish that it's me.

"I'm a little . . . is everything OK, Win?"

"I visited Nan yesterday. At the Home."

She splutters, then says she has to go, as she is at work. Conveniently, she works in intensive care (I've just remembered). I can't remember when she trained to be a nurse. I can't remember why she became a nurse.

I haven't meditated today. I must meditate – try and still my pinball mind.

I have my phone in my hand. I am in such a muddle I can't remember if I'm about to make a phone call or have made a phone call or both. I look at the list in front of me. Both. I just made a phone call to Mum to ask her about Nan.

Next person to sort out is Maddy.

"Hi, Maddy. You rang me."

"Ah, Win. Yes." There's such a long pause that I wonder if she has asked me a question I haven't heard, but she starts to talk. "Win, this is difficult. I think I was being . . . a bit hopeful."

"I don't understand."

"No. You wouldn't. How could you?"

"Um – I still don't understand."

"Fred was so convinced he was right. But he's either lost hope, or lost focus . . . I think maybe this is a lost cause. You obviously haven't found anything, I assume because there's nothing to find. I'll pay the outstanding £400 for your work, and let's leave it there."

"Oh." I feel a hollow where my heart was. Diana's kick to the shin was nothing compared to this. "So Gadd isn't a problem anymore?"

"Oh, he's a problem, all right. He causes havoc in the house; every day brings a new disaster. And I don't mean that literally, Winifred, as I'm sure you know. I don't know why you wrote about him, but we'll just have to put it down to one of those things. And I'll have to find a different way to deal with Fred's problems. I guess I already knew the answer – if I'm honest, I knew all along that you wouldn't find anything."

"If you knew the answer, why did you ask me the question?"

"Because . . . I wanted Fred to be right – just one last time. I so wanted . . .", and it takes me a while to realise that the muffled sound reaching my ears is the sound of Maddy crying. Maddy. Of all the people in the world, I would never have put her down as a blubberer.

"Two more days, Maddy. Two more days – please."

I listen to more sobbing. It seems like a long time before she can compose herself into forming a response. "You'll get paid anyway, Win."

"I know. But that gives me until Wednesday night."

There is a sobby laugh. "Today is Tuesday, Winifred. You have to put your bins out. OK – you have until Thursday – what's the time now? It's almost 10 am. Let's give you until midday Thursday. Whatever happens, come around at midday and I'll give you the rest of your money."

"Done."

Tuesday. Tuesday. It's a special day. I read my calendar. I have to put the bins out, hoover, and go around for sex with Karen; except I can't do that last one as she won't be coming back tonight.

I empty all the bins in the house. I replace the bags with new ones. I put the bins out. I check all the bins apart from the one in Urs's room, as the door is shut, so I guess she's still sleeping. I hoover downstairs. I am hoovering, hoovering. But this time I can't become hoovering. For one, it occurs to me that Marty is suggesting I go around there for sex on the day of Karen's dad's funeral; that's – I don't know – not quite comfortable – and for

371

another, an irritating little version of me (the petty one who interviews me constantly and keeps up a dialogue even when I'm on my cushion) is nagging me now, telling me to get back to the computer. There is ancestor worship to prove. There are trips to Taiwan that must be planned regardless. There are things to do before my mind will be stilled.

I'm afraid that only the downstairs gets hoovered.

I check my emails. Diana has emailed me to say that she has Unfriended me on Facebook; clearly she was worried that I wouldn't notice otherwise. She seems particularly exercised about what she sees as a betrayal by her parents. 'I've told them that far from saving my life, you deliberately caused me to choke. You are no longer welcome at home, so don't come around and bother them again.' I don't think I bothered the Candles; at least, I hope that's not true.

Then there's one from the Pedant English school – in pedantic English:

Dear Zhuli,

We formally thank you for your interest and acknowledge your enquiry. We have had many applications from experienced English teachers with teaching qualifications. We have a preference for teachers already living in Taiwan. If this is your current situation (*bastards – they know it's not*) please contact us again.

Regards,

Gladys

All those names that seem so antiquated to us now get another airing when the Chinese look for Anglicised names: Gladys, Horace. I suppose it would be comforting for old people.

The cheapskates. Having a degree used to be more than enough. The mention of English-teaching qualifications is disingenuous at best. I lost count of the number of times I was approached in Taiwan by people begging me to teach at this or that school. They were so desperate that a couple of times I went out jogging I would hear panting behind me and find a gaggle of English-teacher bounty-hunting women trying to catch up with me. And they looked so disappointed when I said I was already committed to another school.

This is about paying the airfare. Maybe I have to get there first before they'll take an interest. Maybe they could sort out a work visa when I'm there.

Right. One last go at Chinese funeral homes before I give up. I try different ones. I even just have a piece of toast for lunch because it's quicker than the rice cooker. I speed-translate. I'm like a woman possessed. But there's so much to their websites: the British ones are wonderfully simple by contrast. The Chinese ones exploit every feature of internet programming: moving pictures, dancing banners. Some sites have online memorials. For *Qing Ming* day you can buy virtual candles to burn for your loved ones and even little online brooms to sweep your relatives' virtual graves. The mass of information is overwhelming. There are pages on funeral customs for the many minorities. Each website seems to regards itself as a compendium of every funeral history tradition and development. The equivalent on a British website would be pages on how the funeral industry developed from a few carpenters with a sideline in making coffins who gradually starting specialising in selling funeral commodities, and a long history about how the role of undertaking only became a respected craft after the first world war. But we don't do that. Our websites stick to information that is useful today.

I have a quick look to see if other industries' websites in China include such a mass of irrelevant information. But I can't see that they do. All companies seem to have some information on their credentials and their value to the community – but this spewing of extraneous data seems unique to their funeral industry. (The emphasis on credentials/qualifications seems to be a Chinese thing; apart from mall food outlets displaying their certificates of food safety hygiene, the only other industries in Britain that make a deal of displaying credentials are dentists and hairdressers – presumably a hangover from darker days of wielding sharp tools).

Maybe my approach is wrong. I am copying large chunks of text from the websites and then searching for the Chinese terms for ancestors, filial, burn, ghost, reincarnate, and doing a crude translation if I get a hit. I get only one hit:

As the elderly person approaches death, family members should take him from his bedroom to a temporary, specially constructed one in the main courtyard. This is because some people think that if someone dies in bed, his spirit will remain attached to the bed and has no way of being released. In some parts there is the belief that the criterion for measuring the filial piety of the children is whether the deceased was moved to the specially constructed bed. If the elderly person died in his own bed, the children will often be subject to reproach by others.

But no mention of ancestor worship.

I don't know where else to look. I think this challenge is doomed. I am surprised at how this thought drags me down.

Bright light fills my room. I turn around to see my mother

behind me, one hand on the light switch. How did she just appear like that? Is it some sort of Magic Circle trick passed on from Mother to Elder Daughter?

"Win – what are you doing in the dark?"

"I didn't know it *was* dark. I was working on the computer."

She sits on the bed. She is looking strained, unhappy.

"Have you finished work?" I ask.

"Win, it's 10 pm."

"Is it?" Seems like time flies when you feel you've run out of it.

"I think we need to have a chat about Nan, who is in hospital, by the way."

"Oh. Your hospital?"

"No, private for her, of course."

"Oh. Was this to do with my visit earlier?"

"On Sunday? Yes, probably – but it's not your fault – it's mine."

"Sorry. Nan did get a bit agitated. She seemed to think I was in her room – in her house – and when I said I wasn't, she got quite upset."

"Yes, I can imagine." My mother is looking at the carpet, which I haven't hoovered. Next Tuesday I will, definitely.

"I'm afraid I rather used you as an excuse, Winnie. My mother had a few falls and it was obvious that she couldn't live alone any more. We didn't want her to move in, but it was just Dad and myself in a three bedroom house. Initially I agreed, on a trial basis – but it was a disaster."

"Is it her house?"

"No – certainly not. My father gave us quite a bit of money towards the first house – in Tadstone Road – but it was a gift. And we still had a mortgage on it, which became very difficult to pay when your dad lost his job. So we downsized to the three bedroom one."

"Why was it a disaster?"

"She was a difficult woman. And constantly on at your dad to get a job. She just couldn't or wouldn't understand that he had serious problems. When you – when you had to come back from Taiwan, I insisted that she go into a home and that you move into her room. Until yesterday, I let her believe you were still there, being looked after."

"I never needed looking after."

She gives me the saddest look. "You did, Win. I know you don't remember, but you were quite a mess. You still need looking after."

"No, I don't."

She sighs. "Whatever. Anyway, you moved in. Dad just couldn't cope. And left me to it. So now I'm in a three-bedroom house on my own. And I'm probably about as happy as I'm going to be, so . . ."

"Urs lives with you."

"Not really. She's there a couple of nights a week – that's all. It's partly to give her some space and you some space."

"So Nan could move back with you if you wanted?"

"Well, I don't want. I've done enough looking after."

"When did you last see Dad?"

"A few days after you came home. He was in a dreadful state. He discharged himself from hospital and the next I heard was that he was in the Birmingham area – he had taken some sort of overdose."

"Didn't you go and see him?"

"I could hardly leave you. Ursula went. Now that I do feel guilty about. No daughter should have to witness her father in that state. She couldn't do anything. He was awake enough to tell her . . .", Mum sighs and for a moment I think she's about to start blubbing, but fortunately she gets over it. "He told her to F-off. His last words to his daughter." My mother shakes her head. "Fortunately, Urs turned out to be as strong as you, in the end. Thank God, thank God."

I was about to tell her that Dad is in a hostel near Borough station, but something in my head gives a little flutter.

"Were you ever in my room, saying the Rosary?"

She gives a little gasp. "Yes, very likely. But I don't think you'd remember that." And then she gets business-like and stands up. "Do I need to make you something to eat?"

"No, of course not."

"Promise you'll eat?"

"I'll have some soup the minute you leave."

"OK." She looks at my desk and gives a little smile. "I've never known anyone make as many lists as you. I guess it's a sign of trying to . . . of being organised." She frowns. "Does that say Power of Attorney?"

"Ah, yes. I want to get it overturned."

"Win – no-one has Power of Attorney over you. It's almost impossible to arrange for someone else without their consent."

"Really?"

"Really. The law is that people are allowed to make whatever eccentric decisions they want to. Including you. Now – soup?"

"Right away."

And I follow her downstairs. I should be asking more questions. Someone is controlling my finances, and if it isn't Mum, then who?

"Where's Win, by the way?"

"You're Win."

"Sorry – I meant Urs."

"She took the call this morning about Nan. I guess you didn't hear it. She was at the hospital most of the day – poor Ursula."

"Yeah."

Mum stops in the hall. "I'm sorry I lied to Nan."

"Doesn't matter. Whatever."

She looks at me. Quite strangely. Intensely, I guess.

"I'm really sorry, Win."

"What? Why?"

"I just assumed that you were OK."

"I am OK."

"I mean, back then. One of your teachers was really worried about you."

"Mr Fallowfield?"

"No. It was your English teacher. He thought your essays were a cry for help."

"Turner? Why would he have thought that?"

She sighs. "Remember to eat. Please."

I lock the door after her and heat some soup that I have no interest in eating. I am in bed a few seconds before 11:30 pm.

There is no-one tearing tissues in my room. I don't think there will be again.

Chapter Twenty-six

IT IS ALMOST 7 am, but I'm not sure I can be bothered to get up. I'm not sure I *can* get up, my legs feel so heavy I could be wearing wet jeans. I didn't sleep well, and my headache is still with me this morning.

I feel like I died in the night and no-one has told my heart to quit beating.

It takes a supreme effort to get up. In the end I abandon any idea of meditation and wander around the house like an unsettled spirit, picking things up and putting them down again. Strange to think what other people would consider significant once you are dead; I imagine someone walking around here after I had died – wincing at the shoes I wore, the everyday objects I handled, imbuing them with a significance they never held for me when I was alive.

I forgot to set the rice cooker last night, but I'm not hungry and can wait for it to cook now. I try to be mindful – extra mindful – in case someone sees the rice cooker after I've died and bursts into tears at the thought of its importance in my life. I feel I owe this to whomever attends my funeral and might come back to the house afterwards, for a wake or a celebration or whatever it will be: a knees-up probably. I wonder if Dad would come, if he were invited, which he wouldn't be.

I hoover upstairs. Normally hoovering is the best activity to promote mindfulness. Some people who practise Zen get that you have to throw yourself into an activity and lose yourself completely, but few understand that you have to lose yourself in the activity and also be outside of it at the same time, watching the self disappear. It seems as impossible to most people as the circular breathing method of playing the didgeridoo. I can sometimes be inside and outside at the same time, but today I don't feel like I'm here at all.

My phone rings. It just happens to be in my hand at the time, and I find myself in the garden with no recollection of how I got here. Had I come out for a smoke? It is Karen, so I answer.

"You're back?"

"Hello, Julie; yes."

"Are you all right?"

"Yes and no."

"Does that answer count as cognitive dissonance?"

This gets a laugh, at least. "Bloody hell – no it doesn't. I'm going to say goodbye, which is very difficult, but I think we've come to the end of the road."

"Oh. You've only just said hello."

"I'll ignore that, as I'm not sure if you're making a joke or being literal. Anyway, that's the end of Tuesdays and Thursdays. Or at least, you can carry on with the Thursdays if you want. That's between you and Marty. You don't exactly have my blessing, but you two are free to do what you want."

"So you don't want to see me again?"

"I didn't say that. I'm just not sure I'm up to this arrangement anymore."

"Sorry, Karen. I'm not having the best of days today. Just tell me straight whatever it is you need to say."

"I see Goldie Pang has jumped tanks."

Goldie Pang. Fat fish. Broccoli. "Yes," I say. "Um – was that giving it to me straight?"

This gets a bit of a chuckle. "No I guess not. I just mean that I know you were here. It doesn't matter – obviously."

"So it does matter?"

"You haven't done anything wrong Julie. It's just the timing I guess that hurts a bit. I told you how I felt about you and you immediately came round and spent the night with Marty."

"When was this?"

"Never mind – it was a few days ago. It doesn't matter, really. The point is that I'm not up to this relationship any more. It really is just sex to you, isn't it? Which to be fair is exactly what we asked of you."

My mind is squirming. There's a reason I went there, and it wasn't to have sex with Marty. It was something I was trying to do for her, something that was supposed to make her feel better, but it obviously hasn't worked – whatever it was I did or tried to do.

"Are you still there, Julie?"

"Yes, I'm trying to remember. I went to yours for a reason. I can't remember what . . . whatever it was, it was meant to make you feel better."

"Better? Well, I came back and asked Marty why Goldie Pang had jumped tanks, and I have to say that he took some delight in saying that you had stayed over. Which I can't quite forgive him for – considering why I went to Wales. Apparently you asked to come around."

"I can't remember, to be honest."

"The point is, I like you a hell of a lot more than you like me, Julie. So I think best to call it a day."

I thought I'd fixed this.

"Under History, Karen."

"What did you say?"

"You'll find me hidden under History. I can guarantee you won't like me anymore."

"You're hidden under history. Mmm – intriguing, as always. OK. I'll try and find you."

She doesn't say goodbye, but I suppose she's already said it. So that's that.

This must be what grief feels like. I had no idea that the loss of Tuesdays would be so affecting.

Hidden under History. Hang on. *Hidden under History.* I go upstairs and fire up the PC.

There it is. That's where it was hiding. That's where it's been all along.

Thursday at midday on the dot sees me knocking on the door of number 8, Skullbrook Road. Maddy opens it with a thin smile and I follow her into the living room, where Fred sits in an armchair and gives me the faintest nod of recognition. He looks unhappy, beaten – and actually so does Maddy; she slumps down on the sofa and opens her handbag.

"Right. Four hundred pounds, Winifred."

"Hang on. Don't you want to know what I found?"

"You haven't found anything. It's all right. We know."

"But I have. It's all there – hidden under History. I haven't had a chance to translate it properly. I was looking in the wrong place."

Both Fred and Maddy lean forward. Suddenly there seems to be more energy in this disconsolate house.

"All the Chinese websites have a section on history or old funeral customs. I was ignoring those because I took them at their word. But it's all there. Every single step of what to do for the funeral – filial duties – in fact, the information under History is almost the same as the information given under the Taiwanese websites as current practice."

"You think it's deliberately hidden under History to escape the attention of the authorities?" asks Maddy.

"I can't think of any other reason for putting so much detail under those sections. I will do some proper translations for you, but you have the gist already. It's completely androcentric – it's the father who must become an ancestor – it's the father who must be remembered."

Fred takes the news quite calmly, almost smugly. He sits back. "Yes – I thought so. Of course."

It's Maddy who is almost in tears, and Fred who reaches over to pat her knee with a quiet "told you so."

"How soon can we go to China, Winifred?"

"I think we need visas. How soon do you want to go?"

"As soon as possible," says Maddy, firmly. Fred is nodding agreement. "Is next week possible?"

"OK, I'll see what I can find out."

"Well done, Winifred," says Fred. "I knew you'd do it."

It is when Maddy shows me out that the next challenge hits me like a brick. "Hang on, Maddy – that was almost the easy bit. You do know that we have no chance of finding any trace of Gadd, don't you? I mean – even if there were anything left of him – which there won't be – his ashes were probably scattered on a field for extra phosphate or something."

"You'll think of something. You do still have the death letter, don't you?"

I nod. Somewhere.

"There was something in Chinese on it – I assume that's the address."

"I don't remember that there was, but even so, there won't be an urn to pick up, or anything like that."

Maddy moves in closely and grasps my arm. "Winifred, the important thing is that Fred comes home clutching an urn which he thinks contains his father's ashes. Do you understand me?"

"Yes." I think. "I need money."

"Yes, of course. Wait there." She relaxes her grip and goes back into the living room, reappearing with her handbag. "Four hundred pounds. Do you need more for something?"

"I think – I have no idea how much I need. Another hundred maybe."

Her eyebrows give the smallest hop, but she counts out another hundred and gives it to me.

"Oh – visa."

"You need more money now?"

"No – a pen."

She fishes a pen out of her bag and watches me write 'visa' on my hand. She is wearing a half-smile and a half-frown; I realise now that a lot of people seem to wear that expression with me.

"What do those characters mean?"

I have 咖仁 (Karen) already written on my hand. She rang me when I was on my way here. I said I'd ring back.

"Thanks, I'd forgotten that. It's someone I need to talk to."

I ring Karen when I'm in Garratt Lane.

"This list," she says. "Who wrote it? Your sister?"

"Yes. She was upset one day so I told her to write down everything that she didn't like about me."

"Thanks for sharing." She pauses; she is being careful, I can hear. "She actually showed you what she'd written? I'm a bit appalled, to be honest."

"No – to be fair, I found this in the bin. She gave me a fairly short and tame version."

"Glad to hear it."

"Is it that bad?"

"You mean you haven't read it?"

"I've only read the first and last bits. I find her handwriting difficult to read."

"Mmm. Can we meet up? I'm back at work tomorrow, so today would be best."

"Better."

"Pardon?"

"Today would be better than tomorrow – I think that's what you meant."

"Do you want a kick in the shins, Julie?"

"Not really. Anyway, I thought you didn't want to see me again?"

"Come around for a hug and a kick in the shins."

Shins. Carrot. "Say that again to me when I'm there. I've got a funny story about someone choking."

"Er . . . OK. Will do. I can hear traffic. Where are you now?"

"Garratt Lane."

I hear a splutter. "Come now, then."

"Marty's not there, is he?"

"Idiot. It's a weekday. He's at work."

She greets me with a hug (but no kick – so hopefully she was joking about that part). We sit down; there's already a mug of jasmine tea for me on the table – and a list I recognize.

"Want to read it to me?"

"Not sure I do, actually." But she reaches forward for the list, sighs and reads:

"Things about Win that annoy me:

She cannot see a single action through. She cannot turn off a tap she has turned on, close a door that she has opened, or put away anything that she has taken out.

Items under 1. would be easier to put up with if she wasn't so deluded and arrogant as to call herself 'mindful'.

She doesn't notice that every time she has a shower I have to mop the floor afterwards.

She puts dirty washing in the washing machine on top of just washed clothes and adds wet clothes on top of dry clothes in the tumbler drier.

She is incapable of looking ahead. If she isn't cold now she won't take a coat even though it will be cold later. Ditto rain and raincoat.

I have no way of knowing whether her work is any good or complete rubbish. The continuing absence of a cheque for the investment piece makes me wonder whether she is capable of translation.

I can never relax when we are in company. I have no idea if she will say something inappropriate, or obscene, or if she'll ask someone for sex.

She has no morals.

I can't go on holidays because she will refuse to stay with Mum.

She thinks she is enlightened. She is not.

She thinks everyone else is part of an inferior, unenlightened lumpen mass.

She is incapable of the most basic human emotions. She finds nothing funny or sad.

She cannot love.

She has always been obsessed with death.

She has an appalling temper and is incapable of patience.

While she is deaf to conversation she hates music, so I have to live in silence.

She cannot tell day from night and seems incapable of looking out the window for a clue.

She thinks that the house is hers and that I am an irritating house guest. It is the other way around.

She complains that we won't let her move on, when it is the other way around.

She thinks she alone had a special relationship with Dad and is the only one who cared for him. That is so not the case.

She constantly complains that the people around her identify her as she was once rather than what she is now. It is the other way around.

She complains that people cannot accept change.

She complains that people cannot accept their own mortality.

And yet she cannot accept that our father is dead.

She thinks that everything that is oriental is good and everything western is bad.

Everything is a bloody ritual, from boiling the kettle to using that bloody rice cooker to using a hoover (which to be fair she is using more often).

She thinks she is the chosen one at the centre of a mystery

involving someone called Gadd. She is not the chosen one. There is no mystery and it is bloody obvious who Gadd was.

She is like a drunk person trying to pretend that she is sober.

I cannot see what future she has.

I cannot see what future any of us have as long as she is . . ." – Karen briefly shuts her eyes, and looks in pain – "she's scribbled out the next word". She reads again:

"None of this is really her fault, which makes it even harder for us to cope with.

Because of Win, we have had to lie to Nan."

Karen puts the papers back on the table. "Obviously, I have no way knowing if that's all true."

"Some of it's true. I lose track of time. If I'm working on something, I don't know day from night – especially in this country. But I don't ask people for sex, I'm a good translator. I don't like loud music – it's true – but it's only old stuff that I don't like to hear."

"She finds nothing funny or sad." Karen shakes her head. "That's definitely not true. Your sense of humour is just a bit left-field."

"The last one – about lying to Nan – isn't right. I had a chat with Mum about that one last night and she admitted that she told Nan that I need looking after as an excuse for why she couldn't live with Mum."

"Right. And did you once need looking after?"

"I was out of action for a few days. I had a really minor accident in Taiwan. They could have left me there – I had health insurance – but Mum brought me back here."

"What sort of accident?"

"I honestly don't remember."

"You cannot love?"

"What's love?"

"It's wanting someone else to be happy, even at the cost of your own happiness."

"Oh. In that case I can love. I want everyone to be happy."

"And your father?"

"Is alive if not kicking."

"Right. Well, if we stay here any longer then I'm probably going to jump on you, so we need to go out. I cannot tell you how jealous I am of Marty."

"What do you mean? Why do you have to be jealous?"

"It's Thursday today."

Oh God – of course it is. "Right, I'll cancel him. It's not fair, otherwise; I didn't get you on Tuesday." I text Marty.

"You don't have to tell me – but I'm intrigued what excuse you used."

"I said we have to cancel Tuesdays and Thursdays as I'm going to China." Straightaway my phone starts ringing.

"Is that Marty?"

"Yes. I won't answer."

"Right – let's go before I do something immoral."

"Where are we going?"

"I want to see your father."

"OK. I need to say goodbye to him, anyway."

"Why? Where are you going?" She groans. "You're really going to China?"

"Yes, I found what I was looking for. Actually, we've got a few things to catch up on."

Karen says that we need to take the overground from Earlsfield to Waterloo, and then catch two tubes. This means quite a bit of hanging around at Earlsfield. I realise that I haven't asked her about how the funeral went. So I ask. She shrugs.

"It was fine in the end. I think we all did cry a bit – I thought we'd long run out of tears – but I did shed a few in the end. I don't know why."

"Because you missed him as he used to be."

"Yes."

The train indicator says there are still seven minutes before the train to Waterloo will arrive.

"Have you told Marty you're breaking up yet?"

"No. I couldn't bring myself to do it last night; I just didn't have the energy. I'll leave it for a week. I know he won't take it well." She slaps my thigh. "Right – let's see if you've got any morals. Do you ever get something to translate that's unethical?"

"Don't think so. Most of my work involves translating financial reports. They're completely neutral in terms of morals."

"Hypothetically, then. What would you do if you were offered something dodgy?"

"I can't really think of an example," I say. "I think it's unethical to abandon your daughter so that you can have a son, but if I had to translate an article on the consequences of the one-birth policy, I would hardly turn it down."

"That's not what I meant: that's translating something that's unpleasant but true. How about something that you know isn't true, but your translation is going to be used to con people. Like I read that the Chinese say that young Tibetans set fire to themselves to try and reach enlightenment, as they misunderstand Buddhism."

"That's rubbish."

"Yes, I know that. I hope anyone knows that. But that's

what I've read the Chinese authorities say, so someone must have translated it into English. Would you have done that?"

Would I? I don't know. Probably. Or maybe not. My translation course certainly included a section on Ethics – but I have no memory of my reaction to it.

"I haven't read too much discussion on translation and ethics. People are usually too busy agonizing over whether westerners can do any translation without bringing an imperialistic, colonial mindset to it. Which isn't very helpful when you're translating a company report."

"Try. Imagine you've been offered some work on translating some propaganda about Tibet."

"OK. I would do the translation, but I'd use a technique to put doubts in the reader's mind. I would keep citing an authority."

"That's more likely to make people believe it, isn't it?"

"Nope. The reverse. It's a bit of a joke for translators from Chinese that official articles contain multiple references to 'the relevant department', which sounds marked in English. So I would say 'according to the relevant Chinese department the reason Tibetans set fire to themselves is because they think they will attain enlightenment. The relevant Chinese department states that the reason they are setting fire to themselves is because they misunderstand Buddhism. According to the relevant Chinese department, they should stop setting themselves on fire.' That would probably get past the censor because it would sound reasonable in Chinese. But it would jar with a western reader. I've read about translators who say they deliberately stick in bad grammar and spelling to signal that it's a dodgy translation, but I couldn't do that. I'd rather turn down the translation than do a bad one."

"OK. Good answer. I don't think you can be bad at translation, whatever your sister says. You might scrape a pass in Ethics as well."

"Glad to hear I've passed."

The train comes and we get on it and find two seats together.

"So what's all this about China? When are you going and when are you coming back?"

"Going as soon as we can get a visa sorted out – which could be next week – I don't know." I tell her how I found out about ancestor reverence, and that I have to somehow engineer that Fred receives an urn of ashes. "And then, when Fred and Maddy are safely on their flight clutching Gadd's ashes, I'll carry on to Taiwan."

"So you don't plan to come back?"

"No."

"And stay where? And live on what?"

"I'll get a teaching job very quickly once I'm out there."

"What will you tell your mother and sister?"

"I'm not going to tell them I'm not coming back. I'll have to be economical with the truth. I'll say that I'm going with Maddy and Fred for a few weeks – in truth I can't imagine they will want to be there too long – and once I'm reasonably settled in Taiwan, I'll email Mum and Urs."

"What if they are really upset?".

I look at her. "You've read Urs's list."

"And what if you don't like it and you need to come back?"

"I won't want to come back."

"How can you be so sure?"

"I'm tired of being somewhere where I don't feel like myself. It's hard to explain."

~

Karen is very quiet for the rest of the trip; she seems a little upset, though I would have thought that reading the list would have had her thanking her gods for her lucky escape. I wonder if she can hear my phone, which has been going constantly – clearly Marty is not happy about tonight's cancellation. As we are walking towards the ticket gates at Borough station, I spy Dad's figure, with his slightly unnatural stance of holding the magazines away from himself. I take her arm to slow her down.

"There he is."

Once through the barriers, Karen spends a while observing him. "OK. I'll buy a magazine." She turns back. "Give me something on him. Did he like football?"

"Not really. 70s music."

"Of course. David Bowie. Who else?"

"Mott the Hoople. Slade. Sweet. He calls himself Jeff now, by the way."

"What was his name before?"

"Harry."

I watch her go over, buy a magazine and strike up a conversation. He is soon smiling and responding. I can see her mention David Bowie and then they are both grave, but still talking. And he actually *is* talking. I can seem him actually saying something, rather than just giving a bland response to a thread that she has initiated. A special knack of Karen's, maybe? Or is he like this with everyone but me?

I had already been thinking of the things I could say to him, like "Bye Dad, I'm going away", or "Bye Dad, I'm going away and I won't be coming back", but just as a good translator needs to take himself or herself out of the translation, I forget me and watch him dispassionately in his own space, or maybe it's his space with Karen, and I can see that he's sort of happy. I have to accept that this is as good as it gets and will ever get. No second chance. Goodbye Dad.

And then I see her ask who was Gadd? I'm sure that's what she said. And he is thinking, thinking, and then he tells her something, but I can't see what he says. She smiles, thanks him for the magazine and comes back to me.

"Well?"

She looks at me. "Well – there could be a likeness."

"Oh." It hadn't occurred to me that she had any doubt.

"You asked him who Gadd was."

"Mmm. You know, I think you need to ask Urs the same question, as she seems so sure she knows."

"What did he say?"

"You know Gary Glitter?"

"I know he's bald."

She does her forehead-raising expression. "Amongst other things, yes. Anyway, he said that Paul Gadd is Gary Glitter's real name."

"Why on earth would I have written about Gary Glitter when I was a teenager?"

Chapter Twenty-seven

THE NEXT FEW days are crazy. There is a company that can rush through visas at a price. Maddy says fine – she will pay. But we need to send our passports and I can't find mine; nor can I remember when I last saw it.

"Idiot," says Karen. "You applied for a replacement. I was with you."

She's right. It comes through the post; fortunately I get to it before Urs does, for I'm sure she would drop it in the bin or bury it in the garden. She knows something is up, and has clearly passed her concern on to Mum, who has stopped by twice to ask me pointedly if I'm OK.

"Nan's back at the Home, you know. She's all right. It was a minor attack."

I say that I'm glad to hear it and try and look as though I hadn't completely forgotten about Nan.

Urs's and Mum's sense that something is up is only heightened by Maddy's visits, during which we close the door of my bedroom and trawl through websites together. If she has to go to China she doesn't want to devote it entirely to fetching Gadd.

"If we're going all that way, I want to see something. Beijing for a start. Tiananmen square, and, I don't know, somewhere else. What location did the death letter say?"

What location, indeed? I have tried to get some sense out of Fred regarding his grandparents, but really all he knows is that they met in Tianjin where his grandfather was teaching and they then moved elsewhere. I have asked him if he could be a little more specific, but he can't.

It would really help if we had whatever communication Lawrence Gadd received about the death of his own father, Gideon Gadd, but neither Fred nor Maddy came across any such letter when they moved his mother from The Old Vicarage to a Home. It wasn't the Oak Tree Care Home: maybe that didn't exist then. So we have to assume that Lawrence Gadd took whatever he had received to China without sharing the details with his wife.

I am still bugged by the question of how on earth Lawrence Gadd negotiated a trip to China in 1972. Fred is sure his father didn't speak any Chinese; he doesn't even know if his father visited his parents there prior to that, or whether they came to the UK to visit him. It seems that his father wasn't a communicative man; or at least, not when he was alive. He seems to have made more of an impression in his afterlife.

I have now spent hours staring at the death letter:

'LAWRENCE GADD DIED 1974 Heart arresting. Cremated Lululongping, Shanxi province, 1974 May 19'

The faded text in red at the bottom of the page, with its thick traditional strokes in red ink, is near impossible to decipher. Traditional? Why traditional script in 1974 China? But even as traditional script I can't make out the characters.

"It could be Datong . . . something. Sorry, I can't read it."

Maddy (who has commandeered my seat) searches for it.

"Well, that's in Shanxi province," she says. "So what's in Datong?"

"I can't be sure it says Datong."

"Let's assume it does. What's there to see?"

We trawl the net. The Datong area is famous for its Hanging Monastery and for the Yungang cave grottoes, with their many carvings of the Buddha – carved during the Northern Wei dynasty (or during the 5th/6th centuries, if one has an imperialistic colonial mindset).

"Let's do that," says Maddy. "And Pingyao ancient town. I want to do that."

"It means train travel."

"Fine. Just not too much walking for Fred."

The soft seat trains are booked up, and in the end we have to put back the dates of the flights another week to fit around the availability of train tickets. At my insistence, Maddy has agreed that we use a travel agency to book the hotels and trains; I just don't trust myself.

Which leaves the air tickets. I book them using Maddy's credit card, but chicken out of buying a single for myself, in case Maddy checks the amount paid and realizes that something is amiss. I feel guilty about buying three returns, but at least I'm travelling Economy and they will take Business Class ("organizing Fred is a Business," Maddy tells me).

Karen has been completely brilliant. She has double-checked visa applications and plane tickets and the itinerary for China, even though she really doesn't want me to go. I guess that's true love.

"You need a Plan B," she tells me.

"There is no Plan B."

"It wasn't a question. Here is your Plan B. If it doesn't work out, you come back here. By then I'll have moved back to my Battersea flat. You can stay rent-free until you've got either a job teaching translation or doing translation or whatever. OK?"

"OK, thanks." I have told her that Marty is stalking me. I see him from my window on nights he's told Karen he's at football or working late. Urs, fortunately, isn't aware.

"What?" says Karen, when I tell her I remember now that he did the same when I chucked him at school.

"You're going to have problems when you finally tell him."

She frowns. "He does get a bit jealous, but I'm sure he's not that bad. God – maybe he's really in love with you."

"No, he's not. He's just deluded, because he believes no-one could possibly want to chuck him."

"If that's true, then . . ."

"You will need to have friends around."

"OK. I have friends."

There are just two days before our flight. Urs conjures herself into my room.

"Right. What the hell are you up to?"

"Who is Gadd? Why did I write about him?"

"Gadd is Dad. Gadd-Dad – it's obvious. Now what's going on?"

Rubbish. Is that really what she thinks?

"I'm going to China with Maddy and Fred."

She looks appalled. "How long for?"

"Only nine days."

"Where are you going, exactly?"

"Beijing, Datong, Pingyao then back to Beijing for the flight back."

"Don't you need a visa?"

"Sorted."

"Air tickets?"

"All sorted, along with train tickets and hotels."

"Foreign currency?"

"Sorted." Bless Maddy for remembering that one.

"Oh. And you'll be with Mr Fallowfield the whole time?"

"And Maddy, yes."

I can almost see the electrical impulses firing across the synapses in her brain. I quickly start the screensaver so that she doesn't see the email from the Pedant English School, agreeing to an interview in two weeks' time.

"Right. So it's really all sorted?"

"Yes. You have nine days of freedom without me getting in the way."

"Yes," she says, frowns and goes out. I hope she has fun and gets a boyfriend and they can have sex in every room. Except this one. But it won't be my room anymore, so actually she can have as much sex in it as she likes.

A few minutes later, the Mother-Elder Daughter grapevine leads to a panicky phone-call from Mum; hopefully I reassure her – nothing can go wrong.

And then I think more about Urs's response, and I reject it as rubbish: Gadd is not Dad. Gadd is not Gary Glitter. No-one knows who he is. Least of all, me. Then I remember the bags of my Dad's records under the bed and pull them out. There is a single by Gary Glitter. It's a 45 called 'Remember Me This Way'. I find it online and play it – and it is a dreadful dirge: Paul Gadd begging us to remember him as a tower of sequins rather than as the old man he would become. Amongst other things, as Karen said. Dad played it a couple of times, though I have to say that it marks the nadir of his musical taste.

The disappointment I feel almost translates into a physical feeling. Gadd is both Dad and Gary Glitter.

The irony is that Dad had begged me *not* to remember him this way. Mum had taken Urs to her father's funeral and Dad had ended up crawling over the bathroom floor in his own vomit. God knows what he'd drunk or taken. I cleaned up and it was our secret, though not one we ever discussed. Then we moved on, which is all anyone can do.

I tell no-one but Karen.

"Can I actually read this bloody essay?" she says. She comes over on Wednesday, and reads it several times while lying on my bed. Then she shuts the book and stares into space.

"It's really mocking, isn't it?"

"I wouldn't have mocked Dad."

"Forgetting your Dad for a moment, it's quite an extreme reaction against most religions. It mocks all thoughts of an afterlife, it certainly mocks the idea of a static and happy afterlife."

"That figures. I was in a permanent rage against God."

"I thought you didn't believe in him?"

"No. But it seems to me that it's the people who say they don't believe in God who are the ones most angry with him."

The forehead-raising gesture. "Something else for me to think about."

"But I wouldn't have mocked Dad."

"Maybe, not mocking him exactly. Maybe mocking your own feelings about trying to accept the situation. I mean the last paragraph." She looks at the last page.

"The sadder thing was that – unbeknownst to them – they were not grieving for the loss of him as he was, but for the loss of themselves as they were when they thought they knew him as he was."

"That pretty much catches everyone, doesn't it?" I say.

"Yes. I suppose it's quite funny – and very sad – if you were using your essays as self-therapy. But I wish I understood all of these references to people sleeping or being passed between angels – or the sad wretch who stumbled around wailing 'I'm here, I'm here. I've come home.'"

I shrug. "No idea what I was going on about, I'm afraid."

"I don't suppose there was a cemetery that you used to visit? I just wondered if the 'sleeping' bit is a reference to people going to sleep.

"Actually, there was."

We get a bus to Wimbledon cemetery.

"I'm going to have to get a car at this rate," says Karen. "I seem to spend half my time with you on public transport."

I don't like to point out that she won't have to do that for much longer.

Karen also thinks that the sign saying 'The cemetery is open to residents and non-residents' is funny, and neither of us can understand why people walking in aren't smiling at the sign; maybe they've seen it before and laughed the first time. I find my grandfather's grave without thinking about it, and we then wander around reading the epitaphs on his neighbours' stones: a lot of people fell asleep.

"Over here," she calls by a headstone. "This one Came Home."

We wander around some more. There are a couple of Passed Ons and one 'In the Arms of Angels'.

Karen smiles. "Right – I see. You've put them together so that the angels are playing a sort of pass-the-parcel with the dead person. Very you."

The mystery is solved, but I do feel the poorer for it.

Roll on Taiwan. I need to be back to normal.

Chapter Twenty-eight

KAREN SAID THAT she wouldn't see me off at Heathrow, which was a relief; I can't be doing with those pointless scenes. She did actually suggest I ring Marty to say Goodbye, rather than rely on a single text message for closure, so I did. But we didn't get to saying Goodbye, as he simply didn't believe it was happening.

"Has Karen told you to tell me this?"

"What? Karen's has got nothing to do with me going to Taiwan."

"I thought you were going to China."

"I'm spending a few days in China and then going on to Taiwan."

"When are you coming back?"

"I've said. I'm not."

In the end I had to terminate the call, as we were just going around in circles.

The Fallowfields pick me up in a taxi. At the airport, they check in quickly through Business class and then wait for me to check in through my slower Economy queue.

"We may as well go straight to Departures," says Maddy.

"I just want one last cigarette," I say.

She frowns. "I didn't know you smoked. Is that your last cigarette because you're giving up or your last cigarette before a long flight, in which case it isn't really your last cigarette at all?"

"Er . . ." I seem to have developed Karen's forehead-raising expression, for I can feel myself doing it now.

Maddy gives me a twitch of a smile and nods to outside. "Never mind. I saw a group of you desperate people smoking out there . . ." she jerks her head towards a glass panel, ". . . so Fred and I will sit down just by here." We both look at Fred, who seems disengaged, but follows Maddy to the seats next to a door.

Outside, I roll a ciggie and regard the cool spring day. There is always something that feels significant about the last smoke before leaving the country, and if I had answered Maddy's question truthfully, I would have said that I don't know whether it is my last ever smoke in the UK or my last ever smoke anywhere. That really depends on what's to come.

I have alternating feelings of both dread and optimism about this trip, along with the feeling of being a grand swindler about to pull off a last deception, which makes me feel very uncomfortable. Whichever track my thoughts head down leaves me exhausted. But I will allow myself the luxury of hope. It's just possible I can pull off Fred's return to the UK clutching an urn of ashes while grabbing one more chance for myself.

I still feel guilty for letting Maddy buy me a return ticket.

Fred is like a compliant robot. When Maddy tells him to sit down, he sits down. When she tells him to drink water and hands him a bottle, he drinks. If she tells him to eat a Danish pastry, he eats one. Occasionally he lifts his head to check out the environs, but the random movement of people between retail outlets, food outlets and seats seems to usher in the need for him to lower his head, as though the smallest vignette gives him sensory overload. I completely understand: Heathrow airport reminds me of old science films of bacteria breeding, with blobs appearing quickly and randomly, as if the culture dish could support these vast spaces screaming 'Gifts! Gift Ideas!'. Or maybe it isn't sensory overload, but just that he's a nervous flier.

"Has it been a while since he was on a plane?" I ask Maddy, when she has dispatched him to the loo again and is keeping a watchful eye for his re-emergence.

"I suppose it has been some time. We used to go to Italy a lot, but not for years now." She looks at me. "He's never been a nervous flier, if that's what you mean."

"He seems very subdued."

"Yes." Maddy stares at the entrance to the toilet, which takes a long while to disgorge Fred; he shuffles out eventually, looking so bewildered when he steps back into the concourse that I feel compelled to walk towards him, calling his name.

We make our way to Gate 42. It's a long way and I use up so much attention warning Fred about the imminent transition from floor to travelator that he steps on gingerly – but safely – whilst I go flying into a Chinese man in front. Fortunately the man is surrounded by a moat of bags, bulky with duty-free contents, which render him impervious to my onslaught. I apologise in Chinese and he shrugs.

At Gate 42 we sit in a huddle.

"I can't believe you know Chinese but you've never been to China," says Maddy.

"I know. Taiwan will always be my favourite, but China has been on the bucket list."

Maddy looks at me for a few seconds. "You're a bit young to have a bucket list."

"Surely you're never too young to have a bucket list. Otherwise you'll hit fifty with a list of more things to do than you could possibly fit in."

She gives me one of her mouth twitches. "Fifty? Is that your definition of old?"

"Ah. Sorry. I guess I meant seventy."

"Well, I'm certainly not that yet."

And we both turn to look at Fred, but he doesn't appear to be following the conversation.

"Aren't you excited, Fred?" asks Maddy. "Just a little bit? Quest end?"

Fred frowns. "Quest end?" His voice is croaky, as though these were the first words he had uttered for a week. Which might be the case for all I know.

"Quest end. Gadd's ashes." She stares at him intensely, but she speaks so softly I barely hear her. "You do know why we're going to China, don't you?"

Fred nods.

"We're going to collect your father's ashes, aren't we?"

Fred nods again.

"And then he'll stop haunting you, right?"

Fred blinks rapidly then nods. "But she has to tell me what to do."

"Pardon?"

Fred nods towards me and stutters to a halt.

"Winifred?" suggests Maddy softly.

He nods again. "Yes. She . . . Winifred . . . has to tell me what to do with the ashes. To do it properly."

Maddy gives me one of her diamond-cutter looks. "No candles."

"Incense sticks?"

"Not unless you want me to die in a fire."

"OK," I say. I'll have to think of something that sounds ritualistic but flame-free. Except of course that I won't be going back with them. So I need to write out some instructions. And I have to come up with them first. Smells are important. Something easy to buy. Maybe some sandalwood perfume would do it; it smells vaguely eastern and mystical. Ideally, there would be a wooden tablet with 'Gadd' carved into it, except that I can't imagine that Maddy would want to donate anything more substantial than a wooden ruler to the cause. OK: just his name written on paper then. Except that it has to look Eastern and Significant. It's a shame that I don't have one of my yellow-gold little banners with me; I gave them all to Karen to keep. I did offer to tell her the translated meanings, but she waved me away. "I could probably guess if I wanted to – so let's give my imagination something to play with instead." Maybe I could write a letter for Maddy to give to Karen, asking her to hand over one of the banners; I'll tell Fred it means 'Heaven starts with filial piety' – or some equally banal faux-Confucian statement, and hope that the now considerably rotten fruit of my karma isn't further swelled by Fred paying sandalwoody obeisance to a heap of 'ashes' under a banner that says 'Close the freezer door' or 'Pull the curtain across the shower fully' in Mandarin.

"So you do mind?" Maddy's voice.

"Sorry? I mind what?"

"They've just called us. I said I'm sorry that I didn't insist you go Business class as well. I regret it now."

"No need. I'm happy with Economy."

"See you in Hong Kong, then." And she leads Fred to the end of the priority queue, which he accepts without turning around to acknowledge me. I'm afflicted with a strange pang of deprivation: I've been reduced from the most significant person in his life (which I think I was, briefly) to a light that has seen better days.

"I think he's forgotten who I am," I say to Maddy, and when I look up and see the people in the chairs opposite watching me quizzically, I realise that Maddy and Fred have already boarded.

The Chinese man I bumped into earlier gets his revenge by using up all the overhead locker space with his duty-free goods and really-should-be-in-the-hold suitcase, before plonking himself in the middle of the row. In the window seat is a man in jeans, a bit older than myself, who I guess is a seasoned traveller, because he is already busy typing into a laptop and has asked the stewardess how long before food is served. My seat is nearest the aisle.

As flights go, it goes, until we have finished lunch and the stewardesses have asked the window-seaters to pull down the shutters, presumably to usher us away from the Greenwich meridian and towards Beijing time. The young man starts waving every time a stewardess sticks her nose out of their funny curtained zone. Either poor peripheral vision is a requirement of being a stewardess or they are deliberately ignoring him. I and the Chinese man search for an Attendants button on out seat arms, above our heads and on the screens, before shrugging our 'don't knows' at him. I get out of my seat and go to the curtained zone, where I think that two stewardesses are trying to get it on, but then I realise they are merely trying to work together in a small space, and I think that one of them looks a bit like Karen. They look at me expectantly, but my mind goes blank. I came up here with great purpose; I was trying to do something good, but it's just gone.

"Can I help you?" asks the one who doesn't look like Karen.

"I'm trying to help somebody." What the fuck is wrong with my head? My bloody solid head, which right now I would quite happily smash against the stacked metal boxes that have something to do with food, I think – unless they are little mortuary drawers in case a troupe of travelling midgets all die in mid-air.

"Someone in your row?"

"Yes, that's it. A man."

My inability to articulate the situation must have made her think the worst, for she hurries past me and immediately sees the man waving his arms from our row.

"I have to make a phone call," he tells her. "It's an emergency."

The plane lurches and instantly there is a dinging sound and the seatbelt lights go on.

"I can't do anything until the seatbelt lights go off," she says, and returns to the curtained zone. Maybe she's miffed that I led her to believe that someone was having a coronary or something. Maybe I should have asked the one who looks like Karen.

I sit down and do up my seatbelt. "What's wrong?" I ask.

The man rubs a hand over his head. "I've been such an idiot. I don't believe it. I've just realised I've been scammed. I was trying out a new investment company who deal in the Philippines. They sounded really legit. Great website. Very professional-sounding people. The works. I wanted to test the water by putting in a thousand quid to begin with. I gave them my card for the transfer, and it's just dawned on me that I gave them my PIN as well. They don't need that to transfer money. I've just sold my house. Everything is in my bank account."

"You used a credit card? I think they're pretty good at stopping strange money transfers."

"I used my debit card. What a prize bloody berk I am. It's almost five o'clock UK time. If I can just ring my bank, I might be able to stop it."

We both stare at the seatbelt sign. When it goes off, he doesn't see it as he has his head in his hands.

"Hey. The light's gone off."

He looks up and I move out of my seat, followed by the duty-free Chinese man so that he can get out and rush towards the stewardesses' zone. The Chinese man looks at me. I tell him in Chinese what has happened, but he just shrugs. Presumably he only speaks Cantonese.

After a while – I guess after someone has spoken to the pilot to clear use of a mobile phone – the man is led to the back of the plane. Whenever I turn around to look at him he is pacing at the back there – either with his phone clasped to his ear or a hand rubbing his head. His anxiety is palpable. It seems like an hour before he comes back. I get out, followed by the Chinese man to let him take his seat again.

"I can't get through to them," he says. "I have no way of contacting the bank before we land in Hong Kong. They could have cleared out my account already."

"But you don't know. It could be legit."

"No. I looked through the emails, and realise now that things don't add up. They could not have chosen a better target. I thought the guy was pushing me to give the details of my account, but I was rushing for the plane . . ." – more head rubbing – ". . . I can't tell you what a horrible feeling it is."

"I'm sorry. For what it's worth, I've been there. My account was once cleared out. Not the sum of money you're talking about, but it was my life savings."

I don't hear what he says next – though I'm sure it is something sympathetic – because I now have the clearest memory of writing a cheque for St Mungo's. I had just found out that my father was staying in a hostel. It wasn't my mother. It wasn't Urs. It was me. I gave away my savings just like that. A good cause – absolutely – but why did I do that? Was I mad? I must have been. I sink back into my seat. What happened to me?

When did I buy the house in Colliers Wood? I have no recollection of it. I don't even remember moving in. One day – some time after I came back from Taiwan – I was just living there with Urs. I know we don't pay a mortgage. Is it my house? Does it belong to Urs? Did I ever belong there?

At least I will not be Urs's irritating house guest again.

I barely drift through sleep, so desperate am I to walk off the plane and feel that rush of grey, humid heat in Hong Kong. I will start to feel all right then.

Our flight lands in Hong Kong at 7 am. I say Goodbye to my fellow passenger, who is being allowed to disembark early with the rich passengers, who are – presumably – now much richer than him. I panic when I can't find my rucksack, but a stewardess discovers it several overhead compartments behind my seat, displaced by the Chinese man's duty-free.

I don't get to feel the humid air, as we are sequestered from plane to airport in an enclosed tunnel. We should have an hour to kill before our 8 am connection to Beijing, but by the time Fred has reappeared from the first toilet he comes to it's almost a dash to get to the gate in time. He is morose and shows no interest in anything, though the vast spaces in the airport filled with Retail might be disorientating him in the same way as they are disorientating me. I'm glad that Maddy is here.

At Beijing airport I'm prepared to negotiate the train or bus, but Maddy takes one look at Fred's listless figure and leads us to the taxis. The travel agency has booked a hotel in the Forbidden City area, so my proficiency in Chinese is required only to give the driver the address. I know I am a much better translator than speaker, but he seems to understand me.

The hotel is nice enough – in an old area where *laobaixing* ('the common people') still live in hutongs, though with the disadvantage of sharing outside toilets. We eat in a restaurant opposite the hotel, which I'm relieved to find serves real vegetarian dishes, rather than a dish of heaped vegetables with fish tails and greasy pork cubes protruding.

"Point to a picture, Fred," says Maddy, when the options I list elicit no response. Fred dutifully points to the first photograph on the menu – I don't even think he knows it's a salad – which I quickly substitute with a request for a hot tofu dish; the idea of Fred getting a stomach upset at the start of his Gadd quest seems too cruel to contemplate.

Over the course of dinner, Maddy asks me questions about the history of Taiwan and China and I slip into the cloak of tourist guide. But I feel as if I am answering by rote. I talk about the flight of Chiang Kai-Shek to Taiwan in 1949, when the KMT were ousted by the Communist party, but I don't mention that Chinese news reports about Taiwan encase references to the Taiwanese 'president' in inverted commas to show that the role is bogus, nor do I share with her Karen's (probably) accurate prediction that having completely convinced big business of the legitimacy of its occupation of Tibet, one day China will take Taiwan by military and financial force, and the western world will just shrug and say it is an internal matter.

I think about Karen more and more – her stance on human rights now seems like a moral compass, a reliable lodestone. I wish she were with me now so that I could tell her that the warm evening spring air here feels no different from in England, and why that makes me feel further alienated. I will have to see what the next few days bring. I think it is just because I am jet-lagged. Exhausted, in fact.

The next day, after Maddy has taken a short walk near the hotel and declared it to be like smoking an exhaust pipe, she eschews the proximity of Tiananmen Square and the Forbidden Palace for 'somewhere we can breathe'. I ask the hotel receptionist to recommend a park and they call for a taxi to take us to *Yuyuantan* park.

"We have to pay to get into a public park?" asks Maddy, disbelievingly.

"It's only two yuan."

She hands me a wodge of yuan, and I shuffle through different colours of Mao's serenely smiling face until I find a ten yuan note. I get three tickets.

Maddy's mood improves as soon as we walk into the park and see a sign extolling its many cherry blossoms.

"Serendipity," she says. "To be here in spring."

I instinctively take a path down to the river, where a group of men are baring flesh to the sun; they seem to be not so much sunbathing as photosynthesising.

"This feels like a warm spring day in England," she says, approvingly. "And listen to that." Somewhere, someone is singing opera.

Fred sits down on the low wall facing the water – the only decisive action I have seen him take since we left the UK. Maddy suggests that I go for a walk and then come back and keep Fred company whilst she does a turn.

I set off. I don't know if it comes from the cherry blossoms, but the air is uncomfortably filled with white fluffy spores, looking more like giant dandruff. They get in my eyes, up my nose and tickle my face. I do a quick round of the inner track, which circles a very artificial looking lake. A man chugs by on his one-person dust-cart, his face turning around as he goes so that he is continually staring at me, like a malevolent owl. Signs point to non-places in the park, aggrandized by ridiculous names. I think if you let the Chinese loose on London's South Bank they would come up with names like Corner of Paradise, Concrete Oasis, Waterloo Bridge of Harmony and the like.

There are little cliques of women practising tai chi, with fake swords, or ribbons so large that streams of colours are thrown across the path. There are activities I don't recognize, women twirling with curved bats and balls, as if in a sophisticated egg-and-spoon race. Some dance to modern western music, others to Brazilian rhythms. Every clique has its own ghetto-blaster with interlocking circumferences of sound. Above it all is the sound of whips cracking, which I trace to three men dashing the air with chains; if the action has any traditional martial arts significance, I don't recognize it. I come across a kiosk, though I can't tell if it is selling food or renting boats for the fake lake. The bright patches of tulips are the target both of photographers and of men expelling phlegm. I don't think twenty years of meditation on detachment would stop me from feeling revulsion when I hear the tell-tale warning of a male throat being cleared in China. I don't remember it happening in Taiwan.

A small loud-hailer lies on the ground blaring out an item and the price. Despite its unceasing repetition, I can't catch what is being sold, but I know it is *shi ba kuai* (eighteen yuan). Desperate to lose the noise I head in the opposite direction and find four people playing cards beneath a tree. Suspended above their heads is the tiniest cage containing three trapped little birds. My urge to storm the game and release the birds is so strong that I break into a jog back towards the river and walk along it until I find Maddy and Fred, sitting in silence.

"My turn," she says cheerfully, and heads off.

"Is this what you expected of China?" I ask Fred.

He gives the briefest of head movements, but whether it is a nod or a shake is hard to discern.

"Because of course, you are a quarter Chinese."

Again, the same head twitch. But then . . . "It's different to what I expected."

At least he's talking.

I have read of a malaise described as 'Jerusalem syndrome', which results in approximately one hundred visitors to Jerusalem being hospitalised each year with mental problems. Whether this is due to the fulfilment or un-fulfilment of absurdly high expectations is not stated – but I would assume the latter. I am wondering if Fred is suffering from Chinese Syndrome.

"How is Mr Gadd?" I ask, and immediately curse my unskilful question, which sounds so facile that it pains me to believe I said it, but I just can't believe that he is so disinterested in reaching a goal he has been pushing for so hard.

Fred finally raises his eyes to acknowledge me. I expect he is about to say something about nearing the quest's end; he clears his throat and mumbles something about feeling bad.

"Sorry Fred. My ears are still funny after the flight. You don't feel well?"

"I said I feel bad about something. I was never honest to Maddy about one thing."

"What was that?"

"She thought I learnt Sanskrit in my fifties."

"Yes. Amazing. I know some words from Buddhist sutras, but I could never imagine learning it as a language. Really impressive."

He looks at the ground and clears his throat again. "I started learning it at college. I already had a reasonable grounding in it before I took it up again in middle age."

"Oh. Right."

"I don't think I'd have been able to pick it up from scratch later on."

"Yes. I see. I think maybe – no need to tell Maddy now."

"I thought that maybe I should. She thinks . . ." His chin seems to sag below his shoulders.

"Please don't tell her."

Fred slips back into his quiet world and I try and meditate quietly, and with only partial success as cherry blossom gets up my nose and distracts me into wondering what Maddy is feeling. I assume it is negative.

But when Maddy joins us – clutching a camera, which I hadn't seen her take – she is radiant.

"Now I feel like I'm really in China. I love watching the women doing their dancing and flag-waving and singing, ah – it's just wonderful." She waves her camera at me. "And what is all this white fluff? Cherry blossoms?"

"Sorry, I don't know."

"It's like it's snowing. Beautiful."

I always despised the westerners you get staying in Taiwan – and I imagine in China – who are self-appointed ciphers to the mysteries of the Orient, and love lecturing other westerners on 'how to cope'. I have come across a few of these types, and have always taken pleasure in watching their faces fall when they realise that I can speak and read Chinese. But my disappointment in hearing Maddy's delight makes me wonder if I haven't got a touch of that 'cipher arrogance'. I should be pleased that she is getting so much out of a simple walk in an artificial park.

"I think what I really love about the Chinese is that their hobbies are so overt," she says now. "None of these people are going home to tell their loved ones that they came across some strange people in the park."

"Sorry?"

"If they want to dance, they dance; if they want to break into song, they sing. If anyone did that in England we would pretend not to notice, but we'd go home and tell . . ." – she looks at Fred – ". . . well, we'd tell *someone* that we came across weirdos in the park. They would be the point of a story – a subject of derision."

"Right. Yes – I see what you mean."

"And I love the way they give these extravagant names

to areas of the park that we wouldn't dream of naming."

"Yes. It's very Chinese."

"This wind is actually very pleasant, isn't it?"

"Yes, we could be in Cromer."

Maddy hoots with laughter. "Oh God, Cromer. My parents were pathologically scared of foreign places, so we often went there. I didn't get on a plane until I was thirty." Her smile fades and she looks across to a head-bowed Fred. She adds quietly, "He was good for me."

"But I'm not sure why we're here anymore. He seems to have lost interest in reclaiming Gadd," I say.

"I know. All the time you were doing your research, he was like a dog with a bone. But as soon as we started packing, he . . ."

"I do wish you would stop talking about me like I wasn't here," snaps Fred. "I know what we're here for. In fact, the sooner we get it over and done with the better. I don't understand why we're here."

"But we're here to collect his ashes," says Maddy.

"No. I mean I don't understand why we're *here*." He scans the park as if we have brought him to a war-torn Syrian town.

Maddy laughs, I think with relief. "We've been through this, Fred. We're here because if I'm going to shell out thousands of pounds on a trip, I want to make the most of it."

"You should be finding your roots, Fred," I tell him, but he just frowns and looks down. Maddy smiles, and does a forehead-raising gesture, which throws me.

We amble back up the steps and catch a taxi to the Olympic Park, which is not a big enough disappointment to give me Olympic Park syndrome, but is disappointing none the less. There was something so magical about Ai Weiwei's frosty bird's nest stadium when we saw it lit up on TV, but now it just looks like a heap of metal in the sky.

Yet Maddy seems comfortable with the huge concrete boulevard that stretches out in front of us, and even stops to read signs about the layout of the park, and to listen whenever the loudhailers reel off statistics about the construction in English.

"The Chinese are really into surface areas, aren't they?" she says. "All the statistics about the area in the park we were in earlier, and here in the Olympic Park. Metres this and metres that."

I know how many metres the floor footage of my house contains, but when I add up the individual areas of each room, it falls short. Somewhere in this house, there is a hidden room. And somewhere in this house, seventies music is playing. I know it is from the hidden room, so I search and search, exploring every dark corridor, trying to trace the source of the music. Finally, at the very centre of the house I discover a door that I have never seen before. The music blares from within – now almost unbearably loud. As I turn the key in the door, the music stops. I enter to find a small room, with a record player on the floor, the needle now scratching an empty, revolving platter. Behind it is a bed with a figure lying face up, its arms across its chest. As I get closer I realise it is my corpse, and I move closer still, for I can see that my lips are moving. And then corpse-me opens its eyes and snarls, "I want my life back".

I wake up in a dark room and struggle to find a lamp or light switch by the bed.

I still have tinnitus and jet lag from the flight. Tomorrow

we catch the train to Datong. I will be OK once I've managed to get some sleep. I know I'm feeling out of sorts because I am so tired. I will be OK tomorrow.

Chapter Twenty-nine

THE DAY DOES not start well, as I have a rant at the hotel receptionists over their inability to get us a taxi to Beijing station. I am told that no-one will want to do such a short trip – it isn't worth their while – but the subway is convenient. Not convenient for an elderly man, I snap back, completely ignoring the 'don't get angry' rule of engagement. In my defence, I am already a little apprehensive at the thought of manoeuvring Fred around the railway complex without having to contend with the added complications of getting there; I insisted we visit the station yesterday afternoon to pick up the soft-seat tickets the agency ordered online; Maddy took one look at the crowds on the concourse outside the station, blenched visibly, and said, "You were right to come today". She didn't even comment when I took photos of the short route across the concourse to the queues at the turnstiles to show tickets and enter the station.

The hotel reception staff are smiling at me – a sure sign that I have screwed up and embarrassed them. I calm down a bit and ask them if they think one of the unlicensed cabs that wait hopefully outside the hotel would take us to the station. They shake their heads – still too near. Then one of the young women suggests that we quickly get in a cab and don't tell them our destination until we're all in, so that they don't have time to refuse us. The idea of the three of us rushing a cab and boarding it Somali pirate-style is vaguely amusing – I suppose – but impractical. I go and break the news to Maddy that we will have to bribe an unlicensed taxi driver with an outrageous amount of money. It makes me appreciate the Hackney cab drivers' rule that a driver cannot refuse a fare on the grounds of distance.

"Where you from?" The Chinese lady asking me is in her fifties, I guess. Two men in the seats in front get up to watch our exchange; presumably they are with the woman – or maybe they are just curious. Maddy and Fred sit across the aisle from me, Fred looking out of the window, Maddy looking at me.

"I'm from the UK." When the lady looks blank, I say "*Yingguoren*."

"English," cries one of the men, happily. "*Zu qiu*." He mimes kicking a ball, and the other man mimes kicking it back.

"*Zu qiu*, yes." God bless football. As far as I can tell, it is a game we are pretty rubbish at, but in the Far East, they think we are wonderful.

"Rooney."

"Yes, he's very good." I can see Maddy smiling.

"*Ni jie hun le ma?*" asks the woman.

This is tricky. I would quite like to practise my Chinese, but if I admit that I'm not married, the conversation will stop there, as we've already established that I come from the Land of Football, and without family, there is nowhere else for the conversation to go.

I nod. "*Jie hun le.*" It's just a little white lie, surely. I am expecting the next question to be about children, and am inventing a boy who loves football and a girl who likes, oh

421

I don't know, animals. But then the woman asks where my husband is.

I tell them he has left the world and there is a collective gasp of sympathy. She asks how.

A road accident, I tell them. (Another collective gasp.) I tell them that he went to the shops to buy cigarettes and when he came out, a bus mounted the pavement and . . . aagh – my mind has gone blank. I can't remember the Chinese word for 'hit'. They supply it in unison. I see Maddy jump, which is not surprising, as she couldn't have expected three people to punch an open palm simultaneously whilst shouting "*Zhuang!*"

The woman asks if I have a photograph of him, and I quickly say that it makes me too sad to carry one. I think I have told more lies in the last five minutes than in the last five years.

They get off at Xuanhua, leaving me to explain to a curious Maddy what that was all about. When we pull into Datong, I lift down the luggage and motion for Maddy and Fred to leave first. Maddy counters my invitation with a sweeping hand gesture. "Oh no. Please. Widows first."

I should apologise to Mum and maybe to Urs. I can't remember if I openly accused them of stealing my money. I might have done. I think I was polite in my Goodbye letters but I don't think I said Sorry. I won't open them now to check. I will ask Maddy to post the two envelopes when she gets back to the UK.

Then I hope that Mum and Urs forget me and just let me fade naturally from their consciences. Once they know that there is nothing they can do they will be free to move on, readjust their lives and accept the loss smoothly. And I know that my presence is a burden, so my absence will only be the loss of a burden.

I haven't made a will, as I have got nothing to leave. I'm not sure why I have started to think about dying.

We reach Datong, which seems to be nothing but traffic inside a city wall. Our taxi driver is hitting the horn so regularly that it could be in time with his pulse rate. Fred has lowered his head as if he barely dares take in the dashing and darting and hooting of the cars.

"Why are we here?" he asks.

"Your father was cremated in Datong," I say. To be accurate, I should say 'Datong-ish'.

Fred chances one open eye at the world outside, then lowers his head. "Why?"

"Because he was dead."

"But why would he have come *here*?"

"He would have been wherever your Grandfather was when *he* died. I assume your Grandparents moved here after Tianjin."

In truth, I don't know. The characters on the death letter do appear to start with Datong, but they are so faded and creased I am guessing. If Lawrence Gadd were cremated, it is more likely to have been a city, and Datong certainly qualifies on that score. At the hotel reception, I hire a guide for the next day. I make sure it is one who can't speak English, as I don't want someone blurting out "You want to do *what*?" in front of Fred.

We have a subdued meal in the hotel restaurant. Even Maddy's Happy Tourist persona has disappeared. When Fred retires early, she looks after his diminishing figure and sighs. "I'll give him a minute to see if he gets to the room on his own."

"What happened to your dog?"

She sighs. "Lucy was a lovely dog – a black Labrador. We went to Pembrokeshire for a week. I wanted to leave her in a kennel, but Fred insisted she come. We somehow lost her in the forest. We spent the rest of the holiday trying to find her, but never did. And Fred went downhill really quickly. I don't think it was just the emotional attachment: he had been a man who walked a dog, and then suddenly he wasn't."

The next day we meet the guide in the hotel lobby and I outline an itinerary. I want us to do the sightseeing first and then get Gadd's ashes. It worries me that we are going to Pingyao tomorrow, when the job will (hopefully) be done, as it were, but Maddy controls the purse strings and is entitled to some sightseeing, whether it is before or after we have got Gadd.

After I became a widow on the train yesterday, I spent a long time staring out of the window at the relentlessly parched and arid landscape, looking for graves. They were evident outside the villages, usually on the edge of fields: simple mounds of dry earth piled in a cone shape, occasionally with evidence of a grave marker, a red banner. I decided that the large and regimentally discrete villages (so sharp was the delineation between village and farmland) were too big for our current quest; there would just be too many officials who would take a dim view of what I was trying to do.

So I ask the guide to find us a really small village somewhere – (though I don't say preferably somewhere too small to have any officials) and to make this the last thing on the itinerary. He nods, and seemed unsurprised; maybe they get a lot of western tourists (or more likely, Chinese urbanites) paying to see what life is like at the other end of the urban-rural cline.

The Hanging Monastery would be absolutely amazing if it wasn't covered in scaffolding, so we only stop briefly to look up at it. I pass on a few facts from the guide, which Maddy nods at and Fred ignores.

Then we go to the Yungang Buddhist grottoes, and I realise that there is no way Fred can walk all the way from the car-park to the caves. We decide to change our plans and forego the Buddhas. The guide says nothing, but must think that we have exhausted all the things that Datong has to offer. Except Gadd's ashes, which he doesn't know about yet.

We are on the road heading back towards the city. The car's air-conditioning belies the parched air and dirt-dry landscape outside. I wonder whether to point out the many graves I'm seeing by the sides of the road - they're not much more than heaped dry cones of earth - but Fred has his head down, and Maddy seems lost in her own head, so I don't. I ask the guide if it is legal to bury the dead here, and he says: we do it like this, and he closes one eye. Then he gives me a grin.

He stops the car just off the road and points to a little sandstone settlement down an unstable set of steps cut into the dry, crumbling earth. We gingerly make our way down and then across some land to the village. Our progress is slow, Fred walking behind me, with both hands on my shoulders, muttering to himself all the way. The entrance to the village is demarcated by a cement wall with a slogan in red paint.

"What does that say?" asks Maddy.

"Something like 'Strive to be self-reliant'."

"I can't imagine the people have a choice in this place."

A couple of women and toddlers come to greet us – the women in bright red blouses with beads and sequins – beaming with smiles, and holding out little strings with stuffed toys dangling. Clearly, we aren't the first tourists to come here. They respond happily to the guide's words (in a Datong dialect, I assume, as I can make no sense of it) and one beckons us into her little home, dug into the sandstone hill. Although the three rooms look substantial enough, the whole village is clearly being swallowed, reclaimed by the crumbling rock. I am pleased to see that the only men around are elderly. No officials.

The guide tells me that all the children go away to school, and the men to work elsewhere for months on end, so all that is left are a few women and very young children, and the elderly men who want to stay where they were born and brought up.

"Is this it?" murmurs Maddy to me.

"Could be," I murmur back, though I don't know if she is asking the question with any seriousness.

One woman shows us the k'ang (the beds, underheated by hot air from the ovens) and Maddy comes alive again as she looks around the little dwelling with its shrine to plastic figures of Buddha and *Guan Yin*. She spends a while looking at the wedding photographs of the woman's son, but whether this is to marvel at the ubiquity of maternal pride or to mourn her lack of an equivalent trophy, I don't know. Either way, the woman beams when she observes Maddy's interest.

I know this lady will be happy to do what I ask if I buy a few of whatever these dangly things on strings are for. Mobiles for babies? Dangly things for cats to paw?

"Why are we here?" asks Fred.

I am about to start a speech on how this village was much larger in the 1970s, and how Gideon Gadd and his Chinese wife lived here happily with her relatives until he died, when Fred adds: "My family would never have been in a place like this."

There is no point carrying on. I give the charming lady ten yuan for a dangly thing and we make our way back to the car.

The guide takes us back to the hotel after collecting what must be the easiest eight hundred yuan ever.

We have an even more subdued supper that night, though Maddy does say – out of Fred's hearing – "I do appreciate what you're doing Winifred. Do you have another idea?"

Nope. Today's thwarted attempt at locating Gadd was the one I had visualised. I'm a bit lost now.

The next day we get a train to Pingyao, and I point out how the graves we see are changing from simple cones of earth to more substantial structures around the coned earth, with cement tops. Maddy pumps me for everything I know about the Chinese urban-rural divide, which isn't a huge amount, but she is absorbing the few facts I can recite and applying it to the arid scenes we see outside. I can see she soaks in knowledge – lives and breathes for new information – and I like her better for it.

We are staying in the ancient walled Ming 'city' of Pingyao. Our hotel is blessedly quiet. A grand old structure, almost 300 years old, with courtyards, and thresholds across the doorways that tax Fred's leg-lifting skills.

There is a City God temple in the town. As the traditional funeral rites would always have started with the family of the deceased being dispatched to 'inform' the temple God of the death (I guess a bit like the old British 'tell it to the bees first'), I am keen to go, and I explain this to Maddy (who looks enthusiastic) and Fred (who looks glum).

I quite like the temple, with its huge, terrifyingly colourful Daoist figures. A side exhibition, showing one of the nether realms and the measuring of a dead person's account on earth, is pure S&M, with every possible torture inflicted on the poor wretches whose earthly report is presumably poor. After seeing suspended upside-down figures being sawed through from the genitals downwards, the eye-gouging and tongue-cutting scenes look relatively benign. I tell Fred that there is nothing worth seeing in the room, and wait with him outside until Maddy comes out, looking amused.

When we step out to the ancient street, we find the pace has increased. The blasted cherry blossom fluff has started again, and it is as if ten circuses are existing in the same space simultaneously: always the beeps of the little tourist trucks that deliver mainly Chinese tourists to and from sights. A woman attached to a microphone seems to be auctioning huge lumps of meat, somewhere someone plays drums, another a Chinese recorder, somewhere someone is letting off firecrackers (to scare off the spirits for a new business venture?), a Casio version of Happy Birthday plays, and every shop seems to be broadcasting a different tune, and all the while Chinese tourist groups led by someone carrying a different coloured flag clog the streets, compounded by couples wielding selfie-sticks to capture their stay in the ancient town.

Maddy seems to have adopted the pace of a Chinese tourist, a languorous and frequently stopping amble, whilst I sense that Fred, like me, wants to get out of the crowds and away from the frenzy of brightly coloured commerce. And the meat. The little rotating skewers of meat. I feel nauseous.

When we have pressed ourselves to the city wall he looks back with a bewildered expression on his face.

"Chaos is come again."

"I couldn't agree with you more."

"Winifred – when do we get my father's ashes?"

"Soon. Today or tomorrow."

He sighs heavily. "I'm not really sure he was Chinese at all. He hardly saw his mother you know."

"No." I note that Gadd is being re-invented now that Fred is suffering from a good dose of cultural alienation. It means that whatever mumbo-jumbo I come up with regarding settling Gadd's spirit can't be too Chinese. Maybe some offering of English Breakfast tea and Marmite.

"Do you think my father came here? To Pingyin or wherever we are?"

"Pingyao. I don't know, Fred."

"It's horrible."

"Everyone else seems to love it. Including Maddy."

He goes a long while without talking, starting once when a little trolley car beeps at us even though we are pressed against the side with no visible intention of stepping out into the path.

"Do you like it?" he asks me.

"No. I hate it." It slipped out – just like that. That must be what's in my heart. And yet I am sure there would have been a time when I would have drunk in this scene and felt fulfilled and alive. I don't understand what's happened to me.

"What's that cross doing?"

The question makes no sense, but I follow where his head is looking; above the rooftops just a little way away there is indeed a cross. "Must be a church."

"Let's go there," he says, and there seems to be a little spike of energy in his walk. I worry that Maddy will wonder where we've gone, but Fred seems so purposeful that I don't want to interrupt him.

We find it after a few turns. It's quite a sweet little Catholic church with a statue of Our Lady outside. Inside it is empty, and blessedly cool and quiet.

I can see Fred looking around and relaxing.

"I'm just going to sit down," he says. He settles into a pew.

"OK." I wander around the church. Despite the banners and notes in Chinese over its walls, the church is recognisably Christian: stained glass windows with the twelve stations of the cross (text in Chinese), pews, altar.

Although I love its emptiness, I suddenly feel quite sorry that it is so neglected, and then realise that I feel the same about some of the churches back at home: often empty unless there's a memorial service after some disaster, and then people flock in who don't normally come to church because they don't believe in God, but now find comfort in riding on the coat tails of our ancestors who did believe, and who have somehow left an atmosphere of reverence in the cold stone. I shut my eyes, and almost feel a jolt of electricity surge through me. A phrase from Eckhart has just come to me: 'The eye through which I see God is the same eye through which God sees me'. I wonder if I am in the right place.

Fred raises his head when I sit next to him.

"Was your father a Christian, Fred?"

"My father wasn't outwardly Christian," he says. "But my grandfather was very much so."

"He went to Tianjin as a teacher though – didn't he?"

"An English teacher – but he was sent out as part of a mission. Whether they tried to proselytize I don't know. Probably. Colonialism and all that." He gives a sheepish smile and looks around him. "This place does seem strangely familiar to me." He bows his head, though whether in prayer or from fatigue I don't know.

I spot a man tidying around the altar and get up quietly. The man looks up as I approach him, and gives a smile. "I have a problem," I say, in Chinese, and he waits for me to expand.

A few minutes later we both walk up to Fred, who is roused by our footsteps.

"Meester Ge-add?" says the man, softly.

Fred straightens up in his pew. "That's right. I'm Frederick Gadd."

The man says something to me and I say to Fred, "This man says they have been waiting for you".

Some life comes into Fred's eyes. "For me?"

The man holds out a battered little metal box with both hands. "Your father."

Fred reaches forward with both hands and accepts the box with reverence. "My father?"

"Yes."

Fred looks at the box for a long time, stroking the inlaid designs. It would be hard to say if it was silver or silver-coated, but it certainly looks old.

"Thank you. Thank you." And almost to himself. "He was here all the time."

I thank the man, who gives a little nod and withdraws. I have given a small donation to the church. Worth every yuan.

I hope that Fred won't ask me any questions, but he is clearly entranced by the little box. Opening it slightly, he sees the small transparent bag containing the ashes. He shuts it again.

"Yes. Yes. I thought so. What do these characters say?" There are some characters scratched into the tin. I take the box from him and examine the engraving.

"That's his Chinese name. Ge-a-de."

"Yes. I suppose they have to do the best they can with the characters they have."

"Yes. Shall we try and find Maddy now?"

We don't find Maddy, but as she had suggested a contingency plan of meeting at our hotel if we lost each other, that's where we head to, and where she joins us later, carrying all manner of souvenirs. Her good humour improves even more when I forewarn her that we found Gadd in the little Catholic church and that Fred is in possession of his ashes, and seems the more settled for it. We have a quiet celebration dinner in the courtyard of the hotel. Or at least it's quiet until Fred says, "Do you think I should be looking for my grandparents' ashes as well?" and Maddy and I shout "No!" at almost the same time.

"Your grandparents belong in China," I say. "And your father belongs at home."

Maddy escorts Fred back to his room when he says he wants an early night – the courtyard is too dim and the paving stones too uneven to let him attempt the trip on his own – then re-joins me for a final drink. Beer in her case, tea in mine.

"Well done, Winifred. I don't know quite what miracle you worked, but you did it."

"Yes. Best ask no more questions."

"Well – I'll ask just one. And it probably isn't one you can answer. Was that death notice genuine?"

"No. I think Gadd came to Hong Kong to send it himself. I was being an idiot. The faded text in red you mentioned is in classical script – so comes from Hong Kong, not China. It says Datong *bin guan* – which means hotel. He probably used notepaper from the hotel to give it more of an oriental feel. I bet if you hired a decent private investigator, he would find that Gadd changed his name and carried on living in the UK. From what you said, Fred's mother was very passive, and would have been too overwhelmed to find out more."

"Do you think Lawrence would even have been told about *his* father's death?"

"Doubt it. And those mixed unions – i.e. Chinese wife and western husband or vice versa – they weren't seen favourably. The most famous couple was Yang Xianyi and Gladys Yang, and they spent quite a lot of time in jail. So the thought of the authorities informing anyone outside China about the death of someone they once held in prison seems unlikely."

"Yes. It was always impossible."

"Maddy – if you always knew that Gadd wasn't here, why did we come? Why did you pay me to do that research – which now seems irrelevant?"

She spends a long time sitting silently. Her face is barely illuminated by the shimmying candle the staff have placed on our table.

"Winifred, you can't imagine what it's like, always saying No. No Fred, don't do that. You've got it wrong, Fred – don't think that. That's not true. That's just rubbish . . . and on and on and on. Like a miserable small-minded prefect on duty 24-7." She pauses. When she speaks again, her voice is so quiet that I have to lean forward until my head is almost touching hers. "Just for once, I wanted to stop being the one saying No. I wanted to stop being the one always putting obstacles in the way. I wanted to see what happened if I did nothing. I wanted to see what happened if I just went along with Fred's fixation, instead of stamping on it. Just for once, I wanted to get blown along like a leaf in the wind and see where we ended up."

There is a breeze around us now, gently exploring the courtyard and continuing on its way. I wish I was a leaf. I wish my head would go away again so that I could be swept away like a leaf on an autumn day. But my head is still in the way.

"Do you think Fred will be happy now?"

"Happy? You'll still be around, Winifred. I'll keep you posted."

I don't answer.

Chapter Thirty

W E'RE AT BEIJING airport. I want to make sure they have checked in before I break it to Maddy that I won't be joining them on the flight back to London. As soon as they have checked in at Business Class, they return to the main waiting area. I see Maddy's confusion at finding me where they left me, with my suitcase beside me. I have taken out two envelopes, which I've already stamped.

"Winifred?"

"I'm not coming back with you."

I don't know why I was expecting an argument. Maddy looks unhappy, but resigned.

"You did say originally that you wanted to get back to Taiwan. But I thought you'd changed your mind, as you haven't mentioned it for a while." She looks at me. "And I think I did pay for a return."

"Yes. Sorry about that."

She turns towards Fred, who returns a little smile: quite what's going on his head is hard to fathom, but there does seem to be something more calm, less fidgety, about him. Then she notices the envelopes in my hands.

"What are those?"

"Can you post them when you're back in the UK – please?"

She takes them and looks at the addresses on the envelopes. "Hang on. Does this mean your family don't know that you're not coming back?"

"I'm not good at goodbyes." I'm actually fine at goodbyes – I'm just not fine at that protracted 'not really here but still not gone' period where people whimper nonsense and don't know how many times to look back or wave.

Fred moves his head closer to Maddy's and says, "Is she not coming back with us?"

"No Fred. And she's right here. You can say goodbye now."

Fred looks at me. "Goodbye. And well done." He has forgotten my name. I think he has forgotten what I did so well. I look at his hand luggage – an old bag with 'BOAC' in faded lettering.

Maddy gives me a hug and says quietly. "He hasn't forgotten. Gadd is in the main suitcase, by the way. I preferred to have an argument with Fred about that rather than an argument with Security by the X-ray machine." She holds me at arm's length and takes a look at me. "Promise me you really, really have everything sorted?"

"Yes – I've got a job just north of Taipei." Pretty much.

"I can't quite imagine life without Winifred. You always did things your way."

I grin and turn round and walk out of the airport to save them having to go through that polite whimpering stage. The day is so hot that it must be midsummer; the dry heat seems to exacerbate the coughs of the middle-aged Chinese men who are smoking around me: their last cigarettes before they go to wherever they are going. I roll up a ciggie and light it. For a moment I can't remember whether I'm in Beijing or Hong Kong. I wait for some of the men to start talking so that I can hear whether they are talking in Mandarin or Cantonese, but none of them is in the mood for conversation, and the odd grunts they share with each other could be from any Chinese dialect.

I can't remember whether I fly to Taipei from Hong Kong or Beijing. I go back inside the terminal and look around; all the notices are in simplified Chinese, so I must be in Beijing. I find a couple of spare seats together and empty the contents of one pocket of my rucksack after another. There are lists: on post-it notes and ones I've typed out. I can see that items are duplicated ('Buy 2 × Business, 1 × Economy to Beijing'), crossed off in some places, not crossed off in others, sometimes in Chinese, sometimes in English. I can find three entries that say 'Buy ticket from Beijing to Taipei', but I can't see that the route chosen has been crossed out or ticked.

I know Karen asked me about the Beijing to Taipei flight. More than once. I told her it was OK – I had booked a single. Did I? Or did I just add it to my to-do list?

I have got to stop making multiple lists. From now on, there will be just one list and just one record of everything I have to do, and in just one language. As soon as I can get myself to wherever I'm meant to be, that will be my new regime. I don't know whether it would be better to buy a little notebook or put an App on my phone that recognises my handwriting.

I can't see that I've written down anything about a hotel in Taipei in which to spend my first night, but that's less important than not being able to find the air ticket. I know I prepared a short list of hotels. Where is it now?

I count my money, which I've divided between two wallets. I'm sure I visited the bank to buy Taiwanese dollars, but I can't find any: there is more than four hundred pounds in one purse and a wad of yuan in the other, though they're barely sufficient to buy two meals in a cheap restaurant.

This should all be manageable. I need to exchange my

sterling for yuan and buy a ticket from here to Taipei. I just have to take my suitcase and rucksack to wherever it is in this airport that provides foreign currency services. Or maybe I need to find out where to book the flight first, in case they will only accept yuan. I re-pack my rucksack and make sure all the zips are done up properly. Just the suitcase now. I realise it isn't still with me: I must have left it inside the airport when I went out for a smoke and either I've come back into a different part of the terminal or someone has moved it. I can't see it anywhere. I turn my head here, I turn it there, but each new field of vision is filled with families and squawking kids fighting for turns riding the suitcase trolley. Despite all the energy and excitement, everyone seems to have a purpose: either they walk to consult a screen, or they are checking in luggage, or they are walking without their luggage because they have checked it in and now need to buy duty-free or head for Departures. Could I have already checked in my luggage?

My head suddenly feels as if it is throbbing with bloated thoughts, which eventually resolve into an internal scream: I am inadequate.

I close my eyes against the stream of people and find myself and Karen kicking the tin box between us on a street like a couple of delinquent boys. We found it in a shop called Rummages, where we pretty much did what it said on the tin until we found the perfect urn. It is a lovely spring day, cool and bright. When we have scuffed the box enough, we will go back to hers to see if I can engrave some characters, using a compass that she thinks she has in her and Marty's 'God Knows what's in here' drawer. Cremated remains are a bit of a challenge, until we search the web and find a pub in south-west London that advertises a real fire right through the spring months. We're on our way to Richmond now to have a drink and then find out if we can have some of their old ashes. We are happy, lost in our silly little quest, which is another distraction from death, another little flower to admire on our way to the cemetery.

I think I was happy that day.

When I open my eyes I am in Beijing airport, and the only thing I know for certain is that life without Winifred might be easier for everyone, but most of all it would be easier for me.

I go out for another smoke. I am running out of tobacco and I can't seem to get hold of it in China. I should have brought more from London. What did I do last time I was in Taiwan? Did I smoke something different? Did I smoke at all? It's a pretty basic thing to remember. I add 'tobacco' to one of my lists. If I can just find somewhere to meditate for a few minutes, I'll get my plan together.

The noise, the noise. I would kill for a quiet place to lose myself. I wish my head was quiet.

Chapter Thirty-one

Urs:

Saturday 23rd April

I'm afraid that I woke up very happy. I should pity Maddy (as I bet she has underestimated the responsibility), but I must admit that I found the woman rather dismissive of me. Not my problem. Mum of course feels differently – she even asked me to try and find Win's passport and hide it, but there was no way I was going to start going through her stuff looking. I half-expected that she'd have forgotten to take it to the airport and would turn up back here last night. There comes a point where you cannot do any more: it is one thing to make sure the house doesn't get burnt down or flooded, but if she is legally able to make decisions (and to make a big effort to keep those decisions secret), I really don't see what I can do about it.

I wonder if they took out medical insurance. Actually, I wonder if Win is even insurable.

Sunday 8th May

I woke up with a sense of dread that things would be back to normal today, but it's 11 pm and still no sign. She was vague (no surprise there) and said she'd be back in nine days rather than giving an actual date. I wish she would just appear so that we can get it over and done with. This week has been a strange one, in that I have pottered around my little house with a mixture of euphoria and also never wanting to see it again; in my dreams

I move out to a strictly one-bedroom flat on the other side of London. I have really enjoyed not having the smell of rice and cooking oil in the mornings; also the absence of the little scrolls of Chinese characters that I kept walking into. I wonder why she's taken them down. Then again, I never knew why she'd put them up. Her room looks bare without her PC in there – it seemed to be the centre of her existence. I think she was lending it to Karen (?), but I suspect that woman will be straight in there to trawl through Win's life. I still haven't figured out if she is doing a study or a thesis or what, but I can almost guarantee that Win has given her the password. For someone so charmless she can be strangely over-trusting of people.

Monday 9th May

Mum rang me again to ask if Win was back. I suppose I should have tried harder to get a contact number for the Fallowfields. I tried sending a few texts to Win, but with no response; likewise when I tried to call tonight. Knowing her, she forgot to take a charger and her phone is dead.

Tuesday 10th May

Disaster. I got a letter from Win, posted in the UK yesterday. It reads:

Dear Urs,

By the time you read this I will be in Taiwan. I have a teaching job in a school. I don't intend to come back. It's all sorted. Please don't worry about me. I hope you have a good life now that I am out of the way. And please try and get a boyfriend and forget about me. I have sent the same letter to Mum. Thank-you for all that you did.

Best wishes, Win

P.S. You were right. Gadd was Dad. If you ever want to see him he sells the Big Issue outside Borough station and calls himself Jeff. Don't be upset if he doesn't recognise you.

What am I supposed to do with that?

I didn't know whether to ring Mum or not, but in the end decided to call her at work rather than have her come home to the same letter. I wish I hadn't, now, because she has gone straight into panic mode. There's no clue who posted the letters. I guess Mrs Fallowfield, which means she is back in the UK.

I've scoured Win's room for clues, but she's pretty much cleared out. Apart from books, the only thing I can find is that silly exercise book with its story about Gadd. She has crossed out most of the title and just written one word. It now reads: "Dad (deceased)".

Wednesday 11th May

I've started emailing language schools in Taipei to see if any are expecting Win. If no luck then I'll have to extend the search. Mum is beside herself. This is bringing it all back for her.

I haven't told her about my unexpected visitor this evening: Marty Wilcox, in a suit. I guess he came straight from work. I really didn't like him when he was younger, but he seems to have matured very well. He was charming, but very upset. Apparently Win has been bothering him and his long-term girlfriend – so much so that it's put their relationship at risk. I was gutted to hear this – I thought Win had stopped all that, but he says that Win recognised him in the street – just a couple of months ago – and wouldn't leave them alone. I apologised on her behalf and

442

tried to reassure him that she is not in the country, so unlikely to bother them again, but he seems almost traumatised; he just can't believe she won't come back. It's so bad that he wants to take out a restraining order, but he said he can't do that unless his solicitor knows where she is. He doesn't seem to be able to accept that none of us know where she is. Hopefully I have reassured him.

Thursday 12th May

Some of the language schools in Taipei have responded to say that they aren't expecting Win. Maddy Fallowfield came by. She said she wanted to make sure I got the letter OK (she posted both) but then it turned out that she's also been worried about Win. I probably gave her a hard time. I said couldn't she see that Win wasn't able to cope with the most basic tasks, but according to her Win was very competent at organising everything - which I find impossible to believe. So I asked her why she was worried enough to come round, and she said she 'couldn't put her finger on it'. Not helpful! I do at least have Maddy's contact details now. I tried to find out whether the trip had been a success, (I still can't get my head round why they went), and she said 'a qualified success'. I asked her what she meant and she said 'I'll never get my husband back, but the man I live with is more content than he was'. God knows what I was supposed to make of that. She did add that Win had done them a great service, but I wonder if she was talking-up Win's contribution to prove that she wasn't being irresponsible in letting Win escape at the end: Beijing airport, apparently - so we don't even know if Win left China. I did at least get details of the airline and the flight numbers back.

Friday 13th May

It took a few phone calls plus an email and a scanned photograph of my own passport to prove that I'm her sister. It was a forlorn hope of mine that Win might have come back to London on the same flight as the Fallowfields: the airline has confirmed that no-one by that name was on the flight – or was booked on it – and that there were no empty seats. It seems that Win hadn't even booked a return for herself.

I am gutted at the thought of her being lost and confused in China. I'm not sure how I would cope myself, let alone her. She can't even remember to eat or drink when she's here. She will just fade away. It is a dreadful, dreadful thing to admit, but I would be calmer if we knew she was dead. It would save all this worry. I hope this is not wishful thinking on my part, but I am starting to think she may no longer be with us.

I opened an envelope addressed to Win this morning. It looked official and I hoped it would give us some clue. It was a cheque for £743 for the investment piece she did, plus an apology for how long it's taken to pay the invoice – apparently, they had to wait for their chief reviewer to come back from leave. I almost cried – from guilt, I suppose.

She caught me once trying to translate some of her post-it notes, using one of her dictionaries. (I gave up – it was impossible to look up the characters correctly). I know she thought I was being nosey, but I was just trying to figure out if she was really capable of understanding Chinese.

Friday 20th May

Mum looks like she's aged ten years. We actually had a

quarrel: she accused me of not grieving enough (?) and then apologised, and said she'd made the same accusation to Dad once, which seemed to be the last straw for him. Marty came round again to see if there was any news. I tried to persuade him that the more time passes, the less chance of him and his girlfriend being bothered by her. He's seems convinced that I know where she is and that I'm withholding the address that his solicitor needs. He said that I had to tell him as it was a legal matter! Pompous prat. He mentioned his girlfriend's name for the first time – Karen. I said "the therapist?", and I wish I hadn't, because he got quite bolshie and asked how I knew her. It took a while to get rid of him. If he comes here again I won't let him in.

When I heard knocking later I was going to ignore it, but then I heard a woman's voice calling through the post-flap: it was Karen. She said she had news. I told her that Marty had been round earlier and that I mentioned that I had met her and he seemed to be quite annoyed. She just winced and asked if she could come in to talk. I said that if she was also trying to find out where Win was because of their solicitor, I didn't know – and wouldn't tell them even if I did. She looked really confused by the mention of a solicitor. So I let her in, because I wanted to ask her: why had she been hanging round with Win after Win had started pestering Marty and put their relationship at risk? She gave a completely different story. They had propositioned Win – not the other way around. (Why???) Karen has broken up with Marty but has not told him that she was planning on seeing Julie again. I asked who the hell Julie is and she says that Win changed her name by deed poll to Julie Lodestone. Frankly, I don't believe that – Win can barely change a bin liner.

I asked her what this news was and Karen said she knew that

Julie was here and OK. As far as I can tell, Win's phone is now completely dead, so I was a little sceptical of how this fact was communicated to Karen (unless they are on some telepathic wavelength), and Karen rather sheepishly produced a chunk of something she says is bamboo, which had been pushed through the letterbox just before she moved out of the flat she shared with Marty. I asked if this 'message' conveyed where Win was now, and she said not – she was hoping I might have some news.

I'm not sure of any if this is true, and despite Karen sounding lucid, I am wondering if she is quite all there. Especially when she said that they had a Plan B (if Taiwan didn't work out) to live in her flat in Battersea, which is now free of tenants. I told her that if she had the remotest clue what it was like living with Win, she wouldn't even dream of it. Every bloody household task was turned into a weird ritual. Karen laughed and asked if I meant the bowing to the washing-up, to the kettle, to the hoover etc. She said that Win did this to improve her mindfulness and because she genuinely saw these tasks as opportunities to 'break through to a deeper reality'. I told her that she was speaking rubbish and that Win had no idea how bizarre (and infuriating) her behaviour was. Then Karen produced something with my handwriting on – my long list of everything I hate about Win (and which I THREW AWAY) – she said Julie/Win gave it to her to let her know what she was in for if they started a relationship. She also said that Julie/Win had warned her what Marty's reaction would be when they split up; she wishes she'd taken it more seriously now. Finally, Karen asked me what had happened to Julie/Win to make her the way she is, so I told her that Win had fallen off a mountain in Taiwan – or to be more

446

accurate, she had fallen while on a mountain in Taiwan. But I have always visualised Win as actually falling off it. I have horrible images sometimes – even now – of her sliding down the side of a mountain, desperately trying to get a grip, until she falls away from us forever.

Saturday 21st May

Maddy rang me for an update and I told her that 'a friend' believes that Win did come back to the UK, but that I cannot believe it. If it is true, I still don't know where she is.

Maddy sounded worried – she seems fond of Win – or maybe it's just guilt. I asked her how things were and eventually she said that her husband is 'all but gone', but added that at least he is no longer haunted by his father. (Whatever that means). Then Marty rang up, sounding belligerent with his 'Hello' (I cut the call immediately) and then Karen rang, and seemed upset and surprised that I still have had no news of Julie/Win. She made me promise that if Julie/Win gets in touch, I will tell her that Karen's flat is now available. I told her she was living in fantasy land – I'm not sure Win is coming back. I didn't spell it out to Karen – but I said I wasn't sure Win was anywhere she could come back from. 'What? Like your father?' she said. If she'd been here rather than on the phone, I would probably have slapped her. And then Karen went quiet before calling herself an idiot and saying "I didn't think of looking there". I asked what she meant by 'there'.

And so – just for the sheer hell of it – I got a tube to Borough station, with the ridiculous piece of bamboo in a pocket, which Karen insisted I take. And sure enough I saw an old man standing in the entrance of the tube station, selling the Big Issue. Far too old to be our father. I almost turned back before I made it through the ticket barrier, but there was something in the way he had one arm outstretched, holding out a magazine that made me go through with it. I stayed just inside the station entrance to watch him. I still wasn't sure. So I bought a magazine from him and looked into his eyes – a cloudier blue than they were – but it was Dad. Alive. He looked at me and I'm sure there was something. For an instant I thought there was some recognition, but then it was gone. I cannot believe it. I could have burst into tears then – not out of any joy – but because – well, I just thought I was through with all of that.

I didn't know what to do then – whether to try and get him to acknowledge me – or to keep on walking, so I walked out of the station to try and figure it out. There was Win, leaning against some railings watching him. Where on earth has she been sleeping? She looked a little dishevelled, but very much alive. I hate to say that I lost it then, completely lost it. I leaned on the railings and I bawled with my hands over my face, while the great British Public streamed past, and fortunately left me in my own space to grieve. I don't know how long I was like that – ten minutes maybe of non-stop crying. Then someone patted me on my back and I looked up to see Win, staring at me with that funny biting-lip look of concern, and I saw an echo of the sister I once had – the sensible one who could cope with Dad's weirder moments when Mum was at the end of her tether and I went off the rails.

'Hello Win' I said.
    'I'm Julie. Win is dead'.
    I didn't know what to say to that. I told her that I couldn't

448

believe she had been right all along – Dad really was alive, – but she shook her head. "No – he's dead". I turned to look at Dad, selling magazines and oblivious to his two daughters, and she said, "That's Jeff. He's been a good friend".

The bamboo was almost burning a hole in my pocket, but I delayed giving it to her. I don't know why, but I had the strangest feeling that once she had it in her hands, she would be gone forever. In the end I said, "So, Julie. What happened to Win?"

She looked at our father for a while, before turning back to me with her funny little smile. "Oh, you know. I'm sure we all get tired of being saints."

Acknowledgements

THANKS TO: LILLIAN Chia (for being an ace teacher of translation), Liyun Liao (for unlocking the meaning), Stephanie Henry (the real widow on the train), to the man on the plane (I am truly sorry), all at Salt (for taking a chance).

NEW FICTION FROM SALT

RON BUTLIN
Billionaires' Banquet (978-1-78463-100-0)

NEIL CAMPBELL
Sky Hooks (978-1-78463-037-9)

SUE GEE
Trio (978-1-78463-061-4)

CHRISTINA JAMES
Rooted in Dishonour (978-1-78463-089-8)

V.H. LESLIE
Bodies of Water (978-1-78463-071-3)

WYL MENMUIR
The Many (978-1-78463-048-5)

ALISON MOORE
Death and the Seaside (978-1-78463-069-0)

ANNA STOTHARD
The Museum of Cathy (978-1-78463-082-9)

STEPHANIE VICTOIRE
The Other World, It Whispers (978-1-78463-085-0)

ALSO AVAILABLE FROM SALT

ELIZABETH BAINES
Too Many Magpies (978-1-84471-721-7)
The Birth Machine (978-1-907773-02-0)

LESLEY GLAISTER
Little Egypt (978-1-907773-72-3)

ALISON MOORE
The Lighthouse (978-1-907773-17-4)
The Pre-War House and Other Stories (978-1-907773-50-1)
He Wants (978-1-907773-81-5)
Death and the Seaside (978-1-78463-069-0)

ALICE THOMPSON
Justine (978-1-78463-031-7)
The Falconer (978-1-78463-009-6)
The Existential Detective (978-1-78463-011-9)
Burnt Island (978-1-907773-48-8)
The Book Collector (978-1-78463-043-0)

RECENT FICTION FROM SALT

This book has been typeset by
SALT PUBLISHING LIMITED
using Neacademia, a font designed by Sergei Egorov
for the Rosetta Type Foundry in the Czech Republic.
It is manufactured using Creamy 70gsm, a Forest
Stewardship Council™ certified paper from Stora Enso's
Anjala Mill in Finland. It was printed and bound by
Clays Limited in Bungay, Suffolk, Great Britain.

LONDON
GREAT BRITAIN
MMXVII